FAITH'S FORTUNE
The Assurance

BOOK THREE OF THE FAITH'S FORTUNE TRILOGY

by
MATHEW MCINTOSH

Table of Contents

Acknowledgments

❦

*F*aith's Fortune – The Assurance draws its inspiration from the author's life-changing immersion with the warm citizens of the Bahamian Islands–in particular, the fine officers of the Salvation Army on Mackey Street in Nassau, New Providence Island.

I thank my God for circumstances that revealed to me that the Lord is indeed a Loving God, working things in HIS time and for HIS Glory.

To my English friends, Michael and Lindsay Brassington, who, during our time in Nassau, shared their home and the history of the Islands with me. Michael was taken from us by the Tsunami of 2004 in Thailand. We will see each other again.

To our good friends in Toledo, Ohio: David and Janet Kanz, Jennifer Connely, Mike Bankey, Gary Corrigan, Gene and Karen Lapko, Judy Ennis, Susan Perry, Michele Aman, Bonnie Hemp, Dr. "Kwaz", Jennifer Kephart, John and Jennifer Oster, and others who supported this project in a multitude of ways.

To Ron and Lucy Etling who showed me all things were possible through God via a loving family and "Zeke" the dog!

Dedication

This book is dedicated to my sister, Debra.

Disclaimer

Faith's Fortune – The Trilogy, is historical fiction. All characters appearing in these works are fictitious. Any resemblance to real persons, living or dead, is purely coincidental.

About the Author

~

During a thirty-five-year career in Health Sciences as a professor and dean, Dr. Mathew McIntosh has also served as a Board Member for Cedar Ridge Ministries, Drama Director for Tri-State Fellowship Church, and currently is Head Master at Grace Academy School, Hagerstown, Maryland. The author lives with his wife in Chambersburg, PA.

Inside the Cover

In the final book of the Faith's Fortune Trilogy, *The Assurance*, Satan takes care of business himself. Embodied in human form he arrives on the golden sands of the Bahamian Islands supported by soulless merchants of death and annihilation. Standing in their way is one of the most iconic figures in Bahamian history who joins forces with the Salvationists for a twisted reckoning of Good over Evil.

Prologue

With the attic and basement of 354 Davis Street now fully examined, it was time for Mark to turn his attention to the garage. Recognizing the trip to Canada would soon be coming to a close, the kids had asked if Aunt Debbie could take them to a small family-owned convenience store they liked in Bright's Grove where they could get their favorite Coffee Wafer ice cream. Debbie took it one step further suggesting they go ice skating afterwards with their cousins. Mark and Lou agreed and would meet up with them later at the Sarnia arena.

Before she left with the kids, Deb walked with them toward the garage. "The other boys took most of the power tools and the lawn mower, but I think there are a few snow shovels left in there. I set aside a box I think only the two of you would really appreciate," she said with a smile. "It's in the trunk of Mom's Buick, so have at it. And, by the way, Aunt Phalyn is meeting us at the arena. She heard you were here and wanted to talk to both of us," she told Mark with a shrug. "Don't know what it's about but things are always interesting with her. Guess we'll find out. I'm going to pick up my kids and we'll all see you in a couple of hours." After hugs all around, Deb left with the excited children.

Lou fiddled with the door opener, pressing the button several times before the noisy drive shaft finally began to lift the narrow garage door. Mark pulled the keys from his pocket and opened the car's trunk. There sat a blue Hammermill paper box secured with clear tape, and on the top, in black magic marker, was written one word: "Bahamas." They looked at each other and smiled, knowing exactly why Debbie had saved this for them. Nassau, Bahamas, was where they had met.

Mark had been determined to do some traveling before settling down when he turned 30, so when an opportunity had come up for him to do some teaching in the Bahamian Islands, he had jumped at the chance. Little did he know that decision would lead him to his future bride.

The unlikely liaison between the Canadian teacher and a girl on vacation from a small U.S. town happened on the sands of Nassau, Bahamas. After their initial time together, involving complications from an island storm, both felt God wanted them together, but it was a long wait filled with lonely nights, long distance telephone calls and plenty of letter writing. Eventually, though, the two were able to start their life together.

Since the Bahamas was where they met, they were looking forward to going through this box and turning back time, so they sat at the kitchen table with the box between them. Over the past few days they had rummaged through things in the attic and basement leaving them all with a lot of questions about their parents' past, but this box was different. It most likely contained relics only the two of them could value and understand. Lou grabbed the scissors and slashed the tape, anxious to explore the memories.

Mark immediately recognized two folded copies of the *Nassau Guardian,* sealed in clear plastic wrap. One headline read, "The Mystery of Harry Oakes" and the other, "Bay Street Riots!" Mark remembered reading about Sir Harry Oakes in the book "The Boys of Bay Street," basic mandatory reading for every *ex-pat* coming to work in the Bahamas. He was curious about the papers, so set them aside for later inspection.

"You know, I don't think this box has anything to do with us," he said as he rummaged through the memorabilia. "This looks like stuff Mum and Dad stored away. Wow, I never knew they spent time in the Bahamas before I lived there. No wonder they acted so weird when I told them I was going to live in the islands for a while. Wonder why they never told me...."

He turned his attention toward a small brown box Lou was opening. As soon as she lifted the top a flowery aroma wafted over them, and she picked up a wrist corsage made up of bougainvillea and Bahamian yellow elder flowers carefully stored inside. "Mark, can you believe these flowers still smell after all this time?" Lou carefully set it aside as a few petals fell, then noticed a folded piece of tissue on the bottom of the box.

Unwrapping it, she exclaimed, "Oh, my! It's a picture of your mother in a wonderful evening gown! She's wearing this corsage, and her hair...it's beautiful! She looks like a model." On the back was written, 'British Colonial Hotel…with respects, M.N.' "This must be the lobby of the British Colonial Sheraton where you and I had that great dinner," Lou said. "Wonder if M.N. is the photographer."

Mark picked up the picture for a closer look. "But look at her eyes. She seems so sad. It's a shame to be so dressed up and not be able to smile. Looks like she's worried."

Lou noticed something else in the box. "I wonder if this serviette has something to do with it," she said, pointing to the bold lettering across the bottom. "'Lazarus'. What in the world could that mean?

And look, here's a hundred-dollar poker chip folded inside. That was a lot of money back then."

"Who would've thought?" Mark laughed. "Looks like my mother was a fancy socialite… and a gambler, too!"

"Maybe it was your dad's. Did you ever think of that?"

"No, if there was one thing Vaughn McIntosh hated worse than drinking, it was gambling. I bet it was my mother's. Remember, Grandma Harriet was quite a wheeler-dealer in the real estate market. Maybe Mum picked up a few of those traits from her."

Mark was busy looking through the bigger box now. "Look here. It's a packet of World War II k-rations. The way they packaged those meals, we could probably still eat it now!" He said, waving it in front of her face.

"Listen, if our children get special ice cream, I deserve something better than a fifty-year-old packaged meal!"

Lou picked up some plane tickets. "Cat Island? Isn't that where Sidney Poitier was from? Maybe your mother was dressing up for him!"

They both smiled at the unlikely thought that his mother had known a famous actor and continued to rummage through the box. So far they hadn't found anything that had to do with them or that they recognized, but they were still captivated by what they were seeing. It appeared that his parents had quite a history in the Bahamas.

In the corner of the box, under a hardened oil rag, was a cherry wood box with the caricature of a mouse on the side. Lou slid the top off to find a large leather bag tied with a black shoestring. She tried but couldn't open the knot, and reached for the scissors. When she cut the string, the top of the pouch fell open and the most beautiful coral pink sand spilled onto the table. "Looks like the standard souvenir everyone brings back from the islands. We did that a time or two."

Mark reached for the bag. "Here, I'll hold this while you scoop the sand back inside." He began to roll the top down a bit, but stopped short. "Look at the lining. There's something printed on it." They pulled out an old cereal bowl left in the cupboard and, after dumping the rest of the sand from the bag, turned it completely inside out. "It looks like part of a map!" Mark said. "And there's writing: 'Maw.' What in the world could that mean?"

"I have no idea. Maybe they had secret lives as pirates and buried their treasure in the Bahamas," Lou said with a chuckle. "There might be some clues in the letters your parents sent to each other through the years. Deb has them all catalogued, from when your dad went off to war till he was in the hospital the last time. It's hard to believe it's been 5 years since he passed."

"Yeah, I know, but you know we promised Mum we would never read those letters."

"But how can we NOT read them after finding all this?" she asked, gesturing toward the boxes. "There's so much we don't know about your mom and dad. What could it hurt now that they're both gone? Aren't you curious?"

"Let me ask you this question," Mark said with a pointed look. "Do you want our kids reading our letters?"

"I suppose not," she said after a moment's thought. "In fact, whichever one of us survives the other has to burn those letters. I don't want anyone reading them," she finished with a laugh.

"Don't you think my parents would feel the same way?"

"I think they would want us to know the truth. Your mum left a lot of history here, almost as if she wanted us to find it. Your Aunt Phalyn has come quite a distance to see us. I bet she can shed some light on what we found."

"I agree. So let's get these things back in the box and find some ice skates. I have a feeling she could fill in a lot of the blanks about Mum and Dad's past."

Chapter 1

Dark Paradise

Nassau, Bahamas

Sir Harry Oakes put the cablegram back on the silver platter and headed to the library with his copy of the Nassau *Guardian* tucked under his arm. The temperature on this July morning was already high, and Harry planned to follow the Bahamian natives by taking a noon-hour nap, one of the few local traditions he had gladly embraced. He would start with checking out the weekend's yachting, polo and cricket results, then between the boring editorials, the hot weather, and the constant motion of the ceiling fan, would be fast asleep in no time. These cat naps seemed to regenerate him more than his failed attempts to sleep during the lonely sultry summer nights here on New Providence Island.

His wife, Eunice, and their three boys had been in Bar Harbor, Maine, caring for his mother and, as he had just learned from the cable, had decided to stay on there for another week. Their two daughters, the oldest being newly-married, would ride out the month in Vermont. His family's absence actually worked in his favor since he had an important real estate deal on Hog Island to finalize, but he still missed them and looked forward to them all being together again here at Westbourne Mansion.

Westbourne, an audacious 20-room mansion on a sprawling 30-acre estate overlooking the coral sands of Cable Beach, was said to have amenities fit for a king, even surpassing Government House where the Duke and Duchess of Windsor currently resided. But unlike Government House, Westbourne allowed Harry the seclusion he craved in the midst of his hectic business schedule. Today, he would unstrap his suspenders, dangle his bare feet over the arm of a wicker chair and indiscriminately allow bread crumbs to drop on the expensive carpet, escaping the worldly demands of pomp and protocol for a little while.

Outside the first floor louvered windows, bright red royal poinsettias intertwined with the purple flowers of thorny bougainvillea vines, blanketing the area with a sweet fragrance. Toward the beach, white-scarred palm trees hovered over an impeccably manicured lawn, the slender green fronds rustling in the summer trade winds blowing in off the water.

On the backside of Westbourne, where the kitchen and security quarters were located, two 100-foot ceiba, or cotton silk, trees were stabilized by ten-foot high roots that could, when necessary, provide a sanctuary from inclement weather or any other threat that might arise. Local lore claimed the tree would whisper to its owner when it felt the time had come to be cut down to be used for other purposes, but so far, Harry hadn't heard that voice so the trees continued to spider their way up the side of the house without restriction, spreading enormous branches over the roof as if promising protection as long as they survived.

Since being lured to this island, it seemed Harry had not only been protected in this house, he had been truly blessed. The city of Nassau, with its archipelago of pirate and rum-running cays, had become the perfect place for him to hide his Croesus-like wealth. The city was ostensibly controlled by a group of investors known as the 'Boys of Bay Street,' whose dominant members, Trevor Sullivan, a Brit; Axel Salming, a Swede; and Sir Harry Oakes, controlled ninety-percent of the wealth on the islands.

Known as 'Mr. Bahamas,' Trevor Sullivan was the founder and owner of the most prestigious real estate firm in the Islands, T.G. Sullivan International, and along with his brother, Nigel, had spent the last twenty years developing tourist opportunities in Nassau and the out islands of Eleuthra, Berry and Cat Island. He was also instrumental in establishing Bahamas Airways and investing into Pan American's Silver Clipper Air Service from Miami to Nassau, further advancing the tourist trade.

Axel Salming, a German-educated speculator in electrical/refrigeration equipment, was reported to be a friend of Herman Goering, Mussolini and Mexican pro-fascist General Maximino Camancho. The Swedish-born entrepreneur's armament company, Belfors, had paid off handsomely with the re-armament of Nazi Germany, leading to further investments in the United States and Latin America. Then, in the late thirties, Salming moved his entire family to the tax-free haven of the Bahamas with much fanfare. He purchased the world's largest yacht from Howard Hughes and established residence on Hog Island next to New Providence, naming his massive estate, 'Shangri-la.'

Harry thought about the event he was to attend this evening at Government House. Salming had a guest visiting the island and he was insistent that Sir Harry and Sullivan would be interested in meeting him. This mystery man had been escorted from Lyford Cay to Hog Island a few days ago, and after some acclimation to local ways, a gathering had been arranged so 'The Boys' could take advantage of some glorious opportunity.

Harry did not enjoy anything that he did not control. It was only because the Duchess was making an event of the get-together that he felt compelled to attend. Besides, the Duke was one of the few people here who understood his brash and brazen sense of humor, so the evening would not be a total waste. As long as Wallis was being properly attended to and molly coddled by someone, he and the Duke could slip away to attend the informal gathering.

Wallis Warfield was not one of Harry's favorite people. He thought about how she had made it abundantly clear when her husband, the former King George VIII of "The United Kingdom of Great Britain and Northern Ireland and British Dominions Beyond the Seas" abdicated the throne to pursue her love, that she still expected a standard of living on par with most Royals. Granted, the titles 'Duke and Duchess of Windsor' bestowed on them by David's successor, Bertie, were fairly impressive, but they had nonetheless been given a paltry endowment and been assigned as the titular heads of the Bahamas – a virtual exile to the backwash of the Empire which was not her idea of the high life.

Harry's thoughts shifted from the Duke and Duchess to his family. One good thing this evening's soiree at Government House offered was the opportunity to avoid his pesky new son-in-law who had remained in Nassau while his wife had traveled to a cooler climate for the summer. That did not sit well with Harry, but he tried to push thoughts of his daughter's unsettling marriage out of his head as he drifted off to sleep.

After the sun dropped somewhere between the sparkling jeweled waters and the static bulbous clouds overhead, the heat mercifully started to lift. Refreshed from his nap, Harry had his Man, Fitzhue, help him into his formal attire for the black tie affair. Then downing two fingers of Seagram's finest, Harry considered himself ready to face the evening's foibles and fortunes. The best part for him would be the drive along West Bay Street from Cable Beach to the Royal residence. He loved to talk cars with his chauffeur, Alex Ferguson, a former motor mechanic from around the corner at Goodman's Bay.

"Was the problem with the Cord in the transmission?" Harry asked as he settled into the back seat.

"No, sir, it was in the flywheel housing, but she is running smoothly now."

"I had an L-29 Auburn Cord in Niagara Falls and we never had any problem with the casings, even with the snow and cold in the winter."

"Here in Nassau it's the salt air and sand. They grate on all the moving parts. Everything has to be kept cleaned, oiled and greased. When you are gone for periods of time and the car sits idle, or if it gets taken over back roads without the right service and lubrication, the grit builds up and causes problems."

"So, why not drive the Cord when I'm away? You have my permission to take it anytime."

"Well, Mr. Oakes, I'm caught in the middle...."

Harry, known for his fits of temper, knew something was up and cut his driver off in mid speech. "Out with it, Alex! What's been going on?"

"It's Mr. Freddie, Sir," Alex said reluctantly. "He had me drive him all over the middle and south end of the island. This Cord is not built to run on beachfront, ridge roads or lake front."

"What was my son-in-law doing on my developments?" Harry wanted to know.

"He did not say, Sir."

"Let me put it to you this way, Alex, was Mr. de Marigny alone on these drives?"

Alex felt trapped. He wanted no part of the family squabbles, but was fiercely loyal to Sir Harry and couldn't lie to the man who had given him a job, a place to live and a full belly, and the dignity that came with those things.

"Mr. Freddie had a couple of American ladies from Miami with him. I drove them around for days, even out to his chicken farms on Wulff Road. He also took the Cord to Fort Montagu and left it at the cay while he took the ladies to Treasure Island for a few days."

Sir Harry and Eunice had been shocked when their eighteen-year-old, fiery, red-headed Nancy eloped with de Marigny, a man twice her age, twice-married, who had a reputation for womanizing. Although he seemed to be a sound businessman, Freddie was

20

a proverbial gold-digger and apparently had returned to his old ways once Nancy was out of sight.

"Alex, I thank you for being honest, but don't ever forget where your loyalties lie. My son-in-law should be horse whipped. There will be no next time for him, and he won't put you in a tough spot like this again. The man is an embarrassment to this family."

Normally, the beauty of Goodman's Bay was a relaxing sight for both men as they drove to downtown, but today Harry could not appreciate its splendor. He caught a whiff of a woman's eau de toilette coming from the seat cushion. "After you drop me off, I want you to take the Cord home and clean it from top to bottom. Wash and scrub it inside and out!" That would eliminate the aroma, but the vision of Freddie's ladies being in his most sacred of possessions could not be eradicated with soap and sponge. "On second thought, take it home and put a tarpaulin over it. I want you to contact Lefler's in Miami about another Cord...check into a Duesenberg, also."

Alex caught sight of his employer's eyes in the dashboard mirror and thought to himself, I pity the poor soul who crosses Sir Harry tonight!

Chapter 2

Nassau, Bahamas

Arriving politely late as usual, Sir Harry climbed the white-washed steps of Government House, ignoring the salutes from the formally-attired Royal Bahamian police officers stationed outside the door. As a member of the Bahamas General Assembly, he was entitled to a formal salute, but the natives always acknowledged his presence regardless of his standing, because of all he had done for the welfare of the Bahamian people.

It was common knowledge that Harry was the owner of about one-third of New Providence Island, and as such, took the responsibility to care for the people seriously. He built the country's only airfield at Oakes Field, provided jobs on his farms at a wage far above the national average, purchased and upgraded the iconic British Colonial Hotel, and invested heavily in the infrastructure of roads and affordable dwellings for the struggling natives. His philanthropy was unselfish – different from other blue-blooded Brits on the island–and was consequently imbedded in the country's psyche. Sir Harry was beloved by the Bahamians.

As he approached the door he noticed David Windsor inside, sipping on Martell Cognac while welcoming the many strangers who had been invited to the evening's festivities. When David saw Harry, the Governor broke away to greet his good friend, much to the chagrin of the Duchess who thought Sir Harry rude to by-pass her receiving line.

They shook hands and Harry said, "Let's move away from the orchestra, David. I'm not in the best of moods tonight and the music is already annoying me. At least you don't have those incessant steel goombay drums that absolutely drive me crazy. And it's so bloody warm in here. Can we go somewhere else?"

Frowning at his guest's irascible mood, David guided Harry to a side room where he prepared a single malt scotch for his guest. Harry peered out on the moonlight beaming down on an infinitely-stretching sea, but his mind was still somewhere else.

"I heard Freddie took a few friends with him to do some serious fishing this past weekend."

Harry shook his head. "I guess you have eyes everywhere, don't you?"

"Not really," David said, stepping up beside him to look out at the view. "My head bodyguard has a brother who rented the boat to the Count."

"Freddie got that title through heritage and blood, but he has done very little to earn it."

"Well, he did earn the respect of the crew. Apparently, he worked for over two hours to pull in a blue marlin…ten feet and about 200 pounds. That's no small feat."

"Freddie knows how to work a crowd, especially with anything athletic. I'm not really surprised."

"I want to go out myself. I hear the tuna are massive this year. Those blighters are nasty opponents, but with my luck I'll end up with some grouper or cantankerous barracuda. A lot of reeling and jerking for such an inconsequential prize. I've been aching to get to the bonefish off Andros since I had that great fight with a wahoo in the Abacos last year. These Royal Marine legs are still sea worthy and itching to be on the water."

Both men sipped their drinks, and Harry forced himself to put his personal business aside and focus on the purpose of the evening. "So, who is this mystery man we are meeting tonight, David?"

"We have the dubious pleasure of entertaining Mr. Hans Lubeck of the Argentinean Economic Development Commission."

"Who? Never heard of him." Harry threw back the remainder of his scotch and moved to the decanter for a refill.

David followed him. "Apparently Axel thinks it's in our best interest to spend some time with him… and I agree."

Harry's political radar was as keen as his business sense. "Here's what I think. If you and Axel want me to meet this person, there has to be more to this than just business. He isn't another of those Nazi types you two like to associate with, is he?"

"You know how I feel about National Socialism and Hitler, Harry, but since Churchill had me exiled to this backwater colony, I believe he thinks I can do the least amount of damage from here. If anything, the old bulldog should be more afraid of Wallis than of me."

"Regardless, you were highly supportive of Hitler back at the start of the war. Visiting with him didn't exactly endear you to the common folk of the Kingdom. After all, you're from a family of Germans, right?"

"Very funny, Harry. I fought against the Kaiser in the Great War, told Lord Kitchener I would fight in the trenches regardless of what he said. I don't know of too many kings who won the Military Cross in knee deep mud, do you?"

"But giving a full Nazi salute to Hitler in front of the European press? Surely you didn't think that would elevate you in the eyes of your former subjects?"

"All I was saying was I preferred fascism over communism. Hitler and Mussolini both knew how to properly handle unemployment. My government had much to learn from them."

"But you just can't share that opinion with the World Press. And you can't boldly call Joachim von Ribbentrop a family friend, either, and expect there would be no repercussions."

"Wallis was a friend of his long before I came along. I just inherited the amorous baggage."

"David, if you look at what's happening in the war today, things are not going so well for *Das Reich*. They've been booted out of North Africa and are on the run from Stalingrad. The Americans are in the Solomons and soon Guadalcanal. Hitler is on the run…so where does that leave you?"

"Looking to invest with friends who know how to make war profitable, win or lose."

"So, that is the purpose of Herr Lubeck's visit to Nassau? We are going to hide his filthy ill-gotten wealth."

"I know it appears that way, but it is exactly the opposite."

"What? They want to borrow money? Good luck with that!"

"Certain circumstances have arisen that suggest you can do a lot of good things for yourself, your family and this country."

Harry was still uncertain. "Let's meet with Axel and Herr Lubeck, and I want to hear Trevor's opinion on what's being proposed."

"Now, that's the way to start an evening off. I'll introduce you to Mr. Lubeck after the formalities tonight. He is having dinner with Trevor as we speak. They should join us in due course."

Harry hadn't felt his juices flow like this since that first gold train had slithered into the Wyoming station a few years ago. But this was different. He had no idea who he could trust.

Chapter 3

✐

Nassau, Bahamas

Government House was originally of neo-classical design, influenced by the United Empire Loyalists who came to the Bahamas after the American Revolution. For the next hundred and fifty years little was added to the structure save the ten colonnades on the façade and a meager east wing which was essentially an office and bedroom for the Governor.

Then the crippling hurricane of 1929 destroyed almost 80 percent of the island's housing, and despite its firm stone foundation, the two-story, one-hundred-foot long House was not spared from the gusty holocaust. With most of its roof gone, the Governor became as homeless as the forty convicts who were released from prison when that structure was obliterated. Restoration of Government House took three years to complete, at an exorbitant cost, as quality carpenters could not be found anywhere throughout the Islands and needed to be imported. Even with the renovation, the Duke of Windsor inherited a domicile in 1940 that he described as, "a cracked and flaking edifice…with about as much warmth and atmosphere as Wellington Barracks."

So, he set out to refurbish Government House to his own liking. The Duchess's statement, "We have to dish this shack so that at least one isn't ashamed of asking the local horrors here!" did not endear her to the Bahamian people, but she was determined, regardless of public opinion, that her husband should live as a king even though his title was long removed.

Harry Oakes found Wallis's pomposity and aloofness amusing, considering she was the daughter of a barkeep from the obscure village of Blue Ridge Summit, Pennsylvania.

He had never lost sight of his ordinary, down-home roots and felt Wallis was no better, so that's how he looked at her. David, on the other hand, found both Harry and Wallis to be a constant source of amusement considering they were, in fact, both commoners who were regarded here as Royalty, while he was the actual Royal reduced to the level of the commoner. Regardless, Harry invited the Windsors to live at the spacious Westbourne during the reconstruction, and Wallis was only too delighted to accept his invitation after suffering through a brief, but, as she perceived it, unbearable, stay at Sigrist House.

With all the duties and traveling of both families, there was surprisingly little interaction between the Windsors and the Oakes, but on the rare occasions the two families met, the Duke and Harry became fast friends. David Windsor found Harry to be a conundrum. In the morning, Harry would spend time with the locals, displaying his compassion and big heart; at noon he would deride a project manager with a most callous disregard for the employee's personal dignity; and yet later in the afternoon, Harry would enjoy tea service in the most gentile manner with respect to etiquette, traditions, manners and decorum. David was astounded by his diversity. He could swear like a drunken sailor when he didn't get his own way and a few minutes later kiss his wife and children with the utmost gentleness and civility. He also delighted in the fact that Harry had been knighted "Sir" Harry Oakes by his brother, the king, so there was some common ground for regal camaraderie between a Duke and a Baronet, but David's respect for Harry's business perseverance overshadowed everything. It was this quality that brought them together tonight for a meeting with an unknown associate.

As the party wound down, Harry noticed Sullivan introducing a man he presumed to be Herr Lubeck, to the Duchess. He was looking forward to meeting the Argentinean, not only to discuss his business in the Islands, but also to find out where his political allegiances lay. If both Axel and the Duke were for the meeting, he was certain there was some Nazi influence there. With Trevor Sullivan lubricating his guest with drinks and dinner, Herr Lubeck might reveal more about himself than he intended.

Harry had been in the Duke's meeting room on many occasions before and felt comfortable sitting in the Governor's presence. While David sat at his desk completing some paper work, Harry eased into a high-backed occasional chair, crossed his legs and swirled the golden nectar in the snifter he held, careful not to touch the bowl of the glass to avoid warming the fine Napoleonic indulgence. The Duke could always be counted on for serving the best to please the human palate, but Harry had an unsettling feeling the upcoming meeting would not be as satisfying.

A single knock at the door elicited no response from either Harry or David, who continued to concentrate on the papers spread out before him. A second knock was also ignored. The Duke was making a statement and Harry loved his gamesmanship. After a third tap, David placed his sterling silver fountain pen into its inkwell and stood up. He moved to the front of the desk, turned slightly to his left and with a slightly puffed chest, and pulled his vest into place.

"Careful, David, you don't want to pull that stiff upper lip down with your vest," Harry said with a chuckle.

David knew the importance of imperial trappings and would not miss an opportunity to strut its accompanying pretentiousness, especially to an ordinary stranger who, under normal circumstances, would never be allowed to grace any Windsor presence. "Enter," he finally said in his most kingly voice.

Trevor Sullivan, his fedora in hand, opened the door and stepped inside. He avoided eye contact with the Governor who had slipped his hand into his pocket, peering down his nose at his British subject. Trevor stepped aside, conveniently positioning himself beside the liquor cabinet. For the sake of his friend, Harry played along. He held his drink behind his back as he stood at a distance, ensuring the Governor remained the focal point of the room.

The German crossed the threshold in full military stride and approached the Governor. Salming, who had followed Lubeck into the room, stood just inside the door to allow the German sole access to the Duke. He stopped within a few feet, obviously knowing the importance of distance and deference, and remained there with his head down.

The Duke of Windsor hesitated for just a moment, then graced his visitor by extending his right hand.

"*Herr Lubeck...willkommen auf den Bahamas und willkommen in meinem Haus.*"

Spurred on by a salutation in his native tongue, Lubeck clicked his heels and instinctively began the Fuhrer salute. The Duke was quick to intervene, grabbing Lubeck's hand for a handshake before the arm extension could be completed

So, Harry thought, Lubeck is a Nazi! He looked to Trevor for affirmation, who, secluded in the back of the room, had already helped himself to a drink and held his glass high with a wry smile of acknowledgement.

The Duke guided Lubeck across the room. "May I interest you in a night-cap, Herr Lubeck? I trust Mr. Sullivan has taken good care of you tonight. Did you have a chance to meet the Duchess?"

"Yes, I did! Thank you. She is delightful… charming and elegant." The other men in the room chuckled, looking to the Duke for his response.

"Really? Are you sure it was my wife you were talking with?"

At the look of confusion on Herr Lubeck's face, Axel smiled and put his arm on the German's shoulder to let him know the formalities of the evening were now behind them. And when Trevor shoved a cognac into his hands, Lubeck fully realized he was now in the presence of the "Boys from Bay Street."

Chapter 4

A Colossal Disaster

❦

Wellburn, Ontario

Life had moved on in St. Marys after the departure of Picard and Brisbois, and the ceremonial burying of the Amschel gold. It seemed as if the war within the war had finally been removed from Vaughn and Mae's doorstep. Sir Harry Oakes had supposedly used the account pipelines Cate McIntosh had provided to sequester the gold from Canada to whatever destination he had chosen. It was bittersweet, however, to remember that not hearing from Sir Harry was good news.

Phalyn and Will had married under the trestle at the Purdue family's quiet spot and were living peacefully at Science Hill, thinking about raising children along with the goats.

Harriet and George had taken up a rustic lifestyle at the cottage at Point Clarke. They purchased the diner at the Lighthouse renaming the place, "Wyoming Wilma's" and wasted no time in getting their future lives in order by gutting and expanding the place to include a banquet hall and meeting rooms. Following Sir Harry's suggestion, they invested in thousands of acres along the lakefront all the way north to Kincardine, which they were preparing for real estate development.

Fran grew tired of the life of a waitress and was sparking Liam, persistently hounding him about putting a ring on her finger. She kept telling him she didn't want to be a waitress forever, but the burly Irishman, who had decided he needed $500 in savings and a steady job to even think about a proposal, seemed to have cold feet. Rumor had it that Phalyn and Mae had struck a deal, on Fran's behalf, to purchase the Knowles' farm and pond for a song and dance. One could almost see Fran tapping her toes with her hands on her hips, giving Liam the stare as if to say, "Now what excuse do you have?" Liam was as good as married!

Frank Vorstermans served as CNR station master in St. Marys upon the recommendation of the retiring George Beall. True to his military background, Frank was instrumental in setting up the first St. Marys Legion Hall across from Bruce Lindsay's old Garnett House, honoring the needs of returning veterans. On Friday nights he could be seen up the street with Gordon Puttoch practicing the bagpipe chanter while downing a few cold ones. Frank had found a home at last.

Despite the war raging on globally, St. Marys and Wellburn offered some form of emotional withdrawal for all. There were no threats to blow up the town and no reports of murders or missing persons. Church attendance was at an all-time high, and after recovering from Picard and Brisbois influences, everyone began to refocus on a local level, concentrating on home town issues.

With industrial production markedly spiraling for the war effort, many farm families moved into town. Though temporary housing was set up for them near the cemetery at the east end of St. Marys, many townsfolk opened their doors to accommodate the new citizens. George Beall rented his house for a pittance to several families. The Carter house became a boarding facility while the new Furtney Block house became a duplex. The Eddys and the Irvines took in single men and women and treated their new tenants as family.

Phalyn Purdue took a late shift at the Foundry in quality control. Mae prepared victory boxes for the boys overseas while working an occasional shift at Scott's chicken farm. Vaughn began volunteer teaching of mathematics at the local high school due to the teacher shortage, as well as driving cement plant trucks to site locations on King's Highway from London to Windsor. He helped Will with the Boy Scouts and was being solicited to move into a District Commissioner's position.

For the duration, everyone endured meat, gas and clothing restrictions. Will Purdue was appointed Director of the local Combined Food Board by Mayor Thompson, overseeing the rationing of coupons for sundry consumables like sugar, coffee, fruit, jam and fuel oil. Unofficially, through local churches, he was working with Phalyn to distribute as much goat milk and cheese as possible to needy families. Phalyn was a natural manager as she directed all scrap metal and paper drives sponsored by the Boy Scouts of St. James.

After what they'd all experienced, their lives had become somewhat uneventful and normal, and they liked it that way.

Mae was looking out the kitchen window when Liam Boggin came running across the barnyard. She pulled her hands from the dishwater, grabbed a dry towel and hurried to the door. Liam leapt the three steps onto the porch, gave a quick rap on the door and entered in a huff.

"They did it anyway! What were they thinking? After all we went through!"

"Liam, what's the matter? Who did what?" Mae reached out and touched his flailing arm in an attempt to control him.

He took a deep breath and looked around Mae at Vaughn who was standing at the bottom of the staircase. Liam bellowed to his friend, "They went back to Dieppe and got slaughtered. The Essex-Scottish has been wiped out. Stubborn fools! We went there for nothing!"

Vaughn had come the rest of the way into the room and stood facing his friend as he continued. "I just heard it on the wireless–over 500 slaughtered! Maybe a few officers made it back but even the CO was captured. The Saskatchewans, Camerons and Royals were all wiped out! They never got past the beach."

Mae had snapped on the radio, and after the transistors to warmed up, fumbled with the dial to get a clear signal from the Canadian Broadcasting Affiliate out of Toronto. The message was devastating. "*...the main assault failed on all accounts. Tanks were abandoned; infantrymen were slaughtered after a few steps from the landing craft. All told, this is a sad day for Canada as we have lost almost 3,500 heroes...*"

Vaughn stormed onto the porch, pushing the screen door with such ferocity it popped the spring from its eyelets and the door from one of its hinges, and stood in silent frustration. He had had enough. He could give no more energy or emotion to the banality of war. Mae gently reached for his lower back, but the touch didn't even register with Vaughn. The warrior within him was bubbling to come out, but after a few breaths he controlled his anger and spoke softly.

"Liam, we need to contact the Windsor Barracks and see if there's anything we can do."

Mae pointed to the phone. "The number is in our directory book, Liam. Go ahead and give them a call."

Mae moved so she was face-to-face with her husband who just stared past her into the shoulder-high cornfield. She reached out to touch his face and could feel him gritting his jaw in aggravation. Vaughn was oblivious to any type of comfort.

"I am just so sick of this war! More death and more pain. Captain Russell will send out condolence letters from England, I'm sure, but I think I can help by visiting families as directed by the Windsor Barracks Commander."

"Vaughn, don't think ill of me, but I don't want you to leave. I can't be separated from you anymore."

"I don't want that either, but I must do something." His frustration was beginning to wane as a plan slowly took shape. "So, why don't you come with me? Liam can take care of things here. He has Fran, and Phalyn and Will if he needs anything. Not sure how long this will take, but I don't want to be separated from you again." It was a tender gesture that allowed the couple to reconnect, and Vaughn gave Mae a peck on the cheek.

"Liam can work out his frustration on the farm rather than going with us to Windsor. Let's use Frannie as an incentive for him to stay behind. He can even invite her out here for a few days. A female's touch would be good for him." Vaughn turned and went inside to check on Liam.

Mae sat down on the porch steps, straightening her blue plaid dress. She was warming to the idea of going with Vaughn and decided she could use a change and might enjoy a visit to the city, regardless of the circumstances. Besides, there was a Salvation Army Hospital in Windsor she wanted to check out that would work perfectly since Vaughn would be busy.

Just then the men came through the door. "We can leave on the weekend, Liam… I might also go over to Detroit and see a couple of the families from the 25th Platoon. I can stay at the barracks on St. Luke's Road. It's an ugly building, but I might run into somebody I know. There's a motel just around the corner that should be comfortable for Mae. We shouldn't be gone more than a week."

But Mae had her own ideas. "I appreciate the thought, but I'd like to make my own plans. Do you remember the young girl who passed through St. Marys a few weeks ago? She was expecting and had nowhere to go so I gave her the address of our Grace Hospital in Windsor that helps unwed mothers and forgotten children. I thought they could help her out and I'd like to check on her." Mae was excited about venturing into another Salvation Army outreach, especially one that had a warm spot for abandoned or orphaned children. "In fact, I feel sure they could put me up for a few days. The wife of a Salvation Army Captain must have some pull." Vaughn was pleased with Mae's plan.

He stepped back and said, "There's something else. Apparently, there is an official letter from Aldershot waiting for me, care of Captain Russell. Maybe it's my official discharge papers. Can't imagine what else it could be." They stared at each other remembering the last letter he'd gotten from Windsor that called him into military service. There was no real reason for it, but both Vaughn and Mae had an ominous feeling about the letter. It had been over a year since Vaughn had any communication with the military. Why now when things had settled down? Neither of them wanted to think about it.

As the time for their trip grew nearer, some of their anxiety was curbed as details fell into place. Everything was covered at the mission; Will talked Laurie Lane and Mip Duncan into providing a reliable company car for their trip; all the local churches: Holy Name Church, Knox Presbyterian, St. James Anglican and the new United Church of Canada, took up an ecumenical offering to pay for incidentals and expenses; and the IODE, not to be left out, gave them ration stamps for gasoline. The 154-mile trip to Windsor for the sake of the families of boys who had been lost in the war, was a done deal.

The only question remaining was: What was in that letter?

Chapter 5

Abraxas Ascending

Nassau, Bahamas

A quiet scratching on the door drew the attention of the men engaged in a discussion of their observations and opinions of the Nassau culture. All heads turned to see the Duchess of Windsor standing in the open doorway. "I just wanted to say good night, Gentlemen, and let you know the evening was a rousing success! I only wish, Herr Lubeck, you could have met my friend, Mary. There still may be time, though, since she will be staying with us for a few days. Perhaps we can all have lunch." Then looking at her husband, she added, "Will you arrange it, David? I'm exhausted and must be retiring."

David crossed the room to her side and affectionately touched her hand. "So sorry, my dear, for leaving you alone so much this evening. Unfortunate business matters occupied me, but I knew I could count on you to carry on. I will make arrangements tomorrow to clear my schedule to accommodate a luncheon. By the way, you look beautiful. I won't be much longer. We are just finishing up here."

"Take all the time you need. I planned to spend the night with Mary as we are going to the Colonial for breakfast and then for a small tour of Ft. Charlotte. Will you make sure the chauffeur is ready for me this time?"

Then as quietly as she entered the room, she whisked out with a gentle click of the door behind her. David returned to the group, cleared his throat and announced. "The Duchess has given me permission to have our meeting. Only the King can command more respect!"

The men laughed at his quip, but to Harry there was something pitiful about a relationship in which a husband feels free to make fun of his wife in her absence. For sure, her tongue was becoming meaner and sharper toward David, often leaving him emasculated, but he continued to deny the dysfunction through his dry English humor. Harry, in turn, was grateful for the respect and devotion of his dear wife, Eunice. How a man could live such a tortured lifestyle in public and private was beyond him.

Axel arranged the grey velvet channel chairs in a semi-circle around the Duke's desk. Each glass was topped off before they assumed their proper spots, with the guest of honor directly opposite the Governor. Protocol aside, Herr Lubeck took the lead. Surprisingly, he shifted in his seat and directed his attention to Sir Harry rather than the Governor.

"Mr. Oakes, I want to congratulate you on your recent mining successes in northern Ontario. You certainly have led a gilded life. In fact, I would like to talk to you about that discovery in light of transactions I have recently been involved in."

Harry was immediately on guard. There were only two people who he totally trusted and respected – his wife and his former lawyer, George Beall. Why did Lubeck want to discuss his gold? Who was this man with his overblown air of confidence?

"If you will pardon me, Mr. Lubeck, I know nothing about you and have a few questions myself before I will consider discussing my business dealings. Who are you, Mr. Lubeck, and who do you represent?"

Harry was suddenly the center of attention and finally realized the purpose of this meeting was for him to catch up to what the rest of them already knew. The others had obviously met to discuss the agenda beforehand, which incensed the already grumpy baronet. He was not used to being left out of any business venture that involved The Boys, so Harry continued before Lubeck could respond. "Maybe a better question is what is going on here? How dare you put me on the hot seat? You're staring at me like I'm being evaluated and judged. Lubeck, before you speak, I want Sullivan to explain."

The flamboyant realtor didn't hesitate. "Harry, we have to look beyond the war. It's a foregone conclusion that Hitler and Tojo will be defeated, so we need to look at how we can gain and emerge as winners from the fallout."

Axel took up the cause. "There has been a major coup in the banking industry in Europe and we must take advantage of it! Herr Lubeck is here to present our future to us."

Harry could hardly believe what he was hearing. "What type of coup and what does Europe have to do with me?"

Lubeck felt the conversation had come full circle. "The Reich has taken over much of the Amschel banking management."

Sir Harry's chest tightened when he heard the Amschel name again. He needed specifics. "What do you mean by banking management?"

Lubeck looked at Salming to take over. "Most of the historic Amschel investments have been safely hidden in Switzerland, America and Canada; however, with the removal of Jamie Amschel from leadership, a new pipeline exists for us to filter Amschel assets we currently hold, will soon hold, or will acquire in the future." Sir Harry nodded for Axel to continue. "The Reich will expand into Argentina, at least the fiscal infrastructure for now. This means establishing secured accounts–we already have our process in place for South America, but we need a duplicate practice for North America and the Bahamas."

"So, talk to the bankers. Why are you wasting my time? I specialize in the direct acquisition of one commodity only."

"Exactly, Sir Harry, and that is why we need your involvement."

"What could you possess that could even begin to interest me, Herr Lubeck?"

Very slowly and deliberately, the Duke walked around his desk and unlocked the side drawer, lifting out an oily-clothed object which he placed on his desk. He pulled the covering of the item aside while the group kept their eyes on Harry, waiting for his reaction.

Papillons d'or!

Chapter 6

Closing the Ring

❧

Windsor, Ontario

Once in Windsor, Vaughn was directed to travel beyond the Ford Motor Company Food Distribution Center. At the corner of Edna and St. Luke's Road, where the Essex-Scottish Barracks was supposed to be, he was surprised to find a shabby, dilapidated three-story building with several broken windows on the second floor. The wood-chip door was barred with a rusty padlock and there were no lights or any sign of life inside. After double checking to be sure he had the right address, Vaughn began looking around and noticed, across Edna Street, several pre-fabricated wood and corrugated steel huts and headed toward them. He could hear music coming from the middle building, so decided that was as good a place as any to start. Even though it was only noon, there was no traffic in sight as he crossed the street – no vehicles or pedestrians and no signs that it would change in the next few hours. This was a ghost town.

The plywood door opened easily into a seemingly deserted Quonset-shaped area that reminded him of his former quarters in Aldershot. The arched roof had no insulation and, despite the elevated wooden floor, was damp and uninviting even though a boiling kettle sat on a range behind the front desk. Against the opposite wall, three wooden tables, with a bench on each side, sat empty. This place had seen busier days, for sure. Now it was filled with dark green metal filing cabinets stretching all the way to the back of the hut with no illumination of any sort over the storage units. Vaughn thought it the most depressing and uninspired place he had seen in a very long time.

Then, from the dark recesses, a soldier appeared reading an open file and keeping time with the music coming from his radio. He sported a wedge-cap sloped at an angle that was certainly not military approved, with a double chevron on his upper sleeve indicating he was a Lance-Corporal. As he stepped into the light he was startled to see Vaughn, fully attired in his blue overcoat and Salvation Army cap.

"This is Intelligence, Buddy, 'M' shed. If you want Enlistment you'll have to wait till next Monday and go across the street. Be there at 6 AM and make sure you have your civil health records."

"Thank you, Corporal, but I'm looking for Colonel Petrie. He's expecting me. You may tell your commander that Captain McIntosh is here."

Sensing authority in Vaughn's voice, but confused about the visual of the Salvation Army uniform, the clerk wanted more information, "That would be Captain McIntosh… of which Army?"

"Both, Corporal. The 25th Platoon, if you wish."

Knowing the history of the 25th, that's all he needed to hear. He lifted the phone and made contact right away. "Colonel Petrie will be right with you, Sir. Can I offer you some tea while you wait?" The young man was distraught over his previous disrespectful behavior.

"Relax, soldier, I'm not here on official business, but I do suggest you straighten your cap, clean up your desk–and turn down that music–before Petrie arrives. And, yes, the tea would be very welcome."

"Thank you, Sir. Right away. The name is Underwood, Sir." After fumbling to find a clean mug, Underwood carefully presented his offering to Vaughn with two hands. "Begging the Captain's permission, Sir, were you with Major Forester? Pardon me for asking, but we are the Intelligence group and I've done a lot of reading and filing about the Regiment. I only learned the whole story of the 25th last week. Major Forester will be missed. He was a good egg. I thought I knew every soldier who shipped out, but I don't remember you."

Taking a half-sip to test the hot brew, Vaughn replied, "Yes, I knew Major Forester." That was it. The Major would have been proud to know that, if nothing else, the neophyte Captain McIntosh had learned that no extraneous information would be divulged.

Underwood returned to his desk and they sat, for the most part, in a comfortable silence awaiting the Colonel's arrival. A screech of brakes outside prompted Vaughn to place his mug on the Corporal's desk and head for the door. He wanted to meet Petrie on his own terms.

Colonel Petrie was an Amhertsburg boy, born and bred. His father operated the steamer ship that escorted tourists and day visitors between the town of Amhertsburg and Bois Blanc Island on the Canadian side of the southern Detroit River. The 272-acre island was a summer amusement park, affectionately known as Bob-Lo Park to the locals, with a carousel, dance pavilion, Ferris wheel, kiddie rides and car exhibit. Most visitors, however, took the short ride to the island just to enjoy the cool breeze of the river and a day of picnicking.

Thomas Petrie had cut his teeth as a Watchstander's Mate at the very tender age of eight, helping to collect tickets and answer questions as a ship's greeter. Over the years he moved into a boatswain's position, and as the deck crew manager gave the order to prepare for arrival or departure, and in time, his father and fellow mates came to depend on Thomas for all the logistical elements of a successful crossing from fuel to first aid.

This experience eventually parlayed Thomas Petrie into the Logistics Officer position with the Essex-Scottish. His primary task was to prepare the Regiment with tactical, strategic and operational support in order to complete assigned missions. From boots to buckles, khakis to kits and meals to wheels, Petrie was the pivotal man to figure out what the Essex-Scottish needed to be Canada's premier fighting unit. Once the regiment left for England in 1940, his duties were altered considerably to handling enlistment. Based upon the latest news from Dieppe, the Essex-Scottish would have to be refitted and reformed all over again. This task would, of course, fall to Colonel Thomas Petrie.

Prior to the outbreak of the war, Petrie had been good friends with Major Forester, giving his subordinate all he needed to win regimental military marksmanship competitions for almost a decade. It was not uncommon for both men to linger into the early morning hours at the Crown Bar after winning a prestigious competition.

As the Colonel's car came to a stop, Vaughn stuck his head through the back passenger window. "Colonel Petrie…McIntosh here. May I take you to lunch?"

Petrie was curious about the reason for Captain McIntosh's visit and the connection between him and Forester, and would determine through their discussion today whether he could accommodate the Captain. So far he was impressed. "Of course, Captain. Please climb in and we can be on our way. Only a frugal Scotsman can appreciate a meal when another Scotsman buys it for him."

Vaughn's first impression was a good one. He felt this was going to be a comfortable time for both of them.

Raising his voice to his driver, Petrie asked, "Johnston, where would you suggest the two of us go for lunch?" Vaughn noticed the driver's eyes darting back and forth between the road and the dashboard mirror, and smiled. Johnston must have learned his style of driving from Major Forester himself.

"I recommend the Blue Heaven on Ouelette. It's reopened with new management – Albert Kahn, the banker has underwritten it – and I've been told they serve a killer Reuben. And rumor is the apple pie is to die for!"

Both men chuckled at the lack of formality exhibited by the young Johnston. "Then Blue Heaven it is. Are you up for it, Captain?"

Any time Vaughn heard about apple pie he was ready, and was suddenly very grateful for the extra cash that had been gifted to him. "My uniform will fit the theme of the place nicely," he said with a smile.

Thomas returned the smile, thankful that his lunch mate had a sense of humor. "For starters, I'm looking forward to catching up about Major Forester."

"I admired John very much, Colonel Petrie. He was almost like a father to me."

"Well, we can talk more over lunch," he said, reaching into his jacket pocket. "I almost forgot. Here's a letter for you from Captain Russell."

Vaughn realized he had suddenly lost his appetite.

Chapter 7

Windsor, Ontario

Mae stood at the corner of Crawford and University, taking it all in. The Faith Haven House was one of the most beautiful buildings she had ever seen. She couldn't imagine this mansion had housed only one family since it was built almost fifty years ago. Now that it had been bequeathed to the Salvation Army, every one of the ten bedrooms was guaranteed to be constantly full…especially with the sound of children!

The Queen Anne red brick building had been constructed with a very complex roof line including wooden fretwork on both the upper and lower verandas. Floor to ceiling arched windows on each of the three floors, including the third story dormers, ensured that all the rooms would have plenty of natural light. Trust the Sally Ann to give new life to something that had supposedly out lived its time and worth.

As Mae made her way along the semi-circular driveway toward the front door, she was met by a special greeting party–an ambassador about three feet tall carrying a feral kitten her arms.

"Hello, my name is Annie. It's nice to meet you." She put the kitten down and watched it scurry under the front porch through a hole in the lattice work. There was something very comforting about a little girl loving an animal.

"Hello, Annie. My name is Mae. I like your kitten."

"She's alright," Annie responded, "but she only lets me hold her after she eats. I won't see her again till tomorrow. Do you have a kitten?"

"Oh, yes! But they don't come around me much either. They like living in the barn and chasing mice."

"I never saw a mouse. Mrs. Eff says the cats keep them away. I guess that's a good thing."

'It is a good thing, Annie. Mice scare me."

Annie was amazed. "A mouse wouldn't scare me! I could take care of it and feed it cheese. It could even sleep under my pillow."

Mae thought it was time to change the subject. "So, you live here, Annie?"

She nodded. "My mother is away working in a factory. She'll send for me when she finds us a place to live."

"I'm sure that will happen soon." Mae said, though she didn't really believe it.

"Would you like to see my room? I share it with Gail and Marie and Miriam and Patricia."

"I'd like that very much. You lead the way." Annie took Mae's hand and walked with her up the stoop towards the massive oak door.

"Now you have to be quiet so you can hear the bell." She put both of her tender hands on the key of the rotating mechanical bell ringer and twisted it as hard as she could as she gave important first-time directions to Mae. "Now stand back and check your dress so you look pretty. Little girls often find the best homes when they stand up straight… and make sure your hands are clean and your hair is combed. Mommies and Daddies like little girls who are clean. And don't speak until you're spoken to. Nobody likes a little girl with rude manners."

Mae could hear footsteps approaching inside.

"Now, this is the most important part. When they greet you, curtsy with your fingers spreading your dress." Annie assumed the position as the door opened and the mansion Matron appeared. The hostess acknowledged Mae with a wink, but immediately focused on her wee friend.

"There you are, my sweet little girl. And who is your friend?"

"She says her name is Mae. Isn't she beautiful? And she likes cats, but not mice. May I show her my room? Maybe she could spend the night with us."

"You have done such a good job, Annie, by bringing a stranger to our home…"

"I know the Bible verse, Mrs. Eff: Heeboos 2–Be kind to strangers. But Mae is not a stranger, she wears a dress like you."

Both Mae and Mrs. Eff delighted in the innocence of Annie. They looked at each other with a deep sense of recognition – not only from the enjoyment of God's purity within this child, but for the warmth that flowed through them as they touched hands.

"Annie, I need you to wash up for lunch now. Will you do that for me, please?"

"Yes, I will," Annie said. Then added as she turned to Mae, "It was nice meeting you. I'm going to eat a grilled cheese sandwich."

"It was nice meeting you, too, Annie. Maybe we'll see each other again later." Annie nodded and skipped off to the lavatory to prepare for her meal. Both adults stood in awe of this miracle of love who sang on her way, 'He loves me and He loves you, I love Jesus and so should you."

Mrs. Eff graciously took Mae's canvas bag and directed her behind the main staircase. "I'm so pleased you'll be with us for a while, Mrs. McIntosh. We have a small room for you off the kitchen pantry. The old bed springs are a bit noisy, I'm afraid, but you have a window to open for fresh air. The facilities are right down the hall if you'd like to freshen up. Once you get settled we sure could use your help with lunch and getting the little ones set for a nap afterwards." She chuckled. "Nothing like jumping right into things, I always say."

"I would love to join you now. I'll just leave my bag and unpack later."

Together they headed toward the dining room. "I noticed you're using an Army service bag. Was your husband overseas?"

"Yes, but he was discharged a while ago. He's the Captain at the St. Marys Citadel, here on business for the week."

"We have something in common then," Mrs. Eff said with a smile. "Let's check in on the girls and we can chat later." They made their way from the darkened hallway into the light of the kitchen in perfect lockstep, the older woman guiding her with the same attention she would have shown to one of her Faith Haven children. Mae felt very much at home.

Chapter 8

Blood Money

Nassau, Bahamas

Sir Harry was panicky, but like a poker player, refused to show his hand. Herr Lubeck cranked up the heat. "I'm surprised a man of your stature does not recognize the importance of this precious metal?"

"Is there something I'm missing, Herr Lubeck? You've placed this ingot in front of me like I'm to be amazed. Gold is gold."

"Oh, but this piece is special. As you can see by the marking, it's from Napoleon's treasury."

As difficult as it was, Sir Harry remained composed. He stood and took a deep breath as if annoyed by where Lubeck was taking this meeting. He asked Sullivan for a drink refill and approached the gold bar for closer examination. "So, this belonged to Napoleon? Shouldn't it be in a museum? You do have museums in Buenos Aires, don't you? Why are you wasting my time with this?"

Lubeck was not put off. "Because, Sir Harry, I know there are hundreds of crates–somewhere–filled with bars just like this."

"Bravo for you, Lubeck, but once again I fail to see why you have traveled all the way to Nassau for a show and tell."

Now Herr Lubeck was getting annoyed, but the others had seen this before and knew what Harry was doing. He would grill this man to test his mettle, so they settled in. The evening's real entertainment was just getting started.

"The world knows you as one of the pre-eminent speculators in gold and gold supply," Lubeck continued. "You have recently added to your wealth with your finds in Canada. We also know that you have escaped detection, in the past, by moving your gold away from the tax man. You know the methods of how to do so. We need to draw upon that expertise."

Harry turned the tables on Lubeck. "Who are you to ask me to spend my time and expertise on a mythological rabbit trail? I think you should have enough experts of your own to render a plan of action. Besides, I find your world and what you stand for most repugnant."

Axel didn't like the direction this was taking and jumped in. "We're talking business here, Harry, not ideology. National loyalties and political ties shouldn't matter. Hear him out, my friend."

Sullivan handed Harry his beverage, which he held in the air toward Herr Lubeck. "You have the time it takes for me to finish this last glass to sell whatever you are peddling."

Lubeck remained steadfast with his arms tucked behind his back. "Fine. I represent an interest that goes far beyond National Socialism and they have convinced me this gold is real. I've seen a portion of it myself, but the bulk of the treasure has gone missing. We know it was stored in your beloved Canada for decades – and we also know that somewhere a switch was made."

"I believe I will allow this fine liquid to touch my lips two more times, Herr Lubeck."

Lubeck decided he had to be direct. "Mr. Oakes, you know how to move gold without it being noticed. You know those who can make that happen. You did it twenty years ago and we know you are doing it now. We would like you to investigate for us and find out where the rest of the gold is being hidden."

Harry was beginning to enjoy the irony in the situation. "You want me to do what?! Even assuming I have all the connections you're so sure of, why would I help you? What's in it for me?"

The Duke slapped his hand on the desk in satisfaction. "Finally, we get to the crux of the matter! Gentlemen, I think Herr Lubeck and Sir Harry have come to an understanding. Why don't we just call it an evening to digest all that has been presented here?"

Axel and Sullivan acquiesced. They were fine with picking the discussion up the next morning, but Sir Harry thought otherwise. Despite being in a bad mood, bloody tired and tempered by juice that drops inhibitions, Sir Harry surprisingly ratcheted up the discourse. This is when he was at his negotiating best.

"No. I think it's time to drop the pretenses. I would like to speak to Herr Lubeck alone, Gentlemen."

The Duke feared the deal might fall apart if they didn't acquiesce to Harry's request. "Very well. There are some matters I need to discuss with the others, and I should attend to my lovely wife. We will leave you to your own devices. Gentlemen, if you would follow me, please."

When they were left alone, Sir Harry presumptuously sat in the Duke's seat and fondled the gold bar.

"Herr Lubeck, let's get down to brass tacks. I've listened to your struggle between trying to be diplomatic and finally resorting to arrogant demands, neither of which has convinced me of anything. If I was able to deliver what you want—and that's a big 'if'—it would be on my terms, not yours. So, let's begin again with you being honest with me."

Sir Harry was everything Axel and the Duke had said he was. The fact they had even gotten to this point was a business coup in Lubeck's mind so he decided he would play by Harry's rules, at least for the time being, and be up front and honest with him. "The Reich has removed James Amschel as the head of the Cartel and replaced him with Admiral Wilhelm Canaris of the *Abwehr*. As a former Kreigsmarine officer myself, I am trusted by the new head of the Amschel Banks and have been given the sole responsibility to represent Amschel interests here. What the Reich does not know, however, is that the Amschel organization, including Admiral Canaris, is no longer interested in working with them and has hidden most of their investments in Switzerland, Argentina and America where the Nazis cannot reach them. Unfortunately, this *Papillion* gold has eluded us thus far and my job is to find and deliver it to the Amschel Bank."

Harry thought this was a very interesting revelation. "Aren't you worried the Nazis will have other ideas?"

"Admiral Canaris, and many others of the Wehrmacht, know the war was lost when we invaded the Soviet Union. When the Allies take the continent, the outcome will not be good for the Nazis. Already there are plans to kill Hitler, and if that happens the rest of his vermin will scatter. Nazi control of the Amschel will be over and a permanent director will be found."

Sir Harry was a business savant who could smell out an agenda. "Pray, tell, Herr Lubeck. Do you believe that director will come from Argentina?"

"It is the obvious choice if... no, when... I can obtain the rest of the Napoleon gold. I can make it worth your while if you help me find that treasure."

"So, let's hear it. What do you propose?"

Lubeck positioned a pair of wire-rimmed glasses across the bridge of his nose and unfolded a map of the Bahamas on the Duke's desk. It showed the country from Grand Bahama to the Little Inauga Island–over 700 islands, mostly uninhabited. "All this can be yours. The Windsors aren't going to be here forever. Now that you have a royal title, that puts you in line for the position, and with the locals asking for their own choice to lead the country, you would be obvious because you have a sterling reputation with the people. Sullivan and Salming are not citizens and neither are members of the Legislative Assembly like you are. Do you see where this is going?"

"Why would I want to lead this country? I'm no politician."

Lubeck didn't speak, and instead pointed to Grand Bahama Island first, then to others like Eleuthra, The Biminis, Abaco and Exuma. "You already control much of New Providence, but I'm talking about spreading out to these family islands. Think of the future. America will be a big economic winner after this war and the Bahamas will be their playground. It works in Cuba, why not bring it here–50 miles from South Florida? Gambling, tourism, night clubs, vacations, deep sea fishing. There would be employment for all."

Sir Harry added sarcastically, "Drug use, prostitution, crime, gambling addiction and violence. The worst part is the native Bahamians would never be employed in management positions at the hotels or casinos. Cuba proved that. Besides, you're talking about degenerates like Frank Marshall, Charlie Luciano and Meyer Lanskey coming here to set up shop. Those Mafia types don't care about the Bahamians. They just want to suck the life out of the islands."

"But Axel, Trevor and David think it would be in the best interest of the islands for the future. Trevor has already been in talks with them."

"If you have all their support, why do you need me?"

"Sir Harry, you are the very spirit of these islands. With your blessing we could develop this country into something special. So, we learn from Cuba. There is a plan afoot to do just that in Nevada–a town called Las Vegas. We could beat them to the punch after the war is over."

"And what does this mean for you as the new banking head of the Amschel?"

"Off-shore banking for the United States. We become the Switzerland of the Caribbean. Business and investment groups founded in the Bahamas are tax free. This would ensure prosperity in the islands, just like gun running during the civil war and rum running in the last decade. We evolve and give the people in the United States what they want."

"So, if I can lead you to the gold, you promise me the Governorship of the Islands and sizeable ownership in the future development of my country."

"You give me what I need now to claim my position with the Amschel, and I can guarantee you a thousand times your investment over your lifetime. All you need to do is find the gold and we both win."

Sir Harry began folding the map. "I will take this with me and think about it."

"Sir Harry, I have one important question that I must ask you. What drives a man like you to keep going? Was it your youth in Maine, or the gold rush in Alaska, or in the Outback of Australia? Or was it Northern Ontario?"

"Herr Lubeck, there have been various things along the way. Ambition and greed have been driving forces in the past, but lately my motivation to keep going has been prompted by something else. Let me ask you a question. Have you ever played the Thoroughbred Pinball game, 'Favourite'?"

Chapter 9

The Waters of Meribah

Windsor, Ontario

Vaughn's luncheon with the Colonel was excellent. The Reuben was just as promised, including a large Kosher dill pickle–prompting Vaughn to make a mental note to add cucumbers to his garden next year – and topped off with a large piece of Dutch apple pie a la mode. As their conversation wound down, Vaughn knew he could wait no longer to find out the contents of the letter from Russell. Apologizing, he pulled it from his pocket and began to read.

The Colonel occupied his time with his coffee, observing Vaughn's reactions as he read through the three-page manuscript. After a time of sipping, dabbing with the napkin and rearranging the rest of the remaining cutlery, Tom had seen enough facial expressions to warrant a comment. "This communiqué from Captain Russell did not come through usual channels. In fact, it was hand delivered from England to my command here in Windsor. It has to be something important. May I ask, is everything alright?"

Vaughn paused, deciding how to frame his answer. "I have dealings with a banker in London who had handled some transactions for my mother. Captain Russell was with me for one of the discussions and he is forwarding an update to me." Vaughn's answer could not have been more vague, and Petrie knew it.

The Colonel was silent, waiting for the possibility of more information, so Vaughn felt compelled to be more specific. "My mother was quite well off and left me with a legacy of commitments. This letter is a summary of the progress of those commitments.

I believe it was transported directly to you because Russell knew you would respect the security of the message."

Petrie didn't want to press Vaughn further on personal matters. "I'm familiar with your previous let down at Dieppe. Losing a man like Forester does not sit well with me, so I was hoping this letter might give me some closure about what happened to him. And after the recent debacle, enlistment numbers have dropped off remarkably. Morale around here is quite low. You don't lose a whole regiment without the community being affected." Petrie finally got to the point. "Is there anything in your letter that I could share with the remaining men here at the barracks?"

This time Vaughn didn't have to mince words. "Major Forester was actually my father-in-law. It's a long story, but we never knew about the connection until we were in Dieppe, just before we were confronted." Vaughn paused, then looked at the Colonel. "He taught me how to be a soldier, Colonel, and after he was shot right in front of me, I murdered those who murdered him–and I have no regrets about doing so." Petrie was surprised that Vaughn was so forthcoming, especially being a Salvation Army Officer. "Forester's whole operation was a set-up and only one other person survived besides me. It took me a long time to overcome that guilt."

Vaughn slowly folded the letter and then held it up in front of him. "I also carry the responsibility to complete another mission, for which the Major indirectly prepared me, but it's personal and something I can't tell you about. Not because I don't trust you, but it's something my family has been fighting for three generations, and anyone who has gotten involved has faced great danger. So, when I say I will not give additional particulars, I do so for your own protection. I do not want anyone else to be involved."

Petrie was both relieved and, at the same time, concerned for his new friend. "I really don't want to know more Vaughn. I was just wondering about the Major. I'm sorry you lost your father-in-law–I knew him well enough to know his family was scattered – but it is good that you connected before he died. As for your other mission, I know you never trained with us here and that you were awfully young to be given a Captain's standing. I also know you were honorably discharged after the initial Dieppe fiasco. Those three things tell me a lot about you. As the son-in-law of Major Forester, a man I greatly admired, I am at your disposal. Besides we belong to the same regiment!"

"I appreciate that more than you know. I could actually use your help with the task I came here for. With the loss of the 25th Platoon in Dieppe, I'd like to visit any families who are close by who lost boys in the fighting." Tom welcomed Vaughn's support and offered him accommodations in the officers' quarters along with a car and driver to complete his intended rounds. Vaughn humbly accepted and for the rest of the week, while Colonel Thomas Petrie concentrated on rebuilding the 'eeks and squeaks,' performed his own spiritual patchwork.

Vaughn took the rest of the afternoon to walk through the Walkersville district. He needed to be in the right frame of mind to read the remainder of the letter, so with his head down he talked out loud to God, oblivious to what passers-by may have thought. Today Vaughn didn't care who saw him or heard his conversation, and besides, he was not ashamed of his relationship with the King of Kings.

"My sweet Father, I can't begin to think I can stand in Your presence without the shed blood of Jesus Christ. You are my King and Lord and everything under Heaven belongs to You. As I talk with You now, Lord, please give me wisdom to understand what You are trying to tell me. I know You created me and love me. I don't always understand what You are doing so please allow the Holy Ghost to lead, guide and direct me in the path You've set out for me, and I will give you all the Glory...Amen."

He ended up in Willstead Park facing the Tudor manor house of the same name, and strolled in silence through the cool shade of the trees. The shrubs and greenery reminded him of the English gardens close to the Rookery in Clerkenwell–the English laurel with its spikes of perfumed white flowers; the chirping sparrows darting in and out of the deep-green leafed pink euonymus, stealing the fruit from the ripening pods; the spiny leaves of the waxy mahonias that attached themselves to Vaughn's jacket as he passed by; all took him back to his days in England just after he left the war.

What lured him to pause and sit for a while, though, was a towering white elm. He positioned his jacket against the tree between its extended feet and leaned his back comfortably against the deep, cork-like furrows of bark. Vaughn closed his eyes, listening and feeling God's creation all around him. He crossed his arms over his chest and let his jaw relax, wishing he could remove his boots, but thinking better of it. His heart rate began to slow and his breathing was less labored as he drifted off to that singular place between deep sleep and a general conscious numbness.

A gentle breeze blew a leaf onto his face, startling him awake. At first he couldn't focus or remember where he was, then slowly began regaining his equilibrium, but when he tried to move, found his arms frozen from being in a locked position and his backside numb and tingly. The afternoon was noticeably cooler and it seemed darker, and looking at his watch he was amazed to see it was 5:00 PM! He felt refreshed, though, and finally ready to tackle the remaining contents of the letter. So, pulling his knees to his chest and shifting his position a bit, he began to read.

Dear Captain McIntosh:

I am in receipt of the news that James Amschel has been replaced as the Director of Amschel operations. Concurrently, I understand that Phalyn Tremblay has married and is living in St. Marys, Ontario. These are most remarkable events which cannot be discounted and have led to a vacuum and competition for the future control of the House of Amschel.

As you may be aware, we monitor global product exchanges. Outside of South Africa, the most lucrative find, over the past few years, has been in Northern Ontario, Canada. It is to this latter location I will first direct my communication.

I recently met with a Mr. Bolton Tass, a Canadian now working for United Press Services in London. He shared with me the inside history of Sir Harry Oakes and maintains that Sir Oakes has once again removed, undetected and unimpeded, massive stores of product from Canada to his adopted country of The Bahamas. Normally I would discount such a claim, but another circumstance has arisen which gives Tass's speculation credibility.

This is my second point of emphasis. An Amschel aspirant, Hans Lubeck is now living in Nassau, Bahamas. His presence would not be noteworthy except that he is in possession of several Napoleon bars, no doubt from your former treasury. This was divulged by the Amschel Security Head, Etienne Picard (of whom we previously spoke) who was eventually beheaded at Drancy Concentration Camp outside Paris.

This leaves Lubeck and Sir Oakes as the two figures of interest. Our agents who monitor the Duke and Duchess of Windsor have confirmed that a meeting was held between Lubeck and Sir Harry Oakes.

I am pleased that the gold remains within the Dominions of Great Britain, albeit in secret. However, it is only a matter of time until Lubeck will extract the product for his own political advancement.

And now my final point of this communiqué. You have lived up to your end of our bargain. Please consider yourself free of all responsibilities about which we conversed. On behalf of His Royal Majesty, King George VI, I extend our thanks for your loyalty.

Montagu Norman, Bank of England

The relief Vaughn felt was overwhelming! The torch had been passed from his hands to a very capable comrade. Let the big dogs fight it out for their worldly pleasures. He wished he could stand over the graves of his fallen family and friends and proclaim, 'It is finished!' But for now, he would complete his appointed rounds with the families of the 25th Platoon and share the good news with Mae at the end of the week.

Chapter 10

Spare the Rod

Nassau, Bahamas

Sir Harry was pleased that Eunice had purchased the Chinese screen. It not only blocked the early morning sun, but also afforded some privacy when the bedroom door was open to take advantage of infrequent cool night breezes. When he finally awoke, his morning coffee was on the veranda waiting for him, and as he enjoyed the early morning pick-me-up, he thought about his meeting the previous evening. So, the *Papillion d'or* had emerged once again, and with it all the possible accompanying problems. Sir Harry was impressed with Herr Lubeck's drive and ambition, but this Nazi/Amschel was not a person with whom he wished to do business.

Harry preferred the likes of Trevor Sullivan who was affectionately tagged a "Conchie-Joe," born in the Bahamas but with skin color reflecting the white of the Conch shell – a noticeable minority. After a few drinks Sullivan's speech would revert to the local dialect, so he spoke little and smiled a great deal when in the presence of the Duke and Sir Harry. He was just a homespun native who had come out of poverty and would do anything to avoid going back there.

Sullivan had been keeping company with the American crime ingrates represented by Frank Marshall, which Harry did not approve of, but despite that, Trevor and Harry had developed a trust leading them to enormous financial success on the islands. Lately, though, Sullivan had ventured out on his own reclaiming land for an American Air Base and the development of a luxury resort at Lyford Cay. Sir Harry sat back and let him do the leg work during this stage, but at the appropriate time he would come in to seal the deal and abscond with an exorbitant closer's fee. Harry thought about last night's meeting where Trevor had done what he did best–made introductions and then stayed out of the way. Greasing the wheels was his specialty, but he was smart enough to know when to step aside to avoid being an impediment to the others' progress.

Harry frowned as he thought about his son-in-law, Freddie de Marigny. Sullivan and Freddie both enjoyed gambling and the risk that came with it. Once again, this past week, his son-in-law had been acting unscrupulously and immorally as he entertained other women while his wife was out of town. If Harry found out Sullivan had done anything to encourage this latest adventure, there would be hell to pay!

Then his thoughts drifted to Axel Salming. Where the Duke of Windsor agreed in theory with the principles of the Nazi party, Salming was an actual practitioner of national Socialism, and an enigma to Sir Harry. On one hand, Axel had used his boat, the *Southern Cross*, to save over three hundred innocent lives after a U-boat sank the SS Athenia, yet recent claims by British and American authorities suspected his newest bank in Mexico City was being used to filter profits from Nazi armament deals. There was even talk of freezing his accounts until Allied intelligence could prove his intentions. Harry could overlook the Duke engaging in harmless theoretical thought, but Axel was one to keep a close eye on.

Sir Harry did not enjoy all these distractions muddling his mind, particularly on what appeared to be a beautiful day. The humidity was down and there was a slight cloud cover. He would forego his morning stroll to the beach in favor of the golf match the boys had promised Herr Lubeck, but first he had to deal with the issue of his son-in-law's behavior.

He walked along the second floor veranda to the fourth bedroom where he could see the prone body of Alfred Fouquereaux de Marigny in a less-than-dignified position. "Good god, man," he shouted as he came through the open French doors, "pull the sheets over yourself!"

Startled from a deep sleep, Freddie rolled to his side and stared out toward the balcony. Sir Harry moved to the leather-topped coffee table and poured half a cup of java which he forced into de Marigny's hands. "Drink this and listen to me very carefully," Harry said, working hard to keep his temper under control. "I am hearing stories about your dalliances all over the island. May I remind you that you are living in my house while

Nancy is away, and as such, I expect you to conduct yourself with the highest regard for your wife and this family."

"…don't know what you are talking about, Harry. I just got back from Miami. Flew in on Chalk's just a few hours ago."

"You may have been able to pull the fleece over the eyes of your last two wives, but I will not allow that to happen with my Nancy! You will act appropriately or you will be out. My favorite automobile smells of cheap perfume, no doubt from the female company Alex informed me you were escorting."

"I was just showing two investors some property," Freddie said, trying to sit up. "You should be proud of me!"

"I doubt very much that two American girls, barely out of high school, are actual clients!"

"They have connections and will bring their families back to Nassau. Word of mouth and a personal touch goes a long way. At least that's what Trevor Sullivan says."

Harry was livid. "Did Sullivan set you up with these ladies?"

"No, but I saw an opportunity and had to take advantage of it."

Harry wanted to strangle this petulant womanizer, but instead threw Freddie's pants at him. "I want you out of this house till Nancy comes home from Vermont. Go to your friend's house… George, or whatever his name is."

Freddie was dumbstruck. "Are you really throwing me out? I've worked so hard to meet the approval of you and Eunice."

"Her name is Mrs. Oakes," Harry said through clenched teeth. "You have not earned the privilege of addressing your mother-in-law in such a fashion."

"Well," Freddie said, regaining some of his bravado, "as long I have the love of one woman in this family I'm sure 'Mrs. Oakes' will grow to love and appreciate me in time."

"You are more than twice my daughter's age, twice divorced and you never even had the decency to approach Mrs. Oakes, nor me, for Nancy's hand before marrying her. I doubt very much that you will ever gain our good graces. My only hope is that Nancy wakes up sooner, rather than later, and we can send you back to where you came from… all the way to Mauritania."

Freddie slipped his pants on and grabbed a white cotton, short-sleeved shirt, buttoning it on his way to the washroom. Showing his contempt for Harry, he left the door open while performing the necessary function, then unabashedly addressed the King of the Bahamas. "How many years' difference is there between you and Mrs. Oakes, Sir Harry? And you have the nerve to lecture me?"

Harry took a step toward Freddie, bringing a mocking smile to de Marigny's face. Taking full advantage of his father-in-law's reaction, he continued, "Really, Harry, that's how you would handle this situation? Let's be realistic. I'm married to your daughter and she loves me with–how did she say it?–with all the passion of a hurricane. What can you do about that?"

Harry stopped himself short of pummeling this cad, but his tongue was still razor sharp. "Just remember, a hurricane has two parts. You took advantage of my daughter when she was young and played on her emotions–like the beginnings of a storm; but there is also the calm eye of the storm where one takes stock of all that is damaged and determines if anything is worth salvaging. I'm sure you'll eventually slip up in her presence, and after the sheen wears off this marriage, Nancy will see you for what you are."

"And then what, Harry? I'm married to this family. Do you think I would give that up and go away so easily? It will cost you dearly to get rid of me."

By his own admission de Marigny had admitted his real plan, just as Harry had suspected. But he wasn't finished with his analogy yet. "That is where the other part of a hurricane comes in, Freddie! The backside is unpredictable–winds are reversed and damage is usually greater. After all, the first blast loosened things up, and it's the second wind that is more injurious. Trust me, Freddie, you don't want that gale coming on you."

Freddie wasn't stupid and knew Harry had the power and means to make that happen, so he changed his tone a bit. It was time for the de Marigny charm to come into play. He realized he had gone too far.

"Sir Harry, I'm a little hung over and am saying things I really don't mean, so please forgive me for upsetting you. I'm not in any shape for such a conversation so early in the morning. You know Nancy and I love each other very much, so what can I do to make things right?"

"Nice try, Freddie, but it's not going to work on me. My orders still stand. I want you off Westbourne this morning. I haven't decided yet whether to tell Nancy or Mrs. Oakes about this latest incident, so I think it advisable for you to put some distance between us as soon as possible. Oh, and do not ask Alex to drive you into town. Maybe you can call your 'clients' and they can invest in you for a change. And mark my words, if I hear any more rumors about illicit behavior, I will personally horsewhip you myself." With that, Harry turned and walked back along the balcony to his own room.

Freddie was too foggy for any more banter with his departing father-in-law. He knew Sir Harry meant what he said and other accommodations would have to be made, but nobody insulted the Count de Marigny! Freddie would have to decide how he was going to react to Sir Harry after his head cleared up.

Freddie called the chamber maid and gave her instructions as he began to prepare for his departure. He was oblivious to the song she whispered under her breath as she left the room: "Come to da house and sees my gal, Eat my beans and rice as well. Do it, man, and be at rest, But cut me quick, or you lose the bless."

Chapter 11
Passeth All Understanding

❧

Windsor, Ontario

Mae McIntosh found herself in the kitchen after the noon meal at Faith Haven, washing dishes and cleaning up. She had always taken great delight in helping people, doing menial tasks that many others would often spurn. Today she immersed herself, offering her services in the scullery after she finished with the dishes. Mae's heart was open to whatever the Lord laid in front of her. Apparently He would give her a very full first day.

As Mae sloshed her way through ketchup-coated plates, all she could think about were the many blessings the Lord had bestowed on her and remained in a constant state of prayer, listening for His instructions. She drew heavily upon Colossians 4:2: "Devote yourselves to prayer, keeping alert in an attitude of thanksgiving." Today, she was given the honor to work with the 'least of these' – innocent waifs and strays who may never know their real parents. If God had provided her a path to this place at this time, she would be pleased to love and care for the Annies of this world, for however long it would be.

She knew very well what it was like to be abandoned, but God had given her Harriet Blackwell and Sheila Skipper, and through Cate McIntosh she met her husband. More recently, God had provided a new friend in Phalyn Purdue. How could she not praise a God who had provided so much for her, especially when she compared her life to the uncertain futures of these blameless children?

Mrs. Eff and two Salvation cadets were leading the girls upstairs for their afternoon nap when it was announced that an expectant mother was in labor, and had been for some time without their knowledge. The pre-ordained plan was set in motion and the doctor from Windsor General was contacted while the mother-to-be was comforted in a private maternity room at the far end of the first floor. Then Faith Haven was placed on lockdown until the process was completed. Everyone knew their place, including the children, who ushered themselves off to bed in complete compliance and tranquility.

It seemed like Mae was the only one who didn't have a job during this emergency, so she just kept at the task that had been assigned to her. After the dishes were dried and stacked on the wooden shelves she wandered to the basement where she found a mound of sheets, pillow cases, towels, shirts, pants, socks, frocks and underclothes awaiting attention. Judging by the load in front of her it seemed that every day in this place, not just Monday, was wash day. It was a good thing Mae had a very strong work ethic from her early farm days where one of the few things she had done with her two older sisters was helping Harriet with the wash. Laundry was a fairly standard process, and she felt she could easily apply her knowledge to what lay before her here. At least that's what she thought.

As she rolled up her sleeves, she was pleased to see several metal bins into which whites, colors and a few delicate items had already been sorted, saving her much time. Mae pulled out the cleanest clothes which would be washed first in order to re-use the water for the next load. As she sorted the laundry into piles, in the corner of the room she noticed an old copper tub hanging over a brick fireplace, and beside it a posser and ponch that were used to agitate the clothes in the tubs of water. For a moment she thought she might have to light a fire for hot water and use these heavy wooden tools as she so often had done on the farm, but then, to her relief, she spotted a four-legged white, electric Maytag washing machine complete with adjustable wringer, and above it a gas ascot ensuring that hot water would be readily available. She would not scald her hands after all, as had so often happened at home. Mae made a mental note to petition Vaughn to invest in such a wonderful appliance, especially when children came along. One thing she could not avoid, however, was the time-honored washboard where grubby stains would have to be addressed with some intensive elbow grease. Alongside the copper pot was a stone sink with two bars of carbolic soap, a plus for Mae who had been weaned on soap made from a mixture of pork lard, lye and disinfectant.

She stepped into an old pair of work boots and donned a rubber apron, protective clothing that was very helpful when using the washboard, and began filling the washing machine with hot water–without blistering her hands. She decided she liked this invention.

Mae scrubbed piece after piece up and down on the ridged washboard. After a while she heard an odd pounding and realized, to her dismay, it was raining. She would not be able to hang the laundry in the garden to dry, but would have to hang it inside – not the type of thing she was hoping for on her first day. When it rained on laundry day on the farm, everything had to be hung in the kitchen causing the whole house to be damp, and even steaming up the windows. But it couldn't be avoided–the scullery would just have to suffice for the time being.

After a couple of hours, she took a break to check on the progress of the mother and new baby, but instead of the excitement she expected, she found sad faces and a solemn atmosphere. Realizing something terrible must have happened, she looked at Mrs. Eff who put an arm around her shoulders and walked with her to the front porch.

"It seems the Lord has two more souls at His side today. Neither of them made it," she said, her voice catching on the words. "The mother had a cerebral spasm and the baby, respiratory problems. By the time the doctor arrived, a C-section was just too late. If only she hadn't hidden her condition from us for so long." Mae could tell Mrs. Eff was just barely holding her emotions in check.

"What do you mean 'hidden her condition'?" Mae asked.

"Many of these mothers are not healthy when they arrive here at Faith Haven. We try to monitor them, but it's not always possible. When it comes to giving birth, our girls generally fall into two categories–those you can hear a block away and those who remain silent. But they all have one thing in common–they don't know what to expect and they're terrified. This girl today had been ill for some time but we just didn't know it…maybe the flu but we'll never know for sure. We do our best to take care of them, but there is only so much we can do – especially if they don't want the help. Right now we have three girls on maternity watch, but they often sneak out at night for a drink or to meet with their employers, regardless of their condition."

"You don't mean…"

"Mothers seldom stay here with their children. They have to get back to work or they return to their families with shame upon them. We try to share God's love when they are here, but after a few meals and several good nights' sleep, they abandon their children. Many end up back on the streets, especially when all the soldiers were here. The mothers give birth and then move on."

"Judging by the laundry stacked up in the basement, you all have your hands full. What happens to the children?"

Mrs. Eff smiled slightly. "We have 25 here at the moment… five are boys. It's mostly boys who get adopted, or at least the proceedings are started. The final decision comes from the Provincial Court. Boys often are taken by farm families who need labor. In the past couple of years, with the war and all, extra hands are needed to plow and till. And at least with boys the sponsors know they don't have to worry about them getting pregnant."

"Do you follow up on the adoptions?"

"We can't. The records are sealed. I did see one boy in Chatham who I thought was ours, but I can't be sure."

Mae's heart was heavy as she asked, "And what of the little girls?"

There was a lengthy pause, then Mrs. Eff changed the subject. "You know, I used to have a drink at a time like this, and maybe even a cigarette. I had a husband who was a good man, and we were squeaking by before our whole world came crashing down. We split right here in Windsor. Truth be told, I was so ashamed of myself I left him. He deserved so much better."

"But you are one of God's soldiers. I see the warmth in your heart. You mustn't be so hard on yourself!"

"Mrs. McIntosh, you know nothing about me. If I were to tell you the whole truth you wouldn't be so kind in your opinion." Mrs. Eff shook her head and turned to Mae. "For now, I have to make arrangements for this poor family. I let them down. The least I can do is give them a good Christian burial."

She linked arms with Mae and headed back inside. "I'm tired, Mae. Could you attend to the wee ones? I promised them a trip to the park after their nap. The cadets will show you what to do." She stopped to open the door. "The children will like you–Annie will see to that. When I lose someone like this it takes the wind from my sails for a few hours, but not to worry, I'll be right as rain after I lay my head down for a few."

Not since the first time Mae had seen Vaughn had she felt so comfortable with a person. The scripture in Hebrews 13:5 came to her mind: "I will never leave you, nor forsake you." Mae was puzzled by this revelation, but knew the Lord was telling her something and, in typical fashion, she was determined to find out what it was.

Chapter 12
The Devil's Den

❦

Nassau, Bahamas

Axel Salming enjoyed having Herr Lubeck as his guest at *Shangri-la*. It was pleasant to hear German spoken again, particularly in Lubeck's softer Hessian accent, and it seemed to compliment his lifestyle of affluence, station and breeding. The property here, after four years of his influence, was starting to take on the appearance of the famed Chateau de Versailles. Hog Island was being transformed into a silk purse complete with landscaped tiered gardens, lily ponds and marble statues of both mythical characters and real people including Hercules, Mephistopheles, and Napoleon and Josephine. But unlike the great Versailles, *Shangri-la* was bordered on the south by a light-brown-sugar sand beach flowing into aqua-green waters. It was a slice of heaven in the middle of Hog Island, just a small jetty ride from Nassau city proper.

"That beach you love so much, Herr Lubeck, is called Cabbage Beach."

"What an odd name. It does not do justice to such a beautiful place."

"Yes, it is an odd name… comes from the locals and goes back to pirate days when the Spanish ruled this island. The buccaneers who lived here made a popular fish stew they called *cebiche*, and over time the name evolved and became more Anglicized to Cabbage."

"Ah, that makes it a bit more palatable. Might I suggest you also come up with a name other than 'Hog Island' for this paradise, as well? I take it there's an explanation for that name, too, though I'm not so sure I want to hear it."

"Of course there is, but I think it best to dispense with that seeing we haven't had breakfast yet," Axel said with a smile. "I was thinking I could rename this place Ecstasy, or even Paradise Island, but that will have to wait till I can dredge the harbor a bit."

"Speaking of waiting, I wonder what's taking Sir Harry so long to come around to our plan."

"You are in Nassau, Herr Lubeck, where things move at two speeds, slow and stop. It takes some getting used to, but you'll adapt or it will drive you crazy. You'll learn there's no sense trying to rush something ahead of its natural course. Besides, Sir Harry doesn't like to be pushed."

"But you, along with the Duke and Sullivan, have much influence on him, don't' you? Can't you give him a nudge? The *Cosa Nostra* will not wait forever, you know. They have a way of getting what they want whether it's in Chicago, New York, Philadelphia, New Orleans – or here. He needs to be wary of these people."

"But this is not America, Herr Lubeck. We don't rush into things here. There must be an agreement among all parties to preserve the best of what we have if we accept what outsiders can do to help make us better economically. Just as the English Channel is England's protective barrier from the influences of Continental Europe, so the Florida Straits are for the Bahamas from The States. When the deal is done, we'll finally host the DUKES and Ambassadors of the world, but you must have patience, Herr Lubeck."

"I'm afraid that's a trait I do not possess. You must agree, neither of us got to where we are today by being patient."

"Agreed, but remember, this is not our native country. We're virtual strangers here, operating within a foreign culture. I've found the secret to getting things done here is through evolution, not revolution. You know the tumult created in your own Argentina when a strongman dictator forces his will on others. At first he may get what he wants, but over time the tyrant spends his energy trying to prevent others from taking it away in favor of what they want."

"A good reminder, Axel… and speaking of tyrants, whether Hitler is overthrown, or if somehow that madman is able to continue the war, we must be prepared to act immediately. The Amschel were always very good at landing on their feet because they underwrote both sides–it didn't matter who won, there was a result from which they could prosper. That philosophy was put into place so the family would remain powerful and has never been lost. We are proof of that today.

"Our quest now is to acquire, own... and control. Our purpose is in the process, not the direct acquisition of wealth–that will take care of itself when the first part falls into place. Our lives need to be dedicated to an unseen power, one that Jamie Amschel understood. We are a select few who will mold world history."

Axel could not hide his exasperation. "I understand what you're saying, but I can't help but be frustrated. I remain on this tiny island with all the comforts any man could want, yet I have a drive inside for more. Something deep within urges me on every time I succeed. It's just not enough. I need to succeed again. It is almost like Hermann Goering's addiction for owning the art pieces of the Great Masters. When will enough be enough?"

Lubeck could not understand Salming. Here was a successful millionaire who had filled his coffers to overflowing by building an empire based on mundane consumables like light bulbs and vacuum cleaners. He had created a diversified empire that offered him as much money and pleasure as a man could want. Yet, he was questioning what had brought him to this point. The exact thing he had been talking about – the drive for more. "I do not fully comprehend why you are having these doubts, Axel. Your inner unrest seems to be exactly what I'm referring to – a hunger for the quest."

"Perhaps it's because I realize that after almost a decade, one of my closest friends may not share that vision. Sir Harry does not see things the way we do and I fear I may have sorely misjudged the man. Your coming here to Nassau is a critical test for all of us."

"Bear in mind, Herr Salming, Sir Harry took the map and gave all indications he believes the gold is still out there. He also seemed most agreeable to the offer presented to him."

"That's actually what's bothering me. Harry is never agreeable unless it's on his own terms. I both despise and respect him for that trait. Trust me, you can't assume anything yet about where he stands concerning your meeting."

"But surely, if one follows the logic..."

"That's what makes Sir Harry so special. Logic plays a minor role. He is philanthropic but does not have to be. He spends a great deal of effort to be sure his employees, and the Bahamian people in general, receive their fair share, but he doesn't have to do it. I fear Sullivan and I do not have the same heart as Sir Harry, after all."

"But the decision he will make has nothing to do with the heart."

"Ah, but that's where you're wrong, Herr Lubeck. Sir Harry loves to make a profit, but the same conscience that drives his passion to protect his family also comes into play in his business dealings."

"Sir Harry has a conscience on business matters? Is this the same Harry Oakes who cheated the Canadian government out of millions of tax dollars on previous dealings?"

"Herr Lubeck, allow me to give you the true story. Sir Harry actually paid more than his share of taxes to his country, and what he invested in the wellbeing of local communities went far beyond what should have been expected. Have you ever been to Niagara Falls in Canada?"

Lubeck shook his head, and Axel continued. "During the depression he created thousands of jobs in road and railway construction in that community alone. He built athletic fields, public parks and gardens, giving his name freely to city development commissions. The man cared about his community, and now feels the same way here in the Bahamas. In fact, when Sir Harry returned from Canada a couple of years ago, he was even more compassionate than ever before."

"Are you saying Sir Harry might rebuff my proposal?"

"Don't be surprised if he does. I know he's not crazy about anything to do with the Nazis and has told the Duke that on many occasions. He has earned his money himself, legally, and is leery about this proposal for bringing the Americans on board. He doesn't trust them."

"So, he hates the Nazis, will not work with the *Cosa Nostra*, and doesn't take the Duke of Windsor seriously. What are we to do, Herr Salming?"

"As I see it, all we can do is wait," Axel said. "You've made him a wonderful offer, so we wait and watch him closely to see if he can find out anything about the Amschel gold."

Herr Lubeck nodded, and after some thought, added, "Perhaps we should meet again with Sullivan, David Windsor and Frank Marshall for some further discussion, but right now I think I would like to go for a swim to get my day started."

Axel called for his servants to bring in the breakfast table. "I would advise that you stay away from the corals. We have some nasty fish out there – they not only bite but can poison you. Won't you have some breakfast before you go?"

"No, thank you. Better to exercise on an empty stomach. I won't venture too far—shouldn't be more than an hour."

As Lubeck headed toward the stairs, Salming had a final thought for his guest. "When you return I'd like to take you to the main island to see what we call the Queen's Staircase—might help you appreciate what drives Sir Harry to be the man he is. You'll find it most remarkable as it leads to the top of Fort Fincastle, the highest point on the island where the British used to watch for pirates and other such n'er-do-wells." Then, turning back to his breakfast, he thought to himself, but the difference now is, the pirates are already here.

Chapter 13
Tough Love

Windsor, Ontario

As the ambulance drove from the crushed gravel driveway of Faith Haven, Mae interlocked her hand with Mrs. Eff. Annie, noticing this display of love, mimicked the act by slipping her little fingers into Mae's other hand. "I didn't know that lady," she said. "Is she asleep now?"

Mae picked Annie up and placed her on her hip. "Yes, Annie, she is with Jesus now and is very happy."

Mrs. Eff noticed three inquisitive ladies on the other side of the porch and herded them inside. This wasn't exactly what an expectant mother should see, but the matron decided it was a good time to make a point. "Girls, this is the kind of thing that can happen when you don't take care of yourself while you're expecting. The most important thing, though, is when you feel it's your time, you must tell me! Do you understand?"

The three young women instinctively cradled their distended tummies and nodded in acknowledgement. Most were looking forward to having the baby 'out of them', but none were expecting to leave Faith Haven in a pine box. It was a process Mrs. Eff hoped they would now take more seriously. Most would, not because they loved their soon-to-be-born child, but because they wanted their own misdirected lives back as soon as possible. Subsequent laughter from the departing brood told Mrs. Eff her warnings were not taken as gravely as she'd hoped. Each would learn in their own way soon enough.

"Let's have some tea before Vespers," she said, turning to Mae. "The Army doesn't like to call evening prayer such a thing, but I like the good feeling that comes with letting it slip off the tongue…Vesssperrrrss....see what I mean?"

Mae smiled. "You certainly are a mixed bag for an Army type, Mrs. Eff. Cigarettes, drinking and now a Catholic connotation. Don't get me wrong, I'm not complaining, but I would love to hear the story behind who you are sometime."

Mrs. Eff gave Mae a curious look, then said, "If the circumstances are ever right, I might tell you someday."

As they entered the kitchen, Mae plopped herself onto a wooden chair and dropped her head into her hands, closing her eyes. Mrs. Eff smiled. "You've had a tough first day, Mae–dishes, laundry, the park and now this. Welcome to our world. There is no such thing as a good or bad day here because we are always on. It's how you approach each morning that determines if the day will be a blessing or something to be dreaded. Often, just like the past few days, they run together and I lose sight of reality. I guess living on a farm you're used to long hours."

"We have a man who takes care of things most of the time, but come planting and harvest we put in the hours, too. And along with the farm, the mission in St. Marys is our responsibility. I've spent more than a few nights stuck at one or the other. So, I think I have an idea what you're going through."

"Well, judging by your appearance right now, I would say you're just about done for the day, which means there will probably be one or two more crises to take care of before you go to bed. I was going to ask you to spell a couple of the cadets so they could have some regular sleep time, but not tonight."

Mae smiled weakly, for she knew she was at her breaking point. It was one thing to milk cows, bale hay, plant corn, feed the animals, shovel snow and clean the pens. It took another skill set altogether to deliver babies and tend to the children, non-stop. It was a different type of fatigue that required remarkable strength. These servants of Faith Haven were truly angels.

"I know that look," Mrs. Eff said, putting her hand on Mae's shoulder. "Let me comfort you with this verse, 2 Corinthians 12:9: 'My strength is made perfect in your weakness.' And right now the Lord is sure looking strong!"

"You see, that's another thing I noticed about you, Mrs. Eff. What a wonderful sense of humor you have. I've met some very stodgy Army members over the years, who seem to be so heavenly minded they are no earthly good!"

"Looks like we are stuck in the verses of Corinthians tonight, Mae."

"To be honest, I was thinking about the lyrics of a country music song I used to know."

Mrs. Eff let out a laugh and nearly scalded herself as her hot tea sloshed from her cup. Choking just a little, she regained her poise and calmed her voice. "Well, aren't we the pair of sinners? Better not share this with the others. I'm afraid they all have a pre-conceived idea about what a Captain's wife should act like."

"I think I'd be knocked off that lofty perch pretty quickly if they could hear a few of my tales!" Mae told her.

Mrs. Eff relished her visitor's humble nature. Mae McIntosh was something special in her eyes and had earned some new respect and trust. "When I got your call and letter, I didn't know what to expect. To be honest, we occasionally have people who volunteer here, but they don't last long. Laundry alone usually makes them re-think any commitment, but assisting in childbirth is the real acid test," she said, looking intently at Mae. "Maybe I should hold back my judgment of you until you've been through that experience."

"Well, I've done my fair share of birthing sheep, goats, Holsteins and a few foals," Mae said. "I put my dog down at a young age and have laughed at a rooster running around after having his head cut off."

Then without thinking, she added, "True, I don't know what it's like to see a human baby born, but I do know what it is like to take a life…" Too late she realized what she'd said, but she couldn't take it back.

Mrs. Eff put down her tea and stared at her dirty fingernails. Neither said anything for a moment, then clearing her throat, Mrs. Eff looked up at Mae wanting an explanation. "No, No! Not that! I've never killed a baby!"

Mrs. Eff's demeanor didn't change. "We've had mothers here looking for some type of closure after they ended their own child's life. You say 'no' and I accept that. I am not here to judge you. We've all come up short in the Lord's eyes–my life is full of major regrets. Only God knows your heart, that's really all that counts."

"As you said to me earlier, maybe sometime the circumstances will be right and I can give you more details." Mae gave her a slight smile and, thankfully, Mrs. Eff smiled back. Someday there was going to be a very interesting conversation between them, but not today. "I came to Windsor with my husband who is at the Essex-Scottish Barracks offering his services there. Our Board in St. Marys gave us its blessing. I wanted to follow up on a girl who I sent your way after she passed through our town. She had no family–her husband was killed while serving in the Merchant Marine–and she wanted to go home to Charring Cross after her baby was born."

"We have more and more of the war widow stories these days. Sometimes, they have a baby while their husbands are serving abroad, which would be pretty hard to explain when the soldier comes home. Of course there are the girls who perform other services, and we do have some unfortunate ones who are placed here by their families to hide the shame of what they call their daughter's disgraceful behavior…as if she got pregnant by herself."

Mae took a folded piece of paper from the breast pocket of her thick-collared work dress and slid it across the table to Mrs. Eff. "This is the name of the young girl who I mentioned. Did she show up?"

Mrs. Eff unfolded the paper, read it, and handed it back to Mae. Her response was curt as she returned to finish off her tea. "I'm sorry but you missed her. She just left in the ambulance."

Mae was devastated at how coarse her response was. Had the matron seen so much of death that it had become as common place as brushing her teeth and washing her face? Was she oblivious to the pain and hurt that accompanied a tragic end to life? With this in mind, Mae wanted to chastise the older woman, but surprisingly, the words could not come out.

Mrs. Eff could see the turmoil on her companion's face. "Mae, our focus here is eternal. We provide some worldly comfort and care for these girls, and we try hard to find homes for the children many of them leave behind. Those we reach with the message, and who end up caring for their own babies, are a sorry few. We can only share the love our Lord Jesus Christ provided for us. With each meal we serve, each hug and kiss we give and receive, every hour of listening to the fears and dreams of the broken hearted, we try to show the real Jesus. Not the one hanging on the cross, but the one who is resurrected and alive, the One who can change lives and give courage to take on the challenges of birthing a new life and seeing it as a blessing.

"If I seem a little unemotional, it's because I truly believe the Lord is in charge of everything here. I'm just a foot soldier, deep in the mires of human frailty. I do not have the time or the energy to react to all the reasons for the comings and goings of our wards. We all grieve in our own way. Some prefer to openly cry and bellow in real pain. People like me express my hurt when I am alone in my room. It is better for all that I remain publicly aloof, but when I am in my prayer closet with the Lord, my heart just breaks. So please do not be disapproving of me."

Mae was embarrassed for the disgust she had felt for Mrs. Eff and was glad the Lord had muzzled her mouth.

Chapter 14
Honor Among Thieves

❧

Lucas County, Ohio

On its opening day, the Ambassador Bridge was the world's longest suspension bridge spanning the two countries with an apex of 152 feet over the rapidly moving Detroit River. A circus-like atmosphere attracted "odd balls, daredevils and stunt seekers" of many kinds. As the Detroit Free Press reported: "...planes would fly under it, a man would parachute off it, a man would cross it walking backwards, another would push a friend across it in a wheelbarrow, a girl would toe-dance her way across it and couples would marry at its international boundary line...."

Detroit had experienced a boon decade in the 1920s having built some legendary towers of power as a backdrop to the Ambassador, including the Penobscot Building, General Motors and Fisher Buildings, the Detroit Public Library and the massive Masonic Temple. But the crowning glory of the expansion was the finished construction of the Ambassador Bridge in 1929.

Then, during the depression that began only 21 days after the bridge's opening, the amount of paying traffic decreased remarkably to the point

*that the brain trusts of the Ambassador eventually had to default on loans
and reorganize its financial moorings.*

*Judging by the traffic this day, the financial future of the Ambassador
was looking up.*

There was nothing Vaughn McIntosh loathed more than leafing through paperwork,
but as he read through the files of the deceased members of the 25th Platoon, he
learned about the background and personalities of his men which had been previously
unknown to him. Vaughn found his former platoon coming back to life in ways he found
most tragic, but also a little comforting.

One Private, from Toledo, Ohio, had been an excellent baseball player. Tom had grad-
uated from Waite High School and had a character recommendation from a former Chief
Justice of the Supreme Court of the United States. Who knew these non-descript young
men had such exalted connections?

Another soldier, Kenneth, who Vaughn remembered with more familiarity, hailed
from St. Clair Shores in Macomb County just northeast of Detroit. As a youth, the District
Court had sentenced Kenneth to a one-year probation for helping his brother receive
bootleg liquor from the Canadian side of Lake St. Clair. Vaughn remembered the night
he had lectured Kenneth on the evils of the 'devil drink,' but he would never know if his
lecture had any impact.

One of the standouts of the group was an older Corporal, Edwin, who had worked in
the Willow Run Transmission Plant in Ypsilanti before the Ford Company converted it to
construction of B-24 Liberators. He had a wife and one boy, and longed to do something
special with his life, like own his own repair garage. Vaughn and Edwin had shared a
love of all things involving engines, speed and automobiles. Their relationship solidified
around a mutual respect for the famed race car driver, Leon Duray, who competed at the
Indianapolis Motor Speedway. In fact, Edwin boldly displayed a tattoo on his upper right
arm with Duray's Number 26. Though Vaughn was a great fan, he would never go that
far himself, but was impressed with the Duray tattoo, nonetheless.

The rest of the platoon had commonalities that Vaughn now found endearing – dere-
liction, disrespect to an officer, contraband and being AWOL. They were tough Yanks, but

in the end were honored and respected soldiers who paid the ultimate price. Vaughn would travel to northwest Ohio and southern Michigan to meet the families of these fallen heroes, to share his thoughts on what outstanding sons, husbands and brothers they had become. In doing so, Vaughn also hoped for a little closure for himself. This vision for his week would be a perfect complement to the good news he'd received from Montagu Norman.

Captain McIntosh had taken a liking to the file clerk, Underwood, and asked that the Private be reassigned as his driver. Knowing a great deal about the history of the members of the 25th Platoon, Underwood would be a valuable resource in preparing Vaughn with the backgrounds of the men.

Crossing the Ambassador Bridge, Underwood was fairly talkative. "This Bridge is a beauty, isn't it? The wind is not so bad, even in the winter. A lot of people like to take the tunnel, but they miss out on a great view. With the war and all, the amount of civilian traffic is down, but it seems we have more trucks than ever before. The new warehouses in Windsor seem to be one reason for that."

Vaughn tried to enjoy the view, but as they crossed the border, visions of wooden crates with "St Marys Foundry" across the side in big black letters kept clouding his mind. He had to remind himself to put that part of his life in the past and move ahead, so he shook his head and brought himself back to his present task. "Did the men of the Platoon return home much?" he asked Underwood.

"No, Sir. A few did before they shipped out to Camp Borden, but why would you skip three squares a day, cheap Canadian beer and all the good looking women with those lovely accents?" Underwood chuckled, then turned to Vaughn. "I've been noticing, Sir, you don't sound Canadian at all."

"Born in England, raised in Chicago and now live in St. Marys, Ontario. I guess I have a bit of an accent from everywhere."

"I can see why the boys liked you, Sir. Even with all that Salvation Army hoopla and stuff. No offense intended, Sir."

"There are more sides to me than just this coat, hat and the Good News, Private. I think I may have scared a few of them along the way."

"Did you hit 'em over the head with the Bible if they didn't listen?" he said, smiling at his joke.

"I think you're enjoying this drive a little too much, Underwood. You appear to be mocking my position." Vaughn was enjoying the banter, but couldn't let the Private become too casual and familiar.

"I sure am, Sir, and I have every right to!"

Vaughn leaned forward and put his hands on the front seat cushion. "This explanation had better be good, Underwood." Vaughn said in a stern voice.

"Well, Sir," Underwood started, realizing he may have pushed a little too far. "My home town is Ingersoll, Sir, and I grew up in a Sally Ann in Woodstock. My uncle is Gary Pulford who commands the Citadel there. I love to tease our kind."

Vaughn smiled and relaxed back into the seat. "I know of Gary Pulford. In fact, he's pushing for the construction of a dam in that area for water control. The farmers are really hurting with all the excessive flooding. They want to do the same in St. Marys. I love how Major Pulford gets into his community. You have a great man in your uncle, Underwood."

"Agreed, Sir, and, now, if I can compliment you, may I add that what you are doing with this visitation and all, my uncle would be fully supportive. I'm glad you asked me along, I can be a real prayer warrior for you."

Traffic was slowing down as they descended the Ambassador to U.S. Customs, reminding Vaughn there was still a war going on. "Well, we'll need a prayer if we are to get through this Customs stop within the hour. Look at that line up."

The security on the American side reminded him of the hectic activity at the port when the Essex-Scottish first arrived in Scotland. Floodlights had been erected so traffic could be viewed clearly at all hours and in all weather conditions. It was a bee hive of constant motion appearing to have no organizational purpose, with armed personnel everywhere.

Amidst all this random movement, the stationary lines of idling engines spewed such dense carbon fumes the drivers had to keep their windows closed. Willy's Jeeps boxed in all the automobiles as border guards patrolled among the customs lines inspecting each vehicle and its occupants. Any abnormalities relegated a vehicle to a separate area for a more thorough inspection, where identification papers were scrutinized, tarpaulins were removed from payloads for verification and truck cabs were examined for anything suspicious or out of place. In the distance Vaughn could see that soldiers had handcuffed a suspect and were carting him off to a conference booth. His day at the border would certainly be a longer one than theirs.

Suddenly a security guard tapped on the window beside Underwood. "Is this the motor vehicle of Captain Vaughn McIntosh?" he asked. Underwood presented Military IDs for both of them, and was directed to a restricted lane off to the side behind a wooden barricade. They sat for a while waiting for an inspection, but they had learned to wait, and wait in silence…it was the military way. Finally, a Lieutenant came sprinting from the communication building. Pulling down on his tunic, he signaled for the barricade to be moved and gave a salute as the Captain's car came to a halt beside him. "Courtesy of Colonel Petrie, Sir…" and then winking at them both, "…and a crew man of the Bob-lo steamer, *The Promise*! Have a nice day!"

Underwood confidently pulled away from a dozen or so vehicles that had been in front of them moments before. "You see? I prayed and it happened. The Good Lord is using me to help you, Captain McIntosh," he said with a smirk. "Maybe you should tell me your expectations for today and I can ask for some more divinely-inspired guidance. Just say the word."

Vaughn was seeing Underwood as a modern-day blending of Daniel and Philip. His confidence in prayer was uncanny as was his willingness to be led of the Spirit. His sense of humor throughout this trip, on the other hand, would just need to be embraced for what it was. With the meetings that lay ahead of him, Vaughn decided to enjoy any lighthearted moments he could.

"Underwood, I want you to take the Dixie Highway for about forty miles until we cross the Ohio line. We're looking for a place called the Devon Club."

The Private jerked the wheel in surprise. "The Devon, Sir? Are you sure that's not a mistake? Do you know what the Devon Club is?"

Vaughn fingered the badly worn paper and rechecked the address, confirming it with Underwood who suddenly became quiet. "OK, Sir. That's where we'll go, but I sure hope you know what you're getting in to."

In the early forties, Lucas County, Ohio, had become a hotspot for gamblers from Detroit. North of the city limits of Toledo was a group of "entertainment and houses of chance" known as the Old Dix, the Chesterfield Club, the Victory Club and The Academy. These were great places for a quick and cheap steak, but the real action could be found in the rear of the buildings – craps, horse betting, prostitution and watered-down liquor at cut-rate prices. With the war, all the clubs had closed except The Victory – appropriately enough – and it was a favorite with the locals.

But the Mob wanted another club that catered more to the Detroit crowd, so they opened the Devon. The 10,000-square-foot joint featured over fifty gaming tables for craps, blackjack, roulette and other various games, and of course, the traditional horse race boards.

It was strictly off limits for members of the Armed Forces of either country to frequent any gambling venue, but this rule was about to be broken. Underwood was feeling as if he had gone from Joshua, the great and faithful follower, to a doubting Thomas. "Sir, do you know about the Devon and the type of people there?"

"Colonel Petrie and I discussed this visitation and he gave me fair warning. I only want to give a message to one person and this is the address that I was given."

"Maybe you should think about leaving your hat and jacket in the car. That might attract less attention. These boys are pretty turf protective and don't want any of our kind disrupting the patrons."

"I am not there to disrupt. I am just there to tell Mr. Billy Orondorf about his son, Samuel."

Still not comforted by Vaughn's calmness, Underwood gave a hint of what to expect. "They got soldiers there too, Captain, except their ranks go by Muzzler, Slick, Chalky and Lefty…if you catch my drift."

This time it was Vaughn who closed his eyes and asked for God's strength as the car proceeded by the dog track and turned onto Benore Road. Ignoring Underwood's advice, Vaughn headed toward to the main entrance fully clad in his armor of God, past the look-outs under the neon canopy displaying the Club Devon sign. If he wanted attention, this was the fastest way to get it.

Before he could reach the main doors, however, three gentlemen in long, dark jackets, diamond-pinned ties and white fedoras approached him. "Hey, Father, we gave last Christmas. This ain't no charity place."

As other patrons passed by there were giggles, staring and finger pointing that caused a traffic tie-up at the doors. Vaughn had already gained quite a bit of notice without saying a word.

A second greeter backhanded his larger companion to set him straight, and eyeballed Vaughn from toe to military cap while popping a Chicklet into his mouth. "He ain't no Faddah. He's one o' doze Bible types from the Starvation Army! He's harmless. Maybe he's come for a fine steak, no doubt paying with the funds from the mission pot. Ain't dat right, General?"

Vaughn peered into the lounge wanting no piece of either man. "I just want to have a word with Mr. Orondorff. His son, Samuel, served with me overseas."

Both watchmen took a step back deferring to the third member of their party who had moved to the front when Vaughn spoke. Wearing a three-piece dark blue, pin-stripe suit with a red pocket square, this was obviously the person in charge. His eloquence was as slick as his perfectly coiffed head of oily black hair. "Pay no attention to these idiots. I think you will agree with me that you are not exactly like our everyday clientele. Did I hear you say you knew Sammy Orondorff?"

Seeing that things were now under control, the two outriders withdrew from the discussion and concentrated on greeting newly arrived patrons. Vaughn responded civilly and humbly. "I have a message for Mr. Orondorff about Samuel. We served together in the 25th Platoon of the Essex-Scottish. I want to convey to him…"

Apparently enough information had been shared. "I know you! Or, at least I know about you. You are Captain McIntosh, right? Sammy was right, you are pretty fearless. My name is Junior, Benjamin Orondorff, Junior. Sammy was my brother." Vaughn could now see the resemblance between Samuel and Junior. Put Junior in khakis and give him an Enfield, they would almost be twins. "Yeah, I think my father would want to talk to you."

Turning back to his group, Junior gave instructions to get Lefty, Whitey, Billy Jack and Rosewater to escort Vaughn with kid gloves across the Devon's floor to the office. "Take your hat off please, Captain. That way you will blend in and we both can get what we want." Junior was also a diplomat extraordinaire to whom Vaughn would most readily agree.

Vaughn had once come close to examining a world class Casino in Dieppe, and he figured this operation would fit nicely into just a corner of that establishment, yet it was probably every bit its equal in the large number of gamblers present. It appeared there was really no need for a large escort after all, as everyone was intensely fixated on cards, spinning wheels and slot handles. The group dropped Vaughn and Junior in front of a red-velvet-covered door surrounded by floor to ceiling dark glass panels.

Vaughn entered first into a similarly paneled interior where a solitary figure there greeted him with a warm handshake. The fifty-something, slightly balding, thick-bodied man had a likeable but imperial gaze. Vaughn assumed this was Samuel's father. It was also evident that both Sammy and Junior got their looks from their mother, but Junior's personality was all his father. Acting as if he had been reunited with family, Benny embraced Vaughn, delivering kisses on both cheeks. "Please sit down, Captain. Junior, would you please check on the tea I ordered for Captain McIntosh. Take his jacket and hat and see they are cleaned and brushed. I would offer you a fine Cuban and a Scotch but I think they would not do in this circumstance."

Vaughn was overwhelmed by this welcome, but most appreciative. "Your reception committee was very gracious, Mr. Orondorff. Thank you for seeing me."

Benny was amused by Vaughn's courtesy. "You're actually lucky Junior was out there to take care of the boys. If it had been Chicken Charlie or Straight Pants McGuire who met you, you might be holding your breath somewhere near Luna Pier!" Vaughn knew in his heart that an angelic presence must have kept the boys in line.

"Let me begin, Captain, by assuring you that although we come from different worlds, you are always welcome at my place. I am so appreciative of all you did for Sammy. I know this is not what you expected, but I have longed for the day I would meet you."

"Mr. Orondorff, I want to express my condolences about Sammy–that is, Private Orondorff. He served under my command during a ..."

"Stop right there. Mac–isn't that what Sammy called you? You can call me, Benny."

"Well…Benny…you obviously know more about Sammy's service than I thought you would."

"Let's get one thing clear, Mac. You are family to us, so no formalities. And yes, I know a few things from the letter I got from Sammy before he went on his last mission. I think I should read it to you which should answer many of your questions."

Junior returned to the room with a tea service. "Table #4 has a card reader. Frankie wants to remove him." Benny stepped up onto a landing overlooking the tables. He could see the entire casino from behind these two-way mirrors.

"Let him be and monitor his winnings. Offer him a few complimentary drinks and send Eva over there to distract him. If all else fails, close the table. If you look close you'll see that player is the Sheriff's brother-in-law. We might be able to handle this in a more gentile fashion, but keep Butch and Frankie handy, just in case."

Benny returned to his guest and apologized for conducting business during Vaughn's visit. "We have a lot in common, Mac. We invite everyone into our temple and have a product to sell. I bet we both see a lot of heartbreak from the bad choices men can make. But I digress, let me get the letter from my desk."

Vaughn sat straight up and held his cup and saucer on his lap. He didn't realize the men had called him by Forester's assigned nickname. And he didn't know half of them had the sensitivity, or were even capable of writing home.

"Junior, I want you to read the letter, but give Mac a little background on your brother first. That will help him understand better."

"Sammy was my twin brother," Junior said. "Older by a few minutes. He was always a little hot-tempered and loved the ladies. Mama always said she couldn't believe we came out of the same womb. Anyway, Sammy got into some trouble with a girl who is the daughter of a rival competitor… shall we say sort of a Romeo and Juliet thing. The girl lost the baby but a hit was put out on Sammy, so he weighed his options and ended up in your regiment. I guess he figured his life was over anyway, and he wanted to go out taking down a few real bad guys. So then, he wrote this letter." Benny passed the paper to Junior since his emotions would not allow him to read the letter aloud himself. Junior always complied. He opened the thin, blue folded postcard and read,

Dear Papa,

Tomorrow we are off to something special and I don't know if I will return. So, give my love to Mama and Ben. I will always love them too. But I want to tell you a few things about my life and hopefully you will not judge me the way you always have.

For the last year I have served under a Chaplain who is now my boss. He is not much older than me but he can beat the snot out of any man in our unit and can shoot just as well. I have come to admire him very much. You have tried to teach me responsibility and respect for our family but I never really understood it. But here I have learned to take care of myself, take pride in what I say and do. I am actually doing something that you can be proud of. This I owe all to Mac, the Chaplain.

Another thing, he is a man of strong religion and I have watched him live that and I admire him. Tonight, as I say goodbye, I know because of what he offered me, I will end up in heaven. Several of us here are scared and have talked about Jesus and stuff. I want to let you know, I go to war as the son you wanted. I have discipline and a sense of doing something right for the first time in my life. I owe it all to Captain Mac. If you ever meet him, thank him for me and love him as you would love the new me.

I love everyone very much.
Sammy

Vaughn had no idea he had had such an impact on Sammy. Even when he was thinking how war had hardened him, others must have still seen a piece of Jesus through him. He wondered how many others made a decision to accept Christ that night. Regardless, he was very humbled by the letter.

"So, you see, Captain McIntosh, I lost my son when he left home. I had no idea where his life would end up, but I know now. You have returned my Sammy to me. I want you to know that Mrs. Orondorff, Junior and I extend our family love to you. You are always welcome here…although I doubt we will be seeing you much at the craps table!" He laughed, and stood. Then taking hold of Vaughn's hand, he pulled him to his feet and encased him in a bear hug. With tears in his eyes, he stepped back and said, "Junior will see you out." Then suddenly, as if a switch had been flipped, Mr. Benjamin Orondorff was all business again. He grabbed Frankie and headed toward Table #4.

Junior put his hand on Vaughn's arm. "I'm going to take you out the back way–not to hide you from our guests, but because I had the chef prepare steaks for you and your driver." He hesitated just a moment, then said, "There's one other thing." Mr. Benjamin Orondorff, Junior, handed a red and black, $100 High Roller poker chip with *Amico Nostro* engraved in solid gold lettering on the edge to Vaughn. "If you're ever in Miami, Chicago, New York, St. Louis or New Orleans, and need help, just present this chip and we'll be there."

Chapter 15
Look to the Hills

Balmoral Island, Bahamas

Trevor Sullivan, the once-affable shoe salesman, had a deep-seated fear of ending his life the way it had begun... in poverty. Spurred on by this apprehension, he immersed himself in a myriad of diverse business projects designed to ensure his continual wealth, the latest of which being a relatively secret endeavor with the Mafia from Miami about casino development. Less secretive, though, was Sullivan entertaining the proposal with the U.S. Military for two airfields on New Providence. This, he knew, could lead to labor problems if he wasn't careful, but he didn't worry too much because Harry was always there to bail him out.

Besides, he had a sterling reputation as a real estate mogul and newly-elected member of the Legislative Assembly which afforded him unusual access to the board rooms of North America where he had one simple business message for all: Come to the Bahamas! Investments would not be subject to income tax, inheritance tax–or any other type of tax, for that matter. And, between the Duke and himself, residency for investors could be set up through the newly-formed Bahamas International Trust Agency–for the right price, of course. As an incentive, he proudly touted his acquisition of such quality investors as Sir Harry Oakes and Axel Salming. Who could argue with that success?

But, the situation with Hans Lubeck was quite another matter.

For some reason Trevor was not being included in the deal Herr Lubeck wished to conduct with Sir Harry. It was one thing to wine and dine the Argentinian with local customs and flavors to help the Bahamian cause, but, it was a totally different thing to be left out of the business discussions. Sullivan reassured himself he was still one of 'The Boys,' and that in time he would be brought into the fold, but if worse came to worst, he still had the airfield deals. So Sullivan would cut everyone some slack for the time being.

He was also beginning to be concerned that Sir Harry had remained somewhat isolated from the group since their initial meeting. Attempts to contact him were diverted by his staff who unconvincingly said he was dealing with an important family matter, and David Windsor even complained that Harry had missed their regular tee time at the Country Club. Whatever could interfere with Sir Harry's golf game was indeed serious, so it was concluded he had gone off to one of his hiding places. After thinking about their past dealings, Trevor narrowed it down to three possibilities.

The first was the Travelers' Rest Bar on the far western end of the island. Harry could while away the hours there playing backgammon, and even had a permanent room reserved for when his hot streak lasted well into the night. Winning the weekend tournaments, along with large quantities of rum, required a quick exit to a soft mattress. Proprietor Randal Butler took care of the man who had given him the money to open "T.R.'s" during the depression years.

It was here that Sir Harry learned to pay attention to the dreams of the common Bahamian working man.

The second possibility was Doc Cole's Eastern Pharmacy in Grant's Town, just over Government Hill. The Coles were transplanted South Carolinians who came to Nassau in the mid-20s, feeling a call to serve the Lord in this island archipelago. Supported by the National YWCA, Mabel Cole's vision was to set up a pre-school while her husband served the apothecary needs of the Grant's Town community. Although the pharmacy expanded to include a hardware and clothing store, Mabel's notoriety far outshined that of her husband as she became the Head Mistress of Woodcock Primary School and was later appointed to the Governor's Council on Education. Mabel opened her own home to help struggling students, and spent hours emphasizing reading and writing, using the Bible for instruction.

In time, however, she passed the reins of education on to others and went back to working with Doc in the Pharmacy, opening a small counter service for lunch that featured only one item – Cracked Conch with a side of peas 'n rice and coleslaw. The demand was so great the counter top was abandoned and the meal was transported to public work sites and tourist attractions–in the back of any available car Mabel could hire for a few hours a day. Lines for her tasty feast could be seen in front of Government House, Goodman's Bay, Potter's Cay and Fort Fincastle. What Mabel loved the most, though, was serving the machete-wielding grass cutters and pruners along West Bay Street, where she would read stories to the workers as they ate and relaxed in the shade. They told everyone that a Mabel story during lunch was more refreshing than a rain shower in the middle of a steamy July day. Sir Harry could testify to that as he frequently visited Cole's Pharmacy for a special lunch prepared just for him.

It was here Sir Harry learned the importance of supporting private enterprise and personal responsibility in the success of the Bahamian Islands.

Trevor's last choice, and the one he was betting on, was Balmoral Island. Sir Harry had been known to take his wooden Canadian Seabird Runabout from his own white sandy beachfront on a bearing north and west for about two nautical miles to his own personal retreat. When the boat was outfitted with gallons of potable water and toilet paper, they knew Sir Harry must have some thinking to do and was going to disappear for a time.

Harry was the only one who knew of a small entrance through the northern breakwater to the unassuming one-square-acre island, and he shared it with nobody. A multitude of black and white Coppice, Brasiletto and Acasia shrubs along the shore also gave the island an unapproachable air, so it was virtually ignored by locals and tourists alike.

Although lacking electricity and flushing toilets, Sir Harry was no martyr when it came to his personal comfort, and had created a compound with the basic necessities of life. There was a canvas covered lean-to for shelter; gas powered stove and lanterns, a wireless radio, two military-issue canvas cots, mosquito netting, SPAM and canned fruits, a deck of cards, charcoal, mask, flippers and snorkel. Also, within a well-sealed metal container with Red Cross markings was a first aid kit complete with mercurochrome, lotions of all kinds, bandages, tweezers, scissors, digestive charcoal, and even changes of clothing and sandals. In a wooden crate half buried in the sand behind the hut were several bottles of his favorite treasure–Canadian Club and Crown Royal Whisky–for medicinal purposes, of course. Harry may have liked his seclusion but creature comforts would always be a priority.

It was here that Sir Harry learned that although planning and preparation were important in life, there was a higher power that was in control and involved in every life decision.

Although Sullivan had never been invited to Harry's island, he knew about it and kept this ritual to himself. He knew better than to interrupt the island hiatus unless it was a matter of life and death, but felt this time it was close enough. There was a storm brewing that he had inadvertently started that now needed Sir Harry's immediate attention.

Despite the political stability of the islands, there were groups of native dissidents who opposed the ongoing construction of both the main and satellite airports in Nassau. The United States Military looked at them as American projects, and as such, hired laborers from the United States to manage each phase. Plans had been submitted, property had been sub-divided and earth had been bulldozed as if the joint Sullivan/U.S. Military venture was a *fait accompli*. Outside of a few signatures, Trevor had singlehandedly moved the project from being a dream to reality. The usually easy-going Bahamian natives, he thought, would be content to lean on a shovel for mere pennies on the dollar compared to what the imported American laborers were receiving. This turned out to be hardly the case.

For the past few weeks there had been rumblings in Grant's Town, and beyond, about a proposed protest for higher wages for local workers. Rumors stirred emotions resulting in two thousand protestors promising to descend on Rawson Square, the economic epi-center of Nassau, to express their displeasure.

Fearful of such an outcry, the Duke had summoned the Royal Bahamian Police Force to protect Government House which only increased the distaste the workers held for their Governor. All they wanted was a voice, as loyal and patriotic British subjects, yet it appeared the Duke was prepared to beat them down with force. There was going to be a showdown in Nassau-town, and Sullivan needed to quell it and he knew the locals would listen to Sir Harry.

It was inferred by the Westbourne staff that Sir Harry had probably gone to his island, but Sullivan could take no chances, so through the Duke, ordered the Bahamian Defense Force to find and secure Sir Harry Oakes, with Sullivan taking the lead in the effort. The British sub-chaser, *Air Pheasant*, that had been being used as a mail ship to the Eleuthra Islands, was dispatched for the mission. Although it carried a dozen depth charges, a

Hotchkiss three-pounder gun and twin .303 machine guns, it hardly seemed likely they would need such armament to attract Sir Harry's attention.

Once it passed the lighthouse on the western end of Hog Island, the 'Little Ship' cranked up the two Hall-Scott engines to top throttle, and at twenty-five knots was expected to be at Balmoral Island in less than 15 minutes. Sullivan manned the low-frequency radio calling Harry, hoping for an answer but knowing it was a long-shot since Harry only used the transmitter in an emergency. Today he got lucky. Sir Harry came in loud and clear. "Whoever this is, it better be important!"

"Harry, it's Trevor. We have a problem and we're coming to pick you up."

His disgruntled friend answered, "How did you know where I am, Sullivan?"

"I took a wild guess and looks like I was right. Just meet us at the east end of the reef. We should be there in ten minutes."

"Is there something wrong with Eunice or the family?" Harry came back, suddenly worried.

"That is a negative. There is nothing wrong with your family," Sullivan assured him. "We have a situation downtown that needs your attention that doesn't look good for any of us. David has put every police officer on call."

"All right," Harry acquiesced. "I'll close up shop and see you at my launch. Who is with you?"

"Just a few soldiers on the *Air Pheasant*," he said a bit hesitantly, knowing what Harry's reaction would be.

To his surprise, though, all Harry said was, "I take it you'll tow me in?"

"That is correct, I mean, affirmative." Sullivan couldn't hide his relief. Once Harry got involved, he knew things would be OK.

The radio crackled for a moment and then went quiet. Up ahead, the speck of Balmoral Island was coming into view. Captain Pindling gave the order to cut back the engines so they could come alongside and retrieve their important passenger.

As expected, Sir Harry looked miffed, and after receiving a formal salute form Captain Pindling, went straight to Sullivan who held out a whisky flask. Harry, a little sunburned and a whole lot perturbed, stared at Trevor in disbelief. "You've never been to this island, and I only mentioned it to you once. I'm actually impressed you could find the place, and even more surprised you rounded up the cavalry to pull me in. This must be important."

Sullivan was relieved he was talking to a more tranquil Sir Harry who had obviously benefited from his stay on Balmoral.

"The natives are restless, Harry, and they're planning a rally in Rawson Square. We're afraid it might get violent and you need to help us calm them down."

"I'm willing to bet this has something to do with the airports, right?"

"The teachers' talk of unions has stirred up our workers, and two days ago an editorial in the *Guardian* said that 'normally respectful and cheerful' Blacks should be offended that white Americans are being paid ten times the pay on our own soil. The man is inciting a riot. Just last night Cole's Pharmacy in Grant's Town was looted. The Red Lion Bar was ransacked and Bethel's on Blue Hill Road was broken into."

Despite his calm exterior, Harry was incensed about the trashing of Mabel Cole's establishment. "Were Doc or Mabel hurt?"

"No, but the Apothecary was razed along with the liquor store next to it. The Coles had friends who took them in before the trouble began."

"There has to be a ring leader…any ideas who it might be?"

"There doesn't seem to be an actual leader, just a collection of hot heads. They're stirring up the general population and are all planning to come together tonight. I'm afraid the Chief of Police has stirred the pot even more by deputizing the Cameron's Highlanders. You know they tend to be an aggressive bunch. It's a powder keg waiting to explode. We need you there to talk to them. They'll listen to you."

"This has to be more than just locals."

"Well, I've heard some are out-islanders who came to New Providence for work, but were refused because of the American workers. Those from Abaco, Exuma and Andros have no ties to this town and want something for their efforts. You're the only one who can head it off."

Harry's mood was getting darker by the minute. "You started this airport deal without thinking it through, and now you expect me to come in and clean up your mess? And what's going to come about from your 'secret' deal with the Mafia. If we can't come up with a peaceful settlement, the dissidents will go underground, just like they're doing in Cuba."

Sullivan had gotten himself caught in the middle. He knew Harry was opposed to him working with the self-righteous mobsters who intended to turn the Bahamas into another Cuba, but he was also being pressured from the other side of the Florida Strait to make it happen. A riot tonight would delay all those plans, and he knew he'd face repercussions from the Mafia for that.

"I'll do my best to ease this situation tonight–not because I care at all about your Florida friends–but because it's the best thing for the Bahamian people. You have to realize this is straining our friendship, Trevor. I can't keep bailing you out of the holes you dig yourself into."

"Thank you, Harry," Trevor said, too relieved to feel any shame. "I know I can always count on you. I'm sure the Duke and Duchess are going to be safe with all the troops surrounding them, but I'll phone Axel and have him keep Lubeck at *Shangri-la* for now."

With that reminder, Harry thought of the decision he'd made on Balmoral Island concerning Hans Lubeck. The riots could change everything–the Duke could be relieved because of his failure as a Governor... tourism would be hurt even more than the 75% decrease they'd seen because of the war–it might be a very long time before Lubeck's proposal could be operational. Despite all this, Harry decided he was content to stick with his original plan regardless of the outcome of this evening's confrontation.

Chapter 16

Wait on Me

❦

Windsor, Ontario

Mae was beginning to appreciate that Faith Haven could only operate effectively with structure, routine and discipline, which, she realized with a new-found respect, was what Vaughn would have experienced with the Essex-Scottish. In both cases there was a mission that needed to be understood and accepted by all, and each person must commit to that vision without question, fulfilling the daily functions assigned to them. Individual interests were secondary to the group's needs. Mae knew she had to accept that notion if she was going to be used effectively by the Lord.

The more she gave to the collective good of the house, the less she thought of herself. Not that she ever considered herself vain or conceited, but more and more she found the welfare of the mothers and children coming before any self-consideration, including her thoughts about Vaughn.

She was starting to understand the difference between a servant's heart and a sacrificial heart. In her short time here she was being transformed, being prepared for something different that she didn't yet understand. She had always been open to the Lord's bidding, but the way she was being molded was far from anything she had ever known before. Through this experience, Mae was more appreciative of what Vaughn had struggled through when he left her to go off to war.

What was starting to scare her, though, was the feeling the Lord was using her experiences here to give her a different purpose in life. She had come as a volunteer to support

Vaughn with his task, but was beginning to feel more and more that she, herself, was at the center of God's attention. Her focus was gradually being diverted, and she was beginning to sense the future the Lord had planned for her was not going to involve a return anytime soon to the St. Marys Citadel or the Wellburn farm.

Mae found herself nodding off to sleep at the strangest times–while hanging the laundry; watching over the children while they played in the park next door; or strangely enough, while sitting on the toilet. She was that exhausted! Awakening with a start, she would snap back to reality, often wondering how long she had been asleep and what she had missed. Fortunately, nothing serious ever happened since Mrs. Eff was astute enough to send a partner with her whenever she took the children anywhere. She obviously wasn't the first volunteer to succumb to exhaustion.

As the week was coming to a close, Mae was getting excited about her reunion with Vaughn. They had stayed in touch by phone, but she needed to be physically near him. Unfortunately, their plan to spend time together on this trip had not worked out since each of their callings had proven too demanding. He had mentioned something on the phone about a wonderful piece of news he had to share with her, and she was hoping the surprise was a few more days of vacation for just the two of them to enjoy, but she wasn't holding her breath.

Getting up very early every morning was not a problem for the farm girl, but she was used to doing chores with God's creatures providing the background noise while the Lord painted a magnificent new sunrise. At Faith Haven she was lucky to have time to take care of her own bodily functions and needs before her day started. From the time her feet hit the floor, Mae was busy assisting other cadets in waking the children amidst an overabundance of crying, soiled nightclothes and sheets, upset stomachs, fights with other children and the ubiquitous clash over who had the washroom next.

The few boys who were present had it easy in comparison to the girls. They had their own washroom, and while the girls clamored and complained, and had to fuss with combing tangles from long hair and sorting out frocks and leggings, the boys got some extra shut-eye. They could be ready for the breakfast line in a flash with their buzz haircuts, and after slapping some water on their faces and running a tooth brush over their gums a few times, they were ready to go.

Breakfast was always orderly, with the children entering the dining room in silence and standing behind their chairs for the morning prayer led by Mrs. Eff, followed by announcements regarding special visitors or events for the day. Rumbling stomachs waited anxiously for staff to enter from the kitchen with large vats of porridge that would be topped with milk and sorghum sugar, corn syrup or, at holiday time and each child's birthday, a hearty amount of maple syrup. Scrambled eggs, generally overcooked and lifeless, were also on the menu, accompanied by a large slice of Mennonite sorghum bread covered with butter and honey or strawberry preserves. A few benefactors provided these tasty treats on a regular basis and the children were greatly appreciative. The milk was usually tepid by this time, having been poured into ceramic cups long before the children entered the hall, and the occasional flecks of cream found floating on top were usually scooped out and placed on the porridge to make it a bit more enjoyable.

At Christmastime the children were also treated to ham, bacon or 'bangers' as the home's pantry exploded with donations from generous Windsorites at that time of year. Since they didn't have adequate cold storage, the perishable items would be prepared and served at all meals until the supply was exhausted. Although the Salvation Army was not particularly in favor of the excessive intake of meat, they were wise enough to know the value of its consumption as part of a sound nutritional plan for children. Mae secretly wished for some of Harriet's fried chicken. She knew the cadets wouldn't be able to resist it... Army code or not!

Just like everyone else, Faith Haven was subject to rationing, and Mrs. Eff relied mostly on the good will of churches and the fine people of the community to keep the food coming in. She used hoarded stamps to barter for shoes and other clothing for the children, and bundled enough stamps to purchase a Ration Certificate for extra fuel oil and a couple of bicycles. Rumor had it Mrs. Eff was close to being able to buy a car for the Haven, but this was, as of yet, just a rumor. Everyone knew she would do anything she could to get extras for the children, but that usually ended up being special treats like oranges or bananas. A car was way beyond what anybody expected.

When finished, the children put their dirty dishes into the metal bins full of soapy water, and a select few went to the kitchen to begin their daily chores–washing and drying dishes, sweeping the floor or removing any trash from the hall.

Others returned to their rooms to straighten beds, clean the bathrooms and hallways, or fold and put away their newly laundered clothes… socks and underwear in one drawer, pants or frocks in another and shirts in the bottom. Each child was provided three of each item–one to be worn, one in the drawer, and one in the wash – each with their assigned number embroidered on the inside. All dirty laundry was funneled to the basement through a laundry chute – something that fascinated the children. None of them complained when they were assigned this chore, and occasionally, a missing shoe or another essential item was found in a pile of laundry at the bottom when someone got a bit carried away.

The children scrubbed the toilets by hand with a horse-hair brush, but cadets helped them reach mirrors and windows, wiping each down with newsprint and distilled white vinegar. Arguments sometimes ended with an item either flushed down the toilet or thrown down the laundry chute–things found in the laundry were forgiven; those discovered in the toilet, not so much.

Truth be told, the staff overlooked some of this harmless child's play, but for the more serious incidents the recourse was fast, hard, automatic and assured. Physical and verbal abuse were not tolerated, with culprits taken to Mrs. Eff's office to sit for a time to think about what they'd done. Those who were unrepentant or openly challenged authority were either spanked with a barber's strop or smacked on upturned hands a half dozen times with a wooden ruler. The boys may have had their way when it came to the washroom and sleeping in, but they out did the girls when it came to the need for correction.

For the most part, though, incidents were few and far between. The entire staff followed Mrs. Eff's lead of 'loving first and loving always'. They were often referred to a plaque on her office wall that quoted Matthew 18:10: "Take heed that ye despise not one of these little ones; for I say unto you, that in heaven their angels do always behold the face of my Father which is in heaven." Despite the fact that she appeared a little aloof while conducting daily business, Mrs. Eff was known to handle most confrontations, arguments and emotional upheavals with a kind word, a listening ear and a warm hug.

But it had not always been this way for Mrs. Eff, as Mae was to find out on her last night at Faith Haven. The children were in their rooms, and most of the cadets were either in the kitchen or spending time with other cadets visiting from neighboring Detroit. Mrs. Eff used this opportunity to drop in on Mae in her room.

"I hope I'm not disturbing you, but I wanted us to have a talk before you leave tomorrow."

At first Mae thought she was being given a last minute task before turning in–she had learned not to remove her clothing until Mrs. Eff had gone to bed–so she sat on the edge of her bed where she had been working on a crossword puzzle, and nodded her agreement. "Six-letter word, 'to confuse'," Mae said, trying to lighten the moment.

"That would be 'baffle'," Mrs. Eff answered as she closed the door and pulled up a chair.

Mae was impressed with the quick response, especially when this had been another of their long days. Mae laid the puzzle aside and gave the matron her attention. "It took me the whole week, but I think I'm starting to adjust to life here. Every other day by this time, I was dead tired, but tonight I feel relaxed and content… and maybe just a little baffled," she said with a smile.

Mrs. Eff gave Mae a searching look. "I've been waiting all week for this conversation, Mae. You've made quite an impact here and now it's time for you to leave. I just wanted to thank you for all you've done even though your stay wasn't exactly the vacation you and your husband were looking for."

"It's OK, Mrs. Eff. Vaughn has been extra busy, too. Seems he's met some interesting characters in his travels and we agree both of our current situations actually require more attention. I told him I would be fine here and he should take as many days as he needs to finish his visitations."

"I'm looking forward to meeting the Captain. I've been reading a few things about his grandfather."

Mae was elated. "You know about Thomas Martin?"

"Actually made a few calls and talked to some people. Your family has quite a heritage there."

"It's Vaughn's family. I just sort of hitched a ride through his mother and a wonderful family called the Skippers who once led the St. Marys mission."

"When I came back from Newfoundland, I was curious about St. Marys. I actually spent some wonderful time in the area. The news of the Skippers' tragic death was mourned throughout southwestern Ontario. They were good people."

"You say you came back from Newfoundland?"

"I warned you before that I wasn't always the person I am today." Mrs. Eff shifted uncomfortably in her chair. "I left my husband some twenty years ago when we lived right here in Windsor," she said slowly, "and went back to St. John and tried to pull myself together again." A confession of this magnitude might raise some eyebrows, but after all Mae had been through in her life, she didn't think it worthy of judgment.

"Well," Mae said with a reassuring smile, "you're back here now. Is your husband still around here?"

"I have no idea. That was a long time ago and he deserved a better woman than me. I hope he found one. You see, I kept secrets from him and then lost the very thing I was trying to protect. Life has a way of being real harsh like that."

"How did the Salvation Army handle your separation?" Mae asked.

"Oh, no, Mae, I was not Sally Ann at the time. The Lord reached out to me when I was back in St. John. When I told my parents what had happened, they accepted it and loved me in spite of it all, then introduced me to a wonderful Salvation Army couple, and through their influence I joined the Corps and here I am, back in Windsor." She was quiet for a moment, then said, "You know, if I were still a Catholic I would say this is my penance."

Mrs. Eff touched a lace-edged handkerchief to her nose. Her voice was intense and her words slow in coming. "There's something about you, Mae, that pulls at my heart. I don't have an answer for it, but when you arrived here last week, I felt something… as if God was sending me a message through you."

"Well, maybe if we go back to when you joined the Army and go from there, things will get clearer."

"OK…. when I joined the Corps there was an opening in Windsor and the couple who mentored me encouraged me to return here, to Faith Haven. The previous Director had moved to the Bahamas, and I guess you could say I was in the right place at the right time."

"Oh, the Bahamas." Mae was a little guarded but wanted to keep the discussion going, "I know a man who moved to the Bahamas. He was a real character–popped in and out of our lives pretty quickly. Don't know if I'll ever see him again."

"His ways are higher than our ways, Mae. I've watched you work with these children and you have a talent with them that the Lord could mightily use. The mission in Nassau would love a person of your ability. You could start off with a short-term appointment–like what you're doing here. I could write a letter on your behalf to my friend at the Mackey Street mission and see if the Lord takes you there. And you say you already have a friend in Nassau? Maybe that's where you're supposed to head next, to those warm breezes and beaches."

"The Lord would have to hit me over the head for me to make such a move. I can't begin to imagine what Vaughn – or my mother – would say!"

"Well, Mae, there are no accidents in life. Everything under heaven has a purpose and timing is everything."

Mae thought it best to change the subject. "I'm more interested in your story right now, Mrs. Eff. You said you spent time in St. Marys. I was born and bred in that town. Well, actually in the country outside of town. In fact, Vaughn and I own a farm near there."

"What about your parents? Do they still live there?"

"My father passed on years ago, and Mother lives in Kincardine, on Lake Huron. She and her new husband own a restaurant there and are dabbling in some real estate deals."

"I'm sorry about your father."

"No need to be sorry. My father was a mean man. He was an abusive alcoholic and did a lot of other bad things as well. I want to have good memories of him, but they just aren't there." Mae stared past Mrs. Eff for a moment. "At least I can take some comfort in knowing he wasn't my real father."

Mrs. Eff spoke kindly. "So you were adopted? As you've seen this week at Haven, it takes a great deal of love to adopt and love a child as your own."

"Josiah Blackwell never really adopted me. It was only my mom, Harriet, who loved me from the start."

Mrs. Eff sat up straighter. "Blackwell? Is he related to a Jonah Blackwell near Wellburn?"

Mae could hear something odd in Mrs. Eff's voice. "Why, yes. Jonah was his brother. Josiah took our farm over from him when he died."

Mrs. Eff said quietly, "Describe the farm to me, please."

Mae talked about the larch and pine trees, the sloped barn and the expansive corn fields. Her eyes lit up when she told Mrs. Eff stories of drinking the cold water from the pump on a summer's day, and her trips to Knowles' pond. And then there was old granddad, cooing pigeons and, of course, her love for chickens. From the rutted Concession #13 to

Paterson's store, Mrs. Eff just stared as Mae expounded on the delights of her childhood. Occasionally, Mae's words would break through, but for the most part Mrs. Eff just sat, afraid to breathe while keeping her eyes on Mae's face. Could it possibly be? To be sure, the brown eyes and black hair were his, and for certain, the cut of her jaw and shape of her face looked familiar. And finally, as Mrs. Eff watched Mae talking with her hands, she was convinced.

With shaking hands, Mrs. Eff stood up and pulled a surprised Mae to her feet. "Mae, I need you to take a deep breath, and listen to me with an open mind. There's something I must tell you and you have to promise to hear me out."

Mae was taken aback by this reaction. "I'm sorry if I was boring you with my stories. That was rude and I apologize. Please forgive me."

"Oh no, my child," Mrs. Eff said with a shaky smile. "I'm the one who must ask for your forgiveness." Before she could say anything more, though, a voice from the other room called urgently for attention, and she dropped Mae's hand. "We'll continue this conversation another time," she said, turning toward the door and leaving Mae totally confused. Mrs. Eff smiled. The Lord's timing is always perfect.

Chapter 17

Windsor, Ontario

All told, Vaughn visited twelve of the fifteen families of the heroes of the 25th Platoon. The reasons for missing the others were varied: non-existent address, abandoned building, and one family had forced him off the property with a firearm, apparently unable to come to terms with the death of their loved one and blaming the Captain. According to Underwood, though, Vaughn's efforts were successful and most of the families appreciated his visit. So, with a sense of satisfaction, Captain McIntosh set his sights across the Detroit River.

Vaughn thought of his mother when he spoke to the customs official as he re-entered Canada. Cate had always said the Canadians were the most mannerly people she had ever met and when the border guard said, "Welcome home!" Vaughn realized he really was glad to be back home, and in a short 10 minutes he would see a certain lovely lady who would reinforce that feeling.

Underwood was obviously looking forward to an early evening date himself, his impatience showing as he snapped at slow-moving drivers who, in his opinion, had no business being on the road. Then when a beet truck blocked him from making a left onto University Avenue, he laid on the horn as if it would make a difference. So much for Canadian civility behind a steering wheel.

"I'm going to drop you off at Faith Haven, Captain. I trust you and the Mrs. will want to be together, and the barracks is hardly the place to bring a lady. There are a few hotels on Riverside that could accommodate you, or the *Waterfront* on Church would give you

100

a great view of the river. Across the street you can take a stroll along the gardens. It's actually quite romantic."

"I appreciate the suggestions, Underwood," Vaughn said as the grimy green ghost made a screeching right onto Crawford. He couldn't get out of the vehicle fast enough. "I won't be needing your services any longer since Mae has our car. We might go for a drive tomorrow and take advantage of Colonel Petrie's offer to visit Bob-lo." He grabbed his double-strapped suitcase from the trunk and thanked Underwood for all his support. After spending the better part of the week together, Underwood was not offended by Vaughn's quick departure. He knew the pull that a good woman had upon a man's soul. Besides, Underwood now had his own lovely lady waiting for him.

Vaughn made his way up the drive to the front door and rang the bell. A comely young corps officer opened the door and immediately snapped to attention when she saw the stately figure of her superior. She stepped aside so he could enter the foyer then picked up his luggage. Vaughn was careful to wipe his feet before walking across the foyer to hang his jacket on the hook of the black iron coat rack. He intentionally kept his hat tucked under the arm, protocol he had developed from the 'other' Army, and dropped his other hand behind his back in military fashion. He liked the respect the pose elicited as he stood erect with heels together, back straight and chin up, and would incorporate it as part of his social ritual for years to come. He also knew he would have to get through the formalities of the house before being able to see Mae.

Suddenly, staff members began to appear from every room, introducing themselves and welcoming him with hearty handshakes and kind and joyful expressions. Vaughn returned the salutations with equal cordiality, addressing each cadet and officer by title and name. He wondered where the children might be, but before he could ask, someone from the group spoke up. "This is quite an honor, Captain. The children will be excited to meet you also, but at the moment the girls are at the gardens on Cameron Street and the boys are all on visitation with local families."

A pronounced creaking of floorboards caught everyone's attention and the group became silent as Mrs. Eff, decked out in her formal Salvation Army attire, entered to officially greet their esteemed visitor.

"Captain McIntosh, welcome to Faith Haven," Mrs. Eff said, extending her hand. "You will have to excuse our excitement. Your wife kept us entertained this week with stories of the escapades of Thomas, Leah, William, Herbert and Cate Martin and everyone wants to meet the grandson of the famous Colonel from Devon, England." She looked around at the eager faces surrounding her. "Perhaps we could meet in the library later and the McIntoshes may answer some of your questions, but, I believe in the meantime, there are chores to do. If you can finish before the children return, we may have time for the meeting then."

With that incentive, the cadets and volunteers dispersed to their assigned duties. Mrs. Eff led Vaughn to the kitchen, along the same route she had taken Mae a week ago, and there, waiting just inside the door, was Mae, face flush with excitement but working hard to retain her composure. Vaughn couldn't stop smiling.

Mrs. Eff tried unsuccessfully to hide her pleasure. "Mae, you might want to show the good Captain your living quarters... I will come and fetch you in about half an hour. I Corinthians 7 and all that!"

With that Mrs. Eff left the kitchen, closing the door behind her. Finally, Mae was able to take Vaughn's hand and lead him to her room where they could have some privacy.

Precisely 30 minutes later, Mrs. Eff tapped on the door, then escorted the young couple to the library where most of the staff members were waiting. They answered questions for a while, but Mrs. Eff had other things on her mind, so she ended the session short with a promise from Vaughn and Mae to return to Faith Haven another time. Mrs. Eff had some unfinished business with Mae McIntosh.

She took her guests to the front porch where they could speak in private. Under the hanging baskets of gracefully arching Boston ferns, Vaughn and Mae got comfortable and sat back, waiting. Mrs. Eff wasted no time getting to the point. "Mae, I told you earlier I had something important to share with you and, to be honest, I'm a little afraid, so please bear with me." Mae looked at Vaughn who gave a slight shrug, wondering what could possibly be coming.

"Years ago, I had a daughter out of wedlock," Mrs. Eff started slowly. "Well, actually I was married but was forced into a relationship with a very wealthy and powerful man who was not my husband. He forced himself on me the first time, and then told me if I didn't continue to give in to him, he would fire my husband and force us from our home. From that relationship, I had a daughter who my husband loved and accepted as his own. Then, through no fault of ours, our daughter was taken from us and we were forced to move to Windsor in fear for our lives." She paused to catch her breath. "I don't know what ever became of her."

Vaughn could hardly believe what he was hearing. Mae had told him about how odd her earlier meeting with Mrs. Eff had been, but in his wildest dreams had never expected to be hearing this. He looked at Mae and could tell from her expression that she was starting to put the pieces together.

Mrs. Eff took a deep breath and continued. "I felt I had caused all these problems but could not discuss it with my husband. He adored that little girl and was devastated when he found out about the deception, and we never regained our affection for one another after we were driven from the farm. I had lost the two most important things in my life and didn't know how to deal with it. I was desperate, and deserted my man to go back home to St. John. It was the worst thing I ever did."

The normally restrained matron sat with her head down, and when Mae placed her hand on Mrs. Eff's arm she could feel her body shaking. So this is why Mrs. Eff had returned to Windsor. Her work with the children was an attempt to appease her past guilt.

Mrs. Eff looked up, directly at Mae, and said, "When you described your farm, I knew it was my farm. They call me Mrs. Eff, Mae, but my name is Anne Forester. I believe I'm your mother."

Mae could hardly breathe as she knelt in front of Mrs. Eff – or Mrs. Forester – and looked into her eyes. A brief, long-dormant memory came to her mind of a loving woman gently rocking her to sleep, and Mae knew in her heart she had found her natural mother. She laid her head in Anne's lap and let her tears come. Anne stroked Mae's hair with one hand while wiping her own tears with the other. "It's been a long wait, Mae, but the Lord knew what He was doing." They sat in silence for a time, reveling in their newfound relationship.

Vaughn stood, working hard to keep his emotions in check, and put a hand on each lady. "Do you remember what Joseph said to his brother about their deceit? What man intended for evil, God used for good."

Anne lifted her eyes to her son-in-law. "We've stumbled, but the Lord never let us fall."

Vaughn knew the mother and daughter had much to talk about, but needed to add the final bit that would complete the circle. "Mrs. Forester, I have some information about your husband." He looked at Mae who nodded in agreement. Vaughn had told her about her father when he returned after the war, and now she knew her mother needed to know the story, too.

Mae kept hold of her mother's hand as she sat back, and Vaughn pulled his chair in closer. "Your husband stayed in Windsor for a time after you left, then joined the Essex-Scottish and eventually became a Major and an accomplished leader. But I'm sorry to tell you we lost him in battle during the war." Anne gasped. "The Major was admired and respected for his service. You would have been proud of him."

"I called him Johnnie," she said quietly. "Mr. Forester was a good man who lived for me and Mae. Through all these years I never stopped loving him."

Vaughn leaned in and gently said, "I have more to tell you. While we were serving together in England, I discovered who he was and was able to tell him about Mae–and he was overjoyed that his daughter was alive and well, and married to me." Anne looked at Mae who was smiling and nodding at her. "He knew what Lindsay had done to you, but it made no difference in how he felt about you and Mae. He loved you both unconditionally and never blamed you for leaving, though he missed you terribly."

Once again Anne had tears streaming down her face. "All these years I've had questions about my family, and now I have the answers. The Lord has done an amazing thing by bringing you two here, and I will be forever grateful to Him." She leaned her head against the back of her chair and closed her eyes, causing Vaughn and Mae to wonder if they should leave her alone, but just as they started to move, Anne opened her eyes and asked, "What can you tell me about the Lindsay family?"

Taken aback by the unexpected question, Vaughn hesitated for a moment, choosing his words carefully. "They are all gone. Mrs. Lindsay and the boys died in a tragic fire. Bruce was killed in a freak explosion." He didn't add that the same blast had also almost claimed him and Mae.

Anne nodded as if accepting the fate that had befallen them. "And the farm? From what Mae has said it sounds like it's thriving."

Mae answered this time. "I think you would be pleased with it. Before he died, Bruce Lindsay made some major improvements to the house and we're doing well. And, thanks to a deal Vaughn's mother made a few years ago, Mother and I own the place outright now." Too late Mae realized what she had said and apologized for her slip, but Anne just smiled.

"Oh, no! I'm pleased and very thankful you were able to grow up with a loving mother, since I couldn't be there. I only wish your father could have seen you before he died."

"I did show him a picture of Mae," Vaughn said. "Although he never stopped missing her, he was delighted that we were married. I think the Major liked me." Vaughn added with a boyish grin.

The ladies laughed at Vaughn's admission, breaking the tension for them all. Then to deflect their attention from himself, he added, "You must come back to Wellburn with us to visit the farm. It was your home, after all."

"I'd like that well enough," Anne said. "It may give me the closure I need to leave some of my past behind me."

There was much to celebrate today. After years of feeling abandoned by her parents, Mae had been given this gift and finally knew her mother and father had loved her; and Anne Forester had gained a new family, who, despite the shortcomings of her past, readily assured her that she was loved and respected.

At the mention of returning to Wellburn, though, Mae's demeanor had changed and she became very quiet, a fact that didn't escape Anne's watchful eye. "Mae, is there something on your mind?"

Vaughn had actually noticed it, too, and was anxious to hear Mae's answer. He had been sensing a new revelation for the McIntosh family, but assumed it had more to do with him than with Mae. It appeared, though, the Lord had perhaps switched his focus, and he was excited that God was in motion again.

When Mae didn't answer, Anne kept prodding. "Have you discovered something about yourself while you've been here this week?"

Mae finally answered with a Scripture the Lord had placed on her heart the first day she arrived at Faith Haven: "'*For we are HIS workmanship, created in Christ Jesus for good works, which God prepared beforehand, so that we would walk in them.*' I'm not sure, but I don't think I'm supposed to go back to Wellburn. I think the Lord has other plans for me. I just don't know if I'm capable of doing what He wants." She looked at her husband for a reaction, and was pleased to see him smiling. He was happy that Mae was open to God's urging and vowed to encourage her to discover and accomplish this latest challenge.

"When the Lord assigns the task, Mae, He'll give you the wisdom and strength to complete it," he told her in his most pastor-like voice. "He perfectly enables and equips us to be part of His great work, and will guide and give you divine energy for the service you're asked to do." Then, he pushed the pastor aside and reached out and took both her hands in his. "Just think about the chances of meeting Anne after all this time. I think he orchestrated this to show you that you're special in His eyes and He has a plan for you. And I'll be with you every step of the way."

Mae was beaming on the outside, but inside was lacking confidence. She knew it was Satan filling her mind with negative thoughts, but she couldn't stop the flood of doubt. She knew she was insufficient, compared to the other cadets... and who would take care of the St. Marys Citadel? What if she failed? She would make a fool of herself and Vaughn. She was too young to be properly prepared... but most of all, she didn't want to leave her life on the farm.

But then the Lord took over. She realized the only way to overcome her fears was to step right into the middle of them... leaning on His strength and letting Him control everything. She recognized that God could only be glorified if she left the farm and her comfort zone. Finally, for every attack and lie Satan was putting before her, God provided the truth. She would have to let go and let God do His thing.

Vaughn watched Mae's face as she struggled through her inner turmoil. He identified with the feeling all too well and knew it was up to the Lord to lay it all out for her. Then suddenly, he remembered the letter he carried in his pocket, and had a feeling it was going to play a part in whatever this plan turned out to be.

Chapter 18
The Milestone of Change

❧

Nassau, Bahamas

From June to November in Nassau, tropical storms were a way of life. The unpredictable and unreliable nature of this coiled, violent phenomenon, with accompanying driving gales and storm surges, was something to be greatly respected and feared. The Arawack Indians who inhabited the Bahamas before the arrival of Columbus, referred to the tempest as 'a spiritual vision' that brought both death and seeds of new life.

Whether Spanish, French or English, the brigands who operated from the Pirate Republic Port of Nassau for the next two hundred years referred to hurricanes as 'evil spirits within big winds.' There was a sense of spiritual foreboding for those who encountered the 'big blow'.

Captain Benjamin Hornigold, a feared English pirate whose ship was lost on a reef in a 1719 storm, admitted the greatest battle a sea dog could fight was not with another ship, but with the dark forces and demons that drove the 'thunderous and spittin' savage.' Those who lived through its purging forfeited a piece of their soul out of respect for a power they felt was not of this world.

B ahamians who had lived through dozens of hurricanes possessed the fortitude of those survivors who had gone before them, and now that modern science could warn them of an impending storm via radio and telegraph, they had learned to make the proper preparations. Many would try to leave the out-islands for New Providence, Andros or Grand Bahama, but others who chose to ride out the storm in place did the best they could.

They all knew what to expect: the harsh fate of many trees, telephone and power lines, and unusual wind and rainfall patterns that would be merciless to buildings, regardless of their purpose. Fires would break out; schooners, sloops, sharpies and skiffs would be unceremoniously dumped onto Bay Street; crops would be destroyed. Shelters of wood, nail and twine would be leveled as the driving wind found the physical weakness of all man-made structures. Unfortunately, those hunkering down would find their preparations of water, food and clothing meant little once the roof of their shelter was blown off, often times leading to indiscriminate injury and death, many who were never seen again. The damage was final, complete and catastrophic.

On this day, the movers and shakers of Nassau felt another hurricane was coming this evening, but although this was a different kind of storm, it could cause just as much damage. Most of the protesters had made it abundantly clear they loved the Crown and were just exercising their right, as bona fide Englishmen, to present their complaints to the government, but after what had occurred in Grant's Town and beyond over the past few nights, the Duke was taking no chances and had taken precautions. He was aware a large horde had been forming at Potter's Cay, preparing to march the one mile down Bay Street to Rawson Square to present their demands to the government.

Military reprisals would be a quick consequence if any buildings or innocents were attacked by protesters or looters. The Cameron Guard was in place in the square with full military compliment–including bayonets, if the need for them arose – and members of the Royal Bahamian Police Force were scattered throughout the downtown and all along Bay Street. From Christie Street intersection to the main town square there would be dozens of white-clad officers peacefully encouraging the crowd along while watching for disgruntled protestors headed for the town's commercial district. After all, members of their own families might be in the crowd, so everyone had a vested interest in avoiding any type of riotous behavior.

Merchants along the route were not so confident, however, and boarded up windows just as they would for a hurricane, but rather than evacuating as if this were a natural storm, remained inside with personal firearms ready to protect their property. Those owning liquor stores, in particular, asked family members to join them in their place of business, arming themselves against what they feared was to come.

Captain Edmund Wheeler, Superintendent of the Bahamian Police Force, gave the Duke a guarantee this crowd would be manageable with the local police and Camerons. His confidence was based on an incident three nights before when he had dispersed an impromptu rally on Montague Beach just by pulling his pistol and promising to personally take the group's concerns to the Governor. Unfortunately, he had not followed up and there had been no communication via the Colonial Secretary's office to address their complaints, so it was fairly obvious to the average laborer that a show of numbers was going to be the only way to get the Governor's attention.

Leaders hoped if the large number of supporters at the rally could remain peaceful, the Governor would have to respond, but there was also the fear the gathering would devolve into civil unrest. If that happened, a hurricane would explode about Rawson square and spread into the entire commercial district along Bay Street.

Sir Harry would be there to listen to the demands. He was trustworthy in the eyes of most of the protestors, but not all of them. Still, if anything could be accomplished, Sir Harry would be the one to see it through. The masses were tired of promised appeasements and temporary fixes. There had to be substantial changes. The Bahamians were learning to be more than just passive natives. They wanted more control over their lives.

Everybody knew Harry was not the cause of the problem, though he was the one on the hot seat. It was Sullivan and his business cronies who were to blame. Although a native-born Bahamian, Sullivan was white – and had turned his back on his own people. For far too long he and the Governor had ignored cries from the Black majority who wanted more than being second-class citizens in their own country. Instead of promoting those from their own islands, the developers had seen fit to bring in outsiders, mostly white workers, who exploited the country for their own interests at the expense of the locals.

Underneath the screams for social justice was a rising pro-Black Bahamian consciousness. It was a movement that said the *Boys of Bay Street* were not impregnable. In fact, by sheer numbers alone, a crowd could hold the ability to overthrow their economic and political masters that very night.

Prepared to have their say to the protestors, Sir Harry, Sullivan, several local businessmen and a dozen members of the Legislative Assembly stood atop a Fargo platform truck on Rawson Square as the throng approached the plaza. Most lights along the streets were out, so the lamps and torches they carried looked like a long, golden slithery snake undulating toward its prey.

So far, they had been singing national songs of pride, but the ubiquitous pounding of the goat-skinned drums, cowbells and whistles was stirring the group. More than a thousand marchers had joined ranks, including many women and little children, and all seemed transfixed on making it to Rawson Square. They flowed peacefully into the open area, then as the numbers swelled, jammed into any nook or cranny that would offer a view. The Camerons had been pushed back, three-deep, surrounding the Fargo truck where the dignitaries waited. A Turner ham radio microphone, outfitted for public announcements, had been connected for their use, though the cable to the swivel-top mic was too short and required the speaker to sit at a table, looking down on the crowd. They realized later this was not the best set up for an equal exchange of ideas.

The first speaker, Attorney General Eric Holloran, approached the microphone but decided sitting at a table made him look less powerful, so he chose, instead, to stand at the edge of the Fargo and shout his lecture to the people. "I have talked to a few of you before," Holloran yelled, "and you say you represent a union of Bahamian workers, but I look out here and see women, children, and old men who should not be part of this assembly."

Holloran had sorely misjudged the group. They were in no mood for a finger-pointing sermon and their grumbling response reflected it. Then three figures emerged and moved to the front, calling for calm from the crowd. Those close by complied, but the majority of the 1,500 people who had now assembled as far back as Christie Street were not able to hear and were becoming more and more discontented.

"That is where you are wrong, Sir," the spokesman for the three called out. "We have our families with us for a reason. We want you to know we will fight under the flag and we will die under the flag, but we will not allow our families to starve under the flag!" The crowd responded with applause and cheers, but the Attorney General seemed oblivious to the atmosphere and tenor of the situation, and instead of acknowledging their concerns, continued with the haranguing as if the people had no right to challenge his government.

"Nobody is going to starve! Since I have been here, your wages have doubled..."

Comments and questions began to be fired from the group, with Holloran trying to respond:

"We went from one shillin' to two! Deze families cannot live on dat!"

"You should follow the legal and orderly avenue to present your case...."

"Ya, and when is de avenue given to us...only once a seven year? What are we to eat in the meantime?"

"The Governor is aware of your concerns," Holloran shouted back. "He cared for the workers such as you back in Britain..."

"Dey have a big island der. We have only de small one...and, Governor is in Washington now lickin' de American boot he is. Can he hear us from der? Why he be there when we need him to be here?"

Holloran kept trying. "The Governor will be back soon and he will hear your stories..."

"Des not stories. Des are facts. Der are more blacks den whites here, but nobody hears. We be poor in de house, poor fed and poor with de school. De American Company brings in der own workers and take jobs that should be ours. And doz of us lucky enough to get jobs get paid a lot less!"

Holloran was losing ground fast and was beginning to sound desperate. "But it is their project. It is their money they are investing, and part of that money comes to you! Without them you would jus' be sittin' on da blocks!"

A roar erupted from the crowd. "Oh, so now you one of us when you gets to talkin' 'bout de poor! You be wrong! De money do not come to us!"

At the back of the platform, the gathered government group was losing confidence in Holloran's ability to handle the situation and were very uneasy about the direction this dialogue was taking. R.A. Robertson, the Director of Canadian Life Insurance Corporation, decided to step forward to take over from the disillusioned Attorney General who was whistled and booed from the stage. With his hands held high trying to calm the crowd, Robertson tried another approach

"What the Honorable Attorney General was trying to say," he shouted, "is the developers are paying for the privilege of working the land for our good. Think of them as missionaries trying to lay the seed for a promising future for the islands."

"Missionaries do us no good! When dey come, we haf da land and dey haf da Bible. Now we haf da Bible but dey haf da land!"

Robertson had only ratcheted up the distrust, so Reverend Claudius Green, Minister of the island's largest Anglican church, Christ's Cathedral, stepped up to the front to try and calm things. He was very much respected by the islanders, a distinguished Man of God, tall and eloquent, with enough grey hair and lines in his face to show he had experience and was genuinely concerned about his people. The crowd became quiet when they saw him.

"You have talked about the Bible, and it is right that you keep it close to your heart," he shouted to the crowd, then turning slightly to include the distinguished entourage on stage, he continued, "but to the esteemed members of the economic and legal community who stand behind me on this platform tonight, the Bible also tells us that we are to be a people of action."

The protesters were paying close attention now. They liked what Reverend Green was saying. "My Bible tells me that when we are heavenly minded first, we are inspired to do good on earth. Do not deceive yourselves into thinking you are wise in these matters of the world. Rather, be quick to listen and slow to speak. Just listen to your brothers and sisters tonight." The Reverend was answerable only to God, and although generally respectful of those placed in authority over him, was keen to challenge these leaders.

"Tonight I heard from our highest available government representative in the country. I also listened to Mr. Robertson who, I am sure, is the primary insurance broker for the deal and is speaking for the American Pleasantville Construction Company that is building the airports. We find ourselves, gentlemen, serving under two flags. The first is the Union Jack to which we have pledged our allegiance, but the second is the Stars and Stripes which has provided many of us with a good standard of living from tourism, food exports, and, in some cases, as Sir Harry Oakes knows, transplanted farm labor on American soil. But even though that is the case, we must talk about what the Lord Jesus Christ stood for–individual dignity, caring and the value of our own people. I look into this crowd and I see those who strive to make those principles of Christian love come alive. I am surrounded by my brothers named McPherson, Gibson, Cambridge, Fisher, Ford and Kemp who have joined with other laborers, waiters and clerks to peaceably present their demands, in Christ's name, to our leaders who are, in fact, Christ's representatives on earth." He paused to give his final statement full impact. "Do not dissuade us as we are as valuable to Christ in our humblest of callings as you are, whether living at Bain Town or Westbourne."

With that last remark, Harry was afraid the Reverend's comments would only serve to embolden this mob and was ready to bolt onto the stage, but Sullivan grabbed his arm as the crowd began to cheer. With the Reverend's acknowledgment of their plight, the mood had calmed a bit, and now it was time for the greatest Bahamian businessman, Sir Harry Oakes, to work his magic and end this.

Originally dressed in a crinkly white linen suit, Harry had long since removed his jacket and hat, and with his cotton shirt open at the neck, he appeared more like a tourist than one of the officials there to talk down the crowd. If Sir Harry was going to be the savior the Colonial administration was offering, he had better be good.

There was a smattering of applause as Sir Harry approached the front of the Fargo platform. He was comfortable with the words he was about to utter, as they were the truth, but as he looked at all the wide eyes that anticipated something profound, what he saw was a mob, momentarily satiated by the Reverend's words, but ready to change in a moment if he failed to say the right thing.

He cleared his throat and raised his head. "This is your country. We know that, but I was invited here by one of your own..."

Immediately, a voice from the back of the crowd challenged him. "Dat not true. You were give de invite by Conchie Joe..."

The expression of racial division began to stir the crowd once again. Harry paused for just a moment, then continued. "Many of you know that I, myself, came from humble beginnings, and have traveled the world from Australia to Canada working hard to make something of myself. Through the blessing of God I landed here, and you have always accepted me to the islands with open arms. Since I became a citizen of this great country I have used my wealth, my energy, and my ambition for you. I have built our only hospital, paid you above average wages, provided free transportation and built many of the homes in which you now live..."

Some were still listening, but most were not. "We all knows you come here to beat de taxman. Dat makes you de criminal. You came for your own good!"

Harry knew this wasn't good, but he had to keep going. "You're right. I didn't come here under the best of circumstances, but once here I came to love the islands. I give thousands of dollars to…." Once again he was interrupted, this time from the other side of the square.

"…to the building for golfin' and such, polo field and beaches and your big house? It's not like dis black man can ever go where white folk stay. In daylight, we could not be in dis part of Bay Street. If my skin was lighter, maybe I carry your golfin' bag or serve drinks at de club. I say it's time to stand up to you, Conchie Joe! We not gonna lick no white boots no more!"

This brazen response was taking the evening to a place nobody wanted it to go, but Sir Harry kept trying. "Please! Just listen to me! There is justice–it grinds slowly, but grinds fine! We must work together…" This last comment was wasted on the crowd as emotion was replacing reason, and control was slipping away. Still other voices cried from all parts of the plaza.

"You wear da mask that be grinnin' and lyin'. You buy your way to da big gov'ment house. You fire me if I don't tell everyone to vote for you, and you make de laws that say we cannot vote in the secret way like the Conchie Joe. You have no right to be talkin' 'bout justice!"

Things were quickly getting out of control as the crowd began jostling toward the platform, compacting the Scottish Highlanders closer against the Fargo. In a panic, the order was given to fix bayonets. The crowd responded with a cry of black unity referring to other West Indies activists. "Remember Bustermante, Adams and Manley!"

Empty liquor bottles started flying toward the Fargo, and then the worst possible thing happened – gun shots.

Chapter 19

Lull in the Storm

❦

Bob-Lo Island, Ontario

Late summer Sunday afternoons on Bob-Lo Island were meant for relaxation, and since this was the only day Mae and Vaughn would have alone together before returning to St. Marys, they were going to make the most of it. Colonel Petrie had provided them free transportation through his family connections–as long as they remembered to board the right Bob-Lo boat!

During the trip to the island, *The Promise* entered slightly into American waters, then back out again, which caused a bit of a challenge for the crew of the Canadian-owned vessel. Unlike the safety and security precautions at the Ambassador Bridge border crossing, there was no search or interrogation of passengers, but since the boat was technically entering the United States at one point, American authorities were present to check each passenger's passport. The boat's crew felt it impolite to impose on their own Canadian tourists, so it was left up to the American border officers to do their duty.

The crew also never asked for identification from any person wearing a military uniform, Canadian or American, and when they came across the McIntoshes in their Salvation Army regalia they weren't quite sure what to do. Finally, though, after discussing the situation quietly among themselves, they nodded and moved on, giving the officers the benefit of the doubt. Vaughn looked at Mae and smiled. It appeared the Lord had gone before them once again.

Vaughn's interest in anything powerfully mechanical led him to the stern of *THE PROMISE* observing the operation of the shafts and cams, but unfortunately for him, that didn't sit well with Mae. After all, this was supposed to be a day for the two of them to spend together, so she dragged him away from the boat's mechanics to the front rail of the upper deck. Promises of buttery popcorn, a hot dog smothered in deep-brown mustard, and, of course, time spent with her, had been enough to pull him away from the wheelhouse. As they made their way on the ten-minute boat ride from Amherstsbug, they enjoyed the summer breeze on their faces and agreed it was good to laugh again and get away from the mundane and serious, if just for a little while.

There was excitement in the air as they pulled into the island dock where a small ragtime band played outside a souvenir shop, welcoming visitors as they disembarked–and reminding them all to stop and shop before leaving at the end of the day. Many families were return visitors who knew the lay of the land, and they moved quickly to their preferred picnic or beach spot, despite their children's pleas to first head to the Dodge'em Cars, Wild Mouse or Tilt-a-Whirl. The wise–and experienced–parents gave in to at least one tumultuous ride before lunch, knowing the outcome might be unpleasant if they waited till after the children had eaten. Then, once everyone's appetites were satisfied, Mom and Dad would be content with the Swan Ride, the Carousel, or a trip around the park on the miniature train, feeling safe allowing the children to roam on their own as long as they checked in regularly.

Being new to this experience, Vaughn and Mae walked aimlessly around the island becoming familiar with the many possibilities open to them–the Power House, Merry-Go-Round Hall, Dance Pavilion, and even the wash rooms. They both noticed that most of the buildings were constructed of the same limestone as the majority of the houses, shops, and businesses in St. Marys, giving them a sense of hometown comfort. They ended up on the south end of the island where they ate their lunch in the shade of the old Imperial British Lighthouse that had served for years as a warning to river-goers about the dangerous shoals surrounding the island.

With the magnificent beach and lake in front of them, they rested against the white-washed stone tower and nibbled on the brown bag lunch Mrs. Forester had prepared for them–bread and butter sandwiches, carrot sticks, and cheddar cheese blocks. For dessert there was a chocolate bar, proudly wrapped by the Windsor Optimists in shiny silver paper, just like Vaughn had seen shipped to British children during his time overseas. The memory of those days reminded him, when he looked at her, how much he had missed Mae. He leaned in and gave her a kiss, catching her off guard, but she didn't resist and then rested her head against his shoulder, enjoying their closeness.

After lunch they decided to wade in the clear shallow waters off the sandy beach. Mae loved to feel the rippled sand between her toes and thought of Cate Martin's first real date with George McIntosh, and reminded Vaughn about it. "They were both too proud to be the one to make the first move."

Vaughn laughed. "Not a problem with you, as I remember. You were always into first moves. We had never even had a date yet when you kissed me. Very forward, Mrs. McIntosh–or should I call you Cate, Jr.?"

Mae gave him a sly smile. "I don't remember you resisting or complaining, Mr. McIntosh."

"Complain? How could I complain when you nearly knocked my teeth out!"

"Well… at least our first kiss was memorable," she said sheepishly.

"No, I would describe it as unforgettable, but that afternoon in the attic of the garage– now that was something memorable."

Her eyes sparkled in delight as her cheeks flushed, and she leaned over to her husband and whispered, "You know how you love apple pie." Then she splashed the unsuspecting Vaughn, and hightailed it back to safety before he could return the favor. As Mae looked back from the grassy bank at her soaked husband, she laughed and was reminded again of a Cate McIntosh story. Before she could say anything, though, Vaughn was headed straight for her, looking for revenge.

He followed her till she was up against the stone wall of the lighthouse, and when she knew there was no escape, dropped to the grass and hid her face till Vaughn attacked. They giggled together through kisses and tickling like a couple of young lovers, letting Bob-lo work its rejuvenating magic. This was the kind of day they both needed.

They dozed off wrapped in each other's arms, and as the afternoon sun shifted, a chill breeze woke Mae and she reached for Vaughn's coat that had been hanging on a branch to dry. As she pulled it over her shoulders, an official-looking envelope dropped into her lap from the inside pocket. Her movement had wakened Vaughn as well, so she held the envelope in front of him.

"Vaughn, did you know this letter was in your jacket pocket?"

"Yes," he responded groggily. He wasn't ready to come back to reality yet, so he mumbled and pulled his wife close, feeling her warm breath on his cheek, thinking all was good with the world. Then suddenly, he remembered what was in the letter and realized that instead of just good, this moment could be great!

Pushing himself up against the lighthouse, Vaughn took the letter from Mae, and then formally presented it back to her. "I can't believe I forgot! You need to read this!"

Mae pushed her untidy hair behind her ear and opened the letter, a slow smile spreading across her face. "Does this mean what I think it means? We're off the hook? Forever? Completely?"

"I believe so," Vaughn said happily. "Montagu Norman has moved on. Picard is the scapegoat and Sir Harry is now the focus of their attention, though he may not realize it. We all know nobody is more adept at handling gold than he is, so I think our worries are over. We have no idea where the treasure is and Sir Harry has assured us it's in a world that has no connection to us. So, yes, I would say we are off the hook, unless someone comes poking around the farm well."

Mae could feel a lingering tension leaving her body – a tension she hadn't even realized was there until she got this news. She found herself noticing the puffy clouds for the first time. The air smelled sweeter and the raspy call of the gulls was even more melodic. The bright and cheerful music of the distant carousel was calling them to celebrate and they spent the rest of the afternoon enjoying everything they could. This was, indeed, their day and they were going to make the most of it until the last departure time of *The Promise*.

Chapter 20
Pillars of Salt

Nassau, Bahamas

Racial extremism and the herd mentality had come together at Rawson Square, a potent and dangerous combination. The first shot, fired by an unknown protestor, was reported to have been influenced by excessive liquor consumption, but the resulting charge of the bayoneted Cameron Highlanders was the response of training. Usually, participants in a mob have one thing in common–imitation–but the commonality of everyone involved in this disaster was fear.

Sir Harry was pulled down from the Fargo truck by a lieutenant whose pith helmet had been knocked off by an errant rock, and he was bleeding profusely from a deep scalp wound. Several Bahamian policemen had overrun protestors in their haste to usher Sullivan, the Attorney General and the rest of the official party a few hundred feet across Bay Street into the Senate and Assembly Houses on Parliament Square. The statue of Queen Victoria that graced this plaza was deflecting rocks and bottles intended for the retreating party. More gun shots tore into the pink walls of the Assembly House, tearing up furniture and glass-framed pictures of the Duke of Windsor. Orders were given from the armed guard for everyone to stay on their bellies while taking cover.

Harry was feeling more anger than fear, and attached himself to a Cameron peering out a window through a small opening in a closed shutter. The carnage before them was unbelievable: two motionless male bodies on the street, Straw Market stalls, along with several abandoned carts containing very combustible sisal, on fire. Windows had been

119

smashed at the Senate and Police Station, shards of glass sparkling in the light from the fires. The Fargo truck had been turned over and was on fire, the smell of burning oil and rubber wafting down Bay Street, while whirling clouds of black smoke left scorched licks on the light pink walls of the Government Tourism office. Several dray and two-wheeled carts had been rammed into the building, but attempts to use them as tinder had been unsuccessful.

Scores of bystanders were engulfed in the fleeing horde of humanity moving further out onto the cays of Prince George's Dock or down toward the British Colonial Hotel. The lucky ones were taken aboard small private craft or commercial ferries to the safety of the harbor waters where they watched in horror as the vandalism and pillaging spread through the commercial district of Bay Street.

Harry looked around and realized Reverend Green was crouched beside him. "Reverend, we have to get out there and check on those men. I'm sure there are others who need help, too. Will you come with me?" They had all been ordered to remain inside where it was relatively safe, but these two were known for not always being compliant when it came to orders. So, ignoring the command, the two men went back onto the street.

They slowly made their way to the injured men, staying as low and inconspicuous as possible. The first man they reached was already gone, so they carried his lifeless body to a more protected spot, then, amid the sound of gunshots and panicked people darting helter-skelter, they worked their way to the other man, only to discover he was also beyond their help.

Harry noticed tears on the Reverend's cheeks as they moved the second victim beside the first, but then, with stern resolve, the Man of God became a man of action. "Harry, we could take Shirley Street and get to Bay at the intersections–try and get onto the balconies where we can see what's going on. Maybe from there we can figure out how to help."

"Yes, we have to try and do something!" Harry was quick to agree. "There should be officers there and we might be able to help each other."

Sir Harry followed the Reverend's lead as they hurried down the avenue parallel to Bay Street, forcing their way into the back of the Royal Bank of Canada building. Without hesitating, they scrambled up the steps to the terrace where they encountered a young, Bahamian Forces Police Officer huddled in the corner of the terrace. He tried to stand when Green and Oakes stepped out, but fell back, shouting, "Be careful! Dey haf pistols." Harry could see the young man's knee had been injured.

"Are you hurt badly, Corporal?" He asked, bending over him for a closer look.

"Jus' m' knee. Ah gotten to yell at doz who try to enter da bank...and dey shot me!" In his anger and frustration, his roots came through and he spoke like the proud Bahamian he was. "When dey go crazy, der too many. Boss sez jus' get outa da way and I end up here."

Harry examined the knee and bandaged it the best he could. Meanwhile, the Reverend carefully peered over the balcony to get a bird's eye view of what was happening. It was a devastating sight. A hurricane, of sorts, had indeed hit Bay Street. Bethel and Grant's liquor stores had been decimated, the door of iron bars torn from its moorings and thrown callously onto the street. Young boys, not even in their teens, were fleeing to safety with glass bottles held close to their chests. Others openly drank their booty, then broke other merchants' windows with half-finished containers of whisky, vodka and gin.

He could see an empty Coca-Cola delivery truck that had been pillaged, which explained where the protestors had gotten all their glass ammunition. A little girl was dragging two bolts of fabric, stopping to rest for a moment, but determined to make it home with what she had confiscated from the dry goods store.

Damnios Grocery had been gutted, leaving a trail of bent or broken tin and boxed goods from the front door onto the street. Its beveled hurricane shutters had been partially pulled off the wall, and an electrical short caused the lights inside to flash erratically, making the looters look like pantomime figures.

High-end jewelers, art and perfume shops, all owned by the Speaker of the House, which made them contentious targets, were all in shambles. Display counters, soft-back chairs, viewing tables, mirrors and even the carpeting were stacked outside with starter fires sputtering underneath. All the advertised store contents were long gone. The popular Red Lion Restaurant was missing its famous double-paned picture window. Looters had obliterated the place with clubs and iron bars, and the signature bar tables and stools inside had been some of the first things seized.

As Sir Harry joined his companion, the Reverend pointed to a frail older man in a rusty t-shirt and coveralls. He was burning a picture of the Royal Family in front of the John Bull Tobacco shop, shouting above the fray, "Ain't no white man gonna pass me by."

"That man is one of my dearest parishioners, Freddie "Hot Potato" Fawkes. He has a pure heart and normally wouldn't hurt anyone. Just look at him!"

Harry had no words of comfort so simply put his hand on Mr. Green's arm. After seeing the destruction going on below them, they looked at each other and knew they would have to wait things out a bit before placing themselves in danger by venturing out again.

"I understand, Reverend Green, that my man, Alex Ferguson has been well received into your church," Harry said, hoping a distraction might lighten their hearts and ease the tension for a moment.

The good Reverend appreciated the sleight of hand and was grateful for the momentary diversion. "Yes, Alex is a fine Christian man." He chuckled. "His momma would have it no other way." He paused and looked out over the city once again. "When the Duke of Windsor gave us funds to rebuild the church three years ago, it was a dream come true. For over a decade our walls and roof had needed reinforcement and remodeling. We never fully recovered from the hurricane of '29–the crypts under the floor and along the walls are still splintered and cracked open in spots. But we'll be putting in formal pews in just a few weeks. At least we were planning to before this happened. That may have to be put on hold now."

A random gunshot close by caught their attention and they stopped talking, but when no more followed, Harry continued, "Alex talks about serving on a couple of committees at the church."

"Yes, he certainly knows his automobiles and how to fix things, so I asked him to chair the Renovations Committee–and he agreed. He was the perfect choice. He's there seven days a week, checking on progress and making sure everything is moving along."

Another shot, another pause. This time, they scuffled back from the edge of the veranda a bit more.

"When Alex drops me off at the office," Harry said, "he usually takes his sack lunch and makes his way to the church. He borrows one of the cars on Saturdays to do the same thing–basically followed that routine for almost two years now."

"And on Sunday, he's there for both services," the Reverend added. "Whenever a portion of the wall or crypt is ready for closing, he personally does the final touch-ups himself. I think it's his way of putting closure to a very big project a little bit at a time."

"I think you're right, Reverend Green–so very right."

When they hadn't heard any more gun shots for a while, they stood and looked over the railing again.

"Time for us to move... the Camerons are coming down Bay Street. I see at least two wounded people who need attention, over there between Pinder's Candy and the shoe store." They helped the wounded Corporal to his feet, and with Harry bracing under his arm, hurried down the back steps to the side street and waited behind a stone fence until the last of the dispersing crowd raced past them. The Camerons had re-grouped and, in two horizontal lines, marched down Bay Street clearing the district of all persons. Occasionally a few more shots were fired, but the crashing of glass and looting had dissipated – mostly because there was nothing left to destroy.

They rounded a corner and ran into the Lieutenant who had protected him at the outset of the fracas.

"Sir Harry and Reverend Green! You're safe! Please go with Constable Rolle. He'll escort you back to the Colonial Hotel where everyone is meeting."

"Thank you, Lieutenant. The Corporal here is wounded so they can help him back to safety, but the Reverend and I need to attend to those people over there...."

The Lieutenant was adamant. "No, Sir Harry! I'm sorry but this time, I really mean 'no'! You will clear this area. The Attorney General has introduced the War Defense Measure for the next twenty-four hours. Refuse my orders and I will arrest you, no matter who you are. I am in no mood for any discussion."

Recognizing the seriousness of the situation, Harry decided not to tempt fate a second time, so he acquiesced and they headed back along East Bay Street toward the square where it had all begun, this time under the watchful eye of two very nervous, gun-toting Camerons. "These islands will never be the same after tonight, Sir Oakes," one of them commented. "Nothing like this has ever happened here before. You Boys will have to realize the heart and mind of the black man has been agitated. There's a risin' comin' and you better be prepared for a change."

Sir Harry was angry about all the unnecessary destruction around him. He was used to using well-orchestrated strategies, relying on the common decency of civility, to resolve issues. Even in places in his past life that had only boasted minimal formal authority– the Yukon, the Outback of Australia, the Northern Woods of Canada–people had come together in a mutually agreeable manner to discuss their differences. "Violence and willful destruction of property is not the British way. These people have lost everything they ever worked for, and I'm afraid the Government will never trust them again. There will be more blood-letting, for sure, and the next time it will be more sinister and directed toward the country's leaders, Black or White, it won't matter!"

Just as they arrived at the Colonial, intermittent rifle blasts followed by screaming, could be heard coming from Prince George's dock. The guards pushed their important charges into the foyer of the hotel, and after making sure nobody was following them, barred the doors. In the parlor and hallway was a mixture of dignitaries and protesters, both helping to address wounds and comfort each other.

Sir Harry helped the Corporal to a chair, then leaned closer to Reverend Green. "Now this is my picture of our country. People helping each other in times of need. White, Black, Mulatto, Sambo, Octoroons or Conchies–it doesn't matter."

As medical personnel attended to Sir Harry, but made Mr. Green wait, the Reverend was quick to point out the indiscretion that stood before them. Sir Harry passed it off as nonsense, but Reverend Green persisted. "Look around you, Sir Harry. Coloreds are in the hallways and Joe is in the tea room. We sit on the floor while you have the couches and cushions. We get the beer and you get the scotch. We are all in the same house, feeling our pain together, but we are still worlds apart."

Sir Harry could see his point, but wanted to give him a different perspective. "Reverend, doesn't Christ tell us the poor will be with us always. No matter how much we give to people, many will never rise above their station because they just don't have the capacity to do so. It's not just Blacks, it's the same with white people."

The Reverend chewed on Harry's words. "The problem I see is that up until tonight, you were not even aware of the level of dissatisfaction of those who could–and will–make a difference if only given the chance."

"So destroying the foundations of their lives is the appropriate way to start? The Romans achieved much tranquility with their *Pax Romanus*... the British proudly accepted all into their Empire, too. But what do the Bahamians do? They refer to Karl Marx and Lenin to make their point."

Reverend Green was getting frustrated. "Did you not listen to them, Harry? They proclaimed themselves as proud Englishmen first."

"Is that why they burned the picture of King George and shot up the Assembly Hall?" Harry asked. "Sounds more like they wanted a repeat of the Romanoff purge, where you would have been one of us in that case, Reverend! That is no Black versus White issue!"

"That is exactly my point!" the Reverend nearly shouted. "Our people just want a say in the economy and politics of their country. They see people like you paying lip-service with your hospitals, schools and labor projects. They don't want hand-outs. They want the opportunity to build their own roads, bridges and wharfs. All they want is a say in their future and that of their children."

"No," Harry said emphatically, "what they want is a revolution to force us to relinquish what we sacrificed our families and fortunes for."

"Now you sound like an American...."

"At least in America, they still have the pursuit of liberty."

"But that's just it, Harry. Here in Nassau we don't even have the pursuit available to us. That's what I hope you will learn from tonight." Then, from his pocket, the Reverend pulled a piece of paper. "Sir Harry, this is a list of requests we humbly laid out for the Governor and gave to the Attorney General last month. Instead of giving them any consideration, he ignored them, calling them 'demands', and never even allowed them to cross the Duke's desk."

Harry spread the crumpled paper on the bar and began to read: "*One man, one vote...*Development of 'out-island' industry...*No land sold to foreign realtors without first offering opportunities for Bahamian investors...*A fair tax system supported by those who can most afford it...*No Civil Service members involved in politics...*Labour legislation brought in line with current modern practices...*House Assembly membership limited to two terms...*The out-islands have legislative representation."

Sir Harry drained his Scotch and scribbled notes on a bar napkin. Once finished, he handed the paper to the Reverend. "The demands – or requests as you call them–are too vague and impractical. As a member of the Legislative Assembly I feel I can speak for the majority of members. Here's my answer to your list."

Reverend Green read silently. "*They have a vote and chose not to use it... *'Out-island' industry is already in the planning stages...*The Governor, as the King's Representative, will always have the right to determine property usage in the best interest of his people...*There is NO income tax, what could be fairer than that?...*Civil Servants have an oath to protect the government and must always act accordingly in every matter…*Labour legislation and union development promotes mediocrity…*House Assembly membership already has term limitations of seven years…*'Out-island' membership could be considered once industry exists there." Reverend Green silently folded the paper and tucked it into his breast pocket. He thanked Harry for his time and moved to the hallway to aid 'his own people'.

There would be no reconciliation for these two colliding worlds any time soon, and someone would have to pay the price for this calamity.

Chapter 21
While You Were Away

St. Marys, Ontario

The excursion to Windsor had been profoundly successful for both Mae and Vaughn. He was pleased to have some closure with his Essex-Scottish past, and Mae was overjoyed to have re-connected with her natural mother–and she loved teasing Vaughn about his new Mob connections. Romantic memories of Bob-Lo Island, along with the realization that the whole Amschel affair was finally behind them, rounded out their wonderful trip.

Back in St. Marys, Vaughn was busy as ever concentrating on several community outreach projects, including the long-anticipated completion of the Citadel expansion. An ecumenical collaboration to provide comfort for needy people during the upcoming Christmas season was also coming to fruition. The dozens of families moving into the newly-constructed houses on the east end of town provided a mission field ripe with souls who needed to hear how the Gospel could change their lives. He was also looking forward to getting involved in an expanded music program and joining his spiritual brothers who were planning a retreat on the Upper Thames, courtesy of Will Purdue.

Mae returned to run the Thrift Store, but her heart was still deeply pricked by her experiences at Faith Haven. It appeared the Lord was not blessing them with any children of their own yet, so her dream now concentrated on little ones who were lost, forgotten or broken in some fashion. The first letter Mae received from her mother was full of encouragement and advice. Anne urged Mae to follow her heart on this issue and to ask God for wisdom on how she was to be used by Him. She referenced Ephesians 2:10 – *For we are his workmanship, created in Christ Jesus for good works, which God prepared beforehand so that we should walk in them.* Mae knew there were opportunities in the world for her, but she was uncertain about how and when to share her desires with Vaughn now that their lives, once again, had gained a semblance of predictability.

At the Citadel, Mae had tuned in Stratford radio station CJCS, during her lunch hour. Despite being a small town station, CJCS manager, John Squires, was creating quite a following. He gave daily updates on the war, complete with how it affected the kin of all Perth County residents. John obviously did his homework as he lauded those in the Service from Listowel to Thorndale. The inspiring and dedicated personal touch of Mr. Squires was making him one of the most-listened-to programs in the area.

During an early September, 1943, broadcast, Mae was particularly moved: *"…Friends, the battle for Stalingrad has begun. If Hitler can be halted, then the entire momentum of the war may change in Europe. Churchill has done his part by putting his trust in Monty to turn the fortunes of the Allies in North Africa. The Aussies and Americans have stunned the Japanese at Milne Bay in Paupua. These are vital times not to give up the support here at home. Remember your local tin, aluminum, rubber and paper drives. At the end of this broadcast when I read the names of all our men and women in service, I want you to take a look around your house and donate anything you do not need to keep our boys fighting!"*

Before he went into his update on those in uniform, however, Squires continued with another message:

> *"…the children of our country are our future. When this war is over, many of them will have lost mothers and fathers, but lost in its entirety are those who already have limitations. They are the lame, blind and deaf from birth. They are already at war on a daily basis to eek out a living as they hope to grow into independent adulthood. Today, I want to acknowledge the work of the St. Marys Salvation Army, located on the corner of Queen and Peel in the Stonetown. We are going to be visiting our neighbors 12 miles to the west next week to talk about the special project they are about to embark upon. So be sure to join us then…"*

Just as she was shutting off her Delco, Vaughn came through the door, covered in sweat but with a look of satisfaction on his face. "Done! The building extension is finished, as of today. Liam is backfilling the dirt around the foundation and Will is reinforcing the wallboard. We're thinking about cleaning up a bit and joining Frannie and Phalyn at the Grill for some lunch. What do you say?"

Mae didn't answer his question but asked one of her own. "Well, Captain McIntosh, when were you going to tell me the news?"

Vaughn acted dumb and tried to keep a straight face, but Mae knew he could never keep a secret. "The CJCS thing fell into my lap and I had to make a decision." Then he smiled. "I talked to the Board and they all agreed since the monies came from my mother, the new addition would be dedicated to Cate McIntosh, but we are going to re-dedicate the entire building to Ross and Sheila Skipper. Here's some great news: Uncle Bert and Heather are going to try to make it to the dedication service. Unfortunately, the war is too close for Will and Connie to come. I haven't heard from George or Harriet yet, but I'm sure they'll be here. Even your sisters are coming from Toronto. It will be a grand celebration for us all. The IODE ladies are giving us their hall and..."

"Vaughn, stop! When have you had time to do all this?"

"It hasn't been me. You can blame Will and Phalyn for most of it. They're also taking care of the food."

"Please tell me you remembered to invite..."

"Yes, Mae, I did. Your mother is coming up from Windsor. The whole family will be here."

"Is there anything else I should know or do?"

"If you would, please, you could contact the Journal Argus to see if Mr. Irvine can make it. Also, the Eddy's, Doc Munro and the Hollick family... and don't forget to formally invite Frannie. She always said if she could find a good looking man she would even go to church with him, and Liam has agreed. The Lord seems to be doing some pretty incredible things."

"Can you make me a list and I'll take care it?"

"Already done. Phalyn will give it to you at the grill."

"That little sneak! I go on a short vacation and she takes over!"

"We should have almost a hundred people for this event. In fact, I've even heard that with a provincial election coming up we might even be graced with the presence of a few candidates."

"Vaughn, this is a house of God. I can see you letting in Mr. Dickson, he is the current MPP, after all, and even the Conservative, Mr. Edwards, but surely you won't allow Bert Davies to grace our Hall?"

"Mae McIntosh, you sound a little judgmental and legalistic. Since when did you become the filter to say who comes through His doors?"

"But Davies is a communist and all communists hate God. They disrespect and make fun of our beliefs."

Somewhat sarcastically, Vaughn presented the obvious to his wife, "What do you think my mother would want us to do with Bert Davies?"

"Cate McIntosh would say, 'Let me at him!' She went after the General of the Salvation Army at one time when she was only a teenager. She would want us to follow in her footsteps."

"So, we let Mr. Davies come and cast our bread on the water. I think it will be a grand day. Besides, he will be in the Lord's House and terribly outnumbered. What could go wrong?"

"What could go wrong? Just everything and nothing! But it's typical for us McIntoshes. If there's a hard or complicated way to do something, we'll find it." Mae paused, then said, "I want you to remember that when I ask you a tough question later on. OK?" Vaughn was in such a good mood he didn't think there was anything Mae could ask that he wouldn't like, but he missed hearing the trepidation in her voice.

Chapter 22

Spurned

❧

Nassau, Bahamas

Surprisingly, only three protestors and one member of the Royal Bahamian Defense Force were killed during the Nassau uprising, though over two hundred people, both insurgents and bystanders, were treated for injuries. The Camerons had arrested over a hundred demonstrators, but the damage done to the commercial district of Bay Street left staggering economic loss. Now that the ruling elite were aware how quickly the 'docile' natives could turn into a destructive mob, a strategy on how to prevent such an uprising from re-occurring needed to be put in place as soon as possible, but nobody had any confidence in the Governor – the Duke of Windsor – to handle the task.

One of the adverse effects of the riots was the loss of confidence and respect even Members of the Legislative Assembly now held for the Governor. The war had already reduced tourist flow to the Bahamas, but this civil strife caused an economic stranglehold that would take years to overcome–and the Governor was not even on the island when the brouhaha broke out. Fingers were being pointed at him from all angles.

The uproar by the predominantly White oligarchy was deafening. They dug in their heels and refused to take the demands of the protestors seriously. The common belief was, given time, things would return to normal. They asserted that Black anger erupted spontaneously and dissipated just as quickly, which, to them, meant things would go back to business as usual once the mess was cleaned up. But since the feelings of unrest were still

131

fresh, the first dictate from the Assembly was that no free-roaming Blacks were allowed on Bay Street while the damage was being assessed.

The violent behavior had temporarily gone underground, but the seething was still intense. The rioters had caused some five million dollars in damage to a six-block area, and consequently, through what was perceived as their open disrespect for King and authority, had lost their rights to appeasement and *parlez* with the government. A Pandora's box had been opened, though, and Black political action and labor groups could smell blood in the water. They saw firsthand that the "Boys of Bay Street" could have their armor penetrated– they did bleed and were not indestructible. Those having the right to rule had been tested and were found, by the Bahamian Black, sorely lacking in integrity and unworthy of trust.

Regardless, the "Boys" formed an investigative commission to make recommendations to the Assembly to help prevent rioting in the future. Though reluctant to give in to pressure, it was deemed that a few concessions should be granted as a sign of good faith. A two-shilling-a-day raise for the airport project workers was approved, though this was still less than their American counterparts received. Out-island representation would be examined, but nobody thought it would be seriously considered. It was widely noted that Sir Harry Oakes was glaringly absent from the Assembly for the vote on these issues.

Despite his proven altruistic track record, Harry had become the scapegoat. He was the most powerful figure on the island, after all–the largest landowner and most fiscally visible figure. His name was all over everything Bahamian: streets, hotels, restaurants, holding companies, schools, resorts, racetracks, transportation systems. If Sir Harry Oakes was going to lay claim to the growth and diversity of the islands' economy, then he must also be responsible for the cancer within that threatened to take down the White monopolistic primogeniture that had existed without challenge for over two hundred years.

Time was running out for Sir Harry Oakes, and he knew it, but he refused to be part of a system that gave in to thugs and criminals who should have been grateful for all he had brought to the Bahamas. He had invested not only his time, money, and energy, but his total spirit. He continued with his projects that were already in progress–Airport, Lyford Cay, Cable Beach and the South Island projects–but he was noticeably absent at all locales, replaced by mid-level managers who lacked the enthusiasm and credibility Sir Harry had brought to the site. The discord among select Black workers was intense, for they now viewed the "Conchie King" as a tyrant, and Harry feared if they had gone so far as organizing the Bay Street riots, which had given them little personal result, how far would they now go to achieve real economic independence?

Eunice and the girls had hurried home when they heard about the unrest, and had been of great consolation to Harry, but he was a different person since the riots. He complained of headaches and insomnia, and though he attempted to put the whole business in perspective, truth was he felt physically threatened by all that was happening around him.

At home, Nancy was miffed that Freddie and her father were not getting along and the situation was still as contentious as ever. Regardless of his smiling demeanor, Freddie had never forgiven Harry for his banishment from Westbourne. With Nancy's return, he was back at the house, but the marriage was strained, threatening the idyllic sanctuary he had created for himself. What Harry still wondered was how far would Freddie go to protect his own interests?

Right now, though, Harry had other problems to deal with. He knew the current environment in Nassau was unacceptable to the foreign investors from Miami, and Trevor Sullivan had put off Frank Johnson and the Miami Mob as long as he could, hoping to convince Sir Harry to change his attitude about gambling. But now, especially since Sullivan's dealings at the airport project were the real cause for the labor riots, the atmosphere had become even more tense and all the more complicated. And everyone knew how the Mob could un-complicate matters very quickly.

That would have to be dealt with, but the problem at hand was the Argentinean, Hans Lubeck.

From a second floor window, Eunice and Harry stood arm in arm as they watched two stately Daimlers carrying the Duke of Windsor, Axel Salming and Hans Lubeck, enter the Westbourne compound for a meeting they had requested with Harry. Eunice released his arm, kissed him on the cheek, and with great assurance, gave him her welcomed opinion.

"Just pretend they are your former mining partners from Swastika, the Tough brothers, and handle them the same way–find their weakness and exploit it. The Duke, for instance, is all about compromise and will go whichever way the group goes. You won't find an original idea with him, so I wouldn't waste my time listening to what he has to say. Just keep the scotch flowing and he'll be happy. He's actually a non-factor in this meeting, but you already knew that, didn't you?" she said with a smile. "So just send him my way and I'll keep him busy."

Eunice was half his age, but was three times wiser. She was an excellent judge of character and very intuitive about the wants and interests of all who crossed her husband's path. Eunice was his beloved confidante and advisor, and he had learned to listen well to his greatest partner and protector.

She continued her analysis. "Salming, although he appears rather enigmatic, is… struggling. His holdings are being investigated in Mexico City as a possible launder site for the Nazis. Let's be honest. He's a new world order Nazi. He will come down on whichever side wins the war. The British are still watching him, so the presence of Hans Lubeck hasn't helped his stature. He's in it for the table scraps from whatever you concoct. The Americans are tying up his assets in New York and he needs a payday, even if he has to resort to carrying someone else's bags for a while. He's just a porter for Lubeck. I think he'll stay out of it once the Argentinean begins to talk. He might even venture out with the Duke."

Harry looked at Eunice, awestruck. He couldn't imagine how he had survived the past few months without her by his side, and was eternally grateful she was here now. With his thick and straggly eyebrows uplifted, he asked for her assessment of the Argentinean.

Madame Oakes had done her homework. "Let's see… from what I've learned, he speaks several languages which indicates he is well-bred and well-traveled. Herr Lubeck feels comfortable in the company of Kings, so is either related to royalty or is simply arrogant and pompous, feeling he's deserving of aristocratic blood and is open to ridiculing those of unequal social standing. That would be you, Sir Harry Oakes. There's nothing royal about a Yukon stakeholder or an Aussie walkabout. You are so Canadian you will trust to a fault, but, if Hans Lubeck deceives you, that trust will be gone forever. You fight for what you believe because you know that being right is more important than being rich. Be careful of that one. I feel he represents something that is evil."

Eunice turned and put her hands on Harry's shoulders, directing his gaze down to her. She gave him a steadfast, and inspiring look. "I will be down at the beach house preparing lunch for your guests."

Harry waited until he was told his visitors were settled in his study, then he waited a while longer, drawing on his past gamesmanship as Eunice had suggested. When he finally made his appearance, Sir Harry faked a startled look, as if he was not expecting anyone to be there. To add to his salesmanship, he was barefoot, dressed only in a pair of navy blue swim shorts with an open cabana robe on top. He appeared most embarrassed.

"Oh, my! I am so sorry!" He said, pulling his robe closed around him. "I forgot all about our meeting and nobody told me you were here." He walked across the room and shook David's hand and nodded at Lubeck and Salming. "But since you are here, if you don't mind my attire, we can proceed."

Sir Harry topped off the Duke's crystal snifter with another three fingers and asked the others for their beverage pleasure, but they refused any refreshment. Apparently, this was to be all business for them.

"Sir Harry, we need to assess where we stand," Lubeck blurted, ignoring protocol by speaking before the Governor and his host.

Harry was in no mood for this brash behavior and was about to take charge when a servant appeared at the door announcing that Mrs. Oakes was serving conch salad at the beach house. Thankful as always for Eunice, Harry suggested that Axel and David enjoy the beach while he and Lubeck completed their discussion. As expected, the two were only too happy to let them hammer things out between them.

As the door closed behind them, Sir Harry wasted no time and turned to Lubeck. "I know about you, Lubeck, and the hateful family you represent. I also hate goose-steppers and everything you symbolize. So that is two strikes against you right from the start. Despite that, I still considered your proposal concerning the gold and my future here in the Bahamas….and frankly, I found you have nothing to offer me."

Showing no reaction, Lubeck sauntered up to Sir Harry until their faces were just inches apart, then very quietly and confidently said, "I don't think you totally grasp the situation, Sir Harry. I have the power to crush you and your silly little enterprise here if I want to, and I understand there are others in line to do the same now that you've allowed these riots to happen…"

Harry took a few steps back, scoffing at his rudeness. But Lubeck was not finished. "It seems, Harry, you forget we've toppled kings and countries all over the world. We are currently working on a Jewish state in the Middle East so we can control the Zionists once and for all… Argentina is already ours and soon the rest of South America… we are in the final stages with gaining control of the Bank of England and the Federal Reserve in America." At the lack of reaction from Sir Harry, Lubeck smiled. "Perhaps you should consider the welfare of your family. I know how important they are to you." He walked to Harry's desk and picked up a picture of Eunice that was sitting there. "With all this stacked against you, Harry, I think your best protection is to reconsider my offer."

Nothing made Harry angrier than his family being threatened, but he maintained his poise and decided now was the time to take charge. "OK, Hans, you're right. I know about the gold, and I also know how badly you want to be the new Jamie Amschel. But I think you're over-estimating your influence here. I could make one telephone call and both the Americans and Brits would sweep you up... right along with your good friend, Axel. You can pretend you deserve to wear the royal Amschel robes..." Harry paused and gave Lubeck a piercing look, "but you have to get off this island first."

Harry poured himself a club soda. "No response? Well, then let me say, the biggest mistake you ever made was threatening my family. By this time tomorrow I want you heading south, and don't ever come back or I will use you for tarp bait."

Lubeck seemed unfazed by Harry's threat. "I was warned about your stubbornness, Harry, so now, you will listen to me. I am in a position to take over all your companies, removing you from all positions and accessing your holdings, with the help of your dear 'friends' out on the beach," he said with a sneer. "They sit on most of your corporate boards, and will do whatever I say – and once we gain trustee access to your operations, any influence you have will be over. So, you are the one who has made a big mistake, Harry. You're a prisoner of this little island. After the riots, nobody will care if you are gone, or who removed you." The look of triumph on his face was almost embarrassing.

"Really, Herr Lubeck? Your threats don't scare me. This isn't the first time I've encountered a personal threat such as yours. I've stared into the face of evil before and prevailed. This meeting is over."

Lubeck was indignant. In his anger he reached into the pocket of his white linen jacket and menacingly drew his Mauser 34. "I could just as easily get rid of you right now, Harry, and be done with it."

Harry wasn't expecting this, but appeared to take it in stride. "Do you really think any of you–Axel, David, Sullivan–could find my gold with me gone? I'm way too smart to allow that. My holdings are so scattered around the world that even your next generation of thugs could never discover it all."

"I think you're bluffing. It took months for Picard to move the gold, and you couldn't just move something like that without being noticed. Even Roosevelt sent three destroyers to South Africa to pick up British Gold to pay for lend-lease. We noticed that, and your treasure is measurably more cumbersome. I'm sure it's in one place. Your ruse of using four colleagues and their banks did not fool us. It's in one place–and that place is here."

"Lubeck, you're not going to shoot anybody, so why don't you put down the pistol? You look ridiculous." Harry began moving across the room without taking his eyes off his companion. "Now, I'm going to plant myself in that big, green chair over there and we can continue playing this game in comfort. Besides," he said, glancing pointedly at the gun, "the safety is still on."

It had been a while since Lubeck had unshouldered his pistol so he knew he could be a little rusty, but when he checked and the safety was indeed off, he was embarrassed that Sir Harry had been able to plant doubt in his mind, and his anger grew by the minute. This Bahamian was indeed a fine poker player. He knew, just as Harry had guessed, he wasn't going to shoot anyone, so he put the gun back into his jacket, swallowing the humiliation of Harry's smile.

"Good choice. I have guns myself throughout this house, Herr Lubeck, and could have used one on you any time while you fussed about, but I was enjoying our little banter. I learned a lot about you and it was most entertaining."

Lubeck had not been the target of such berating since Kapitan Langsdorff had threatened his officers off the dying Graf Spee. Back then, the abuse was taken from his superior out of respect. The rebuke from an *untermensch* like Harry Oakes, though, was almost more than he could bear.

"Let's say, just for the moment, that the gold you're looking for is in one place. Now where do you think that would be, Herr Lubeck?"

Lubeck had no intention of playing Harry's game, so he stood still and quiet, waiting for Harry's next move. "No thoughts? Oh, that's right – that's why you need me! Well, maybe those two maps on the wall will give you a clue."

Lubeck reluctantly crossed the room and stopped in front of two, three-foot square, glass-covered charts. As much as he hated following Harry's orders, he realized this just might be his chance to learn something about the gold. This underling wasn't as smart as he liked to think, and there was a good chance he would slip up if Lubeck kept him talking long enough.

"The one on the left is, of course, the Bahamian Islands," he began. "I never realized how extensive Grand Bahama was until I researched it before coming here. Andros is nothing to scoff at either, and here we are on New Providence." Lubeck ran his sweaty finger disrespectfully down the glass plate. "Eleuthra, Long Island, Ackins, Inauga... Yes, they all seem to be here."

Sir Harry found Lubeck's rudeness to be childish and refused to comment on the indiscretion. "Look at the boot shaped island...Cat Island, we call it. What do you know about it?"

Lubeck recited, "Cat Island got its name from Arthur Catt, a less-than-renowned pirate or it could possibly be due to the many feral cats that live on the island. It's the home of several failed plantations."

Lubeck then added, "There are also stories of lost spirits and such..."

In spite of himself, Harry was impressed. "You know my islands, well, Herr Lubeck. But what can that map to the right tell you?"

"That is, of course, your Cat Island. Wait!" he said, turning back toward Harry. "Are you trying to tell me that's where you've hidden the gold?" When he saw the mocking smile on Harry's face, he knew it was another of Harry's distractions. "And we could have become modern-day pirates, digging for buried treasure."

"Listen, I suppose you want me to think the gold is hidden on Cat island, but I'm aware of the tales of all those who have wasted their life's fortunes looking for their 'booty' in and around that island. It's too obvious, too impractical and frankly, beneath your intelligence level. I can tell by your expression I'm right... Yes?"

"You seem to have the answers for everything, but are you sure? Let me give you a hint. In that middle cabinet behind you is an acacia wooden box. Go ahead and pull it down, but be careful, it's quite heavy."

Lubeck hesitated for a moment, but finally did as he was instructed. He had to use both hands as he slid the box to the edge of the shelf and then let it slide against his chest before sitting it on the desk. He slowly lifted the lid to find a polished gold ingot prominently displaying the stamp of the Bahamas. Lubeck picked it up, turning it over in his hands while almost licking his lips.

"You see, Herr Lubeck, if you were not clever enough to account for the deception of Monsieur Picard, how can you be so sure the gold is all in one place? You have in your hands a bar of the finest product ever made, but where is the rest of the family? And why would I show you this piece?"

Lubeck would not give Harry the satisfaction of a response. Obviously, he had been prepared for this meeting and had planned his steps carefully. "Ah, no answer again?" Harry said. "The answer is actually quite simple. You will never learn where the gold is and this is the only piece of it you will ever see. Why don't you take that bar back with you when you leave tomorrow–as a consolation prize?"

Lubeck had finally had enough. "Sir Oakes, it's time for you to face facts. The forces mounting against you are insurmountable. Are you willing to put your family at risk? I tell you, I'm willing to do anything to force you to reveal the location of the gold."

Harry stood, and took a menacing step toward his guest. "Do you wish to leave this room as a living creature?" he asked.

"Don't come any closer. I still have my gun, and for all your bragging, I can see no weapon in your hand."

"I don't need a weapon, Herr Lubeck. You have already done yourself in." Just then Alex Ferguson appeared from the patio. His fists and jaw were both clenched as he took a step closer to Lubeck.

Lubeck laughed. "Surely a man of your proclaimed taste and stature would not resort to this type of bawdy exhibitionism. Where is the scheming Sir Harry Oakes I've heard so much about? Can't you think of a classier and more creative way to your end game than having your man use his fists on me?"

Harry never took his eyes off Lubeck. "Alex, please tell Herr Lubeck how he brought about his own demise."

Alex looked at the black face of his alligator-strapped Rolex and then looked at Lubeck. "You touch da gold bar. It be cover wit da poison of lion fish and ciguatera fish."

"You see Herr Lubeck, I might not have had a problem doing business with you, until you brought my family into it. I don't care about disagreements. I might even sometimes stray ethically and legally myself, but I wanted to see just what type of man you are. Would you stick to the original deal, or would you change it and push me? When you threatened my family, you went too far. When I do business, it's all business. We never make it personal. So, even if I wanted to keep our deal, you ventured into sacred waters and I can't have that. You could never be trusted." Harry paused, and looked at Alex. "So, like I said, you brought about your own demise."

"Yu got less dan a minute or so," Ferguson told him.

Lubeck could feel his head begin to pound and braced himself against the back of a white wicker chair, trying not to panic.

"Da head poundin' is da brain swellin'."

Lubeck stumbled against a book shelf, wide-eyed and afraid as he fell to his knees.

"Da konfussion be settin' in about now."

"I can..not..feel..legs," Lubeck stammered.

"Not long ta go now. Ciggy give you da pain in da gut, but lion fish be the one killin' you."

Lubeck grimaced and took his last laborious breath. With his eyes open, he dropped to the floor.

"Alex, you know what to do," Harry said quietly.

The massive native wrapped Lubeck in a white sheet and carried him over his shoulder to the beach where he changed Lubeck into a bathing suit and placed him on the sand where he could be easily found. Then he hurried back to Westbourne to let Sir Harry know the task was complete.

"I tink da poor man really tot he be dyin'," Alex said, flashing Harry a broad grin.

Harry chuckled, too. "He'll wake up in about an hour with a most terrible stomach pain."

"I'm afraid he be havin' other pains, too." At Harry's questioning look, he said, "I lay him out on da sand like a piece of scorched conch. He be getting' a bit too much sun."

Sir Harry slapped Alex on the shoulder for a job well done. "Go tell Mr. Salming and the Duke that Hans went for a swim down the beach so they'll go looking for him. I'm sure Mr. Lubeck got my message... and by the way, the Bahamian backwater talk is very humorous."

"Yes, Sir Harry. I enjoyed it just as much. I will take care of things."

Harry put on gloves and carefully oiled and rewrapped the bar of gold and placed it back in its acacia box. He thought about the times in Wyoming listening to Frank Vostermans and Mae McIntosh share the story of the Amschel gold. Those who wanted it wouldn't hesitate to kill anyone who got in the way. Sir Harry was not about to sacrifice his family for it, but he was relieved to know he was not quite ready yet to take a life.

Lubeck was out of the way, at least for the time being, but one thing he had said stuck with Harry. There was a lot of distrust of him on New Providence now–starting with his own family. Freddy was still very angry at him, and although the riots had been quelled for now, there was still a great deal of unrest bubbling under the surface, and Trevor had done a quality job so far in holding off the Mafia, but that couldn't last for much longer either. His greatest apprehension, though, still had to do with the Amschel gold. He had bought a little time today, but he was sure there was eventually going to be a showdown.

He tried to push all those thoughts aside as he ventured to the beach house to share his Lubeck encounter with Eunice. He wanted to involve her as little as possible, but this was just too good to keep to himself.

Chapter 23

Omega and Alpha

St. Marys, Ontario

The dedication service at the Citadel was so crowded that Peaker's Restaurant across the street opened their parking lot as an act of support for the Salvation Army. The IODE ladies sent warm wishes in the form of a monetary gift to be used for supplies and equipment, while the St. James, Knox Presbyterian and Holy Name Catholic churches sent both trustees and laymen as a show of solidarity in the faith. As expected, the politicians were present, glad-handing with as many constituents as possible, but sadly, neither Bert or Will had been able to make it because of heightened U-Boat activity in both the North and South Atlantic.

On the bright side, Liam and Frannie arrived together–as a couple! Although feeling totally out of their element at first, after finding Phalyn and Will they began to feel more at ease, and soon Frannie's infectious laugh could be heard all over the Hall. With the Call to Service, everyone found their seats, and Frannie, always the hostess, stayed by the door to help late arrivals find open chairs.

The service began with "*Give me the Faith that Jesus Had*," an unfamiliar song to the newcomers, but Liam seemed to catch his stride later on with "*It's Grand to be a Soldier*," and could be heard singing quite loudly, if not melodically. The Hollicks, Monroes, Irvines, and Eddys added amplitude to the voices, and Vaughn thought this place had not been so gloriously graced since the Promoted-to-Glory service for Ross and Sheila Skipper.

George and Harriet arrived late, explaining they had to park a few blocks away due to the wonderful attendance. Despite the fact the service had already started, Will left his seat to greet his friend who he hadn't seen in quite some time. He and George had been through so much together, their bond of friendship could not be broken by either time or distance. Though they tried to be discreet, their reunion caused a bit of a distraction, something Vaughn wasn't going to allow to pass, and, to be honest, it played right into his plans. This was a great opportunity to change this from a stuffy church service to a time of friendly fellowship.

He looked at Will, and then at George, and said with a smile, "Well, everyone. It looks like these two have hijacked my service. I've always had trouble getting them to listen to me, but I thought maybe here, of all places, they might let me have the floor."

The congregation snickered and then broke into applause when George responded, "Well, we're just trying to be consistent!" Just as Vaughn had hoped, the atmosphere was lightening and becoming more like a family reunion than a formal Sunday service.

Laughing, Vaughn threw up his hands in resignation and said, "Tell, me, please, when did I lose control of this service?"

Liam was quick this time, to everyone's delight. "Who said you ever had control, Captain?"

The atmosphere in the Hall had become one of true celebration. Good friends, good music and the Good News. Vaughn had never felt so assured the Holy Ghost was making his rounds in and among everyone gathered there. This had been intended to be a time reflecting a traditional Salvation Army service, but Vaughn's instincts had been correct.

"So, now that we've started this, is there anyone else who would like to say a few words about what it means to be here today?"

To everyone's surprise, Candidate Davies, an avowed agnostic, responded. "I just want you all to know I've never been in a church service before that showed so much love and friendship." Davies' comments were shedding a light on his human side and Vaughn smiled and made a mental note to try and follow up with him.

Then, as the laughter subsided, a middle-aged lady in a Sally Ann uniform stood in front of her chair. She had been holding Harriet's hand, and dressed in her formal garb, Vaughn thought she looked as dignified as the pictures he had seen of his Grandmother Leah that used to grace Colonel Martin's office in Chicago. When all had quieted again,

Vaughn and Mae arrived at her side to help her to the podium. Once in front of the group, they stepped aside and she began to speak softly.

"Good morning. I am Lieutenant Forester, but some of you may remember me as Anne Forester. Before I joined the Army my husband and I used to live on Vaughn and Mae's Wellburn farm, back when it was owned by Jonah Blackwell. We were tenants who worked the land before life took us away from this area and our daughter." Whispers and hushed comments rippled through the congregation, each one trying to remember this dignified lady. Anne Forester continued in her quiet manner which silenced the congregation who wanted to hear more.

"I'm here today at the invitation of the McIntosh family–something I never dreamed would happen. I was warmly greeted by all, including Harriet and George Beall," she said, smiling and nodding in their direction. "In fact, I've become instant friends with Harriet because we have something great in common. We share the same daughter – Mae Blackwell-McIntosh." Looks of dawning recognition were sprinkled throughout the crowd, but voices were quiet.

"My presence here today is proof positive God has a plan for all of our lives. His plan may take you through heartache, like what we are experiencing with this war, but if you wait and trust Him, you will end up where you're supposed to be.

"If you want to make God laugh, just try and tell Him the plans you have for yourself. I never expected to leave my native Newfoundland. I never expected to marry the fine man I did, or to lose him through an injustice caused by others, but that is the way life, and God's plan, sometimes goes. Then, when it's all said and done, despite all the misfortune and hurt, God restores people. He finds value in each of us. Just when you think He has unjustly dumped all of life's woes on you, He asks you to trust him a little longer–to wait and let Him direct and guide your path. Life was not smooth for me, but the suffering has brought me back to my family, with a heart that is grateful for all He's done to sustain me."

She turned and said quietly to Vaughn, "I'm sorry if I'm speaking too long."

But before he could answer, from the back of the room, Mr. Davies, of all people, spoke out. "Go ahead, Mrs. Forester. We want to hear more."

Vaughn smiled and nodded, so Anne continued. "I can think of nobody who suffered more than Ross and Sheila Skipper, whose names will grace this hall today. Some people think Ross's greatest gift was his heart to serve others without question. Others, like our fine ladies from the IODE, were also impressed with his handsome looks…" It was just the comment to lighten the moment. "And Sheila… can anyone deny her wit and caring heart for others? She took my daughter in when Mae was struggling and introduced her to a person who was a great influence on her life. All this she did without her eyesight. Just think how the Lord made her better through her disability.

"So, be assured as we dedicate this building in the memory of these two fine people, when you give your heart to the Lord be prepared for the ride of your life. He will give you strength and power to do things you never expected of yourself. I believe Ross and Sheila Skipper were promoted to glory for a greater good that has been realized here this morning. Thank you."

With that, Anne turned from the podium and Mae guided her to one of the chairs arranged behind the podium. Suddenly, the silence in the Hall was broken by clapping coming from a single person–Candidate Davies. Slowly then, as if the dam was now broken, the rest of the congregation began to stand and applaud until everyone was on their feet. Vaughn was most pleased, since it appeared that God had used Anne Forester to win hearts–including Mr. Davies.

Additional testimonies from Harriet, Mae and Mayor Thompson concluded the first part of the dedication ceremonies. Next was a luncheon served in the basement kitchen, where Anne Forester was surrounded by people she had never expected to see again. They were all older and a bit more stooped, but their memories were keen. They shared stories of Mr. Forester's good heart, his work ethic and volunteer work for his farming neighbors. Vaughn knew he could have added stories of Major Forester's fine accomplishments during the war, but this was a day that belonged to the Wellburn Farm Forester and not the Dieppe Soldier Forester.

After dessert was served, everyone was directed to the new addition for one final observance. This was a fine, 3,600 square-foot auditorium complete with all the necessary comforts to provide temporary housing for a small number of traumatized families or individuals. There was a section of built-in wooden bunkbeds, two toilets and a shower, space for additional cots and plastic mats for children if needed, and three large lounge chairs. A Philco radio playing soothing classical music had been placed near the back of the room creating a homey atmosphere that invited everyone to relax. Against the back wall was a military-style metal cabinet full of blankets and pillows, with a section at the bottom for some games and toys. A white General Electric refrigerator rounded out ame-nities needed to help a person in need feel at home for a while.

It was a tight squeeze, but nobody who was here for this second dedication really minded. The formality of the first service had been replaced by a friendliness felt by everyone in the group, regardless of affiliation. Vaughn could tell this was a very special moment, and knew the Holy Spirit had invested in this time and place. For Candidate Davies to be so moved, for Frannie and Liam to say this felt like home on their first visit, for the normally-private Ann Forester to be so eloquent in a public setting, and for the outpouring of community help, there could only be one explanation. God was moving in the hearts of the people of St Marys and Vaughn could only wonder what the Good Lord would be up to next. Whatever it was, it had to be monumental and Vaughn would ride that wave all the way home if he had to, but for the moment, he would just enjoy the loving atmosphere of being with his friends and family.

When it came time for him to speak, Vaughn issued a light-hearted challenge in the spirit of the day. "Now I see that George and Frank have settled themselves in the easy chairs. I know how these men operate, so I need everybody's help to make sure they don't doze off and start to snore!"

As the laughter died down, Mae had come to the front to stand beside Vaughn. They had planned to tag-team their remarks since both of their lives had been so impacted by Cate. Vaughn began.

"My mother, Catherine McIntosh, originally came to this town to fulfill a promise that her father had made years before–a promise that transcended several generations. Today it is my pleasure to reassure Catherine McIntosh," he paused and raised his eyes toward Heaven, "that the promise has been fulfilled." Vaughn and Mae had designed their remarks to include a double entendre regarding 'the promise'. The general public would conclude the promise had been about this building and its purposes, but as Vaughn looked around the room, he subtly nodded at all the others who had helped carry out her 'real' mission, silently thanking them for the part each of them had played.

Mae continued. "Like Mrs. McIntosh, or Cate as she liked to be called, I am not a formal officer in the Salvation Army. But even though she never felt the call to wear the Blue, after moving here she worked, mostly behind the scenes, to give generously to this town that came to be her home. I believe God brought the two of us together so I could help her record her life story – and maybe for another reason, too," she said, glancing at Vaughn "and let me say, her life was fascinating! All the places she had been and the people she met–from the Fjords to the Alps, from Nazi Germany to England and Bonnie Scotland, and then to the States and finally to Canada. She led quite a life!"

Now it was Vaughn's turn again. "Yes, my mother was an amazing person, but through all that, there was something else even more important to her. It was slow in coming–God allowed life to whittle away at her pride and her heart – but, in what turned out to be her last days, she shared with us the greatest pleasure she ever had was giving her life to Jesus Christ." As he paused to let his words sink in with the audience, the impact of what he was saying about his mother and her spiritual conversion hit him. Then his gaze rested on the friends who meant so much to him, all sitting together and smiling at him, and he couldn't continue. His emotions were getting the best of him. Mae noticed and quickly stepped in, laying her hand on his arm.

"Cate realized that life doesn't happen alone, and we believe that God brought us all together to help her finish her task to its rightful conclusion." Once again the double meaning was clear to those who understood. "But it is the spirit of everyone's presence here today that is the real reason for Catherine McIntosh coming to St. Marys. God worked through her heart and she touched all of us in one way or another. She gave freely to the people she met along her journey, but she left the best for last. This wonderful sanctuary," Mae raised both hands, indicating her surroundings, "where all can come and know God's unconditional love in times of trouble and crisis. And so, we give thanks to God for using Cate McIntosh as a blessing upon this town."

Mae led the way, giving the Salvation Army salute with her finger pointed upwards, and was instantly joined by the rest of the group, including Candidate Davies. He was in good spiritual hands as Ross Skipper's uncle was standing beside him, whispering into his ear. Regaining his composure, Vaughn broke out into the doxology, filling the room with a sense of peace and joyful celebration as the last words were sung in wonderful harmony, "Praise Father, Son and Holy Ghost."

As the afternoon drifted on, most of the congregation had departed, but small groups still lingered here and there, either in the 'Ross and Sheila Skipper Citadel' or 'Cate's Place' carrying on quiet conversations. A few even found their way back to the kitchen looking for something to drink or nibble on from the lunch leftovers.

Noticeably absent from the Citadel, however, were the hosts, Mae and Vaughn. They were both drained after the Memorial and Dedication services, so they decided to take the short walk to the rebuilt Furtney Block–the place where Cate and the Skippers had lived, and where they had first met–to recharge and talk about their amazing day.

The burned-out ruins had been replaced by a brown brick replica of the original, right down to the floor-to-ceiling windows on the Queen Street side, but the inside of the building was a different story. It was still virtually empty and would remain unfinished until the Board could decide what they wanted to do with the place. It was obvious, though, from the basic framing, that the downstairs was going to be more open than before. The Skipper's downstairs bedroom and the closed-in porch that had run along the King Street side of the house were gone. The mahogany staircase had been replaced with one of lighter heart pine, but it was not yet stable so the couple couldn't venture upstairs, but they were happy to see that Old Napoleon, the trusty wood burner they had huddled around so often on cold winter days, had been refitted and was ready to be re-installed. They stopped beside the stove, memories flooding over them both, until Mae grabbed her husband's hands and gave him a kiss.

"Vaughn, I have something to say, and I want you to just listen and not comment till I'm finished. I don't have it all totally thought out yet, and I'm still struggling to find the right words, so please, be patient and let me work my way through it."

Vaughn nodded, returned Mae's kiss to her forehead, and sat down on Old Napoleon with arms crossed, ready to listen.

Mae began quietly but found the open space swallowed her words, so she spoke louder. "You know that even before we went to Windsor, I was thinking about where the Lord wants to use us next. After all we've been through with the gold and the war and all, things seem to be settling down and we're getting comfortable–and that scares me."

Mae began to walk around the room, searching for the right words. "All my life, I've gone from one task to another… never settled… always in motion. I have a lot of energy and want to use it to serve the Lord. So, I find that as soon as I start to settle down and can take a breath, I get the urge to start with a new challenge." She stopped and looked at him. "I guess that's why when you were called to the Essex-Scottish, I felt left behind." She paused again. "I'm sort of afraid to say this, but I sense the Lord wants me to be more than just a wife and a helper to Captain Vaughn McIntosh of the Citadel. I mean no disrespect," she added quickly.

"None taken," Vaughn said, playing his role well. "Please continue."

"I loved my youth and the home Harriet made for us. I love this town, and our farm, and the friends we've made. The logical thing would be to settle into this life, make it through this war, and start a family. We could serve this community for decades and I know God would honor that." Mae was expecting, at this point, for Vaughn to offer an opinion, but instead, he continued to be a man of his word. He dropped his chin and said, "Go on."

"I feel I'm being called to other things than serving in St Marys," Mae blurted. "With Mrs. Forester... Anne... my mother... coming into the picture again, I feel now I'm as much her daughter as I was Harriet's growing up. I seem to feel the same thing Anne feels. I sense another calling and it's not in St. Marys. I don't know yet what it will be–and I don't care what it is–but I do think God may be calling me to something way beyond what's easy and comfortable."

Vaughn recognized "the call" when he heard it, and Mae knew it. Now he had to say something. "Like my leaving you in the middle of the Amschel crisis to go to war?" he asked. "Mae, I recognize the bidding. We've both been through this before, except now the shoe is on the other foot, and although it scares me a bit to think where he might take you, I love you all the more for it. Following His guidance will never steer you wrong. Let's both pray about it and watch for how He puts a 'lamp unto our feet'."

Mae was dumfounded. "You aren't upset?"

He stood and gave her a hug. "Who am I to be angry or upset? I hated going to war, but I felt it was the right thing to do, and so many pieces have come together as a result of it. Look at the people we know who have been impacted by the Lord using us during that time, and I'm willing to bet there are others out there we don't know about. That's what it's all about, Mae. If I got upset, I would only be thinking of myself. You have so many wonderful gifts and, truth be told, I've been waiting for the day you could be mightily used of the Lord. I'll be honest, though. A part of me has also feared the day He would decide to take you, or me, or us, to something else. But we both know we love Him first, and if that means giving all this up to be used in another way, to give Him glory, then so be it! I will be your helper this time, no matter what happens next."

Mae couldn't stop smiling. She lunged at Vaughn, enclosing him in a tight hug. "I love you so much!" she cried, then stepped back, still holding his hands. "So we pray and wait and trust the Lord. You know, it wasn't just my heart that was pricked today. Did you notice the reaction of Mr. Davies? Don't know if it will be a lasting change, but we should keep an eye on him."

"My mother was probably the angel pulling at his heart strings. She was there, alright, and would have been very proud of all that came about."

"I feel in many ways an anointing took place today. Vaughn, am I crazy in feeling there's something else God wants me to do, and that it involves both your mother and my mother, Anne, not Harriet?"

"Well, it's possible, but let's not bring God's soldiers into this until we hear from the King. I think we have some hard work to do on our knees first."

Mae was pleased with Vaughn's support and believed this was the 'blessed assurance' that the Lord was bending her path in a new direction one more time.

As they headed back to the Citadel, they sang quietly in perfect harmony, "Perfect submission, all is at rest, I in my Savior am happy and blest. Watching and waiting, looking above. Filled with His goodness, lost in His love." Then Mae had a thought. The problem was that goodness oftentimes comes at a high price.

Chapter 24
At Your Service

❦

Quebec City, Quebec

William Lyon McKenzie King thought the weather was quite mild for a Quebec City August. The locals would be walking the old town seeking a brewed beverage and some tasty fare at the fine selection of old-world auberges… lovers would saunter arm-in-arm along the wooden Boardwalk overlooking the St. Lawrence River... the Terrase would soon open its door for early dinner at the Chateau Frontenac Hotel... but for the moment, Mr. King would continue to sit on the terrace between Winnie and Frank while photos were taken. Not exactly what he wanted to do on this late afternoon, but here he was.

Even though he was the Prime Minister of Canada, and his country had made enormous contributions to the war effort, his sole function at this Quebec Conference was to act as host. He and the Governor General had felt less than useful being relegated to a titular position on their own soil, and even though Canada had invested much in the way of munitions, food, raw materials and manpower, Winston Churchill, the British Prime Minister, had mostly ignored him. As the cameras flashed and newsreels whirled, the smoke from Churchill's Cuban 'Romeo y Julietta' cigar found Bill's nostrils. It was the only thing the British Bulldog had shared with him since his arrival thirty-six hours previously.

On the other hand, the American President had been much more affable. McKenzie-King and Roosevelt had actually become rather chummy over the past three years after successfully completing several collaborative deals–the Alaska Highway project in the Yukon, Air Bases in Newfoundland, and agreeable border protocols from Windsor, Ontario to Ogdensburg, New York – benefitting both of their countries. His participation in this Conference had at least made it bearable.

Then mercifully, Governor General of Canada, Lord Athlone, joined the group and took over much of the conversation with Churchill. Dressed in military garb, Churchill found Athlone to his liking and steered the conversation toward Stalingrad, Lord Louis Mountbatten's appointment as Commander in Southeast Asia, and Monty's push to beat the American General Clark to Rome.

Fortunately, President Roosevelt's personality was quite another story. Without turning his head, he addressed his host as they sat side by side waiting for the next flash. "You look a bit glum, Bill. Just a few more minutes and these newsie-types will be done. You need to put a smile on your face. Let me help with that."

McKenzie-King found FDR's interest in him most refreshing, so he was curious to hear what the President had to say. "Last week we were at Val-Kill with Winston and Clemmie, and their daughter, Mary," he began. "We did the picnic thing – some fishing, swimming–I even got a picture of the esteemed Sir Winston Leonard Spencer Churchill in his swimsuit and a ten-gallon cowboy hat. Now, if the thought of that doesn't put a smile on your face, maybe this will. Harry Hopkins told me this story. Winston takes a drink of ice water and says, 'This water tastes very funny.' So Harry says to Winnie, 'Of course it does, it's got no whisky in it. Fancy you a judge of water!'"

Not only did a smile replace McKenzie-King's rather droll expression, it took all his willpower to keep from laughing out loud, and Roosevelt saw it. "That's the spirit, Bill! Maybe I can find a ten-gallon hat for you, too!"

Just as they were finishing up the photo shoot, everyone was startled when a Royal Canadian Air Force flying boat buzzed a low descent over the Quebec Citadel on a flight path to land on the St. Lawrence River. Winston jumped and dropped both ash and live sparks onto his lapel, then looked at FDR, who nodded. "Sounds like we should be ready to move ahead soon, Winnie. Anthony and Cordell have been waiting for that plane to arrive."

He was referring to Sir Anthony Eden and Cordell Hull, the State/War Secretaries for each country and the informal spokesmen for both Churchill and FDR. These two did the leg work, first listening to the logistics people and gathering as much information as possible, then rendering their diplomatic and military opinions to each leader on how a situation or strategy should be handled. There had been many issues discussed during the weeks leading up to this conference–sharing secrets on atomic bomb research... the Balkan guerilla line of attack... the future home for a Jewish Nation in Palestine–but at the top of the list was the implementation of a second front against Nazi-controlled Europe. They were ready to move ahead except for one detail, and they all hoped the arrival of this plane meant things were about to change.

Operation Overlord had been on hold for the last few months with hundreds of thousands of Yanks and Canucks stationed in Britain–waiting–and with the removal of the Germans from North Africa, and the landings of the Allies on Sicily, the time was right to go. There would be an invasion of Europe on the coast of France. They just needed to figure out how to finance it.

Britain was in bad shape economically, having never fully recovered in the two decades since the Great War, so all this current conflict had accomplished was bankrupting the nation. Though the lend-lease plan had helped initially, it cost the Brits their remaining gold reserves in the Dominions of the Empire. It appeared it was going to have to be up to the Americans to underwrite the invasion–but FDR wanted to hear options of how Churchill planned to ante-up. Hopefully he would soon hear that a plan had been agreed upon.

That afternoon, Eden and Hull met with their secret emissary in the Governor General's informal meeting room. It was here in 1759 that British North America took shape when James Wolfe defeated the Marquis de Montcalm, and Sir Anthony was counting on another successful venture today. He looked at the wall above him, drawing inspiration from Benjamin West's world famous painting of the death of the General, depicting Wolfe as a Christ-like figure. Sir Anthony knew there was to be a second battle today and he would have to emerge, like Wolfe, as the conqueror of Quebec.

A red-vested Northwest Mounted Police officer ceremoniously knocked, then opened the door to admit their guest. The impeccably dressed gentleman stood with Fedora in hand, straightening his striped bow tie then slowly stroking his grey goatee as he surveyed the room.

Sir Anthony immediately rose from his chair to greet their visitor. After shaking his hand, he turned to his colleague. "Mr. Cordell Hull, I would like to present the Governor of the Bank of England, Mr. Montagu Norman, Distinguished Service Order and member of King George VI's Privy Council."

Hull greeted Montagu with a hand shake and offered him some tea or coffee to ease into the proceedings. "No, thank you, Mr. Hull, caffeine makes me jumpy and affects my heart, so I will pass for the time being as I have something very important to share that I think is the answer you're looking for."

"Our Federal Reserve man, Allan Sproul, speaks highly of you, Mr. Norman, and I don't discount your expertise or your connections, but I will reserve judgment until I see what magical sleight of hand you have to offer."

They settled into their seats and Norman began. "I understand you need assurance from Britain, Mr. Hull, that we can come up with the financial reserves to carry out an invasion of Europe?" Hull nodded. "What I am about to explain to you may seem unbelievable at first, but I assure you it is true, so bear with me." He paused, then quietly said, "I can get you the Amschel gold."

Despite his artsy, flamboyant style, and air of dignified self-confidence, it was rumored that Norman had suffered a nervous breakdown the previous year due to excessive use of morphine to control his numbing joint and neck pain. He was a man who was fighting ghosts, yet had one of the most brilliant minds in the global marketing economy and was highly respected, but had also at one time claimed he could walk through walls. Montagu Norman's truth lay somewhere between myth and reality, so it would take shrewd analysis to determine if the story he was about to tell would be a viable solution to their problem.

Eden could see that Hull was on the verge of calling off the meeting. "Give him a chance, Cordell," he said quickly. "Listen to what he has to say before you make any quick judgments."

Pulling his chair closer to the table, Hull moved his tea service aside and shoved his finger into the face of his counterpart. "I don't have time for any shenanigans from either of you. I've heard the stories of the Amschel gold going all the way back to Benjamin Rush's early days with the Federal Reserve. Don't forget, I was in London in '33 when we tried to piece together a world economy after the Amschel-contrived depression. My health may not be what it used to be, but my mind is perfectly fine. I've listened to all the economists in the world trying to explain the mess we find ourselves in today, but because I have even less confidence in any of them, I will hear you out. So, if you have some new information I haven't heard already, then we can go ahead with this meeting, otherwise I have other places to be."

Norman had prepared himself for the Tennessee mountain skeptic. "What will it take to convince you, Mr. Hull, that the Amschel gold exists – and that I can lead you to it?"

"That's a very good question, Mr. Norman, and I don't have an answer. I suppose you'll just have to go ahead and try to convince me. Where I come from we're used to people spinning tales."

Sir Anthony was disturbed that Hull could be so dismissive of a man of the Governor's standing, but was quick to remind himself the no-nonsense Hull could sniff out a fake at a moment's notice. Ever since the government had ignored his pleas to prepare for a Japanese attack on Pearl Harbor, Hull had absolutely trusted his instincts, and very little else. He would weigh all the facts before deciding if this story passed the stink test.

Fortunately for them all, Norman seemed unfazed by Hull's cynicism. "I've done my research also, Mr. Hull. If you are the good old boy you claim to be, you know there have always been legends that can't be explained–the witch that talked to your own former President Jackson; the unexplained death of your great explorer, Meriwether Lewis and, of course, the hundreds of ghosts that haunt your plantations. These may all be myths, but I can assure you, the story surrounding the Amschel gold is real and you will want to hear me out."

Hull decided to give in and at least listen, but he couldn't resist one last mocking comment. "Well, if McKenzie-King can openly admit to having séances to seek out his mother, then I might as well have temperance with your story, Mr. Norman, while I am in this Land of Oz that we call the Dominion of Canada."

Montagu Norman stood to emphasize the seriousness of his findings. He reviewed the three-hundred-year history of the banking Amschels, ending with the securing of the Napoleonic gold and Romanoff treasure within the last century. When he got to the involvement of a German POW Commandant and the camp Chaplain, Mr. Hull's interest was piqued.

"Are you telling me a simple clergyman was given the task of keeping the gold from the Amschels?"

Norman nodded. "Though hard to believe, it was a promise Colonel Martin made to Nathan Amschel, and for three generations, from Martins to McIntoshes, the family kept the gold in safekeeping. The last McIntosh involved is a Salvation Army Captain in a small town in Ontario. He's also a war hero who I met personally after he participated in a most regrettable French coast raid. He told me what he knew about the gold and asked that he be given a chance to take care of the matter himself, before turning it over to me. I agreed, and came to find out later that he did, indeed, keep the gold from returning to the Amschels, by passing the responsibility on to someone a bit more adept at maneuvering through the financial world."

"OK... who is it and where is he?" Hull had heard enough.

"That would be Sir Harry Oakes of Nassau, Bahamas."

"What? The back woodsman who struck it rich in Canada."

Norman nodded once again.

"Well, how do you know for sure this transfer succeeded?"

"When Jamie Amschel was deposed as the family banking head, he was replaced by Admiral Wilhelm Canaris, who is actually a double-agent for us. The good Admiral has assured me the attempt by the Amschel to secure the gold from Canada failed, but they figured out the deception and are zeroing in on Oakes themselves. Those loyal to Jamie Amschel have someone ready to replace Canaris–if he can find the gold and return it to them. He is in Nassau as we speak.

"So you believe Sir Harry Oakes has taken the gold to Nassau?"

"I can't say that for sure, but I believe he knows where it's hidden."

"That Amschel scoundrel searching for the treasure wouldn't be Axel Salming, would it? We've had our eye on him for some time."

"He may be part of it, but the Amschel surrogate and ringleader is Hans Lubeck, a former German officer. He's the one who discovered that Amschel security chief, Etienne Picard, had faked the gold shipment to Argentina."

"Picard? Never heard of him, but I wouldn't have wanted to be in his shoes when they found out about a double cross."

"Agreed. From what I hear he was tortured and died in a Nazi detention camp in France, but he never veered away from his story–that the McIntosh family, along with Sir Harry Oakes, set the Amschel up for a double cross, and Picard was the scapegoat."

Hull couldn't help but laugh. "A bunch of Salvationists pulled this off? That is just too hard to believe!"

"I suppose we shouldn't underestimate the good people of St. Marys, especially when they have God on their side. Just like the President should not have ignored the boy from Pickett County, Tennessee regarding Pearl Harbor."

Hull looked from Norman to Sir Anthony, and back to Montagu Norman. "I'm beginning to believe your story, but in my position, I must have proof of something before presenting it to the President."

Norman crossed the room, opened the French doors and asked the four Mounties stationed outside to bring a covered crate into the room. He pulled off the cover, exposing large black lettering: "St. Marys Foundry...Box 1." He then instructed the Sergeant-at-Arms to pry open the wooden case.

"This is the very first box that Picard escorted from St. Marys across the American border. Canaris found it hidden in his Paris flat after he was taken to the camp. It seems that Etienne Picard had his own fingers in the till all along. Mr. Hull, if you will do me the honors."

Cordell Hull approached the box and lifted the cover. Pushing back the oily cotton cloth, he beheld what kings, queens, and princes–and now a simple country boy from Tennessee–knew was real...*Papillions d'or*!

Chapter 25

Tekel Tekel

❧

Nassau, Bahamas

Sir Harry felt like the whole world was closing in, which was a new sensation for him. He knew the Black Bahamian wanted a greater say in government, which was bound to lead to more conflict between the people and the island's leadership, but as bad as that could get, it wouldn't happen in isolation. The Amschels, led by Lubeck, would take advantage of any government struggle and make it work to their advantage. So, central to his concerns at this moment, was the future of the Amschel gold. He had a plan to handle it but needed a cohort he could truly trust to make it happen, and right now he had no idea who that might be.

As if that weren't enough to worry him, a new player had been added to the table–the Florida Mafia. He knew their success in big American cities had made them bolder, and they were determined to essentially take over the Islands with gaming, hotels and racketeering, and Sullivan was pushing him to get involved. That struggle alone was enough to give him an ulcer, but right now was more of a secondary worry to the Amschel threat. Although he was well entrenched in these islands, all of this happening at the same time was almost too much, and he felt the winds of change would eventually displace him.

To this point he had been living large, finding purpose and gusto in all aspects of his life. Each day presented a new goal for him to achieve, and then over the evening meal with Eunice and the children he would recap his day and celebrate his successes. But now everything was changing. There were fewer successes to observe, and, more times than not, his grown children were off pursuing their own interests, like tonight. It was just the two of them having dinner, nibbling at mutton stew and Bahamian journey cake, so he had little distraction from his torturous thoughts.

Eunice was concerned about her husband's sullen demeanor. Through all her years with him, Harry had always put aside his troubles at mealtimes and had something positive to share with those around him. But tonight he was not only deathly quiet, he couldn't even seem to make eye contact with her. It was time to find out what was bothering him.

"You missed all the excitement today. Mr. Lubeck certainly put a scare into Axel and David. They say he must have stepped on some spiny lionfish or stone fish–and the man was red as a lobster from lying out in the sun so long. Axel said the doctor at General Hospital advised him to stay in bed for few days." Eunice couldn't believe she got no reaction at all from Harry. "Alex told me you were called away on business after your meeting with him."

"Trying to get the curbing right on the round-about on Wulff Road," he said, briefly looking up then quickly returning to his stew. "I pay these engineers a bundle to move the process along smoothly, but they can't even make a decision about a sink hole or boulder they have to address without asking my opinion. Then the workers want extra pay for the extra time it takes to correct the mistakes they made in the first place. They're starting to get belligerent with the contractors, too. I swear there's some serious sabotage going on. I may be forced to fire a couple of crews–and that won't sit well with anyone after what just happened in town."

"Maybe you should take some time off… play some golf for the next few days. I know David is always keen to tee-up whenever you are."

"I guess I should pay my respects to Axel, too."

"You mean Hans Lubeck?"

Harry took a drink of water without answering and Eunice was losing patience with him. "Harry, what happened with Lubeck?" she asked, kindly but sternly. "I know very well the whole situation was contrived. He was found unconscious at the far end of the beach, an area a visitor would never go to. And when he was revived, he wouldn't say anything other than he wanted to get away from Westbourne." She waited, but Harry was not going to volunteer any information. "How did your talk go?" she prodded.

"I drew out his real character," Harry snapped. "He's a cutthroat – the worst kind of businessman! Do you remember before the war when we talked about the banking industry in Europe?"

"You were thinking about putting reserves into Swiss accounts." Eunice said, searching her memory. "I seem to remember you also talking about the National Banks in London, Paris and Frankfurt–you made a big deal about their battle with the… Atold… Amstel…"

"Amschel banks!" Harry blurted.

Eunice was confused. "I found it all very fascinating, but what do those banks have to do with this now?"

Harry was trying hard to rein in his frustration. "Lubeck is a representative of the Amschel banking dynasty. In fact, he may be next in line to run the empire if he has his way with me."

"What do you mean?" She was starting to get really nervous. "What are you not telling me?"

Harry pushed his food aside and leaned forward, finally giving Eunice a straight look. "Seems that our little treasure chest in paradise has caught the interest of a whole host of international parties."

"But isn't that what you always wanted? Progress? To be the Switzerland of the Caribbean? The whole world is finally coming to you Harry, and you made it happen!"

"I can handle the ones who want to talk about resorts, hotels and vacation homes, but we're talking here about something very different. They want to take something from me they think is rightfully theirs."

"Trevor hasn't been making promises he can't keep, again, has he? It's bad enough that he caused what happened downtown. What more damage can he do?"

He looked at her and shook his head. Eunice was his staunchest supporter. "No, it's not anything about Trevor and his wild promotional tours."

Harry moved his chair closer to Eunice. He looked downright forsaken. "Harry, you're starting to scare me…."

The time had come to fill her in on what was going on, but he was having a hard time making himself say the words. He didn't usually involve Eunice in his business dealings, especially something as potentially dangerous as this, but she needed to know what might be down the road for them. "Do you remember the trip I took to Canada when I began operations at Swastika?" She nodded. "Well, there was more than that to the trip. I was helping a friend out of a jam."

"Harry, the only person in Canada you would go that far for is George Beall. Is it George? Is he sick or in trouble?"

"Yes, I met with George and he is fine... now. I've never seen him happier than when I left him. But he and his friends were mixed up with the same Amschel group that Hans Lubeck is representing."

"What?! How in the world did that happen?" When he didn't answer right away she knew this story wasn't going to end well. "Why are you telling me this now?" she asked nervously.

"I made a promise to George to take care of their problem–and I did, at least for the most part, but now the Amschels think I know where their gold is – and they want it back." There was no way Harry could side-step the subject any longer.

Eunice jumped to her feet. "Gold? What gold?"

"You've heard me talk about the missing Napoleonic gold that disappeared after the Great War. Well... brace yourself... I do know the whereabouts of that treasure."

"Good lord, Harry! How did this ever... actually, I don't want to know how you got involved with this. Just let me ask you, why are you telling me about this now?"

"Because Herr Lubeck threatened our family. He threatened to kill me, you or the children, unless I tell him the location of the gold."

"We don't need the money, Harry. Just tell him and be done with it."

"You don't understand. Even if I tell him, they'll still kill us. The only way out is to kill them first." He paused long enough for his wife to absorb the shock of what he'd said. "I could have disposed of Herr Lubeck today, but I just couldn't do it!"

"At least that explains what happened this afternoon. Does anybody else know where this gold is hidden?"

"Only Alex, and I trust him with our lives. Somebody had to help me move it. It involved hundreds of international agencies to complete piecemeal transfers through scores of banks. Over the past year I've created thousands of new Bahamian accounts for company sources from Singapore to Stockholm to house the transfers. Apparently they tracked those – that's what put me on their radar–but that whole thing was just a ruse to get them off my back. So far they have absolutely no idea how I got the real gold out of Canada."

"Sounds like the work of one George Beall."

Harry smiled, but quickly turned serious again. "Eunice, I need you to pack up the kids and go back to Maine until this blows over. It could be too dangerous for you here as long as Lubeck is still sniffing around. It might take some time, but promise me you'll stay in Sangerville till I contact you."

Though she wanted to, Eunice knew she couldn't defy Harry on this. "I don't like it but I'll do what you ask – but it's only because I know Alex will be here with you. Why don't you just come with us?"

"No, I'm their primary target and this has to end here. I know I can depend on Alex, and there are still some I can count on in the Defense Force who are loyal to me. I need to know you're safe and far away from this evil." Harry felt that in time the darkness would have its way with him, but his family would not suffer for his decisions. Thankfully, for once, Eunice didn't put up a fight so he could breathe a bit easier and get on with the job at hand.

—⟊⟊⟊—

Trevor Sullivan had made himself scarce since the riot, and claimed he was too busy to join Lubeck, Axel and the Duke during their last visit to Westbourne. In actuality, he was meeting with the Mob in southern Florida.

Frankie Johnson, a Harvard-trained lawyer, was the prime promoter representing Myer Lansky in what they called the 'Bahamas Dream'–making the Caribbean island nation the next Cuba. He was renowned for his love of Flamenco, both music and dancing, even going so far as to sponsor the master of the Flamenco guitar, Vicente Gomez, for American citizenship. Hanging in his office in Hallandale was a large portrait of the Hollywood star, Rita Hayworth, in her Flamenco costume. He was proud to tell anyone who would listen that Ms. Hayworth's name was really Margarita Carmen Cansino and she was the daughter of Eduardo Cansino, the most famous artist of Spanish Flamenco. Johnson was indeed a passionate man who could not be moved from an idea once he had it in his head.

Myer Lansky knew this about Frankie and used his crony's enthusiasm and legal knowledge to grow his most lucrative gambling business, along with his satellite interests in horse and dog racing, jai alai, and prostitution. Barrister Johnson was Lansky's mouthpiece on all transactions.

This first meeting between Sullivan and Johnson since the Nassau uprising would be held in the second-floor conference room at the Imperial High Rise on Collins Avenue, and Trevor was not looking forward to it. He figured he would have some explaining to do.

When he arrived, Trevor was offered a cocktail by the Cuban server behind the rattan bar. The "Flying Tiger" was actually the perfect beverage for Trevor—gin for his English palate, Bacardi's for his Island spirit, grenadine for his adventurous pirate soul, and some bitters to quell the sweetness. He declined, however, refusing to drink alone and, since the day was young, he knew he could always revisit the possibilities after the meeting.

Frankie steamrolled into the room in a cloud of foul-smelling cigarette smoke, removed his tortoise-framed sunglasses and embraced Harold with a pincer-like grip as if to say, "this meeting WILL BE productive." With Harold's stoic English sensibilities now additionally off guard from a kiss to his cheek, the lawyer had claimed the high ground.

Johnson didn't waste any time. "Now what's this I hear about some Kraut wanting to horn in on our plan? Don't mess with me Sully. You know how we work. When we give our word, there's no going back on it."

"The 'Kraut' you refer to is Hans Lubeck, an Argentinean banker who is pressuring Sir Harry. He represents a larger European corporation and has brokered a deal, through the Duke of Windsor, to grant land rights to Sir Harry from Eluethra to Exuma in return for something he wants. Whatever the 'something' is, it must be valuable, but none of us know what it is."

"What could be more important than land to a country made up of islands? Forget what Mr. Whats-his-name wants, Sir Harry cannot be allowed to control any more real estate, especially in Nassau or Grand Bahama. Those are our spots, Sully. Didn't we make that clear?" His menacing tone definitely made it clear to Trevor.

"I know, Frankie, but Sir Harry seems bent on keeping you and your gambling interests off the island, but he's sending mixed messages." Frankie waited. "Harry refused the Lubeck offer and ordered him to leave Nassau."

"So, what's the problem? Harry has taken care of this interloper and we move ahead with our plan."

"Lubeck won't leave. He's digging in his heels and Harry still refuses to speak to me about your offer."

"Surely, he doesn't plan to play us off each other? That's just too obvious – and dangerous for him. I could have half a dozen boats and a few hundred of my soldiers in Nassau within hours – not to mention my men who are already there."

Sullivan shook his head. "I don't think so. Harry isn't stupid – but neither is Lubeck, and he won't give up easily. He has connections with both the Nazis and the Amschel."

"The Amschel! What are they doing in Nassau? They don't go in for resorts and sports entertainment like we do."

"That's the big question, isn't it?" Trevor said. "There's something Harry knows, but isn't telling anybody. Whatever it is, it must be worth far more than the deal Lubeck has offered him."

Frankie snapped his fingers at the barkeep who poured a cold Atlantic beer into a tall, frosty Pilsner glass and handed it to him. Frankie drained most of the contents before making his next statement. "If Sir Harry is hiding something that's worth fending off Lubeck–and us–we'll have to protect him till we can find out what it is. We can't wait till the war's over to make our move. Besides, my people hate Nazis, too. In fact, we've worked with the Genovese family in Italy to get the Allies off Sicily and onto the mainland." He paused to drain the remaining contents from his glass. "Yeah… I think we can have a little relationship with Sir Harry for the time being. What do you think?"

Trevor was relieved at Johnson's insight and desire to protect Harry. In truth, he was ecstatic that the Lubeck issue had distracted Johnson from questions about the riot – the topic he was really dreading. It was quite apparent that whatever information Sir Harry was holding, Lubeck was prepared to kill for. And it would be very interesting to see Harry's reaction when he learned his main defense was going to involve being in bed with Johnson/Lansky, Inc. after all.

Sullivan was relieved and, patting himself on the back for a job well done, was just getting ready to accept the previously offered cocktail when Johnson shattered his dreamland. "Now that that's taken care of, Sully, explain to me why there was a riot that destroyed half of Nassau."

Chapter 26
Twice Smitten

❧

St. Marys, Ontario

The last decade had been most tumultuous for Montagu Norman. Dealing with the Amschel Bank and the never-ending circus of monetary foibles of the Americans, French and Germans had taken a toll. Then there was the great depression and that nasty little thing called "the war" that had skewed his ability to make precise predictions and decisions. His latest report to Churchill bluntly stated that Britain was essentially broke, although they still had a few options–properties and interests in the global dominion, untapped stashes of diamonds in South Africa and oil from the Middle East, extension of military property leases, emerging countries possibly buying their independence from the Commonwealth–but in order for any of these options to be viable, Britain would have to be victorious in the war. Operating from a base of conquest increased the probability of an economic upturn… if the war could be won.

Now his final contribution to Britain's security would be to obtain the funds to win the war. Montagu Norman had given notice to King George and the Prime Minister that he would be stepping down from his position at the Bank of England sometime during the next year. With almost a quarter of a century as the Governor of the National Bank, his health had deteriorated and he wasn't able to adequately handle the stresses of this job anymore. So, at the insistence of his wife and two stepsons, he finally agreed it was time to step back and think more about himself. And to be honest, he was beginning to look forward to passing the problem of fiscal uncertainty on to the new Bank of England Governor.

Montagu had come up with a concrete plan to deal with the Sir Harry Oakes/Hans Lubeck situation, but had heard a troubling report recently that a new player, the Florida Mob, was at the table, and he knew they could be just as brutal and undermining as any Amschel or Nazi. Anthony Eden and Cordell Hull were sold on the idea of extracting the gold from the Bahamas, but the precise details would be left up to him as he was familiar with the history of the persons involved. He had already made contact with some influential people and a ring of protection was quickly being established around Sir Harry by the British Secret Service of MI5 who had already been surveilling Salming, and now were keeping an eye on Lubeck as well.

Everyone agreed there was no use in trying to forcibly pry Sir Harry from his home unless the gold came with him, so, if they were going to convince Sir Harry to escape with his life – and the gold–they would need to send someone who had a lot of influence with Harry, understood the situation, and was completely trustworthy. As much as Montagu hated to go back on his word, he knew who that would have to be.

Using the excuse that he had never seen Niagara Falls, Norman, accompanied by his two plain clothes security officers, planned the 600-mile trek up the St. Lawrence and around the western tip of Lake Ontario. Realizing the importance of this mission, the Prime Minister agreed to provide Montagu's entourage with the Royal Hudson Train #2850, the regal blue and silver cars and engine that were used by King George VI and Queen Elizabeth when they toured Canada before the outbreak of the war. With the new train station now operational in Montreal, the only expected stop would be in Toronto, which provided time for a good night's rest and a hearty breakfast for the travelers before they were re-directed off-line toward Stratford, and then the final twelve miles to St. Marys.

The banker had been hoping to arrive under the radar, but after attracting attention along the way just by passing through the small towns, he realized accepting this mode of transportation, though obviously very comfortable and luxurious, may not have been his smartest decision. As they got closer, the conductor informed them they could either disembark at the St. Marys station, or travel on to London and drive the 24 miles back to their destination. Either way, the train would attract some attention, but the Governor decided the smaller station at St. Marys was most likely the lesser of two evils, a prediction that proved true.

Norman was relieved to see there was no fanfare to greet them – their only wel-coming committee being just a few boys playing road hockey against the red-bricked wall. He was hoping to complete his business and be on his way before too many locals took notice of them.

The train had arrived on schedule at 8:15 AM, and in less than five minutes had dropped of the party and was on its way to London. Norman had come prepared with a map of the town, telephone numbers for the police and the Mayor–and the address and number for the McIntosh residence in Wellburn, but his real source of information was going to be the station master who was walking toward them.

"Welcome to St. Marys, Gentlemen. I'm the Station Master, Frank Vorstermans. I see you don't need any help with bags, so how can I serve you this fine morning?"

Montagu was encouraged by the British inflection in Frank's greeting, and let himself relax just a little. "Good morning, Sir. I see I'm in the company of a real gentleman," he said with a genuinely warm smile. "We have come to town to meet a comely couple at the Salvation Army headquarters."

"Oh, Brits are we? We haven't had many visitors from the homeland since the war broke out, so I say again, welcome to St. Marys!" Frank Vorstermans played his role to the hilt. "Well, we have lots of couples who go to church there, but I'll need a better descrip-tion than 'comely' for they are all comely to us," he said with a chuckle.

Montagu laughed along with Frank. "Well perhaps I can find them myself after all. If it wouldn't be a bother, do you have telephone service inside that I could possibly use?"

"You and your friends, Sir, are no bother, and of course you can use the phone." Frank turned and headed for the office door, with the visitors following. "If there's anything else I can do for you, just let me know. A lot of folks come here for our festivals, others just to swim at the Quarry or walk the bridges over the Thames. You don't want to miss seeing the Flats and the dam while you're here. Watching the water spill over the dam is one of the most soothing sights around."

Norman nearly choked. That infamous dam! Soothing? Vorstermans obviously didn't know its history. Yes, he thought. I think I should see that dam before I leave here. "Well, if we have time, maybe we can enjoy some of the sites, but for now a telephone box would be much appreciated. And then, if you could just point us in the direction of a reputable hotel to stay the night."

Frank smiled and pointed to the station, "Help yourself. The phone is beside the telegraph desk and there's a list of local numbers in the black three-ring binder in my first drawer if you need it. I'm going to be out here sweeping for a bit, so when you're finished come on back out and we'll see if we can't find you a 'reputable' place for your stay in town."

Missing his good-hearted sarcasm, all three visitors were amazed at the trust shown by this St. Marys ambassador. If the rest of the town was as welcoming as this fellow, Montagu could see why Vaughn and Mae McIntosh didn't want to leave this place, and he hated that he would be the bearer of bad news.

Phone calls completed, Norman and his companions made their way to the 'reputable' Windsor Hotel recommended by the station master, and after settling into their rooms and changing into more casual clothes, lunched at the Prince Edward Pub then spent some time at the dam over which the Thames River flowed. Norman could hardly believe the role this innocuous setting had played in the intrigue he was still trying to unravel. He was, once again, saddened that he had to drag the unsuspecting McIntoshes back into this business, but at this point he saw no other way to proceed.

As he set about to locate Vaughn and Mae, he made his way through the downtown where the sights and sounds seemed familiar and reassuring, reflecting his heritage and loyalty to the King and Empire. The Salvation Army's main facility, the Skipper Center, was closed, but a small note jammed into the corner of the door directed them around the corner to the Thrift Store where, the note said, Mae was conducting business. Montagu's anticipation grew as he got closer to meeting the wife of Vaughn McIntosh. To him, Mae was legendary.

He discovered the Thrift Store in the basement of the IODE Hall, directly across Church Street from the Citadel–a modest storefront flaunting the red shield of the Salvation Army on its gunmetal-gray door frame. Montagu dismissed his men to enjoy a coffee at Peaker's Restaurant so his first meeting with Mae McIntosh would be private.

He pushed the door open silently to reveal an assortment of tables covered with various pieces of neatly folded and sorted clothing in a full range of sizes. Down the middle of the shop were a half dozen black and chrome clothing racks holding assorted hanging items–women's dresses and blouses, men's suits, winter coats–with shelves on top where belts, ties, gloves and other accessories were neatly displayed. Along the back wall were slanted shoe and boot shelves offering varied sizes and styles, from house slippers to work boots, children's oxfords to ladies' dress pumps.

A separate section on the right contained housewares–towels, curtains, rugs, vacuums, standing lights, a couple of springy off-blue prams, shovels, an old phonograph and radio; and finally, on the left was the item Montagu Norman had been searching for. In front of the counter was the sales lady, unaware that a customer had entered her store as she continued folding and taking inventory of the items before her.

Montagu allowed himself a moment to study Mae before stepping toward her and clearing his throat. Startled, Mae spun around and stared at this man who was smiling as if he had found a long-lost friend.

"Hello. Sorry I didn't hear you come in." Mae began to feel uncomfortable when the gentleman still didn't speak, but just continued to stare and smile. "I'm sorry, but do I know you?" she asked nervously.

Montagu realized his smile might be a bit off-putting, but he couldn't seem to stop. Why was she having this effect on him? Before meeting Mae, he had been mindful and respectful of her role in the Amschel story, but now that he was seeing her face-to-face, he was mesmerized. Slowly, though, Montagu was able to rally himself, despite being so hopelessly smitten.

"Mrs. McIntosh? My name is Captain Norman…"

"We are always here to help our boys in uniform," Mae answered cautiously, wondering how he knew her name. "Did you serve in the Great War?"

"No, I go back a little further, to the Boer War, but my title of Captain is really not germane to my business here."

Mae could tell by his word choice and accent, and the style of his clothes, that she was not dealing with a veteran looking for a warm bed and a hot meal. Her radar was fully active, especially since he had known her name. Not only was this man not a veteran in need, his bearing indicated he was worldly and definitely not from Ontario.

All of the latent fears she had been trying to put behind her since returning from Windsor rose to the surface. Mae moved behind the counter to create some space between them, then quietly stood facing him. It was obvious to Montagu that Mae didn't trust him, and who could blame her after all they had been through. He knew it was up to him to win her over.

"Mrs. McIntosh…" he began

"How do you know my name?" she interrupted, demanding an answer.

"Please just give me a few minutes to explain. Your husband, Vaughn, and I met in London at the Rookery several years ago, with your brother-in-law from Halifax and the McIlheneys. My name is Montagu Norman."

He felt this information should have cleared up the matter, but Mae would not be so easily convinced.

His assured manner and easy delivery just made her more skittish. She knew a smooth talker could belie the devil himself. But then she remembered the letter Vaughn had showed her on Bob-lo Island – the letter from this man saying they were free of the Amschel. Why was he here? She prayed he hadn't traveled all this way to tell them things had changed. She didn't want to speak fearing her suspicions might be true, so she remained quiet and waited for him to continue.

"I understand that you are hesitant to trust me, but perhaps if I tell you some of what I know about you, it will ease your mind. You are Mae McIntosh, wife of Vaughn McIntosh, formerly Captain and Chaplain of the Essex-Scottish 25th Platoon who scouted Dieppe for us. Your husband has a scar on his chin and right cheekbone from a knife fight when he was a boy in Chicago, with one Liam Boggin who became his friend and confirmed his exploits in France. Captain McIntosh is quite a boxer and can handle a knife as well as anyone. His ribs were fractured when he was young and rib number three did not re-attach properly to the sternum, but to the rib above which still causes him tenderness. He has three loves in his life…His God, his wife and his apple pie."

Mae was taken aback by all this information. This stranger either knew Vaughn or had done his homework well, just as Picard and company had done last year.

Norman continued. "You are Mae McIntosh…formerly Blackwell, and Forester before that. You love your farm animals – all animals actually–and had an Indian bicycle you refurbished yourself. You love jazz and have a beautiful singing voice… you used to work with Vaughn's mother, Cate McIntosh, in fact, that's how the two of you met."

Mae was still not convinced. She knew there were any number of ways their adversaries could have found these things out. She continued to stare at him.

"You're looking for proof that I'm not with the Amschel, aren't you?"

Hearing the name out loud again made Mae jump, and Norman noticed her reaction. Were they never going to be rid of this? She thought it was finished – at least for them. This Montagu Norman was quite convincing, and he was obviously well rehearsed, but could he be trusted? She was still afraid to say anything until she knew for sure.

"Maybe I can resolve this whole issue for you, Mrs. McIntosh, with two words that only a friend would know – Harry Oakes."

Mae was shocked, and still wasn't a hundred percent sure he could be trusted, but those last two words, along with everything else he knew, told her she needed to learn more about who this man was. She pulled the curtain and locked the front door, and although she knew she needed to talk to Vaughn soon, first she needed to learn more from Mr. Norman.

Mae suggested they talk during a walk along the Thames to enjoy the St. Marys fall afternoon. The maple and elm trees starting to turn into all their variations of oranges, reds and yellows, and the honking Canada Geese and shrill call of the soon-to-be-departed red-winged blackbirds always drew her to the river this time of year.

Norman's security guards kept watch from a distance while the two tried to sort things out. So far, Mae had felt at a disadvantage in this conversation, but now it was time for her to go on the offensive. "Now, it's my turn to learn about you, Mr. Norman. You've told me about both me and my husband, but before we go any further I want to know who you are and why you've come here today. And please tell me why you continue to look at me that way!"

"Let me start with your last question. I sincerely apologize if I've offended you, but when I saw you – the look on your face, your hair–you reminded me so much of my wife, Priscilla, when I first saw her at a Chelsea Borough Council meeting years ago, I was stunned. I thought I'd slipped into H.G. Wells' Time Machine. You have a double in London, my dear," he said with a smile. "Again, I apologize for my rudeness, but since coming to Canada, I've had more than a few surprises."

Mae visibly relaxed. "I suppose that's a plausible explanation, Mr. Norman, but please stop. I find your ogling extremely unsettling. Now to the first part of my question. Who are you and why are you here?"

By the time Montagu Norman finished his story, Mae was convinced he was who he claimed to be, and that she should trust him, though now she had a new dilemma. "I must say, I find the situation with Sir Harry concerning since he promised to never contact us again so we couldn't be connected with his dealings from here on out."

"Bookends, my dear, bookends. Your husband has told me the history of the gold coming to St. Marys, and I know quite a bit about its removal through the claims of an Amschel security officer, Etienne Picard."

"We certainly had our fill of that man! What ever happened to him?"

"Well, it sounds like you might be pleased to know the Nazis took care of him, but not before, as they coarsely say, he spilled his guts." He stopped walking and turned to Mae. "I know you and your husband, along with Sir Harry, had something to do with the double cross that fooled Picard. What I don't know, though, is what Harry did with the gold. And that is why I'm here."

"I will leave it to Vaughn to give you more details about what happened here in St.Marys, but I can tell you we don't know where the gold is. That's why Harry wanted to break all contact with us, so we would be free and clear and couldn't get sucked back into the mess. I'll tell you what little I know about Sir Harry, but you'll have to build your own bookend then."

With that, Mae locked arms with the older gentleman as a sign of acceptance and began to tell her Harry Oakes tale, which took two circles around the Flats to complete.

"I'm very sorry all of you had to go through such an ordeal," Montagu said. "I can't imagine what more Vaughn could add, but I look forward to talking with him. I would also so very much like to meet Phalyn Tremblay-Purdue. I've heard much about her in banking circles, but have never spoken with a flesh and blood family member of Jamie Amschel. You say she's changed, and I have to believe you since there's no way your family would have accepted her otherwise."

"That can definitely be arranged, Mr. Norman."

"I also have something else to ask you and your husband about, and would like you both together when I present it."

"Would you come to the farm for dinner tonight? We'll invite Phalyn so you can meet her. When was the last time you had some country cooking?"

Montagu was feeling guilty for accepting this kind hospitality when he had such an unsavory request to make of them, but this did seem like a golden opportunity so he graciously accepted. Mae grasped his arm again. "In the meantime, why don't you tell me more of London and the Rookery? I've only been there in my imagination and would love to learn more." And then as they turned and started another lap around the Flats, Mae added, "By the way, Mr. Norman. I think deep down inside I was always expecting someone like you to show up again."

Chapter 27
Thief in the Night

❦

Nassau, Bahamas

From the outset of the war, the *Kriegsmarine* knew the only way to bring Britain to her knees was to destroy access to her oil reserves. Britain had been relying on several major suppliers in the Caribbean including the Royal Dutch Shell Refinery in Curacao and Pointe a Pierre in Trinidad. If four tankers didn't make it to Britain each day, the country would find itself in an industrial wasteland, so, from the Lesser Antilles to Bermuda, some sixty-four Axis submarines trolled the warm waters, indiscriminately attacking single ships and convoys alike.

The Allies had countered with two dozen anti-submarine squadrons and one full-fledged Navy fleet to cover the 3,000 miles of the Caribbean theatre. Over one million men, in all, had been assigned to protect the islands, and with the advent of sub-chasers, depth charges and advanced warning systems, the bulk of U-boat activity was eventually pushed into the North Atlantic, making U-Boat attacks in the Caribbean nothing more than a nuisance.

Regardless of the tight security surrounding the Allied oil tankers, one German submarine, U-128, was committed to another task for the Reich that was just as deadly. The sub had entered the deep fishing waters off Bimini, following the direct flow of the Gulf Stream, running undetected as deep and silent as possible. Passing by two British tankers at Barnett Harbor that, under different circumstances would have been theirs for the taking, the boat continued stealthily along the Little Bahamian Bank destined for Nassau some 100 miles away.

The Bahamas was like a maze through which U-Boats and merchant ships alike had to maneuver to reach the US Coast and Gulf of Mexico. The thirty-mile strip was well monitored by the Americans for any enemy U-boat activity, but German Captain, Ulrich Heyse of U-128, was a veteran of these waters who, in the past month alone, had ventured north to sink the American flagged PAN MASSACHUSETTS and CITIES SERVICES EMPIRE off Cape Canaveral. Without reprisal, U-128 then returned to the Caribbean to send a lethal torpedo into the Norwegian O.A. KNUDSEN off the northern tip of Andros Island.

On this particular evening the attention of the Allies was being intentionally diverted by a seemingly random wolf pack attack near the Bahamian island of Mayaguana. The 3,200-ton US MARIANA, carrying sugar from Puerto Rico to Boston, and Norwegian bulk carrier, GUNNY, delivering mahogany and manganese ore from Trinidad to New York, were the victims intended to take many eyes off U-128, giving the *Kapitan* enough time to complete his task.

With distractions in place, the 250-foot *unterseeboot* inched toward New Providence Island with no resistance. If there was an attack she was fully prepared to counter with her twenty-four forward and aft torpedoes, thirty-two mines and, when surfaced, her experienced crew on anti-aircraft guns and canon, but it appeared their tactic was working and the sub's movements would be unimpeded.

Heyse checked his watch, then kissed the tips of two fingers and briefly touched the five-arrow tattoo on his muscular forearm. This had been his habit ever since joining forces with the Amschel, and he wasn't going to abandon the practice now. He needed all the luck he could get to successfully complete this mission.

In five minutes he would have to surface for oxygen for his men and motors, so he gave the order to climb to snorkel and periscope depth. Turning his cap backward, he took hold of the periscope's training handles and set his forehead against the faceplate, circling slowly, trying to determine the horizon or water level. As he moved, he adjusted the range and focus controls looking for any concrete object, or better yet, some man-made light, straining to get some type of visual bearing, but so far there was nothing in sight.

The *Funker* silently got his attention and motioned for the *Kapitan* to put on his headphones. The transceiver was picking up music, though Heyse had never heard anything like it before. He could only understand a few words–Andros… spiritual… rhyming… sponge–but was sure, with what he was hearing, that Nassau must be very close.

As the radio chatter became more pronounced on all channels, to everyone's surprise Heyse gave the all-clear and ordered the crew to prepare to surface. A scruffy-bearded *Oberleutnant* Kroesen was the only one brave enough to voice his concerns. "This is highly irregular *Kapitan*. I must express my objection."

Heyse didn't even give the young lieutenant eye contact. "It does not matter what you think, Kroesen, but rather what you do," he said firmly. "And right now I want the boarding party ready to go."

"But we have no orders to drop these men off," Kroesen persisted. "In fact, we had no orders to take them aboard in the first place. The whole boat is being put in danger if we surface. May I remind the *KorvettenKapitan* that Nassau is a British colony? We are moving into the dragon's teeth and you have given us no reason for such an action!"

"Since when do I need to explain myself to you?" Heyse snapped. "These men are highly trained *Kampfschwimmer* under my direct command, and your job is simply to do as you're told."

"But *Kapitan*, they are not regular *Kriegsmarine*. I did not say anything when we picked them up from the Florida Keys two days ago, but this mission was not discussed with the Senior staff as is normal practice. I demand to know what you are up to, *Kapitan*."

Heyse gave him a withering look, then decided to change his approach. "They will be gone soon enough, *Oberleutnant*, so you needn't be concerned. We will be out of here before you know it and then maybe can tune in some American jazz or big band music– Harry James and Tommy Dorsey? Think on that instead of the fear you are projecting to the others."

Heyse felt his attempt to diffuse his junior officer's questions was somewhat successful as the lieutenant returned to his assigned station, in a huff but fully engaged in his immediate duties once again.

"Leveling to 20 meters, *Kapitan*. Preparing to pressurize ballast. Topside in one minute."

Heyse retracted the periscope bars and stood by the ascent ladder to the conning tower. Behind him emerged four special forces operators who, for the past two days, had been isolated in the Officer's quarters, separate from the rest of the crew. Once the white light appeared at the depth range station, they began their ascent. The last man shoved several duffle bags to the others in the tower and Kroesen left his station for one last look at the mission departure.

In the distance, strands of lights encircled the trunks of the palm trees lining the beach. Although Prince George's Wharf in downtown Nassau had been under blackout protocol for the past year, the north end of Hog Island was a world of its own. The coral reef that surrounded the island prevented a torpedo from entering the newly-hewn harbor, so restrictions were much lighter and locals were much less cautious. And, on this night, one very large pleasure craft floated in the water, seemingly unfazed by the possibility of danger.

In their small craft, the five *kampfschwimmers* pushed off from the submarine into the warm Bahamian waters, carefully navigating the coral reef that could so easily rip through their rubber dinghy. When they reached the beach, they hid in a cabana until they were contacted by their shore party. By *Kapitan* Heyse's estimation, they should have been able to make land in less than twenty minutes, so when that milestone was reached, the order was given to blow ballast and be on their way.

The only causality of the operation was *Oberleutnant* Kroesen, whose naked body had made fine shark bait.

Chapter 28

Laban's Contract

❧

Wellburn, Ontario

Vaughn and Liam had spent the week baling hay on both the Wellburn farm and at Tom Bonnell's property. Rising much earlier than usual, they had the laborious task of gathering the square bales from the rows laid out by the Fore Cart and stacking them into twelve-foot-high sections. As the day progressed, and the dampness of the hay dissipated, the bales became easier to throw and pile, but it was still back-breaking work.

Everyone agreed that nobody had a purer heart than Tom Bonnell. He was the helper who always went above and beyond for neighbors in need, and in return the Wellburn community rallied around. Since his girls had moved on, and he and Betty had aged, they needed more and more help on their farm and folks came from miles around, pleased to lend a helping hand. This week Tom had been promoted to driving his old orange Case tractor while Vaughn and Liam did the heavy work for him.

By the time the bundles were set to be stored in the haymow, the real dirty, sweaty and lung-clogging work was just beginning, so the three of them agreed to sit a while to eat, drink and maybe even catch a quick nap. Vaughn was grateful for the new machinery that cut their baling days in half, but it was still exhausting. After days such as these, he would generally come home to supper and then go straight to bed, a schedule that left very little time or energy for work at the Citadel or in the community. His parishioners knew when the good Captain had spent time baling, for his sermons were a bit less creative and were delivered with a lackluster spirit.

Mae approached the three sitting in the shade of the almost-filled hay wagon, with a large pitcher of lemonade and some sorghum biscuits and cookies. "You all look like it might be time to call it a day. Maybe some nourishment will perk you up."

When they all had a cup of lemonade and some cookies, Mae took Vaughn aside, and while picking pieces from his blonde hair, said, "Any chance you can knock off a little early and save some energy for a few guests this evening?"

Vaughn stifled a groan, thinking that all he wanted was a bath and bed. "What's the occasion? Who's coming?"

Mae refilled his glass and waited till Vaughn stuffed another cookie in his mouth before she continued.

"We're going to have a very special visitor tonight. Phalyn will be coming, too." She took a deep breath.

"Governor Montague Norman is in town and I invited him for dinner."

Vaughn nearly choked, and Mae slapped his back till he could breathe and speak again. "Why would Norman want to see us?" he asked nobody in particular. "He sent that letter releasing us from any duty!" Now he started pacing. "When did you meet him? Where did you meet him? What did he say?"

"He showed up at the shop this morning and we spent some time together. I was just as shocked as you at first, but he's been a perfect gentleman so far, but..." she hesitated just a moment, "...Vaughn... he knows about Harry." The look on Vaughn's face made her fear he was going to choke again. "He wouldn't tell me any more without you being there so that's why I had to invite him to the house. You can ask him all your questions when you see him. It's odd, but he seems just as interested in meeting his first Amschel face-to-face as he does talking with us. Since Will is out of town with the scouts, it's actually the perfect time–and Phalyn is just as curious about him. It should be quite an evening. I have a feeling."

Now that Vaughn had some time to digest the news, he reluctantly agreed. "I'll go along with your intuition this time, Mae. After all, you're the one with the unsettled feeling lately, the one looking for a new purpose for your life. Right now I have no more energy to put to the matter. I feel like God has us on a coaster ride that just won't end."

Mae knew it was mostly his work exhaustion talking. "Buck up, Vaughn. This may not even be about you or me at all."

"When the Governor of the Bank of England comes, in person, to our little part of the world, he wants something pretty bad. He could just as easily have sent a messenger. Remember, the Amschels showed up in person and we know where that led. Norman would not be here...."

Liam had been standing silently during their exchange, but now spoke up. "Because he trusts you, Vaughn, and respects what you did in Dieppe. He was amazed when I confirmed your story from over there. Norman looks at both of you with great admiration—whether with the war or with the Amschels, and I agree he's most likely here to ask something of you. That is my Irish intuition," he finished with a smile.

"Well we won't know what he wants till this evening so I would like you boys to come back to the house now and get cleaned up. Look at Tom over there. He's fallen asleep under the wagon. I don't think he'll mind if you call it a day."

As they headed toward the house, Mae was deep in thought. She appreciated Liam's intuition, because she had the same feeling. There would be a decision to be made alright, and she knew it concerned her. After all, the Governor had spent time with her today instead of requesting to see Vaughn straightaway. She had a giddy expectation about tonight. Maybe, there was one more step involved in putting this whole adventure to rest. But she wouldn't know till this evening, so she needed to get home and get prepared.

Mae was nervous as the evening gathering approached, but acknowledged the tinge of excitement in her anticipation as well. She had advised Phalyn to stay out of sight until Vaughn could reconnect with the Governor and they had a better idea as to what this visit was all about, so when Norman and his two associates arrived, Liam kept the security officers busy with a tour of the farm while Captain Vaughn McIntosh was reunited with Governor Montagu Norman. The banker was quick to pay his respects to his most hospitable hostess, and his never-ending gratitude to his host, the war hero, but once they were all seated on the front porch with some cold iced tea, he wasted no time getting down to business.

"I'm pleased I could release you from your family's obligation in the Amschel situation, Captain. When you asked if you could have a chance to dispose of the gold in your own way, I was, I admit, leery of the outcome, but you proved yourselves and handled it quite successfully, and we're extremely appreciative for what you and your family have done. We do know, however, that you used the services of Sir Harry Oakes to dispose of the gold." He caught the look between Vaughn and Mae before he continued. "If it were just His Majesty's government that had uncovered Sir Harry's involvement it wouldn't be such a dire situation, but there are several other unsavory players who know as well, which is putting your friend in great danger."

Vaughn was silent, working very hard to maintain his composure. This was not good news and he wanted more information before responding, but Mae had no such hesitations. "You told me earlier that some of your information came from Picard, but there must have been something else that led you to Sir Harry." She moved behind Vaughn's chair and put her hand on his shoulder.

Vaughn broke his silence, "Picard? What do you mean you got information from that weasel?"

"Sir Harry hid his tracks well, but with a personality like his, it's very hard to operate in the dark. He is world renowned–married a girl from the Commonwealth and spent a lot of time in Australia, South Africa, Canada–and government attention is always drawn to any business transaction he makes. And, regarding Picard... let's just say that when the interim operators of the Amschel Bank and the Third Reich discovered that he had double crossed them, they used their talents to acquire any information he had of how and when the gold was removed from Canada. Did you know Picard even kept one crate for himself? Its discovery was his death knoll."

Vaughn finally shifted forward. "We had heard through a source that he was taken into custody and that, for the most part, our plan had worked, but none of us knew his ultimate fate. But I still don't understand how you have access to information gathered by the Nazis."

"Let's just say we have our ways," Norman answered cryptically.

Vaughn looked at Mae. "You know what? I don't even want to know. I'm just pleased he's behind us."

"So you should be, Captain. Problem is, an even more despicable cad appears to be poised to take control of the Amschel interests, and he has targeted your friend, Sir Harry Oakes, as his first step in solidifying his claim to replace Jamie Amschel."

Phalyn had been listening from the kitchen and silently slipped through the screen door, unable to stay out of the discussion any longer. At first site, with her blond hair pulled into a low pony tail, wearing her dungarees and red plaid shirt with rolled up sleeves,

Phalyn Tremblay Amschel Purdue looked more like she was prepared to dispense information on soil samples than world politics and banking. Regardless of how she was dressed, though, Montagu knew immediately who she was and was not going to let this once-in-a-lifetime opportunity slip through his fingers. He could barely contain his excitement.

"Nobody replaces an Amschel, but an Amschel," Phalyn said as she extended a hand to Montagu Norman. "I'm sure you have questions for me, Governor Norman." Mae and Vaughn looked at each other, noticing a marked change in Phalyn's tone and demeanor. This was the worldly Phalyn, not the woman they knew and loved. Quietly they moved together and took hands, praying silently for their friend and the situation.

"Madame Amschel," Norman began as he grasped Phalyn's extended hand. "This is an experience I never dreamed would be offered to me. Yes, there are many things I would like to learn from you. Might we sit and chat for a while?" Phalyn looked at Vaughn who nodded. He and Mae moved to the other side of the porch, staying close by but separating themselves from the immediate conversation about to take place.

After the two were seated, Phalyn looked at the Governor. "Let me begin by telling you why I came to this town in the first place." Then, for the next while, she walked him through her original mission, her cohorts and their ultimate failure, and her change of heart that led to where she was today. She ended with what she knew about the current state of affairs in the Amschel family.

"After things were under control here, I visited Paris and had a long talk with Admiral Canaris–and saw Etienne Picard. I know the good Admiral is your double-agent, and I also know that Hitler keeps him on a short leash. Since my father's death there have been a lot of changes in leadership, and now this person you talk about – the newest heir apparent to my family's business–must be Hans Lubeck, former Kriegsmarine, *n'est-ce pas*?" Norman affirmed her guess. "Canaris is totally bound to him and will play this out as long as it takes to see if Lubeck succeeds in finding the gold, or if Hitler wins the war. Either way, Lubeck feels he's in a position to help himself to the spoils."

"It is to that point, Madame, that I have come to your new homeland. You are right about Herr Lubeck, and I know the gold you removed was your family's *Papillion d'or*. We know that Sir Harry was in this town, or somewhere nearby, when the gold was removed, so the belief is that the gold is with him–back in the Bahamas perhaps. And Herr Lubeck is hot on his trail."

Now it was Phalyn's turn. "We were part of the plan when Sir Harry transported the gold from here to his Swastika motherlode, and then used the routing plan set by my grandfather to secretly filter it out of Canada. He had done the same thing before, though with a less complicated system, to avoid Canadian taxes. Using my grandfather's system to disburse the gold through many Canadian banks would leave it widely dispersed, and recouping it to a single place again would be most difficult, but, I wouldn't sell Sir Harry short–he could have used something very obvious to transport the treasure. I really don't think you should waste time on how he did it, but you should look at where the gold could be most safely kept to be used for Sir Harry's purposes. That's where you should concentrate your efforts."

The Governor was impressed with yet another member of the group who had hood-winked Picard, Brisbois and company. It was apparent that Phalyn had been reborn into this country girl, and her loyalties were quite evident. She loved her new life and would do anything to protect it, but she also had a reserve of knowledge that Montagu intended to use.

He turned to Vaughn and Mae. "I'm sure you can see that Sir Harry is a targeted man. He has little time to live if the Amschels have made it into Nassau."

Phalyn nodded in agreement. "You can't trace the gold to find where Sir Harry has hidden it– you have to go to Sir Harry to find the gold before they get to him."

Montagu then proposed the scheme he had never wanted to put to the McIntoshes. "I need someone to make contact with him. Someone he trusts, who is of little or no notable consequence to draw minimal attention to themselves. We could take Sir Harry into formal custody, but he will never divulge the whereabouts of the gold to any government agency."

Phalyn hated what she was about to say, but knew it was the only thing to do. "Sir Harry was doing a favor for this family, and his only motivation was doing what was right. Now he's in great danger, and, unfortunately, we are back to the task of preventing the Amschel people from getting the gold... again. It's a curse for our families, and now it includes Sir Harry." She paused to take a deep breath, then looked at her friends. "Remember, the Amschel will kill him in a heartbeat. You know they have no morality – just a lust for power and control."

Montagu summed it up. "Sir Harry must be convinced to come under protection, but he will only listen to someone he respects. He knows your hearts are pure in this matter—you don't want the gold and have no agenda. If we can protect him, we protect the whereabouts of the gold.

"We must find a way to stop the Amschels once and for all. They already control governments and banks all over the world, and have even made inroads into the Bank of England and the Federal Reserve of the United States. If they get that gold, it will go to finance Hitler's war and then there will be no stopping him from his dream of world domination."

Mae's excitement was growing. She knew in her heart this was the mission the Lord had been planning for her. "It appears there's only one power great enough to stop the Amschel, and fortunately, we have direct access to it. Although it scares me, I agree we're the only ones who can do this." She looked at Vaughn. "We thought this family mission was behind us, but it seems the Lord has other ideas and we still have work to do for Him." She paused to look at Vaughn. "If I know Sir Harry, he has a plan, and I, for one would be glad to go to Nassau and be part of what he's concocted." Mae didn't even solicit Vaughn's opinion before making her decision, but she felt sure he would be on board. Now it was his turn to follow Mae's heart and be confident that God had it all planned out—and she knew in her heart that the Lord—and Sir Harry—would not disappoint.

Chapter 29
Joined at the Hip

❦

Nassau, Bahamas

A lex Ferguson could trace his blood lines back to the end of the American Revolutionary War – to an ancestor who was in slavery to Donald Cameron David Ferguson of Goose Creek, South Carolina. Donald Ferguson was a bit of an anomaly for his day. He had discovered that the silty and low-lying terrain of the region allowed for the cultivation of a most atypical crop for the American south – rice. Goose Creek had all the requirements to make rice a viable commodity – abundant rainfall along with the humid summers and mild winters made it the perfect environment. The only thing lacking was manpower to maintain the water sluices and flooding rotations, so he purchased half a dozen slaves from the West African nation of Sierra Leone, through Portuguese drivers, to work his land. These were Alex's ancestors.

Ferguson claimed his accomplishment as the Tidewater Method and was actually amazed at the results his new property achieved. From April through September they planted, hoed, weeded and supported the strict regimen required for a good crop yield, then when harvesting began, large sickles, or rice hooks, were used to cut the stalks, which were first dried, then collected into sheaves and sent to the threshing floor.

Donald Ferguson took great pride in his product and had his slaves husk and clean the stalks by hand – a most time consuming task. Many of the working songs Alex remembered his granddaddy singing came from the long hours that his granddaddy had spent flailing the stocks. It was worth it, though, for by the time the rice that heralded from the fields of Donald David Cameron Ferguson of Goose Creek, South Carolina, made its way to market in CharlesTown, it was clean and already barreled for overseas shipment, and brought top dollar.

But the Revolutionary War meant Donald Ferguson had seen the last of his glory days along Goose Creek. He was a Tory–loyal to King George – a traitor to his neighbors, but he preferred to call himself a United Empire Loyalist. So, when the Colonies won their independence, he lost his 600-acre plantation and lavish way of life. It was impossible for him to start life anew where he was, so the household was moved to the Bahamian Islands.

King George had promised free transportation for all Loyalists in South Carolina who would emigrate to the British-held Bahamian Islands, and although Donald Ferguson had put almost forty years of his life into his South Carolina home, the preservation of his honor was more important. So, in 1783, with the assurance he could duplicate his lifestyle in the Caribbean, Ferguson began to dismantle, pack and transfer his property to Cat Island, Bahamas, which was no small task. It included dismantling his two-story, five-bedroom brick mansion, complete with fireplaces, wooden floors, doors, staircases and cabinetry. Nails, wooden bolts, shingles and drain pipes were barreled; kitchen pottery, pans, kettles, utensils, and cutting tables were methodically catalogued and packed. The only items left untouched were the slave quarters – an indication of what was truly unimportant to Donald Ferguson.

Hundreds of wagons set out on the 30-mile trip to the CharlesTown harbor where "His Majesty's Ship Royal Oak," whisked his family and belongings off to the free, un-granted island lands guaranteed by His Majesty's government. Settling on the north end of the boot-shaped Cat Island, it didn't take long for them to realize the South Carolinian lifestyle they had enjoyed could not be replicated in this place. Before long, rice paddies were replaced with cotton fields, and in just a few years a blight destroyed all hopes of making this another successful plantation. Finally, a thoroughly discouraged Donald Ferguson took his family to Nova Scotia, leaving behind some forty slaves and what was left of his property to be divided up among them.

Thus began the diverse history of Alex Ferguson's family. From cotton farming to fishing–and even some pirating–from Arthur's Town to Orange Creek, the name of Ferguson was pervasive. Life was reproduced with little variation in the fifty square miles of rolling hills and pink sand, the tropical paradise with the seemingly endless sea and sun–but Alex Ferguson wanted more.

As a boy he had crossed the island from the north coast to the southern tip, pretending to spy on imaginary pirate ships, usually ending up on the island's highest point, Como Hill. He would spend time swimming and spelunking in the sea caverns known locally as 'boiling holes' that got their name from tides that caused burps and bubbles to erupt in the chiseled caves, which also gave rise to the myth that a sea monster inhabited the island. After extensive exploration, however, Alex had personally debunked that belief, but as long as it kept others at bay, he perpetuated the story to keep the area as his own.

There were other deeper caverns on the island, 'Big Blue Hole' for one, that was reported to contain some other-worldly creature that partially devoured local farm animals then left their remaining body parts wash out to sea on the very strong undercurrents from its multiple grottoes. The foul smelling waters around Big Blue were well known and were enough to convince Alex keep his distance.

Alex was often called upon to offer tours for the Mt. Alvernia Hermitage, a monastery on the island that attracted pilgrims looking for a peaceful retreat, and soon learned to parlay his abilities into a small business. He would include historical facts about the vine-covered ruins of the Ferguson House, DeVeaux Mansion and the Armbrister Plantation, and regaled stories of runaway slaves hiding in the Griffin bat caves and then being helped by mermaids who lived in underground passageways and unexplored caves.

His father, Rummie Ferguson, was mostly absent from Alex's life, preferring to fish around the coral reefs all day, and play his guitar on the main street of Port Howe for donations in the evenings. Alex's mother, Aurora, did her best to provide a loving home for Alex and his three step-sisters, but being the oldest, Alex was often called upon to help put food on the family table. With his active imagination, the skill of oratory and a sense of responsibility and hard work, Aurora was proud of her son, and though she knew it would be hard for the family without him, she supported his plans for independence and at sixteen years of age Alex left Cat Island to seek his fortune in the city–Nassau.

He arrived in New Providence with ten dollars in his pocket and a small suitcase, provided by his mother, that held a change of underwear, long pants, a dress shirt, bow tie, comb, bar of Solvol soap, toothbrush and his dog-eared Bible. He sought out a cousin,

Rambling Ferguson, who had a garage near Goodman's Bay and was in need of an apprentice mechanic.

For almost a decade Alex Ferguson learned the automotive repair business from his cousin. He could tear an engine apart and rebuild it with great aplomb, and he gained a reputation as one of the strongest men west of Ft. Charlotte. All of his swimming, diving and running during his youth had built him into a muscular adult, and he built on that by working for hours at a time lifting, pulling and prying his way through automotive servicing. When his cousin, Rambling, decided to live up to his name and move to another island, he and Alex settled on a deal that gave the garage to the younger man for a minimal investment. Alex was more than happy with the arrangement, but his most important accomplishment, in his eyes, was that he was recognized as a loyal man of integrity, sparing in words, but speaking volumes by his deeds. He became a deacon at Christ's Church, donating his services for rebuilding everything from wooden carts to an occasional truck.

Alex first met Harry Oakes on a Sunday afternoon. Harry loved to drive his silver Pierce-Arrow to Goodman's Bay, across the road from Alex's garage, once every two weeks where he would apply wax to the vehicle. Because of the grit of the sandy roads and the ubiquitous salt air, the body of most high-end vehicles would begin to rust early so Harry was meticulous about waxing the Pierce-Arrow to prevent this decay. It was as much a rite of passage for Harry as it was a chance to get away to his favorite beach and relax for a few hours of therapeutic handwork.

On this particular Sunday, Harry was approached by some rude American tourists who had claimed his favorite cove for themselves, and they threatened to remove him forcibly if he didn't move on. Not one to take kindly to being given orders, Harry ignored the brash interlopers, hoping they would be distracted by the rum they were drinking and the scantily-clad females who were with them. But it was not meant to be.

Alex was pumping gas for a customer when he heard loud voices coming from the beach, and putting the two dimes for the gas into his overall pocket, he crossed West Bay Street to Goodman's beach where he saw three strangers arguing and physically threatening a lone man standing beside a car. What happened next would be forever etched in the memories of both Alex and Harry, and would be re-told late at night to family members and good friends.

"Can I help you, gentlemen?" Alex asked, walking toward the altercation.

The belligerent male tourists turned from Harry and glowered at Alex, spurred on by their female companions. "Get lost, boy. The old man here is about to shove off or play chauffeur and give us a tour of the island."

Alex noticed that Harry didn't seem bothered by the rudeness and insults, or their threats and close physical presence, but Alex believed in standing by his fellow man and remained courteously insistent.

"I don't think the gentleman wishes to offer you his services at this time. I have some cool sodas at my station across the street. Come with me and help yourself to a free bottle for everyone."

Alex's presence had been a distraction to the men at first, but now was becoming an annoyance which they thought would be a good warm-up for the main event.

"Maybe you didn't hear me... MON! Stay out of our business." Alex could smell the liquor, and with the girls egging them on, feared they were in for a fight. Harry just seemed to remain aloof and unconcerned. He nonchalantly put his hands into his trouser pockets where he grasped the pocket knife he had carried since he was a boy. If the mechanic needed help, Harry would be ready even though the last time he had been in a fight was decades ago in a Yukon bar. He remembered it usually only took one thrust to stop the blustering, overbearing cowards in their tracks, but he hoped it wouldn't come to that. In the meantime, he would stand ready.

The oversized work clothes Alex wore belied his physical presence – something these men didn't realize they should respect. He didn't know much about formal fighting, but knew how to defend himself with a well-placed blow to the neck or groin, and if they got too close, Alex could administer a strangle hold to render any man unconscious for a few minutes. He knew the Good Book told him to turn the other cheek, but Alex also knew that Joshua and David had been mighty warriors for the right reasons.

The spokesman for the thugs took a step toward him. "Who are you to offer us anything for free? I have enough money to buy your whole piddly gas station a hundred times over if I wanted."

"Well, I thank you for the offer, Sir, but it's not for sale."

The smallest of the three men who had been standing off to one side tried a sucker-punch to the side of Alex's face. He saw it coming and stopped the punch with his hand, then pivoted the man, face first into the sand. The battle had begun, but Sir Harry released the knife in his pocket and leaned comfortably against the lid of his Pierce-Arrow to enjoy the show. He was fairly sure this man was going to be able to handle the situation.

As the larger man in front of him started moving toward him, Alex reached out and wrapped him in a bear hug and dropped him onto the sand when his body went limp.

"Do something, Charlie!" the ladies screamed at the only fellow still standing. "Don't let him get away with that!" But instead of rising to the challenge, Charlie turned and ran in the other direction.

Alex began to laugh at the retreating man, but suddenly sensed a presence behind him and turned just in time to see a 100-pound female with a bottle of Bacardi's Rum aimed straight for his head. He extended his arm to protect himself, catching his assailant just under her nose, sending her sprawling. With a lot of screaming, crying and cursing, her two companions helped her to her feet, and joined their escorts in a retreat from the beach.

This last bit of vaudeville was too much for Harry. He bellowed as he clapped his hands for the brief but most satisfying moments of entertainment. Once Alex was assured the group was definitely leaving, he turned to Harry to make sure he was OK.

"I didn't mean to hit the lady," Alex said apologetically.

"Sir, she ceased to be a lady – became more of an animal–when she attacked you. You protected yourself masterfully and with controlled civility. Even if those cowardly men had had half her resolve, I'm sure you would still have bested them."

"That's very good of you to say… thank-you."

"No, I'm the one who should be thanking you. I'm impressed that you didn't get rattled. You gave them viable options, which they should have taken, by the way. That's ingenuity. And you only fought in self-defense when they attacked you first. That, my good fellow, shows me you are a gentleman."

"I only did what any God-fearing man would have done. I'm glad you're alright. I'm Alex Ferguson," he said, extending his hand to Harry. "You know, I've seen you come here almost every week for some time now, and have watched you go about your business and then leave after a few hours."

"Ah, another quality to be admired…you are a man of great perception."

"You're embarrassing me now, so I'll stop talking, if I can ask just one more question. Who services your Pierce-Arrow? These twelve cylinders create a lot of power, but its low ride can be treacherous on our roads. She probably has power steering and brakes like the earlier models, but are you having problems with the drive…that is the crankcase or camshaft?"

"Well, Mr. Ferguson, I see you know your cars as well as your strangleholds. How would you like to drive this beauty? Let's get some of those sodas from your place and then you can take this jalopy for a spin. It's the least I can do after you saved my skin." As they headed toward the garage, Harry stopped and turned. "Oh, by the way, I'm Harry Oakes."

"Yeah, I know who you are," Alex said, "but you know what? You may have a lot of money, but you could still use somebody like me around to watch your back." Harry didn't stop laughing the whole way to the garage.

That was the beginning of their friendship, and in due time Alex was totally absorbed into the Oakes household. He sold the Goodman's Beach garage for a respectable profit, and with Harry's help, had a trust fund set up for his family back on Cat Island. Taking up residence in a small brick house on the Westbourne property, Alex was not only the chauffeur but acted as body guard for the entire family, often accompanying them to Miami, and even a few times to Maine.

He loved the autumn colors in New England, but wasn't so sure about winter. He found his first snowfall amazing but refused to drive any vehicles on the slushy roads. He abhorred wearing wool hats and heavy overcoats but loved to split wood and sit before a roaring fireplace. And after the intense heat he was used to in the islands it was very tough to pull himself from his warm bed on the cold winter mornings. All in all he was content, but was always happiest when they returned to Westbourne.

Just like Sir Harry, Alex did not approve when Nancy married Freddie de Marigny, and was guilt ridden for not having seen the romance developing. From that point on he vowed to make up for his oversight by shadowing the activities of their new son-in-law, and in addition, made it his mission to monitor any threats that might arise against Sir Harry.

With all his connections in the Nassau community, Alex knew the locals were talking about Sir Harry after the riot. The Duke of Windsor might have been responsible for the political atmosphere, but most people blamed Sir Harry when there were economic problems, whether he was at fault or not, so Alex was always listening and paying attention to the talk on the streets.

One of his ventures included attending meetings held by prominent Black leaders where they discussed what influence they might have over the political and economic future of the islands. The world was in turmoil – democracy vs. communism vs. socialism vs. fascism – and the Bahamas was not immune to the changing times. A world war was being fought over these ideological beliefs, but Alex could see it was really all about who would ultimately control and benefit from global natural resources. Alex saw it simply as whoever controlled the money, controlled the world, and in Nassau, the native Blacks wanted their piece of the fiscal pie.

They demanded higher wages, shorter work days, safer working conditions, access to affordable and competent health care, better housing, improved schools, safer neighborhoods, and in some cases, all they wanted was access to potable water. Union organizers, church leaders, and some black members of the Legislative Assembly had been conferring for the past year attempting to construct a strategy for improved social justice. A residual effect of the meetings, unfortunately, was the development of an overtly para-military faction headed by one Sydney Albury.

Sydney was the only son of Stanley and Mila Albury of Marsh Harbor on Abaco, where Stanley was the Postmaster and Mila was the Assistant Headmaster at the Seventh Day Adventist Long Bay School. By Bahamian standards, these positions put them in the upper class of Black society, but unfortunately, the prestige didn't filter down to Sydney who spent most of his time servicing the sport fishing and sailing interests of the recreational elite at various yacht clubs. He eventually came to hate the disparity that existed between the floating middle class and those black Bahamians whose lot in life appeared to be economic servitude, and secretly determined to do something about it.

The riots in Nassau were a rallying cry for young Albury. He moved to Nassau and, using the uprising as a springboard, dedicated his time to the task of gaining the islands' independence from Britain and stopping the unregulated influx of American resort and tourist development in the Bahamas. He could see, though, that if anything was going to happen in a reasonable amount of time it would have to be through revolutionary methods. Post-riot concessions by the Duke and Legislative Assembly only fanned his hatred for the existing political structure, but his real venom was aimed at Harry Oakes whose overbearing character was paternalistic and degrading, at least in his opinion, and represented everything that had to be removed if the Bahamas was to attain self-governance.

At the meetings, Albury was eloquent in his pleas, but frightening in his demands. He was often shouted down by the assembly who took his plans for independence as nothing less than treason, and in this time of war, many felt he should be jailed for his anti-democratic views. Committee members who were dubious about his methods and motivations equated him to Harry Pollitt, the General Secretary of the Communist Party of Britain, a most hated and vilified politician. The clergy dismissed Albury due to his atheistic views, Labor Union proponents felt threatened by his aggressive para-military tactics, and the Black MLAs ordered informal surveillance of his daily activities.

Yet, there was a group of young men who were attracted by his rhetoric. Interestingly enough, Alex knew most of them from his home on Cat Island. He related to them through bloodlines–cousins, aunts, uncles named Wilson, Adderley, Poiter and Bain–and was able to have discussions with them about the dangers of associating with Mr. Albury, but his pleas fell on deaf idealistic ears.

Congregating at Pinder's Bar on Blue Hill Road after formal meetings, the exuberance of the youth, fired by excessive rum consumption, often erupted into shouting matches and occasional fist fights between Albury's Cat Island supporters and the more moderate factions, over how best to strategize the fight for independence. Albury convinced them all that Sir Harry Oakes should be their target, and knowing that Alex worked for Sir Harry, they advised him to warn Harry that his blood would be sacrificed as soon as they got the chance. 'Chopping the head from the beast' was how Albury put it, knowing it was a symbol with which his flunkies could readily identify since Cat Island was the home of the tradition of Obeah – the Bahamian version of Hoodoo. They were very familiar with flying witches, zines-priests, hag-vampires and human sacrifice. Stories of ghosts and gravediggers abounded, but the one practice that was becoming the talk of the group was the candle-lit ceremony washed in rooster blood, feathers and fire, which was performed to take the life and spirit of an enemy.

Alex sensed an evil within these young men, and knew they could be very easily manipulated by Sydney Albury for his own purposes. The boys didn't seem to be thinking clearly, as if they had fallen under a spell, and totally rebuffed Alex and his warnings against associating with the radical. All Alex could do was observe and report back to

Harry – the obvious target of the satanic ritual. They just needed an excuse to put it into practice. Then late one evening at Pinder's Bar he heard them singing:

"On da blood-moon Thursday Night,
 Uncle Duckie was going to Goodman's
 He heard a rolling in the West,
 It sounded to him like an evil.
 Then he said, "Oh, Duckie, visit da Say-man,
 And hide youself in the pines and palms
 Duckie go high to meet da Say-man's lair,
 And hide him forever with blood and fire."

Alex knew he would have to be very vigilant.

Chapter 30
Beyond Honesty

Wellburn, Ontario

"I think Liam is being an excellent host. Your men seem to be enjoying their farm tour." Phalyn joyfully waved at her friend who rode on the wheel well of the Case, encouraging his guest to 'wind it out.' "Mr. Norman, this may seem odd to you, but I've never felt as alive as I have since living on a farm. To see the cycle of life in plants and animals is something that pulls at your soul. Will and I live that life now and I couldn't be happier. We take pleasure in what God has provided for us, to know His presence is all around – in the sunrise over the grain fields, the wind blowing through the crackling corn, the dead silence on a side road in the wintertime when all life appears to go underground–these are all things I had never experienced before coming here, and now can't imagine living life without."

"I must say, Mrs. Purdue, you are not at all what I expected. I thought I'd find a self-absorbed Amschel, but what I see before me is someone who respects, values and cares for all that is decent and simple. It is a delight to be in your presence."

While her friend accepted the kind words with quiet grace, Mae was quick to return the compliment on behalf of her husband. "Vaughn spoke very highly of you when he returned from the war. The fact that you gave him… us… the chance to finish our family's legacy shows extreme faith, something we were grateful for. We thought your letter would allow us to close that chapter of our life once and for all – and we enjoyed that for a while – but, even though I didn't want to admit it, I always felt it wasn't really finished.

"Now I see how the Lord was working, even when we were in Windsor, by opening my heart to the opportunity in the Bahamas I learned about at Faith House. I loved working with those children, and Mrs. Eff encouraged me to consider following her friend to Nassau. Now, you come along with this proposition and I can see the pieces coming together. Just as Vaughn felt he needed to travel overseas, I feel the Lord's calling for me to go to the Caribbean–where I can help both the children and Sir Harry."

Vaughn had been sitting quietly while Mae spoke, his head resting on his hand and a slight smile on his face. Montagu looked at him for a reaction to Mae's declaration, and was surprised to see none. "I agree, Mrs. McIntosh, that this may be a 'God thing,' as you faithful people call it. There are very few people Sir Harry would accept assistance from, and I believe you might be in that group."

Mae was trying to make this decision on her own, so avoided looking at Vaughn. She didn't want to take a chance on him disagreeing with her. "So, Mr. Norman, the big question then is, what can I do for him?"

Montagu hesitated just a second. "First of all, you must go to Nassau and connect with Sir Harry."

Before Mae could answer, Phalyn jumped in. "Mr. Norman, my friends are good people and although we know Sir Harry is in danger, I've given this more thought and now believe what you are asking of them is unthinkable. None of this was ever their idea, but they've stood fast in the face of adversity when this whole thing should have been over a long time ago. You had no right to release them from their vow and then come back and try to renegotiate a new deal. It's cruel to send peace-loving people on such a heinous mission. There must be somebody else you can send."

Then she turned to Mae and Vaughn. "If you go, you do know you will probably have to kill the ones who are trying to kill Sir Harry and his family, right? It must be done without feeling or remorse, without hesitation. Are you willing to do that… again?" Vaughn knew he was capable of murder, and Mae believed she had been given no choice when she left Picard's men on the Sarnia trestle, but neither had ever envisioned pulling a trigger again.

Before they could answer, she continued. "You must know there is a real difference between you and anyone who works for the Amschel family! I lived the evil and, thankfully, was saved by God's goodness. I know darkness because the struggle is still within me. I fight it every day–as any Christian does – but this is worse. The Amschel is pure wickedness. They have no conscience or morality. If you are to survive, you must kill them first–or be killed. They murder, Mae, and I don't want to see you and Vaughn be their victims."

Norman jumped in to defend his position. "There is a distinct difference between the Amschel and us, as well, Mrs. Purdue. That family, as you well know, exists for the sole purpose of self-perpetuation, while we exist to serve the common good of millions of people. I'm a banker, of course I make money, but I do it by investing in people, not destroying them."

As Phalyn glowered at the banker, he continued. "War is cruel, Mrs. Purdue. There is no doubt. But Mae and Vaughn have great faith and I am confident they can finish the race that's before them. To be quite frank, I don't think you are in any position to judge me, considering that it's your family who is responsible for all this in the first place."

Mae had been waiting for a chance to speak up. "Excuse me. Have you forgotten that we're still here and are able to make our own decisions?" She paused long enough to be sure she had full attention from both of them. "Phalyn, I appreciate your concern more than you know, and your questions are legitimate. Mr. Norman, we understand your dilemma but she's right that it's unfair of you to come back and ask us to do this after all we've already done for you. But you're both missing the biggest point here – this is a battle between good evil, and, to be honest, we may be the best equipped to finish it off.

"Take the story of Joseph in the Bible. He found himself in dangerous situations not of his own making, but in the end, he triumphed and realized 'what man intended for evil, God intended for good.' Vaughn and I know the realities of what you're proposing, but, unfortunately, now there's something else that needs to be completed before we can truly put this behind us. We need to put our fear and doubt aside and have faith that God will see us through. Peter said, "be not surprised at the painful trial you are suffering, we must go through many hardships to enter the kingdom…"

Even though Vaughn hadn't said much throughout this discussion she knew he supported what she was saying and the look they exchanged then could have moved mountains. They were on the same page as far as understanding God's role in the life of a sacrificing servant. Mae had understood the situation when Vaughn had to go to war in Europe, and now it was his turn to embrace Mae's task to reconnect with Sir Harry. This time, though, God had forged a solid bond between the two of them. They would travel as a couple to a strange land because God had told them to. Neither was afraid, being bolstered by Philippians 1:21, "to live is Christ and to die is gain." The only question remaining was whether their resolve would hold at the moment of decision.

Chapter 31

Island Belly

❧

Nassau, Bahamas

Imperial Airlines Flight 234 touched down at the fledgling Duke of Windsor field at the west end of New Providence Island after a one-hour flight from West Palm Beach, Florida. Twenty people were on board including several businessmen looking for migrant Bahamian workers, one honeymooning couple from Miami Beach, and a combination of U.S. and Canadian servicemen bound for further training at the Royal Aviation School at Oakes Field. Stuffed into the rear seats was a young couple wearing a different type of military garb. Captain Vaughn McIntosh and his wife, Candidate Mae McIntosh, had arrived in Nassau to present a cheque for $1,000 to the Nassau Salvation Army post on behalf of the Cate McIntosh Trust and the Canadian and British Governments.

Although the propeller-driven Dakota had taxied to a stop there was no movement anywhere in the airport yard to either open the doors or remove the luggage. After a few minutes the pilot asked for everyone's patience as local customs now applied, which meant things worked more slowly, and with the heavy rains, the Bahamian service worker's operating speed was reduced even more. So, sit back and wait for the storm to pass.

Mae reached out and touched Vaughn's knuckles that had been cut and scraped while retrieving a few gold bars from under the Wellburn farm water pump. Norman had been able to liquidate the gold so they could use it to fund their mission, and just a few calls to Ian McIlhenny in London took care of their cover when the International Salvation Army came through with a donation that Mae and Vaughn were commissioned to deliver to its expanding outreach in Nassau.

Mae felt a clear calling to be here in Nassau and was thrilled to be part of the Salvation Army heritage of Colonel Mary Booth who had begun this mission just twelve years ago, but right now the Harry Oakes mission was just as important. They expected Sir Harry, who was well known for his philanthropic endeavors, to be drawn to them when the donation they were presenting made the front page of the *Nassau Guardian*. Since the Salvation Army could always be counted on to be part of a healing process, whether in the forefront or behind the scenes, a presentation of this sort was not unusual and shouldn't attract unwanted attention. As they waited for the weather to clear, Mae thought through the plan once more, and prayed it would be successful.

Finally, after a twenty-minute wait on the tarmac, passengers were led to the customs area. Very few questions were asked of either Vaughn or Mae, their uniforms apparently speaking for themselves, before the official snapped his fingers and a concierge gathered their luggage and steered them to a waiting area for pick-up to the city.

"I don't understand where Mr. Stubbs is. He was supposed to meet us here at the terminal," Mae worried. "We're already later than we planned, so he should have been here. I hope he hasn't had any trouble." Vaughn had to smile at Mae's nervous chatter. This was the first time she had ever been out of Canada, and that, along with the task they were about to undertake, had put both of them on edge more than usual.

They were trying to decide what to do next when a grey-haired, grey-vested porter approached and without saying a word, picked up their bags and started to walk away. "See here, fellow," Vaughn demanded, taking hold of the man's arm. "What are you doing? That luggage belongs to us!"

"Last ride leaving for da night over here. No more till mornin'. You gotta go if you want ta get der tonight."

"Well, what about our ride? We're waiting for someone to pick us up."

"Dis be the last ride for da night. Don't know about any other." Vaughn and Mae decided they'd better follow this curious fellow, especially since he still had their luggage, and they'd sort out the rest of it later. After adjusting his burgundy and grey military cap, he slowly and most deliberately placed each piece of luggage on his rolling trolley, then began the slow journey to the street. With every squeak of the metallic wheels the couple was becoming more irritated.

He didn't say a word to them during the good five minutes it took him to load four pieces of luggage into the 16-foot yellow taxi, one piece at a time, while he told the taxi driver his life story–how his day had been, and how his knees and back were bothering him, and how his wife was giving him grief–didn't seem to matter who overheard the conversation. After all that, he had the gall to hold out his hand to Vaughn for a tip. The dime Vaughn reluctantly handed him seemed to be satisfactory, and the wispy fellow ambled back to the terminal.

The servicemen had disappeared, possibly taking a military vehicle to their check-in station, and the businessmen were being detained in Customs, most likely until a few dollars could be slipped to the agents to allow them passage, but the newly-married couple from the plane had joined Vaughn and Mae and they all climbed into the taxi together.

"We be going by Bay Street to downtown," the taxi driver informed them. The aroma of rum wafting from the front seat didn't engender trust that they would reach their destination in one piece, but at this point there was no alternative. "Where you stayin'?" While they answered, he pulled a white cotton Bull Durham tobacco pouch and cigarette paper from his front shirt pocket, opened the small bag, tipping and gently tapping the bottom until a small mound of crinkled tobacco rested on the zig-zag paper, then with one expert whip of the tongue he moistened and finger-rolled the cigarette before planting it in the corner of his discolored mouth. Lighting up the smoke stick, he inhaled the first blast of nicotine deep into his lungs, then with a great blast of smoke hitting the foggy windscreen, he was ready to roll.

The humidity after the rain was nearly unbearable for these rookie islanders, so windows were all pushed wide open as the driver chugged and grinded his way along the six-mile trek to the heart of Nassau. The crushed gravel road from the airport to the coastal by-way was riddled with bumps and potholes, and scrub brush continually slapped against the sides of the vehicle, but once they were on the east-west passage to town, the ride was remarkably smoother. This was Mae's first exposure to driving on the left side of the road, so each car that came toward them caused her to nervously squeeze Vaughn's hand. He, on the other hand, was re-living the first time he drove with Major Forester to Aldershot. It seemed like a lifetime ago.

As the skies cleared, the moon shuttered in and out among the foliage, and passing scenes changed quickly from the outlines of cottages to momentary sightings of moonlit sparkling water along Cable Beach. The driver's next words brought them both quickly back to attention. "We be coming up on da big man's house, on da left. It be home of Sir Oakes and dat is his own golf course to da right." There wasn't much they could see in the dark, as Westbourne was well shielded from the road by an eight-foot brick and plaster wall imbedded with a large black wrought-iron door. They could hear dogs barking, probably keeping guard along the wall, and Mae suddenly had an eerie feeling knowing that Sir Harry was so close to them again, but now they were in his world – a world that was totally foreign to them.

The taxi swung around the Colonial Hotel to drop off the honeymooners, then proceeded east down Shirley Street, running parallel to the downtown section of the city still under repair after the riots. Unbelievably, they noticed the driver steering the taxi with his knees while he prepared another cigarette and giving a running commentary about the riots that had happened just one block away. Vaughn and Mae had read reports about the unrest in the London Free Press but figured there was more to the story that Sir Harry would fill them in on when they saw him. For now, though, all they wanted was some rest. One of the original officers sent to the islands, Divisional Commander Jeremiah Stubbs, was the one supposed to meet them at the airport, and they were still confused about how they had missed the connection.

"Here we are at Meadow Street," their driver announced. "Jus' knock heavy on the door."

Vaughn took their four pieces of mismatched luggage from the underside of the taxi and searched his pocket for a tip, but the driver refused, saying something about the Army giving him something that has no price. It was a most heartening way to end their drive – until the taxi drove off and they turned around. Surely this could not be the site of the Salvation Army Headquarters!

There were no street lights and they could clearly hear the roar of propeller engines indicating they must be near the other airport at Oakes Field. The building that stood before them appeared to be some sort of storage or small hanger for engine repairs, but as their eyes adapted to the dark, they could see a small opening in the building wall with a corrugated tin door that had become unhinged at the frame. A large concrete bar blocked it and was fastened into place by two padlocks. Vaughn was ready to explode. What had they gotten themselves into? He shook the locks out of frustration while Mae walked to the other side of Meadow Road trying to find any building that didn't look totally deserted.

In the distance she could see lights from downtown reflected against the remaining low-lying clouds, and fighting down a rising panic, she returned to Vaughn's side. After a brief discussion, they decided to head toward the light, so to speak, though they would have to walk a good mile or so through a strange area to get there. Mae tried to tell herself it was really no different than a midnight trek through the cornfields or a walk along the Wellburn concession from school to home, and they agreed that as long as they kept moving, they would be alright.

They started out with each carrying their own luggage, but after about fifteen minutes of the heat and humidity–in their heavy Army uniforms–Mae could barely walk, let alone carry heavy bags, so it all fell to Vaughn. With a piece tucked under each arm, and one in each hand, he leaned forward to put the strain on his legs and not his back. In the smothering humidity, his clothing was already soaked through, and just when he thought he could go no further, Mae spied a communal water spigot at the side of the road. They both drank heavily and wiped their brows and hands at the oasis God had provided for them... the Bahamian Waters of Meribah.

As refreshed as they were going to be at this point, they took one last drink and started out once again, but an approaching vehicle gave them hope of rescue. Mae waved her arms above her head until the car came to a stop with its headlights nearly blinding them. Through squinted eyes, Mae could see two silhouettes approaching. "Welcome to Nassau! Captain and Mrs. McIntosh, I presume. I'm Captain Stubbs, your welcoming committee, and this is Hector Rolle, an invaluable part of our team." Turning to Hector with a broad grin, Captain Stubbs said, "I told you they would drop them off on Meadow Road. Nobody knows about our living quarters in Palmdale."

Vaughn and Mae stood in stunned silence. He was acting as if it were the most natural thing in the world to come across two strangers overloaded with luggage, at the side of the road in the middle of the night. Before either of them could answer, though, the smile on Stubbs' face was replaced with a look of concern. "Did either of you drink the water from that spout?" When they both nodded, Hector began to snicker and quickly put his hand over his mouth, and Jeremiah said, "Well, then, we better get moving and get you settled in. I think you only have a few hours before Armageddon hits."

With no more explanation than that, their hosts hurried to collect their belongings and pack them inside the dark green GMC pick-up. Mae took the passenger seat while Vaughn and Jeremiah sat among the luggage, paint cans, ladders and stained drop cloths in the back. Hector stomped the accelerator causing the truck to fish-tail until the four wheels finally took hold of the slick pavement.

"I'm sorry I didn't make it to the airport to your liking," Jeremiah said to Vaughn, "but it's the way things work here. You'll get used to Bahamian time. If we set a meeting for 4 PM, folks might start to show up at 4:15 if we're lucky, and the meeting might finally get started by 5. By your expectations we were 45 minutes late to pick you up, but by the custom here, we were right on time!"

Vaughn was in no mood for chit chat. "I get it, Jeremiah. Now what is this Armageddon you mentioned?"

Captain Stubbs became very apologetic. "Normally when someone new arrives we try to ease them in to island ways gently. We talk about sunburn, animals, left-side traffic, ocean hazards, and crime, but the first thing we always tell our new arrivals is...don't drink the water!"

Vaughn's face turned white. "What do you mean? Is it contaminated? What's wrong with it?"

"We don't filter or purify the water here and it all comes from cisterns, so yes, it's full of parasites and bacteria and, unfortunately, they are currently finding a nice home in your digestive system. Before this night is through you and Mrs. Mac are going to be making quite a few trips to the loo. It starts with a general rumbling in your gut and then you won't know which end to put in the toilet first – but trust me, both will have equal time." He stopped as Vaughn lowered his head and wiped his face with his hand. "It should last about two days, but the good news is when you're past this you'll be a real Bahamian, able to eat and drink anything you want!"

As Vaughn digested this information, Hector swung the truck west down Mackey Street, traveling a little too fast for Mae's liking. "Hector, you almost hit that man back there! Didn't you see him?"

"I see 'im jus' fine, Ma'm, but he need to be watchin' out fo' me. If we made it firs', den we had de right to go."

"You're taking these corners awfully fast. May I remind you that both Captains are in the back of the truck along with our luggage?" Then she had a revelation. "Hector, have you been drinking?"

"Oh, yesss, Mrs. Mac...every day. I drink from de well of livin' water and give tanks for His never-endin' love."

"Hector! You know what I meant–have you been drinking liquor?"

"It be ma legs, Ma'm. I have de pain all de time. Mos' days I no feel ma feet, and my toes be turnin' black. I take a little nip to get me started in de morning, then I jus' need a wee bit to help me tru de middle mornin'. Sompin' wit lunch makes de food tase better, and an afternoon shot keep me goin'. Of course, I like to be social fo' dinner and it helps me talk to people, and dere's a night-cap before I goes ta bed ta help me sleep. Dat's all. Udder dan dat, I don' drink de liquor no way!"

Mae smiled. Hector had a big heart, but he had problems beyond her abilities. She remembered from Cate's writings the advice Leah Martin had given to her daughter about adjusting to different cultures, so for now, Mae would not judge, but rather look at the good that Hector was doing, in spite of his malady. Besides, she suddenly felt an urge to upchuck, and knew it wasn't from Hector's erratic driving. Her vision was becoming blurry and her heart felt as if it were pounding through her chest. Hector had been expecting this to happen, so when he came to a skidding stop in front of the residence, he quickly ushered her through the red-painted doors and into the women's lavatory, with Vaughn close behind.

All Mae remembered about the next few hours was alternating between hugging a metal toilet and sitting on it until every ounce of liquid her body could expel was forcefully driven out. She vaguely recalled someone washing her face and rubbing her neck with cold compresses, and then sensed strangers removing her clothing and washing her to cool her body down. And then Mrs. Mac passed out.

Welcome to Paradise.

Chapter 32

Perdition in the Coral

❦

Hog Island, Bahamas

For Axel Salming, Hog Island was the ideal place to live. The waters of Prince George's Sound offered him the isolation and independence he craved, and had kept his property immune from the effects of the Bay Street riots, yet it was just a short launch ride to Prince George's Wharf in the heart of downtown Nassau when he needed to be there to conduct business.

His wife, however, did not see it the same way. For her, this island and the Sound were barriers keeping her from the rest of the world. At least before the riots she had been able to take advantage of the reasonable shopping and recreation along Bay Street – the finer things that had been there for tourists and the predominately white population of the town – but now even that was gone. Bay Street was not supposed to be a place of protest, but rather a site for cultural enjoyment and tourist attraction, and she, for one, had had enough. She was sick and tired of living in these islands. She had thought it provincial before, but now it was unbearable – and she didn't hesitate to let her husband know how she felt.

Axel had promised that once his 'business associates' were settled, meaning the Amschel special force from the U-128, though he didn't tell her that, he would take her on a trip. Salming's job with the Nazis would essentially be complete, and truth be told, he didn't want to be around to see what was going to happen next, so his wife's whining was a convenient excuse.

"I was glad to be of service to the Reich, Herr Lubeck, but now I'm going to take my wife away from the islands for a time. She's been very unhappy here since the riots, and seeing as I have some business dealings in Mexico I must attend to, I think the change will do her good."

"You should go, Axel. The proper introductions have been made and we're grateful for the use of your house. It's the perfect staging area for our mission. We feel very safe with the security guards on the docks to keep their eyes on any curious boaters who might venture too close."

"Well, you know where my allegiances lie and I will do whatever I can to help further the cause."

"The men have had an opportunity to scout the town and Westbourne, and have been studying our target and his routines for some time now. All I ask is, when our task is successfully completed, you help in the logistical transportation of the acquired goods."

"I'm sure we can come to an arrangement when that time comes, but for the moment I have a commercial crisis elsewhere that needs my attention. The place is yours. You and your men seem to have things under control. Just watch your back with the local defense force."

Lubeck chuckled. "You must learn to have faith, Axel. We only need to ask Sir Harry Oakes a few questions. Besides, my men were known as the Hunting Group back in Germany and were considered the best of the best. They are trained for espionage, sabotage and assassination – they are experts in the use of most firearms and artillery, and are skilled with watercraft, automobiles and motorcycles. They're expert swimmers, parachutists, and are specialists in hand-to-hand combat." He looked at Salming and smiled. "I think we'll be fine."

"I know your intentions, Lubeck, and it makes me nervous, but that is not my concern. What is of immediate importance to me is getting Mrs. Salming back to her native America. Like the Duchess of Windsor, she longs for a cosmopolitan lifestyle, and the riots have left little in town to interest her. Maybe the ladies can connect in Florida while I handle my business in Mexico City."

"Depending on the answers we get from Sir Oakes, we may be ready to leave by the time you return. Then, with your help once again, we can be on our way. Perhaps we will do business later on—when the war is over?"

Ever since Lubeck's associates had arrived Axel had felt like a stranger in his own house. The Nazis were constantly holding meetings in secret so he had to be careful not to overhear or stumble into a conversation. They had obviously devised a plan to deal with Sir Harry, so Axel was more than happy to leave for a while. The riots were a sign that things were slowly changing in the islands, but he knew whatever Lubeck's plan entailed would cause changes that would be immediate and permanent.

He knew the Argentinean would stop at nothing to get the Oakes gold – Lubeck would be the heir apparent to the Amschel Empire and his men could retire any place in the world they desired. This group was indeed highly motivated. Sir Harry had no idea the threat he was up against, and Axel Salming wanted to be far away so he didn't have to face what was going to happen to his friend.

Chapter 33

Made Men

〰

Nassau, Bahamas

Stretching for 60 miles into the Atlantic Ocean from Palm Beach, Florida, to the tip of Cuba, lie 700 islands with balmy weather, the clearest water in the world and fishing that leaves sportsmen breathless–but there's an underlying sinister side to this Garden of Eden. Pirates, slavery, disease, ship wrecks, arms and rum smuggling had all left a trail of debauchery and lewdness over the years, but through it all the Bahamians had persevered and carried on the heritage of the islands. Although meek and poor by the world's standards, they were proud their way of life had withstood the many cultures that had invaded the islands. But now there was a new type of enemy coming to their homeland. This foreigner came, not to take the land and water that gave the natives their souls, but rather, offering to give them a new way of life while promising to keep the best of what they already had, and Trevor Sullivan was the one opening the city gates.

Sullivan was glad he had arrived at the airport early since the Chalk's flight from Miami was ahead of schedule. Maybe the winds over the Gulfstream helped them along, but whatever the reason, he would be happy to have this over with and be able to get out of the already blazing hot sun.

Trevor watched the silver seaplane circle for its landing and thought about how war veteran, 'Pappy' Chalk, was chiseling out quite a name for himself in the islands. Flying lessons, sightseeing flights, junkets to Miami–not bad for a fellow who had sold his first tourist tickets from a lawn chair under a beach umbrella. Pappy was his own man

– Trevor's kind of guy–making his way according to his own rules. During prohibition the authorities had turned a blind eye when he flew alcohol to the mainland, and in spite of the war, he still took trips to Bimini when all flights were supposed to be suspended for security reasons. The daredevil pilot was a modern-day pirate who didn't give much thought to the legalities or rules of aviation.

This morning Pappy Chalk would be bringing other pirates to the island, but these buccaneers would be wearing top-of-the-line suits with matching shirts, silk ties and hand-kerchiefs. With mixed feelings, Trevor watched them descend the stairs from the plane adjusting wide-brimmed hats to shield their eyes from the bright Bahamian sunshine, and hoped he was doing the right thing.

After a quick greeting, he herded them into the limo and they were off along Bay Street to the British Colonial Hotel for brunch and an important meeting. When they pulled up in front of the hotel's newly refurbished entrance, Frankie Johnson was waiting for them. With the gang all together, Frankie was ready to put his plan into effect, and Big Joey, Sammy the Boot, Kid Kane and The Grocer were all about making it so.

When the last of the waiters left the room, Big Joey bolted the door and gave a nod to Frankie to begin. "Fellas, our purpose for being here is quite simple–protect Sir Harry Oakes from Hans Low-bek and his associates. I've been watching Hog Island, and Herr Lube-job appears to have free run of the place as the Swede has temporarily gone to the mainland. Mr. Sullivan here has informed me the Kraut will not be leaving Nassau any-time soon so we need to keep close watch on this fella. He knows something, and we need to find out what it is."

Sammy had an inspirational thought. "I think we should just whack the guy and make this Harry hand whatever it is over to us."

Sullivan shook his head, Frankie looked at his crony. "Sammy! When the time comes for you to think, I'll let you know. In fact, I'll send a little birdie your way and he can chirp instructions right into your ear."

Like a child, the beast of a man with no neck and pointy black cowboy boots was appreciative. "Gee, Boss, that would be great, but make sure he don't come before 8 AM. I really like to sleep in late."

Frankie reached across the table and slapped him on the back of the head, "Sammy, do you not recognize sarcasm when you hear it?"

"Sure I do, Boss. I even put money on Sarcasm at Hialeah last week. It was part of the trifecta for him to win." Lucky the guy had muscle, Frankie thought, or there would be no good reason to keep him around.

Sullivan chimed in. "We'll have a chance to see both Sir Harry and Lubeck tonight. There's a Good Will soiree at Christ's Church–some do-gooders from the Salvation Army in Canada are bringing a big donation from their office in London and they're having a ceremony to help quiet the town after the riots. Sir Harry will be there and they're hoping he'll open up his pocket book, too. The whole thing should attract Lubeck's attention, so maybe then we can see what firepower he has with him."

Frankie was enthused. "You see, boys, this is what we call an educative moment. Finally, someone who thinks through things. You boys will join us tonight, but you'll have to lose the suits. You're supposed to be on vacation–and stay outa trouble!"

"The Duke was supposed to be there tonight, but I think he went to the mainland with Axel for a few days. That means Sir Harry will be front and center, and there's no way Lubeck would miss it – it'll be your chance to see him face to face."

"Wouldn't that be somethin'? You know I have a brother with the 7th Army in Northern Africa. I'd love to have a few words with that goose-steppin' galoot!"

"You might want to change your approach a little. He's very refined and intelligent."

"So, I'll switch to lawyer mode. You'll see–I can polish up the rough edges and parlay with the best of them. My gut tells me with Salming and the Duke gone something big is about to happen, so we need to stay so close to Sir Harry that we can tell what flavor of gum he's chewin'."

"I thought you said you'd stop with the mob talk?"

Frankie chuckled. "Just one last swipe, Sully. When you see me next, I'll be so polite and gentile even the Duchess of Windsor would invite me to tea."

Chapter 34

Fleece

❧

Nassau, Bahamas

The early afternoon summer sun was hot enough to send everyone into the shade for a few hours, but the newly arrived Captain and Cadet's recent introduction to Bahamian life had left them feeling cold and weak, and still feeling a bit nauseous but with nothing left to expel, all either could do was sit in the sun, warming their frail bones.

Hector had seen this necessary purging before, and knew what it was like for missionaries to go through the island belly, but this stupidity he couldn't understand. "Why you in da sun? You be burned to a crisp! You haf to be da craziest I see in years. Skin can't handle da sun when you new here. I'm gonna haf ta watch you two before you do sompin' really stupid. Now git inside. We have breakfast fo' you."

Without a word of objection, the still woozy and imbalanced couple helped each other from the wooden bench, slowly and deliberately turned their feet, and shuffled inside. They made it just inside the door before collapsing into chairs beside a small table. Once they were relatively stable again, Captain Stubbs and two volunteers, Aurora and Bernadette, came bearing gifts–their first meal since arriving in the islands. Mae and Vaughn were both looking forward to eggs, and maybe some bacon, but the smell of fish came with the smiling servers.

As they proudly presented the breakfast to their new friends, Captain Stubbs explained. "The ladies made this especially for you–corn porridge with tuna and sardines. We were going to use corned beef but it had already turned. Bernadette wanted to try and save it by spicing it up a bit, but after what you've been through already, we decided the fish would be safer. Aurora felt the sardines would taste better so we mixed them in a broth with potatoes and onions, though they didn't have time to soak the fish in lime. Hopefully the salt and pepper will help with the taste, but I think you'll like the way the porridge mixes with the tomato paste, flour and oil. They also wanted to make some sheep tongue souse for you, too, but couldn't get to the market in time. On the side is some Johnny Cake–it's like soda bread. Think of it as toast. Enjoy!"

Aurora and Bernadette stood silently despite Captain Stubbs' attempt to usher them out of the room, waiting until the guests approved their meal. Doing her best to smile, Mae broke off a piece of Johnny Cake and put it on the tip of her tongue, then swallowed immediately without tasting it. Vaughn was a little more adventurous, taking a spoonful of the hardened porridge and downing it with expressions of "Umm" and "Yum." The ladies were satisfied and the three finally left the McIntoshes in peace.

Once alone, they considered each other's sorry state–puffy eyes, unwashed faces and hair, and a general sense of disarray–then looked again at the meal in front of them and both burst out laughing, though they quickly got themselves under control in case anyone could hear. After what their bodies had been through the past few days, just smelling and looking at the plates before them was enough to send them back to bed, but it was good to be up and walking around again, and feeling a little better, so they would find a way to cope, though Mae wasn't sure, at this point, how they were going to survive here.

Captain Stubbs returned. "Now don't say a word! I know this meal is a little over the top–considering all you've been through – but their hearts were in the right place. They only meant to please you."

Mae was most apologetic, "Captain Stubbs, it's not that we don't want to eat, but everything here is so… we're very grateful, but I don't know if our stomachs are ready for this…"

Captain Stubbs knew what she was trying to say. "I spent many a year in London's East End before coming home. I know what it's like to adjust to the culture and the food. Don't tell our cooks but I have a special present for you." Jeremiah was truly an angel. He pulled a serviette from his coat pocket that held two hard-boiled eggs and an apple. It looked like manna from Heaven to Vaughn and Mae.

"While you enjoy this, I'll dispose of the other plates. Bernadette and Aurora have gone to market and there are a couple of souls outside who will make short work of that breakfast. Meanwhile, you can drink the tea they made. It's hot and shouldn't affect you now that you've survived the worst."

Vaughn was quick to thank Jeremiah again. "Please understand, we are not unappreciative–just really hesitant about what we'll be putting into our bodies for a while. Give us a little more time, we'll come around."

Jeremiah smiled. "I know you will. At least you've been through the worst of it. In the meantime, why don't you clean up a bit. The washrooms are empty right now, but come dinner time it will be full up. Once you're finished I'll show you what we do here. See you in about thirty minutes in the Meeting Hall?"

As they began to unpack they both realized the woolens they had brought with them were going to be way too heavy to wear in this heat and humidity, so decided at this point the best they could do was their working denims with a checked shirt for Vaughn and a white short-sleeved blouse for Mae. Though the clothing didn't quite fit their roles at the Mission, at least they would be reasonably comfortable while they adapted to the climate. With a good wash, some palatable food and clean clothes, they were starting to look and feel more like themselves.

When they entered the meeting hall, Captain Stubbs was waiting and smiled broadly. "Well, you won't be mistaken for Sally Ann officers in those clothes, but you do look better than I've seen you since you got here! Do you feel like going for a little ride with me?"

With Jeremiah behind the GMC steering wheel, Mae and Vaughn were taken back to the storage building near Oakes Field where they had been dropped off their first night, but they were amazed seeing it in the daylight. The two walls facing them were covered with Suriname cherry bushes that were loaded with fruit just beginning to turn a blood red color. "We should be able to pick these soon–our second crop this year," Jeremiah told them. "Bernadette uses them for pies, jams and jellies, though we did catch Hector once fermenting them into wine. He's no longer on harvesting detail," he ended with a chuckle.

"On the other side we have some Jumbie plants. The red bark and leaves can make a tea to help calm the nerves. There's also Pretos for sores and cuts, and sea grapes for stomach upset. Over by the corner of the lot is sarsaparilla that Hector mixes with olive oil and rubs on his jumpy legs when they keep him awake at night. The rest I'll show you another time, but for now, I want you to see what we have in storage."

He removed the padlocks and slipped the bar from its moorings, and the tin doors swung open letting the sunlight flood into the dusty barn. Everyone was relieved to step in out of the boiling sun.

"When the Colonial Hotel was refurbished a few years ago, Sir Harry Oakes made donations of the old furniture to various organizations, and we were fortunate enough to be on the list and received these beds, lampstands, dressers and mirrors. We were also given leave to take what else we could from the third floor," he said, waving his arm around. "We've worn out the pillows and blankets over the last couple of years, but these mattresses and box springs are still safe and secure, along with the wooden chairs and cabinets that we hope to put to good use in a dormitory for children we're developing on Mackey Street." Mae's ears piqued at the mention of children.

"Most children born here in Nassau are illegitimate, usually being raised by a mother and grandmother. Though some fathers take interest in their children, it's not uncommon for women to have children by several different men. Unfortunately, children born with problems, or deformities, are often abandoned at an early age…especially the blind. They are the ones who will be our focus with the grant money. We want to establish a school for the blind children of the Bahamas, with a bed and personal living space for each one. Your donation will finally make putting a roof over their heads a reality."

Mae forgot all about being sick. She couldn't have been happier, and was convinced her short time in the Bahamas would have more purpose than she could ever have hoped for. It was humbling to be used as a vessel to carry the good news to this mission and she couldn't wait to share her experience with Mrs. Eff when she returned to Canada.

"I have a niece and nephew, both blind, who I've taken into our care and raised for the past decade. So, my gratitude is not just from another Army officer, but comes from a personal level as well." He slowly walked around the room as he talked. "I've been praying for this for so long I never thought God would answer and actually got to a point where I just stopped praying about it. It's not that I didn't think God could do it, but it had been so long I thought His answer was 'no' and he wanted me to be content with what we had – like Paul said, 'I have learned to be content in whatever circumstances I find myself.' Only thing was, I started becoming bitter. I found myself yelling at God some nights, and it was pretty difficult to believe in His greatness with all this poverty and despair around us. I asked him why these little children had to suffer? What have they ever done to deserve this?"

"And this donation changed your mind?" Vaughn asked him.

"Oh, no. What changed my mind was working with the children. I listened to them talk about the many blessings God was pouring out and realized I was the one who was blind. All I was looking at was the injustice–kids with no future, no means of taking care of themselves, no chance of things ever getting better than they were..." Mae and Vaughn found a couple of chairs and sat down, sensing that Jeremiah's story was far from complete. Captain Stubbs had snapped into preacher mode and with each statement his voice became more intense and passionate. The Holy Spirit had grabbed him this morning and was extending a life-line to Mae and Vaughn...and they loved every minute of it.

Stubbs continued. "I listened to the faith of these who had nothing and this is what I heard: they honestly believed that God was working for good in their lives... they accepted that the Lord's ways are higher than theirs... they focused every day on the good things God provided, not the blindness that was holding them back... they were grateful that God had given them someone who loved them, who put clothes on their backs and gave them a place to live... they were content to give up their lives to a trusting God who promised to care for them. They laughed, and were not surprised, when I told them a new home was finally coming for them because they never doubted God would provide for them as He had always done."

Captain Stubbs was totally oblivious to their presence, speaking with unwavering conviction as he poured out his heart. "They know the Father is in control of everything and look at their lives as an adventure, not a crisis... they were not angry, but joyful that God had chosen them to carry this burden... they are grateful for those who read the Bible to them and hopeful that someday they will be able to read it themselves... they are especially happy to know that someday they will have perfect bodies... and they never take their eyes off Jesus – because all they ever need for that are the eyes of their hearts." Then, after a few more minutes of 'preaching,' Jeremiah was finally finished. Empty of all that God had stored in his heart. He was sweating profusely as he stood with drooped shoulders and his hands set firmly against his thighs.

Mae looked at the gentle face that seemed to be glowing in this darkened room. Vaughn noticed it too, and thought of the night in a field near Dieppe when Good had prevailed over Evil. Right now he could feel God in this place and dropped to his knees, with Mae beside him.

Neither of them knew how long they had been in prayer until a gentle hand on their shoulders brought them back to awareness. There stood Captain Jeremiah Stubbs as if nothing had happened. "I also believe in the strength of prayer and have been watching you two for a while. It's encouraging to see young people so penitent and worshipful."

As they rose, his appearance and attitude caught them off-guard. "We were inspired by your Spirit-empowered sermon about the faith of the blind children. It was like a Sunday morning message."

"I don't understand," Captain Stubbs said, rubbing his chin. "You say I was preaching? Just now? I've just been standing here watching in amazement as you two were totally caught up in your communion with the Lord. You were in solemn prayer together and I was overwhelmed by your sincerity. Is this what's happening in the Citadels of the Salvation Army in Canada? If it is, I want more of it!"

Vaughn and Mae looked at each other, then back at the Captain. "We all seem to be a little confused as to what just happened," Mae said.

"My dears, whatever we just experienced was inspiration from God," Stubbs said, a smile lighting up his face. "We asked the Lord this morning for your health to return and to set all our feet straight upon the path we should go. It appears He has spoken but there is one more piece to fill in. We will meet a true angel tonight at the donation ceremony."

"Is that tonight?" Mae shook her head. "I've lost track of time."

"We can talk more about it at our next stop. I'm fairly sure that egg and apple I gave you have worn off by now, so I'm going to treat you to another heavenly experience. You haven't lived until you've tasted Momma's homemade potato salad, peas 'n rice, and her sun-touched chicken. It's the best thing to heal you and give you strength for the days ahead. Praise God!"

Captain Stubbs locked the storage facility and decided to make one more circuit around the building to check on the herbs and gardens. Vaughn and Mae waited for him in the shade, still trying to make sense of what had just happened to all of them.

"Whenever God has appeared to me like that in the past," Vaughn said, "it was to equip me for something special He had for me to do. I expect, in the next few days, we will have an encounter with evil that we may not be able to rationally explain. Mae, I don't know what's going to happen, but we have to be prepared for just about anything."

This was the first time Mae had experienced the actual breathtaking and unexplainable presence of God face to face. He had revealed himself to her in this extraordinary way and she silently prayed that the next time she felt His presence, she could be used as His helper and less as an observer. She hoped the meeting tonight would give her some clue as to where and how God wanted to use her.

Chapter 35

Confounding the Wise

❧

Nassau, Bahamas

Alex had just visited Christ's Church as part of his daily routine and was pleased that most of the restoration and remodeling of the building was in its final stages. He was particularly happy he had been able to seal the last tomb so the stone masons could complete the flooring, and the old mahogany pews could be returned to their rightful place. They had been removed for the floor repairs, and to continue holding services, temporary pews had to be brought in and then removed each Sunday, and he was relieved that soon that practice would no longer be necessary.

The renovation Alex had been involved in was not the only one for this church. Not long after the original wooden building had been completed, a hurricane had devastated a large portion of the structure, then through subsequent decades it had been rebuilt several times after similar storms until it was eventually replaced by a quarried limestone block structure that folks hoped would stand up better to Mother Nature. Problem was, the building was not held together with any type of cement or mortar, but rather by the fit and sheer weight of the stones. So, when the storm of '29 hit, flood waters shifted and corroded the foundation, and to everyone's surprise a dozen deep graves memorializing military officers, distinguished landowners and government executives from days gone by were found under the floor.

Church officials agreed the tombs should be preserved, but the repair work moved at a snail's pace. The depression and subsequent war left little funding to underwrite the extensive and ongoing overhaul needed in the foundation, walls and floors, so the bulk of the recovery didn't begin until Sir Harry Oakes returned from Canada in the forties and agreed to provide the necessary funding for the restoration. His closest associate, Alex Ferguson, had led the undertaking as an act of good will toward his Anglican friends, and soon he and his crew began to remove the Italian granite tiles covering the graves, exposing various plaques and memorial engravings that nobody had even known existed.

Then, working with Reverend Green, Alex proposed a plan to set the tombs straight and reinforce them with rebar and cement, and he would personally oversee and re-seal each tomb to maintain the respect and dignity they deserved. With the floor then fortified and safe to bear weight again, the pews could be reset, thereby inviting all to worship God in a safe haven. Now, after several years of work, the church was almost ready to accept parishioners into a sanctuary restored to its original splendor.

Now that he had his church back, and with the riots still fresh in everyone's minds, Reverend Green had proposed an ecumenical service for peace, and had talked the Salvation Army into including their donation ceremony at the same time. The Army would still be receiving the donation from its international benefactors, it would just take place in the comfort of his almost completely refurbished Christ's Church. He believed God's work could be done both in the sanctuary and on the streets.

The event had been promoted by the *Nassau Guardian*, and word had spread so more than the clergy and parishioners would be attending. Esteemed members of the legislative and business communities, along with military personnel, tourists and other guests would be present. Notably absent, however, would be the Duke and Duchess of Windsor who sent their regrets from abroad. Regardless, the evening's festivities would culminate in a gathering in the Garden of Remembrance to the east of the building, where, under torch-light and with respect for the quiet and tranquility of the garden, all would be encouraged to meet, greet and eat to the glory of God, the Provider of everything under Heaven.

Reverend Green ascended the stair for the reading of the Gospel and looked out at the vast array of faces. In the front pew were members of the Legislative Assembly, Sir Harry Oakes and Trevor Sullivan, along with a few other clerics and dedicated Christ's Church patrons. On the other side of the aisle was his friend, the smiling and excited Captain Jeremiah Stubbs, who hugged and conversed with many of those around him. Beside him was Hector Rolle who had already nodded off, but, he thought, it's good, nonetheless, just to see him in a church. The Reverend had been confused when the young Canadian couple with Jeremiah had wanted to wait in the side room off the sanctuary until time to make their presentation. Their explanation that they didn't want to distract from the main purpose of the service seemed a bit odd, but reasonable enough for him to acquiesce.

Toward the back of the church was a collection of men Reverend Green didn't recognize. They were all Caucasian which, in and of itself, made them stand out from the crowd. One group sat at full alert with shoulders straight and backs against the pews, hands on knees, looking straight ahead. Each had blondish-brown hair, impeccably styled with shaven sides but a bit longer on top, and they all wore black, long-sleeved shirts that were buttoned to the neck. The clothing made them look out of place in the heat, but, strangely enough, they did not appear uncomfortable. The Blackshirts, as he thought of them, engaged in no small talk–amongst themselves or with those around them. Their faces were stoic and unmoving, totally transfixed, Reverend Green noticed, on Sir Harry Oakes.

The other group was totally different. There were five men, all but one heavy set, with thick black hair heaped high on their heads. They were slouching in the pew, one biting his fingernails, and the man on the end had his black boots stretched into the aisle. Aside from their general slovenly appearance, they stood out because of their multi-color floral shirts – all different patterns. The Reverend marveled at how different God's creatures could be.

"I want to thank Pastor Phillips of West Hill Baptist Church for sharing the Epistle to the Romans from St. Paul," Reverend Green began. "I'm honored to have a man of his faith come to God's House and preach on honor, humility, love and charity–all the attributes that promote love, unity and tolerance for all. The Gospel of Matthew also shows us that a community that bases its life on the teachings of Jesus Christ will likewise not fail. This Church has withstood fire and water and is still standing and, I dare say, will flourish despite our community struggles. Many of you have had a hand in this renovation project even though another church is your home, but I am here to say that he who builds a foundation fortified by Jesus Christ will find a home no matter which church he attends.

"We are called to Christ's Church because all are accepted here. You symbolically rebuilt this church as Nehemiah rebuilt the walls of Jerusalem, but the essence of this church is not the new building, but the souls who inhabit it. There is something wonderful within these walls–something greater than gold itself. It is the faith that each of you bring tonight to make this church, this town, this country better than it has ever been. May we truly be moved by the Spirit of Christ, both as individuals and as a community, to bless Christ's Church for His appointed glory. Here endeth the Gospel...please rise for the reciting of the Apostles' Creed."

The congregation stood and spoke in unison–some profoundly, some whispered in deep reverence, others mouthed words they recited only on Christmas and Easter, others remained silent with heads bowed, and a few sat through the recitation in great discomfort. At its completion, Reverend Green descended from the pulpit and informally addressed the congregation. "I see before me quite a mix of persons, many of whom I've never seen before though I've been in this community for over thirty years. I look forward to meeting all of you, so on behalf of Christ's Church, I invite you to stay for refreshments after the service. Before we move along with that, however, we have two important matters to take care of.

"First, let's sing a hymn I know everyone is familiar with, 'Hark, the Herald Angels Sing.' I know, you think of it as a Christmas song, but let me give you a little of its history. Charles Wesley wrote it in 1739, then a hundred years later Mendelssohn changed it a bit to–believe it or not–commemorate the invention of Johann Gutenberg's printing press. It is the fourth most popular song we sing in the Anglican Church, and Handl proclaimed it a recessional of joy and thanks to the Lord. So, it is fitting tonight that we celebrate with 'Hark, the Herald Angels Sing' as we close the service."

As the church's organ thundered its way through the chorus into the six verses, some disquiet in the back pews began to spill forward. A few white-collared Bahamian Defense Force officers were attempting to corral several dissidents, but they refused to be quiet. As the youths were being dragged from the church screaming praises to Loa and Damballa, Sydney Albury broke free and ran past Reverend Green to the chancel, holding a live rooster by its claws! The organist immediately fell off key and stopped playing, a few parishioners standing next to the aisles headed toward the door in fear, but most just stood in shock.

Albury climbed on top of the communion rail and made a bold pronouncement. "Death to all Bay Street Boys! Death to Harry Oakes!" Albury's eyes were blood red and his hair had been spotted with white paint. As he held the rooster high above his head, the creature's wings began to flap, sending feathers everywhere. Reverend Green tried to stay calm and comfort the congregation, but it was no use. Sir Harry made a move toward the young man with his fists clenched, but Sullivan held him back.

The policemen had followed Albury to the front of the church, but stopped at the communion rail as Albury danced to the altar. Then, pulling a blue-handled knife from his waistband, he severed the rooster's neck with one swipe, dropping its head onto the altar, and then ran toward the front pew, spewing the pulsating blood over all their faces and clothing. The one he sought, however, was well-protected from him now.

Momentarily stunned by the act of blasphemy, Reverend Green finally responded by lunging at Albury, but lost his balance when he tripped on his ankle-length cassock and fell to his knees. Albury gleefully scattered the remainder of the rooster's blood onto the Reverend's pure-white clerical robe, then dropped the carcass and ran, disappearing out the north transept onto Shirley Street into the chaotic crowd.

Trevor Sullivan had disappeared in the melee, and during the original confusion, Vaughn and Mae quickly decided this was not the time for Harry to discover they were in Nassau, so along with Jeremiah, they had slipped out with all the other terrified con-gregants. They stopped, however, just outside the door and stood off to the side praying and trying to make sense out of what had just happened. Being from the islands, Stubbs was familiar with this type of overt evil, but it was new to the Canadians. They thought they were prepared for just about anything after dealing with the attacks from Picard and the Amschel, but this had brought Satan to light at a whole new level. Jeremiah told them that rituals like the one Albury had just played out were fairly common on the out islands where the old practices were alive and well, but they weren't usually as blatant in the city since development had driven them mostly underground. Jeremiah could tell the young couple was shaken to the core, so he laid hands on each one and prayed for God's protection over them. Then they headed back to the relative calm and protection of Mackey Street.

Once Albury was gone, the pandemonium inside Christ's Church began to subside. Everyone who was going to bolt had done so, leaving Sir Harry, Alex Ferguson, and the strangers Reverend Green had noticed from the pulpit, who turned out to be Hans Lubeck and his henchmen, and Frankie Johnson and his boys.

Sir Harry, now awash in sweat, took off his linen jacket and, along with Alex, moved to check on Revered Green. As they helped their friend to his feet, Sir Harry addressed the only other face he recognized. "I'm surprised to see you here, Herr Lubeck. I see you recovered from your unfortunate accident at Westbourne, but you didn't take my advice to leave the island and instead have brought reinforcements?" Not liking the tone Sir Harry had taken with them, the Germans stepped from the pew like cats moving in on their prey. When Lubeck raised his hand to stop them he heard a metallic click behind him.

Frankie Johnson and his men all stood with arms extended, pointing their respective weapons straight at Lubeck. "I don't know who you gentlemen are, but there's no need for you to draw on us," Lubeck said with a smile. "We have no business with you and mean you no harm. So please, put your weapons down, whoever you are."

The German accent was enough to set Frankie off. "You must be da Krauts we heard about. I know all about you, Mr. Lube-job, and your dealings with Sir Harry over here. I don't think you are in any position to tell me what to do."

Reverend Green was furious about the guns being drawn in the church. "This is a House of God! We've had enough bloodletting this evening. Whoever you are, put your weapons down!"

Frankie responded. "Sorry, Padre, but no can do. I might listen to a real Priest, like Father O'Byrne, but you hold no water for me."

"This is outrageous!" the Reverend spluttered. "Harry, tell them to put the guns down."

Sir Harry didn't want to contradict Reverend Green, but he needed to be realistic. "I would love to, but I just don't trust Herr Lubeck and his crew. Something tells me they may be packing, too, and I think right now it's in everyone's best interest to ally ourselves with what I believe are some of Sullivan's investors from Miami."

"Right you are, Sir Harry," Frankie agreed. "After tonight, though, I think you and I have some business to discuss, or would you rather break bread with Hermann Goering over there?"

"So what would you have us do?" Lubeck asked. "I think this is what they call a 'stand-off' in your hoodlum language."

Frankie wasn't fazed. "Oh no, Herr Goebels. This ain't no stand-off. We have the firepower and judging by the color of your clothes you're all ready to be put to rest."

"Then I agree with the Reverend. We should not take life within God's sanctuary. We should all leave peaceably."

224

"There you go, again, Lube-job, tryin' to tell me what to do. I do believe my boys' fingers are gettin' kinda itchy. Big Joey, Boot and the Kid did some work for me last week, but Grocer's been on the shelf for a while." The boys all snickered at the pun Frankie stumbled into. "I bet he'd like to see some action. "What d'ya say, Grocer? Should we bag 'em now?"

"I dunno, Boss, but this pistol is getting' real heavy and my finger is pretty itchy."

Lubeck sought a compromise. "We will slowly remove our firearms and place them on the floor. Then we can leave this holy place in an unblemished state."

Harry couldn't believe Lubeck was being so compliant, but was hopeful he really did respect the church and wouldn't try anything while still inside. "There's a Chalk's flight to Miami leaving tonight," Harry said, looking at Lubeck. "You should be on it and never come back."

"Of course," Lubeck agreed and placed his blunt-nose Mauser onto the marble floor. The other four did the same, then lined up in the middle of the Nave and slowly started toward the door.

Frankie and his men were all in one pew, with Frankie on the end–without a weapon. The Blackshirts pulled a maneuver known as 'Crossing the T', and once they were in the perfect position, Frankie and his boys were doomed. With their inability to fire directly into Lubeck's line without hitting their own men, the counter attack was on and it was quick, bloody and commando efficient.

As if on cue, the Blackshirts catapulted at the gangsters, driving their miniature naval daggers at their unsuspecting prey. Necks and chests were their targets resulting in instantaneous death for all but Frankie, who was left standing with the slaughter all around him. He stared at Lubeck in disbelief while the head German retrieved his Mauser.

"Don't be afraid, Frankie. I am not going to kill you. I want you to go back to Miami with a message for your Boss. If you stay out of our way until we complete our business here, the Bahamas is open for you to do whatever you want. Our work should be complete by the end of the week. Now, I think you need to hurry as I was informed, earlier, a plane is leaving for Miami this evening – and you should be on it."

"You're going to shoot me the minute I turn my back, you stinkin' Kraut!" Frankie screamed.

Unbothered by the insult, Lubeck lowered his gun and allowed Frankie to hurry toward the Narthex. Then turning to his men, he asked, "Did you get the joke about the grocer?" His men remained stone faced as they cleaned and replaced their daggers to their straps. "Only one problem, the store is closed for the night." Then Lubeck raised his Mauser, and from a distance of twenty steps, cracked a shot at Frankie, purposely grazing his upper arm.

"Now that's how you tell a good joke!" he laughed.

The lone survivor of the onslaught lurched, but kept moving on his knees until he was safely into the narthex. Holding his hand to his bleeding arm, Frankie got to his feet and eased himself through the door and into the throng outside. He had to get to the Colonial Hotel a few blocks away to regroup and make a very important phone call.

Momentarily caught up in his success, Lubeck suddenly realized Harry, Alex and the Reverend, had managed to escape out the transept entrance. Lubeck looked at his men who gave him no indication that they had seen the others leave, and took a deep breath of resignation. "This was actually a very productive evening, don't you think? We can tie up the other loose ends tomorrow. Now I think we should rewrite the last line of this evening's closing song to be, '...Hark, my herald angels sing, Glory to this Amschel King.'"

Chapter 36

❧

Nassau, Bahamas

Sir Harry knew the safest place to be was Government House. Although the Duke and Wallis were in Florida, everyone there knew Harry, and he was always welcome. The trained and armed British regulars surrounding the mansion and grounds offered ample protection against any of the forces who were out to get him, so he decided this was the best place to hole up until he could figure out what his next move should be.

The Salvationists had made their way back to the Mackey Street building, but were in a much different situation from Harry. For the second time this summer the downtown was being rocked by unrest, but instead of the rage being taken out on local businesses, the brunt of the destruction this time was focused on foreign entities in the city – which could include the Citadel. There was indeed an evil that had been permitted to enter Christ's Church, and if it had been able to perpetrate its horror in a centuries-old bastion of sanctuary and praise, how vulnerable could the Army's Mackey Street building be?

It was determined that everyone associated with the Citadel would remain in groups of three at all times. Nobody would work, travel the streets, drive a vehicle, eat or sleep in less than a threesome, which allowed limited privacy for everyone. Until some good news broke, safety would not be compromised. Mae and Vaughn were separated during the day so that each would have two Bahamian assistants, but when it came to meal and bed time, Vaughn and Mae fell under the watchful eye of Captain Stubbs himself. Rumors spread very quickly in Nassau that Sydney Albury, who was still on the run, was the culprit who was causing all the trouble, but when Captain Stubbs and the McIntoshes had heard of the horrific acts that took place after they fled the church, they knew the Blackshirts were the real problem. They could attack anywhere they chose and be gone before authorities could be activated. It was more obvious than ever that Mae and Vaughn had to make contact with Sir Harry as soon as possible.

Over lunch, Stubbs tried to give them an out. "I would completely understand if you just want to go home, Captain McIntosh. You've done your best to deliver the donation. I know we were hoping others would piggy-back on your kindness, but the timing just isn't right. Nassau seems to have turned inward for the time being."

Mae was not ready to let the children's residence go so easily. "I'm disappointed that your ceremony didn't work out, Jeremiah, but can't we at least try and get the building under contract for the children's home? What if we contacted Sir Harry ourselves and explained the situation? Surely he would consider being a follow-up benefactor to our donation for such a worthy cause."

"I'm afraid the time for such things has passed, Mrs. McIntosh. We should just move on."

"Well, I'm not ready yet to give up. If nothing else, I would like to meet Sir Harry. After all, he is one of our Canadian icons, and I would love to meet him even if we can't do business. Can you maybe try to arrange it through his associate?"

"The person you speak of is Alex Ferguson, Sir Harry's driver and right hand man. He spearheaded the restoration of Christ's Church on behalf of Sir Harry and Reverend Green, so I'm sure the recent events there have caused him much pain. Being a devout Christian, he usually made his way to pray at Christ's Church most weekdays during the noon-hour break, but I would guess recent events might have changed that practice, at least temporarily. I'm not sure how to find him otherwise."

"Can you please at least try?" Mae knew she was being pushy, but they had to get in touch with Harry and she couldn't see any other way to do it.

"Well, one thing's for sure. Find Alex and you will find Sir Harry. The two men are almost joined at the hip."

"So maybe we can go to Christ's Church over lunch hour and see if Mr. Ferguson shows up?"

Stubbs could tell Mae wasn't going to let this go. "Mrs. McIntosh, that whole building has been cordoned off by the authorities so I doubt we could even get close, but I suppose we can try. Please understand, though, that nothing short of a miracle is going to get you close to Sir Harry Oakes today."

Mae smiled. That was just what she was counting on.

— — — — — —-

Although Sir Harry felt safe at Government House, he didn't want to tempt fate so he stayed away from windows and arranged for an armed guard to be outside his door at all times. After a few days of this, though, he had had enough of being a reactionary, and surmising the Argentinean would be hiding out on Hog Island, he pulled enough strings to commandeer select members of the Bahamian Defense Force and devised a plan with Colonel Mylo Wilson to go on the offensive. Just knowing he was finally being proactive energized Harry, and he decided it was time to return to Westbourne. There were some important documents he wanted to collect.

Knowing Harry was safe at Government House for the time being, Alex walked down George Street to Christ's Church to see for himself what was happening so he could report back to his boss. As he approached, he could see the place was still abuzz with police, reporters and the general public looking for a story. Since he was a well-known associate of Sir Harry, he decided not to go any closer and ducked into the Shutters Pub across the street where he could see the church without being spotted. He settled in at a table near the window and ordered a slice of key lime pie and coffee.

He didn't pay much attention when the door opened, but then a voice behind him said, "Hello, Mr. Ferguson. Sorry to interrupt, but I'd like to talk with you if I may. My name is Jeremiah Stubbs."

Alex turned slightly in his seat. "I know of you Captain Stubbs. I saw you at the church the other evening and am happy to see you were one of the survivors. Are your guests alright? That was quite something for them to have to witness."

"Yes, thank you. We're all trying to make sense of it."

It suddenly hit Alex why the Captain might have tracked him down. "I'm sorry your ceremony for receiving their donation was spoiled and you didn't get to make the public appeal you were hoping for, but I'm afraid now is not the time to be asking Sir Oakes for the favor of a matching contribution." He would not give Captain Stubbs the chance to argue. "I admit I do admire your persistence, though. Come, have a piece of pie with me and we can discuss more pleasant things."

Alex asked the waitress for a second dessert, and Jeremiah lowered himself onto the wooden bench beside him. If ever there was a day an ale could cut a man's thirst, this would be it, but of course, the Captain would refrain from strong drink in favor of cold water with a squirt of lemon juice.

"I have not come seeking money for our mission, Mr. Ferguson. I'm here to ask a favor," he said, pulling an envelope from his pocket. "My guests have written this note to Sir Harry and would like you to give it to him. They would very much appreciate a chance to see him before leaving the island."

Alex was amazed at the request. "You do remember that Sir Harry was threatened twice–we barely escaped with our lives, so Sir Harry is in no position to entertain guests. I'm sorry, but he prefers to remain in hiding until this blows over."

"Of course, I understand that. Those black shirted men are fervent killers and intent on their mission, and they showed no restraint at all, so the possibility that they will attempt another attack is very real."

"Pardon me if I sound a little sarcastic, Captain Stubbs, but don't you think Sir Harry has already thought of that? The entire Defense Force is out looking for these men."

"No, actually I think they are looking for Sydney Albury," Stubbs said calmly. "Not very many people saw what the Blackshirts did. Sir Harry may appear to be dodging the threats from Albury, but in reality he's more concerned about the Blackshirts, and he has every reason to be. You saw it for yourself. So, if Sir Harry is quarantined and safe from harm, just give him this letter. Please," he said, holding out the envelope once again. "I can't explain it, but I have a feeling he'll want to see what's inside. What can it hurt?"

Alex took the message from Jeremiah and turned it over in his hand. "I will be seeing Sir Harry within the hour and will give him the letter. As you say, what can it hurt, but I will not guarantee anything."

"I don't know its contents, Mr. Ferguson, but these folks haven't had the best of times since coming to the island, and it would be nice for them to leave here with at least one positive experience. I'm sure your word carries some weight with Sir Harry."

"I am just the messenger, Captain Stubbs," Alex said dismissively.

Jeremiah didn't wait for his pie to arrive and stood. "Well, we appreciate anything you might be able to do." He hurried out of the den of inequity, anxious to tell the McIntoshes the news.

For a brief moment after he left, Alex thought, John the Baptist was also a messenger and look what happened to him. Alex and Sir Harry had come too far to let Lubeck stop them now. They were so close to completing a promise Harry had made… a promise to people Alex had never met. Then he picked up the envelope from Stubbs. Was it possible this letter had something to do with that promise? Why did he even have that thought? If there was even a chance, Alex should take up his cross and give the letter to Sir Harry.

Then a final thought came to his mind. The *Collect* from the *Anglican Common Prayer Book* that he had read last night, "*It is meet and right so to do.*" With that etched on his heart, Alex felt the Lord was trying to tell him something about what He was preparing for them. Alex couldn't get back to Government House fast enough.

Chapter 37

Nassau, Bahamas

Lubeck amused himself with the irony of his situation. He and his men were having a relaxed day on the main island in a private beach residence near Lyford Cay at the expense of the owners–Salming and Oakes International–while in the process of planning the demise of said owner. He had wanted to go back to Hog Island after the night at the church, but his men convinced him it would be too dangerous, so he tracked down Axel Salming who arranged for them to stay at this place. It was not as luxurious as the house on Hog Island, but Harry Oakes would never think to look for him here.

While his men tinkered with the motor launch, Lubeck sat idly by waiting for the phone call he knew was coming. He had slept well the last few nights knowing that a pesky group of mafia *untermenschen* had been dispatched–a group he had not even been aware of until last evening. In his mind, it had been a good thing, since Sir Harry had seen what would happen to him if he didn't cooperate. Lubeck was pleased knowing that at this very moment Sir Harry had to be feeling terrorized.

The phone finally rang and Lubeck picked it up. "Lubeck, you could have gotten out of this peaceably. What were you thinking?"

"Not to worry. Sir Harry now knows the price of not doing business with us."

"The island is upside down. This is worse than the riots! All you needed was Sir Harry for a smooth transition, but you had to grandstand. If you had just gotten Harry out of the way, the rest of the board and I could have eased in and found what you're looking for without all this bloodshed and drama."

"Please remember it wasn't us who drew first. It was those *dummkopf* that you brought here that forced the issue. They said they were there to protect Sir Harry, so a showdown was inevitable."

"Well, you took care of that problem for now, but you and your men left the others escape, and now Reverend Green is bedridden in shock and Harry is hiding out at Government House."

"So he's not at Westbourne! How did you find him?"

"I came back here to Westbourne from the church to wait for him, but he never showed up. His son-in-law was here, though, so I bribed Freddie to go out and look for him, and he finally found out where he is. Guess he figured you couldn't get to him there with all the soldiers around the place. It actually was a pretty smart move, I'd say."

"Fairly smart, but not smart enough," Lubeck said. "He has to come out sometime, and we'll be waiting for him."

"I have news about that, too. A man I have on the Defense Force told me today that Harry thinks you went back to Hog Island so he's mobilizing an attack there tonight. Someone else I know at Government House told me she overheard him say he's coming to Westbourne tonight before the attack – I don't think he wants to risk those papers being out of his sight for too long. There's your chance to get to him."

"Ah, a man with connections. I like that. Then tonight it will be. You know, there's one thing I can't get out of my mind. During the confusion, I saw a young couple at the back of the church with a robust black man. They were all wearing formal military-like uniforms."

"That was Captain Jeremiah Stubbs, local Salvation Army. The couple were his guests from Canada who were supposed to present a donation for their work."

Lubeck's sixth sense was kicking in. Salvation Army... Canada... young couple... surely it was coincidence, but he didn't believe in coincidence and couldn't shake the feeling that it meant something more. "You know, I think I should talk to those people. They might have some connection to Sir Harry." Lubeck said.

"I can't imagine what they might have to do with this, but I could have them picked up if you want."

"Not yet," he said slowly. "If they are who I think they are, the horse will come to the trough on its own."

"I don't understand, Herr Lubeck."

"Of course you don't. Just have someone keep an eye on Sir Harry and his movements for the rest of the day. If anything happens, let me know immediately."

Lubeck replaced the receiver into its cradle, then scrabbled through his briefcase to find his notes on Etienne Picard. Could it really be that simple?

———————-

Sir Harry refolded the note and stuffed it in his trouser pocket, then threw back another scotch and soda. He was angrier than he'd ever been. He couldn't believe how everything around him seemed to be spinning out of control: the riots, Sydney Albury, Lubeck, the Duke and Salming gone, the murders and evil ritual at Christ's Church... and now this note. He looked at it again–all it said was 'Wyoming' and was signed 'M. Mc.' He told them to stay away! Why was she here? What in the world was she thinking?

"I know you got this from Jeremiah Stubbs, but do you know where the person is who gave it to him?"

Alex was confused about Harry's reaction to the note. "I didn't ask, but most likely at the Salvation Army Citadel on Mackey Street. Harry, I saw them with Captain Stubbs at Christ's Church. They were the international representatives for the donation."

Sir Harry muttered to himself as he walked in frustrated circles. "I told them to stay away. I warned them that no good would come of them being here. But they didn't listen. What are they doing here?"

Alex could only speculate. "It must be important if they knowingly put themselves in harm's way."

"Use the Duke's car and take a couple of regulars with you to Mackey Street. Pick them up and bring them here. I'll wait for you. This could change my plan – they might need to be brought in."

Alex couldn't believe what he was hearing "But why, Harry? We need to keep this between us. The fewer involved, the better!"

"These are not ordinary people, Alex. They're the ones who helped me take the gold in the first place. They actually have every right to be here, even though I told them to stay away. They are good people and deserve to be out from under the weight of all this." As Harry talked, his anger at the McIntoshes faded. Yes, Mae and Vaughn were good people, and if they had come here against his wishes, they must have a good reason.

"Sir Harry, please listen to me! Don't go to Westbourne. If you leave this place, you put yourself in danger again. Lubeck will stop at nothing to kill you now. Wait until the Duke and Mr. Salming return – maybe they can talk some sense into Lubeck. And what about Trevor Sullivan? Those three together can make a strong case that Lubeck will have to listen to."

"You're fooling yourself, my friend. Don't you see? The Duke and Salming are gone on purpose, and I haven't heard from Trevor since we escaped from Christ's Church. I'm alone to face this evil, but it appears God has sent me an unlikely support team in Mae and Vaughn McIntosh. If nothing else, it will be a great showdown."

Alex was getting perturbed listening to his normally confident employer. "You sound like this is already over."

Harry ignored Alex's comment. "Alex, you have to realize you're not immune to this either. They'll come after you once they get me so you have to protect yourself."

"But the job is almost done! We shouldn't let anyone else know about it."

"Alex, I've made up my mind. The McIntoshes would not have gone against my wishes unless there's a very good reason, and they deserve to know what we're doing. Especially after the events at Christ's Church, we need a back-up and I know Mae and Vaughn will be up to it."

Alex finally gave in to Sir Harry's logic, although the idea of more innocents being involved in their plan was not sitting well with him. "If these McIntoshes are as savvy as you say they are, then let's move ahead."

As the full weight of what was coming registered with each man, Alex caught Harry's eye and asked, "Before we do this, Sir, may I speak openly to you?"

Harry topped off another Scotch and whirled the ice cubes in his crystal glass. "Of course, Alex. This isn't a time to hold anything back."

Alex took a deep breath. "You know how much I appreciate all you've done for me and my family. I've always done my best to follow your instructions to the letter, without question, and now all I ask is that you listen to what I have to say."

Harry put his glass down and turned to Alex. "I think I know what's on your mind, my friend, and you don't have to say it." He paused for a moment, searching for the right words. "You want to talk about spiritual things, am I right?" When Alex nodded, Harry motioned for the two of them to take seats before continuing. "This is why I feel strongly about including the McIntoshes in our plan. I'm sure you've felt how this isn't just a simple fight we're in–it's a battle against pure evil. There's a reason Mae and Vaughn have come here. They have a very close relationship with God, and it's just what we need right now to win this. You look surprised." Harry finished, with a feeble smile.

"It's just that I've never heard you talk this way before. I had no idea you were so open to spiritual ideas."

"Well, I'm still searching for answers, but when I look at you, and my wife, and now am reminded of the McIntoshes, I see selflessness and unconditional love toward everyone – including me – and I want that, too, but I still have a ways to go. Hopefully I'll have the time to get there. So, can you be patient with me, Alex?"

"That's the least I can do, Sir Harry," a wide grin brightening his face. "And I'll pray for you, too."

Harry stood up and put his hand on Alex's shoulder. "I appreciate that more than you know. I have a feeling prayer is the only thing that's going to get us through this." Then, ready to get back to the business at hand, he said, "Well, you have friends of mine to pick up, right?"

"I will get them, Sir. You can count on it."

When Alex had left the room, Harry stood alone in the Duke's library, and held his Scotch glass up to the picture of the King. "As my last act of loyalty, I salute you, my King." Sir Harry gulped the bitter liquid, then put the crystal down and turned his eyes toward the heavens. "And to You, my new King, that will be last time I drink of that cup."

Chapter 38

Nassau, Bahamas

Sydney Albury had been watching Westbourne from a distance, waiting for Sir Harry to return. His men had been monitoring security measures, including comings and goings of Harry's service workers from grounds crew to cooks, searching for anything that could work to their advantage.

Freddy de Marigny had logged in and out of Westbourne several times to look for his father-in-law. His bar buddies believed he had a death threat out against Sir Harry for encouraging Nancy to leave their struggling marriage.

Trevor Sullivan was hiding out at Westbourne, taking advantage of its great walls, gates and security guards who patrolled the estate with their Rhodesian Ridgebacks, waiting for Sir Harry to return so he could talk some sense into his friend.

The bulk of the Bahamian Defense Force was preparing to deploy to Hog Island with a shoot-to-kill order in effect against Lubeck and his men. The locals had had enough of this outside meddling in their country and wanted to put an end to it in their own way.

Since Lubeck's call about a new place to stay, Salming and the Duke had ignored all Bahamian communication, immersing themselves in their own affairs, including dinner with the Mexican President, Manuel Avila Camacho, where they would discuss "Bracero" or temporary labor contracts for the proposed Hog Island Harbor project and possible bridge construction from Nassau City to the adjoining island. Anything to keep their minds off what was happening to their friend back home.

Reverend Green had slipped into a coma following an unexpected stroke.

Frankie Johnson, nursing his wounded arm at the hotel, had been informed that help was on the way–Animal, Diamond Jim, Hoggie, and Clutch would be arriving by Chalk's that night. Frankie couldn't wait to get another shot at Lubeck and this time the Kraut wouldn't walk away.

Lubeck and company were preparing their triple-cockpit Seabird motor craft for a venture of their own. They had repeatedly reviewed the intricate steps of the operation over the last few hours until, when darkness finally came, the men coordinated their watches and began their six-mile trip.

At the Mackey Street Citadel, Mae and Vaughn were summoned by two khaki-clad corporals and ushered to an awaiting vehicle. Captain Stubbs' demands to accompany them were unceremoniously refused, his protests filling the air as the vehicle hurried away.

Sir Harry heard the Duke's Bentley Mark IV pull up under the canopy and wondered what emotions would prevail when he saw the McIntoshes again. Though he was one of the world's richest men, and associated with some of the most influential individuals on the planet, this unlikely farming couple from rural Canada were two of the people he respected the most. Neither possessed an outstanding pedigree, especially Mae–a throw-away child who had, against all odds, landed solidly on her feet, and Vaughn had survived and matured into a man of great integrity despite life-changing incidents that would have turned many men cynical with life. Both had been forced to make the ultimate decision when it came to taking a life–something Harry had not been able to do with Lubeck when he'd had the chance. Maybe it was their resolve to do what was needed in a dire situation that was the basis for his great respect for them.

He glanced out the window as they approached the door and admired how distinguished they looked in their Army uniforms–and thought about how differently they approached life. Harry wanted to mold a world in which he controlled everything around him, but lately, what used to please him gave him very little satisfaction. The McIntoshes, on the other hand, gave up their personal desires to be controlled by something they felt was bigger than this world, and that seemed to give them peace. He didn't fully comprehend that attitude, but he appreciated it.

The door to the library was open so Harry could hear Mae and Vaughn coming down the hallway, and as they entered the room he realized how happy he was that they were here. The time and distance that had separated them dissolved as Harry reached out to embrace Mae. In return, she hugged Sir Harry like a long-lost daughter clinging to her loving father, but she could feel something different about this man. Was he more comfortable being on his own turf… or was he exhausted after the Christ's Church incident? She wasn't sure until he released her and she looked into his deep brown eyes. There she saw a softening of his soul.

Vaughn had been standing alongside Alex who watched this unexpected display of affection with mixed emotions. He didn't know the whole story about what had happened in Ontario, but he was aware of Harry's close relationship with Mae's mother, Harriet, and determined that this young woman was like another daughter to his boss. He relaxed just a bit knowing that Sir Harry was no longer fighting this battle alone.

As Alex stepped back to close the door, Harry released Mae and with an arm still around her waist, extended his hand to the other young McIntosh. "I'm very glad to see you both, but what are you doing here? I told you to stay away for your own good, and especially now that things are out of control. I appreciate the visit, but I can't guarantee your safety and you should get back on that plane and leave as soon as possible."

"Sir Harry, we know what you said, but circumstances have changed," Mae began. "We're here on behalf of Montagu Norman who asked for our help. It seems that everyone and his brother knows about you and the gold, and they all want it–the Amschel is ready to kill you to get it. The British feel they have first rights – I don't know about that, but to be honest, we don't care who gets it as long as it isn't the Amschel. Montagu Norman asked us to come here and convince you to get out of here with your life so you can let them know where it's hidden. So, will you please come with us back to Canada right now?"

Harry couldn't help but smile. This was quite a speech for the usually reserved Mae McIntosh. "Mae, and Vaughn, I am so grateful for your concern for my safety, but surely you realize that Lubeck will not stop coming after me, even if I leave here. I don't care about the gold for myself, either. All I care about at this point is stopping Lubeck, and the Amschel, from getting it–and that needs to happen right here, right now." He paused and looked at the two of them. "So, rather than any of us leaving, and since you're already here, I could use your help with a plan Alex and I have been working on since I returned from Canada. Will you help me?"

Mae looked at Vaughn, and an understanding passed between them. They could tell Harry wasn't going to budge, and he was obviously right about the Amschel. They wouldn't give up even if Harry left with them now. Phalyn had been right. There was going to have to be a showdown. "Of course we'll help, Harry, but can you tell us where the gold is? If we can give Sir Norman that, he can throw the resources of the King our way to help."

"Hmm. That's not part of my plan, but let me think about it. I have to leave you now for a time to make some preparations, so stay close to Alex till I see you again. He knows what to do and will bring you to me soon."

They looked at each other. "Where are you going?"

"To Westbourne, of course."

Chapter 39

Nassau, Bahamas

The night turned darker as clouds rolled in to smother the usually radiant full summer moon, driven by a surging breeze – the harbinger of an impending thunder storm. The approaching weather was affecting the birds and animals in and around Westbourne. Gulls on the beach were flying lower or hunkering down along the dock, and throughout the compound the guard dogs were yelping and barking incessantly, as if an enemy was about to storm the gates. All seemed to be keeping vigil for something ominous coming from the west.

These were all forecasters of natural phenomena, but the perfect storm about to descend on Westbourne was a mix of both natural and human forces. The only thing missing was Sir Harry Oakes, and he was just two minutes away rounding Goodman's Bay. Like most men his age, Sir Harry could feel weather changes in his bones. His left shoulder and elbow were aching more than usual and he could feel the beginnings of a migraine coming on. It was obvious something ominous was on its way.

His safe haven was in sight as the drab olive Austin 10 Cambridge was cleared through the entrance to Westbourne. Once inside the gates, Sir Harry was ushered to his front door by the British Regulars who had accompanied him from town along with an overly-noisy Rhodesian Ridgeback. This vigilance was indeed re-assuring to Harry.

Once inside, he hurried up the front staircase to his bedroom, and had just closed the door when he heard a voice in the next room. He was supposed to be alone in the house, so he reached for his service revolver and held it steady and level as he headed toward the door to the guest room, but lowered it when he realized he recognized the voice. "Trevor! So this is where you've been hiding!"

"Harry…you made it back – finally! I haven't been hiding, exactly. After all the nonsense at Christ's Church, Reverend Green and I ended up at police headquarters for a while answering questions, but the Reverend wasn't feeling well and they offered to take us both home. I wanted to come here to check on you, and when you didn't show up decided to hang around to be sure you were OK. Where have you been?"

"Government House – seemed like the safest place at the time. This is serious, Trevor. Lubeck will not stop until I'm dead. I'm only here to get some things and meet some people."

"A meeting? With who? Everybody we know is off-island."

"Not that it's really any of your business, but Alex is bringing a young couple who were at the church during that horrible business. I need to talk to them."

"Do you mean the Salvationists? You picked a heck of a time to get religion."

"Well, again, it really doesn't concern you, but I can use all the prayers I can get at this stage. Besides, that's not the only business I have to do with them."

"At a time like this you want to be a do-gooder? Harry, there are much more important things for you to worry about–like preparing for Lubeck, not to mention that crazy man, Albury."

"Don't worry, I haven't forgotten. But I just need a little bit of normalcy in the middle of all this craziness. Besides, we're probably safer here right now anyway."

"What do you mean 'safer here'? Is there something you're not telling me?"

Harry looked at Trevor, deciding if he thought he could trust him. "Trevor, the BDF is planning to assault Lubeck's base of operations on Hog Island in a few hours."

"Lubeck on Hog Island? He's far gone from that place."

Sullivan's response was so quick and sure that Sir Harry sensed something awry. He approached his friend pointing an aggressive finger at his chest. "How do you know that, Trevor? It's my turn now, what are you not telling me? What do you know?"

Trevor, realizing he had slipped, sidestepped the question. "I was talking to Frankie Johnson last week in Miami. His guys were sent here to protect you from Lubeck!" He explained Lubeck's plan to stage a coup with Harry's banking, trust and real estate boards if Harry rejected his proposed offer. "Whatever Lubeck wants from you is far past the negotiating stage, but the Mafia wants a piece of the action, too. They don't care about you, Harry. All they want is your secret, and then they'll try to do you in as well."

Harry didn't take his eyes off his friend. "And what do you want, Trevor? Seems like you've been working all sides against me. You were the first one who met Lubeck–on your own and then brought the Duke and Axel in on it. You fool around with the Miami Mafia… you made deals with American companies behind my back–deals that caused the riots, by the way. Seems like lately I'm only your friend when I can pull you out of messes you create."

Sullivan stepped nervously from foot to foot, rubbing the back of his neck while searching the air for an answer. "The world is coming to our paradise, Harry, and there's nothing we can do to stop it. We can get on board the gravy train and be part of it or be bowled over when it comes."

"You wouldn't be where you are today if it weren't for me," Harry was quick to point out. "I breathed life into this country when it was just salt water brine. I trusted you and now I see you playing both sides off the center…" Then Harry had a deeper revelation. "You're here to keep an eye on me, aren't you? Why? What's going to happen tonight… Judas?"

"Harry, that's ridiculous! I'm just here to help you – I'll stay all night if you want. Lubeck, the Mafia, or even that Albury kid – none of them can separate me from you."

Sir Harry knew what was in Trevor's heart and felt pity for him. "Really… you'll stay with me till the morning?"

"Of course, Harry. We're friends."

"No, Trevor, it's done. I don't know the role you're playing in this tonight, but now I'm telling you what you're going to do. You're going to go from here – now." Harry looked at his hand that still held his gun. "The only thing keeping me from pointing this gun at you right now is our past friendship. So, if you want to survive this, leave now – get off Westbourne and never come back. The storm is almost here. Go!"

The wind was kicking up and Harry noticed the lights of the Duke's Bentley pulling up in front. He needed Trevor out of here before the others arrived.

"I'll go, Harry, but I will be back. You may think this is over, but it isn't." He headed toward the door as Harry called the guard house to alert his men that Mr. Sullivan should be escorted through the gate.

Chapter 40

Nassau, Bahamas

Harry was relieved when Alex delivered the McIntoshes to his library. He had feared they would be delayed since road washouts were common during storms, and he knew they didn't have a lot of time to set his plan in motion. He was also aware he was welcoming wonderful friends to his home for the first time. When they walked through the door with Alex, he tried to put on a sincere smile. "Well… it isn't the wonderful atmosphere of the Wyoming station, but welcome to Westbourne! I would be honored for you to consider it home!"

Between Government House and now Westbourne, things were a little over the top for the small town McIntoshes, but Mae gave him a heartfelt response, "Anywhere we can be with you, Harry, is like home for us."

While Vaughn and Mae were settling into their chairs, Harry led Alex back to the door, whispering something to him along the way. Alex pointed to the two glass-plated maps on the wall then quickly left the room and Harry returned to his guests.

"Cat Island is where Lubeck must go for the gold. Since it's Alex's home island, he knows every nook and cranny of that place, and there's plenty of lore and history there to attract treasure hunters – and to convince Lubeck. Some say it's where Columbus first landed, but we're sure Blackbeard and Arthur Catt made frequent stops on the island. The Spaniards lost plenty of ships in and around the shoals. Put them all together and you have enough tales of lost doubloons and ghostly plantations to lure someone like Lubeck there. Supposedly the deep caverns, inland lakes and sink holes hold hidden treasure and restless spirits who protect the loot. Most pass it off as tom foolery, which is what Hans Lubeck thought when we discussed the subject in this very room."

Alex returned to the room and gave a thumbs up to Sir Harry.

"That is until Alex over there showed him what he might find on Cat Island." Alex and Sir Harry shared a wry smile remembering their encounter with Lubeck, then Harry turned and faced the couple.

"Lubeck needs to reconsider Cat Island for the gold and lead his men there. Whatever treasure they find, if any, they can have…but… here's the trick: it won't stop Mr. Montague Norman from having his gold."

"How is that possible? Have you split the gold up?" Vaughn and Mae were thoroughly confused by his vagueness.

Harry sat down across from them and looked them both in the eye. "I know you are people of faith. You trust that God has your best interests at heart. I'm asking that you have that kind of faith in me and our plan. You being here is no accident. Since you arrived, I revised my original plan and have now built it around you. Will you trust me and Alex, and do this for me as your friend?"

"What role are you going to play in all this, Sir Harry?" Vaughn wanted to know.

"I'm afraid that is where your faith begins. Alex, show them the box, please."

Alex reached into the white cabinet and pulled out the same Acacia box that Lubeck had been given, and placed it on the end table beside Mae. "I want you to take this box with you when you go back to the Citadel tonight. This is very important–do not open it or touch anything on the inside! If you do, harm will come to you. You will learn the rest soon enough." Harry paused and studied them again. "You haven't told me yet if you can trust me and I need a definite answer to that."

Vaughn looked at Mae and then back at Harry. "I honestly thought it was more of a rhetorical question that didn't require an answer. Sir Harry, we put our lives in your hands once before and have absolutely no qualms about doing it again now. Of course we'll trust you and do anything we can to help."

Harry nodded, but then added. "Give me your word that you'll do as I ask regarding the box."

This time Vaughn answered for them. "Of course, you have my word."

Harry looked toward the window. "It's starting to rain harder now, so you should probably get back to the Citadel while you still can. I'm sorry I can't let you stay here at Westbourne, but under the circumstances, we don't want anyone to know of our relationship – and I'll feel you're safer under Captain Stubbs' watchful eye. Alex will take you now."

A tear came to Mae's eye and she rushed to embrace her friend. "I don't have a good feeling about this, Harry. What are you going to do?"

"Nonsense, Mae. I'll be fine." A crack of thunder caused the windows to rattle. "Go now, both of you. We'll see each other again soon, I promise you."

Vaughn gently pulled Mae from Sir Harry's side, and they followed Alex to the waiting car. The crushed corral in the driveway scattered as he sped to the exit gate, double-checking as he went that the guards and dogs were still in place, despite the storm. Alex hoped that nobody would attempt to invade Westbourne under these conditions, but he, too, had an ominous feeling about this night.

Unfortunately, he and Mae would have known their feelings were right if they had seen what was silently gliding up to the Westbourne dock–and what was moving through the bushes across from the Westbourne entrance. The evil that had demonstrated itself at Christ's Church just a few nights previously was closing in on Sir Harry as the dark skies poured out its heavy rain.

Harry closed the blinds in his study and took the maps of the Bahamas from the wall and carried them upstairs to his room. As he passed the guest room he noticed a light had been left on in the window. Apparently Trevor had been planning on remaining at Westbourne, but that was before Harry had discovered he was a traitor. Harry turned off the light and, closing the door behind him, moved on down the hallway to his own room.

He could still hear activity downstairs and assumed it was his night crew battening down the hatches now that his guests were gone. The maid was being extra diligent this evening, Harry thought to himself, as he heard the French doors of the library clicking into place. Looking out of his bedroom window he could see the reflection of the sitting room, dining room, and hallway lights being sequentially turned off, the usual practice of the maid heading to her quarters. Listening between thunderclaps, he could hear the occasional barking of the dogs, so was reassured that everything was as it should be, and he began to get ready for bed. He was looking forward to sleeping in his own room again but missed Eunice being there. No matter. This business would be over soon and his family could come back home and things would get back to normal.

As Sir Harry buttoned his night shirt he glanced out the window and thought he saw a ghostly silhouette moving from the beach house towards the mansion, but decided it was his eyes playing tricks on him through the rain. Then there was some intense barking that reminded Harry the security detail was making their rounds, even in the heavy weather, and he relaxed a bit more.

The silk sheets had a fresh ocean fragrance that the maid knew Sir Harry liked. He moved to the center of the bed and propped several pillows behind his head and shoulders, then reached over and extinguished the lamp. It felt good to close his eyes and drift off to sleep to the beat of the rain against his window.

But just as Harry was about to nod off, his eyes flew open – there was someone in his room. Quietly moving to the far side of the bed, he reached for the revolver in the night stand, then remembered he'd left the gun in his study. His only chance was escape, so he silently slid out of bed, and balancing himself against the Chinese screen, he vaulted for the bedroom door as a bolt of lightning illuminated the room.

The last words that came from his mouth as he saw his assailant were simple, "It is finished." Harry felt a thud on the side of his head and all went black.

Chapter 41

Backlash

❦

Nassau, Bahamas

The largest armored clash of World War II was raging around the Soviet regions of Kursk and Pokrovska, with a staggering 200,000 lives lost in a monumental slugfest that drove the Germans back to the Homeland. Operation Husky had also begun–the American and British invasion of Sicily with an additional sacrifice of 30,000 allied soldiers... but in Nassau, Bahamas, the only talk was about one man's life–Sir Harry Oakes.

The morning after their fight, Trevor Sullivan discovered Sir Harry's body in a most macabre state.

The body of the Patriarch of the Bahamas was lying on his back on top of the bed sheets; his body had been doused with gasoline and set on fire, with one of his bed pillows ripped open and the feathers spread around him in a ritualistic style. If not for the rain that drenched the room through the totally broken bedroom windows beside the bed, the body would have been completely charred.

Unofficial reports from a myriad of officials suggested that, because of the excessive blistering of the skin, Sir Harry had still been alive when his body was set on fire. Subsequent cable reports circulated around the world confirmed that an autopsy revealed he had received triangular-shaped wounds to the back of the head indicating that the murder weapon was a blunt object with a defined edge. Blood stains across his face indicated that Sir Harry must have been face down for some time during the night.

The Duke of Windsor returned to Nassau when he heard about Sir Harry's death, and immediately activated the War Measures Act giving himself the power to do whatever he felt was necessary. As was his prerogative to do, but rather ill-advised and unpopular, he ignored the Bahamian Defense Department and Scotland Yard, and instead hired a pair of American Private Investigators to take charge of the inquiry.

The prime suspect was Sydney Albury, who had basically disappeared into thin air, and despite the efforts of the BDF on Hog Island, Lubeck and his men were also totally off the radar. Sullivan was questioned, but on the orders of the Duke of Windsor, was ruled out as a person of interest. The only other obvious suspect was Harry's son-in-law, Freddie de Marigny. His tirades and threats on Harry's life were well known in Nassau social circles, and could lead to his possible indictment, especially if he had no alibi for the night. At this point, officials had no other clear suspect, so only time would tell who would be charged for Sir Harry's murder.

Mae and Vaughn were horrified by the news. The fact that they had been with Harry such a short time before his death, and the grisly way the deed was carried out, made it so much worse. Their hearts went out to Harry's wife and children, but they knew George Beall and Harriet would be devastated as well. It was a somber day for all.

Alex Ferguson had spent the night at Government House when he returned the Bentley after delivering the McIntoshes back to the Citadel. The weather had been just too ominous for him to venture back on the roads to Westbourne, and as it turned out, that just might have saved his life. Now he was at the Citadel with Mae and Vaughn, sharing his grief with the only other people he knew who had loved Harry as much as he did. As they were finishing their tea, Jeremiah joined them.

"I really don't have any concrete news about Sir Harry's killer," Alex told them. "The whole inquest is a mess. I heard that at first the Governor was going to call it a suicide, but he obviously wasn't thinking straight, and for him to ignore our own police force and call in outsiders is mind-boggling."

"I've been asking around," Jeremiah said, "and nobody knows where Albury is–and now two of the night watchmen from Westbourne are also missing."

"They say Sullivan had guests in and out of Westbourne all day long, but nobody saw anything strange. Guess they all left before Harry got there. Considering all that went on that night, you'd think someone would know something!" Alex disappeared inside himself for a moment, then slowly added, "According to the maids, when Sullivan found him, he thought Sir Harry was still alive. Even propped him up and tried to force-feed him some water. Can you believe it?"

"No, I can't even begin to imagine. Alex, do you think it was Albury – the feathers and all?" Vaughn asked.

"I don't know. It's anyone's guess right now. It's also amazing that the maids said they heard nothing at all during the night – nothing–and then they were allowed to run in and out of the room in the morning. Heaven only knows what they did then.

"I walked to the beachfront this morning with one of the security guards to check out the dock area. He said Sullivan was in the bathhouse for a long time last night – he must have come back after I made sure he was off the grounds. One of the dogs nearly got away from the handler to attack him thinking he was a prowler. And then, the guard told me, when he wanted to inspect the house and dock, Sullivan got really angry and ordered him to take the dog and get lost. Seems pretty suspicious to me."

"As long as I've known Trevor Sullivan," Jeremiah added, "he's always tried to cover things up."

Hector appeared and pulled Captain Stubbs to handle a mini-crisis in the kitchen, giving Alex a chance to address the more pressing issue with just Vaughn and Mae. "Even though Sir Harry is gone, we have a job to finish. I trust you still have the Acacia Box."

Vaughn nodded.

"And you haven't opened it?"

"Of course not! We had very firm instructions."

"That's good, Captain McIntosh. Your innocence from knowing what's inside could be your grace card."

"We are definitely in this now, Alex. We put our trust in Sir Harry–and now in you. Don't you think it's time to let us in on just a little of what we should expect?"

"I appreciate the trust, and… you're right. You do need to know more." He paused to gather his thoughts, then began. "Let me start by saying I'm certain it was Lubeck who killed Harry, and I believe Trevor Sullivan was his accomplice. When I checked the library at Westbourne this morning, the map of Cat Island had been taken out of its frame and the bookcase where the box had been kept was torn apart. Sullivan probably told Lubeck about our visit there last evening – he was the one who brought Lubeck to the island in the first place and introduced him to Sir Harry – I'm sure they're in this together. Everything else – the feathers, the burning–is a distraction. Sir Harry always said to go with the simplest answer, so I go with Lubeck being the one. I'm sure he figures one of us has the box, and he'll be coming for it and what's inside.

"Sir Harry asked you to trust him, so let's finish this. He was determined to get rid of the gold once and for all without anyone else being harmed, and he was willing to sacrifice his life to protect his family, me....and you."

"So are we supposed to just sit here and wait for Lubeck?" Mae wanted to know. "We know he isn't on Hog Island, so he could be anywhere!"

"No, we won't just sit here. I've booked you a flight to Arthur's Town on Cat Island for this afternoon – and take the box with you."

"So we're the mouse in the Cat-Island-and-mouse game? What happens when we get there?"

"There's an illegal gambling hall not far from the air terminal in Cat Cay called The Palace. Just walk in and give the box to the proprietor. That's all. Then, later tonight, you already have reservations on a flight to Miami from Cat Island–and you're done. Go home to Canada knowing that Sir Harry's plan will leave you in the clear forever."

"Sounds too simple…which means there's more to it than you're telling us. Is something else going to happen to us there? Shouldn't we know what to expect?"

"No. You're probably better off not knowing what to expect. Think of it as having the privilege of being used for a greater good, and know that your life is in someone else's hands. My best advice is just deliver the box and get out of there."

"Why aren't you coming with us? Cat Island is your home, after all?"

"I have to stay here. I promised Sir Harry I would do one more thing for him." They were all silent for a moment, then Alex had one final suggestion. "I think you should walk into the Palace in full uniform."

Vaughn snorted, "I entered a gambling hall once in full regalia and not only came out alive but ahead in life's game."

"Then draw on that experience and go for it. I have a feeling the Palace has something special waiting for you."

"Because of our uniforms?" Mae asked.

"No, because of your faith."

Chapter 42

Out-Island Illusion

Cat Island, Bahamas

M ae had spent her whole life living in a rural community where change came slowly and was met with much resistance, but since meeting Vaughn her life had seen nothing but change. She knew Vaughn wanted to put down roots, but it seemed ever since they got married that God had designs to either keep them apart or send them on missions that defied the very nature of life in sleepy old southwestern Ontario. Mae was just a simple farm girl who God had thrown into the worldly fray. She had thought she would live out her life serving the people of St. Marys, but surrendering herself to God's will in her life had certainly taken her on a different path. Now, here they were, winging their way to Cat Island, Bahamas, of all places. If nothing else, God also had a sense of humor.

Looking out the window, Mae could see the outline of the north end of the sixth largest island in the Bahamas. Stretching almost fifty miles in length, Cat Island was, at its widest point, 4 miles wide with most of its 900 inhabitants living in either the south or the north end of the land mass.

The beauty of the wavering blues and greens of the shimmering waters in the setting sun prompted Mae to utter a prayer of thanks for God's creation. Just before the sun disappeared behind the flat horizon, she had enough time to see large limestone bluffs outlining the shore, inland pools of blue water, and as far as the eye could see in the mid-section of the island, lush green forests. A strong westerly wind bounced the Dragon Rapide side to side causing Mae to feel nauseous on their final approach to Arthur's Town Port. Just as they were about to touch down, the engines revved and the nose of the bi-plane suddenly launched skyward again.

The pilot was quick to apologize, "Sorry folks, but a road crosses the airstrip and a couple of cars were coming into AT from the east. Not to worry, though. It's something we always watch for. We'll just take one more pass and then we can touch down. If you're here a while you'll find this end of Cat Island tends to be a little wild and untamed."

A passenger across the aisle from Mae laughed as if he'd seen this before. "Leas' dey not goats! Can't ever get goats ta move – we be up here all night," he said with a chuckle. The comment was met with grunts and groans of approval from other locals on the flight.

Then he turned to Mae. "Wha'chu doin' in da Cat, nice Missy gal?" Bones Deveaux asked, looking over her uniform from top to bottom.

Mae was uncomfortable with his unwelcome appraisal and attention, but did her best to be friendly. "We're here to deliver a message to some friends."

"Mebbe ah can help. Ah bin heah ma whole life. Who it be dat you want to see?"

Just then the plane touched down and bounced up again several times, not unlike a roller coaster ride, before starting a smooth taxi. Mae's air sickness had been with her throughout the entire flight and the rough landing hadn't helped a bit. She couldn't wait to get her feet on solid ground again.

Bones Deveaux wasn't ready to end their conversation yet, though. He stroked his curly grey chin whiskers and touched Mae on the shoulder. "So, where you an' your man be headin'?"

"We're going to a place near Bain Town – The Palace."

Bones raised his eyebrows. "Really, now? Dress' like dat?'

When Mae nodded, Bones loudly announced, "Dis fine couple is headed fo' da Palace!" causing the other passengers to erupt in hoots and laughter.

"You sure you have da right place?" Bones asked again.

"Yes, I'm sure. We're supposed to meet a man there."

A wizened old woman sitting behind Bones chimed in, "Der be lotsa men, but dey no good fo' uze."

Mae was already nervous about what they were doing here, and the reaction of these people made her worry that much more. Vaughn had been sitting quietly watching all this, but now touched Mae on the arm and put his finger to his lips so she would stop talking. He knew from experience you were better off listening more and speaking less. Mae got his point, so she smiled at Bones and sat back in her seat.

The pilot gunned his left engine and the plane spun around, coming to an abrupt stop in front of a one-room building with yellow walls and a red roof that glistened in the blazing island sunshine. The door slowly opened and a man came toward them, moving a couple of rusted bicycles aside before placing a step beneath the airplane door for the passengers.

The natives stayed seated allowing the beautiful couple to disembark first, and Mae and Vaughn decided that what had first appeared to them as prying, could very well just be a genuine desire by the locals to be friendly, so when Bones followed them toward the building, they weren't concerned until he suddenly stepped between them and took hold of the handles of their suitcases. Vaughn stopped and grabbed his arm. What was it with people here? Didn't anyone think to ask before intruding into another's personal space?

Bones looked at him in surprise. "Don't go in dere," he said, motioning toward the terminal. "Dey won't do right by you. I know a better person to take you to da Palace–my cousin. I help him out."

Against his better judgement, Vaughn nodded and released Bones' arm, taking hold of Mae's elbow as they followed the Bahamian past the clamor of several aggressive taxi locals to an impeccably clean and polished black Chrysler Crown Imperial limo.

The driver, decked out in black suit, spit-polished shoes, military cap and white gloves, stood beside the open passenger door. As they approached, Bones said, "It fits eight but jus' for you this time, so you have lotsa room. Mostly here for big rollers from da mainland."

From the corner of her eye Mae could see him looking her over again. "You be busy all weekend wi' dat outfit, I guarantee it." Mae looked at Vaughn, beginning to think this may not have been the smartest decision, and when the driver handed Bones some money, they had even more doubts.

As Bones danced away from the vehicle back toward the terminal, the driver said, "Bones works for the Palace, just like me. He usually meets up with the gamblers in Miami and Palm Beach and flies in with them, but this trip was mostly empty so he brought some of his family who work in Miami back with him – and you, of course." Then he gave Mae the same type of look she'd gotten from Bones. What were they getting themselves into?

Though the driver seemed pleasant enough, Vaughn couldn't shake the feeling they were walking into a really bad situation. Given the remote location of this island, he was pretty sure that whatever was going on here was escaping notice from any authorities and he was beginning to think Alex Ferguson may have set them up.

He loaded their bags into the trunk, and kept talking as he sat behind the wheel. "With the Americans building the New Bright airport on the south end of The Cat, the girls we fly over during the weekends are very welcome... but I guess you know that." He stared at Mae in the rear-view mirror. "Don't know what your cover story is, but you look like a pair of missionaries...highly creative. We don't usually get naturally pretty girls like you here, so you should score well for a few weeks."

When the realization of what the driver meant sunk in, Mae was shocked. She looked at Vaughn, expecting to see anger, but instead caught a twinkle in his eye that quickly infected her. After all they had been through recently, rather than taking offense, the absurdity of the driver's assumption took hold and their laughter was so uncontrollable he was embarrassed and shut the sliding panel between them–and kept it that way for the remainder of the ten-minute drive to Arthur's Town.

After a while, Mae thought Vaughn was enjoying the situation a little too much and nudged him in his always-tender ribs. It was no use. The laughter had breached the gates of carefully pent up emotions, and Vaughn wasn't able to stem the flood quite yet. He opened the side window to let the ocean breeze wash over his face, which seemed to help, and he began to calm down, but he couldn't help one last comment. "I'm just wondering now how I'm going to explain this on your final Cadet evaluation!" That comment earned him another painful poke to his side.

The limo began to slow, then stopped, and when they looked out the window any remaining laughter suddenly died. "There must be some mistake, Vaughn," Mae said fearfully. "Could this dive actually be the Palace?"

"Let's just play this by ear, Mae," Vaughn did his best to put on a brave front. "Just stay close to me and keep that box out of sight!"

A windowless, yellow-painted cement block structure stood in front of them with its roof outlined in blinking Christmas lights. Two large oil drums stood on either side of the open door with groups of men standing around each one, slamming dominos onto a make-shift flat cement tile.

As they took it all in, their driver said, "Pay them no mind. They are out here all day and night, playing games. Consider them part of the ambiance of the place. I think the person you want to see is inside."

Vaughn carried their suitcases while Mae clutched his arm with one hand and held the box close beneath her jacket with the other. Pushing their way through a black beaded door curtain, they slowly entered a room that was anything but a palace.

Directly in front were three very sweaty, very bare-chested older men telling stories to each other, a series of empty Bull Dog Stout bottles lined in front of them. Behind them on the wall was a hand-painted sign declaring them to be "Sir Arthur's Rake 'n' Scrape Band." As best as Mae could tell, the only instruments around were an accordion, a carpenter's utility hand saw, a butter knife and a goat-skin goombay drum. The trio paid no heed to the new arrivals.

To their left, several patrons appeared to have their elbows glued onto the L-shaped linoleum-topped bar. Two were nursing half-filled, suds-stained glass mugs while their companion had given in to gravity with his head resting on his folded arms. The bartender was a barrel-chested behemoth who shouted every time he opened his mouth, but it appeared everyone mostly ignored him anyway.

The assortment of bottles on shelves behind the bar were plentiful, in varied colors– green cameo, white porcelain, opaque blue; rusty brown – and shapes–glass pigs and penguins, deflated jugs, big-armed boxers, laced-up boots, laughing clowns – it was all too much for the teetotaler couple to comprehend.

On the back wall, a blinking red neon sign reading 'PALACE' hung above a large black metal door with the push bar wrapped in chains with locks on either end. Whatever was behind that door needed to be protected and most likely had something to do with gambling. Even though gaming of this kind was illegal in the Bahamas, joints like this would never be totally shut down, and Cat Island was far enough away from Nassau, and was so insignificant politically, that the Boys of Bay Street paid no mind to what went on here. On the other hand, it could simply be that the powers-that-be were getting a cut of the take. Whatever the explanation, there was never a shortage of customers for whatever game was available.

While Mae and Vaughn stood trying to work up the nerve to move further into the room, a nondescript door at the end of the bar opened and out walked a man with his left arm in a bone-colored sling. He smiled at the new, albeit out-of-their-realm, patrons and said, "He said you would come. I think it's time for us to have a sit-down. So, please follow me."

Mae gripped the box even tighter while Vaughn's luggage burden was relieved by two rather menacing compatriots who motioned for the Captain to follow his wife through the door. They passed through a half-empty liquor storage shed that turned out to be a passageway, through another door to a winding sandy trail to the beach. The fresh air was welcome and revived the Salvationists as they were encouraged along, with a few shoulder pushes, to follow the 'slinged' fellow to the wide open seashore where two other gargantuan men tended a colossal crackling bonfire. The heat was so intense that everyone had to stay a fair distance away, but they kept adding more dry driftwood that was instantly engulfed in the searing flames.

Then, in the brilliant firelight, Vaughn suddenly recognized the man from the night at Christ's Church. "You were at Christ's Church in Nassau. I heard about what happened to you. I hope your wound is healing and I'm sorry about the loss of your men. We were never introduced... I'm Captain Vaughn McIntosh and this is...."

"I know who you both are," Frankie said to Vaughn, and then turned to Mae. "I also know, Cadet McIntosh, you have something for me. So, without any more ado, I will take the box now."

Mae looked apprehensively at her husband, who nodded his approval, so she removed the box from inside her jacket and gave it to the closest guard. The thug sloughed through the coral sand and placed the cube firmly into Frankie's hands.

"Have you taken anything out of the box?" Frankie wanted to know.

"No, we were instructed not to open or touch anything inside," Vaughn said, stepping in front of Mae.

"That's good. Alex Ferguson said you were trustworthy."

This was one of Vaughn's worst fears. "What has Alex got to do with this?"

"Let's just say that when we talked, he was very cooperative. We know Sir Harry was hiding a big secret and our goal was to make sure that secret never ended up in the Kraut's hands."

"Since when do you care about Sir Harry?"

"We don't care about him! We only care about our future investments in the Bahamas. I think this box will go a long way to making those ventures become a reality."

"You're talking about gambling and casinos, right? Sir Harry always fought that."

"I know...ain't it ironic? Sir Harry is dead and here you are, giving me the key to the very thing he hated? And, judging by your outfits, it appears I have God's blessing, too." Adjusting the uncomfortable sling, Frankie Johnson gave his men the nod and they turned toward Mae and Vaughn. They pulled their guns, aiming them at the young couple, waiting for the final signal from Frankie.

Before anyone could move, though, a sudden collapse of the wood in the fire caused a fountain of sparks to burst into the sky causing enough of a distraction to grab everyone's attention, then repetitive pistol fire started from further down the beach. Bullets began ripping through the sand and whistling past their ears as the men scattered away from the fire into the darkness. Frankie was in a quandary—with only one free arm he couldn't hold the box and draw his weapon, so he ran with the others

Relying on his instincts, Vaughn tackled Mae to the ground, both of them staying as low as possible while bullets whistled by above them. When Frankie's men began returning fire toward their attackers, Vaughn knew he and Mae couldn't stay where they were. He whispered in her ear, then they jumped to their feet, zig-zaging across the sand away from the firing. They were stopped, though, by a flurry of bullets ripping into the ground in front of them, and for a second time, dove flat onto the sand. To Mae's amazement, she realized she had landed right on top of the Acacia box, and suddenly had an idea. With the sounds of war whistling around her, Mae did the unthinkable. She stood, presenting herself in full silhouette against the fire, and hurled the Acacia box into the raging flames!

Instead of causing the fighting to stop, Mae's action only increased each side's determination to rescue it from its fiery death before the other side could move in. Forgotten for the moment, Vaughn and Mae saw their opportunity and raced into the shadows—and never looked back. The sounds of gunfire receded as they ran inland with the moon giving them just enough light to stagger through the sand and beach grasses, but it wasn't long till the vegetation began to change and taller bushes and small trees drastically reduced their ability to see the path ahead. Vaughn was just about to give up when they stumbled upon a roofless, obviously abandoned, old stone house where they could rest for a while.

With nothing but the moon to illuminate their surroundings, they leaned against a wall to recover, just grateful to be alive.

"Mae, are you hurt anywhere?" Vaughn asked urgently.

"I can't really see anything," Mae answered haltingly, "but I don't think so. At least nothing big. My knees and knuckles are scraped up, and I'm exhausted, but nothing that really matters. How about you?"

"I seem to be fine," he told her, but something in her voice was concerning him. Vaughn moved closer and despite the warm Bahamian night, could tell Mae was shivering. He had seen soldiers in shock before and quickly put his jacket around her shoulders and briskly rubbed her arms. Mae was strong, and with her stubbornness, should bounce back quickly, but they couldn't stay here forever. He was sure either Frankie Johnson or Lubeck – or both – would be sending men to track them and he couldn't take a chance on being caught again.

With her mind slowly clearing, Mae had an ominous thought. "We were set up!" she said. "Meeting in front of a bonfire? And what does Alex have to do with all this? I'm assuming it was Lubeck's men who started the shooting but where did they come from? They were going to kill us!"

Vaughn was quick to agree. "Well, thanks to you we managed to get away, so they can fight each other all they want, but I'm afraid they won't let us get away without trying to catch us. I just wish we knew what was inside that box." Vaughn was truly amazed at the formidable warrior she had demonstrated herself to be in a time of great stress, and that increased his confidence that they might actually get out of this situation alive.

Mae had a sly smile on her face. "I don't have the box, but will this do?" So proud of herself, Mae pulled a sealed white envelope from inside her jacket and held it out to her husband. "I took this out of the box after Sir Harry died."

Vaughn was stunned. "But we swore not to open the box," he said.

"I know and I'm sorry, but that promise was to Sir Harry and he's gone. Besides, back at the fire they only asked you, not me, if the box had been opened, so I never lied to anyone about it. I only wish I could see their faces if they manage to get that box out of the fire and open it." Mae had proven once again that she was the more collected of the two, and reminded Vaughn of her capability. "You aren't the only one with good impulses–and you can put that down in your Cadet report, thank you very much! My intuition told me I needed to open that box, and I did."

"Oh, and one more thing," Mae said, reaching into another pocket. "I noticed these as we passed the bar at the Paradise and had a feeling they might come in handy, so I slipped it into my pocket. What do you think?" In the darkness she groped for Vaughn's hand and slid a box of wooden matches onto his palm. "Maybe we can find something to make a torch so we can see where we're going when we leave here."

Once again Vaughn was stunned at his wife's ingenuity, and poured out all the awe he felt for this amazing woman in a deep and lingering kiss. It was a stolen moment that gave both of them hope that their lives were still waiting for them when they got off this island.

"I have no words to tell you how wonderful you are," Vaughn stammered. "We need to keep going to get further away from here, but I was worried about going in the dark." He kissed her again. "Thank you."

"Don't thank me, thank the Lord. I'm sure He's the one who prompted me to pick those up, but if that's the way you show your appreciation, I'll take it any time!" she ended with a chuckle.

Vaughn lit a match and they saw their retreat for the first time. Numerous good-sized tree limbs were scattered across the floor, so Vaughn picked one up and wrapped a shredded curtain he pulled from a window around the end, then touched the flame to it. Within seconds they were ready to go.

"We need to get moving. I'm sure they're looking for us and it'll be easier for them to find us with this torch, but we'll just pray hard. I think I saw a path behind this building heading inland which seems to be the best thing to do right now." Mae agreed and Vaughn led the way.

It was rough going, even with the torch, as they trudged away from the deserted house. After a while the path started to climb as they left any remnants of the beach behind for more difficult terrain where the sand was replaced by clumpy dirt and outcrops of lichen-stained rocks. They were making decent time until suddenly in front of them rose a rocky granite wall. Vaughn searched in both directions but could find no way around, and they came to the realization it was either climb or turn back—which they both knew was not an option – so they made their plans for the climb.

The biggest issue for Mae was how she could maneuver in her long skirt, but between the two of them they figured out a way to hike the back through her legs to the front and secure it in her waist band. The other problem was the torch. Even if Vaughn could manage to carry it while he climbed, they realized the light would make them sitting ducks for anyone who might be in pursuit. So, reluctantly, Vaughn extinguished the flame and prayed the moonlight would be sufficient for the climb and they'd be able to find another sturdy branch when they reached the top. Then, after a heartfelt prayer for safety, they slowly began to make their way up the rock face using anything they could find for steps and handholds.

When they reached the top about half an hour later, they were rewarded for their tenacity. There before them was a large tree with several low-hanging, partially-detached limbs that were perfect for their purposes. This time Mae tore some strips from the hem of her slip to wrap around the end of the branch, and with a lit torch in their hands once more, they both felt proud of themselves for what they'd accomplished, and from this vantage point they could look out toward the ocean, over the ground they had covered.

Mae suddenly grabbed Vaughn's arm and said, "Is that a light I see down in the trees?"

Sure enough, as they stared into the distant darkness, they both saw a dim light bobbing along toward them. "You're right and they're not far behind us. We have to get off this cliff right now."

Vaughn lowered the torch so it was closer to the ground, and when he turned around to find an escape route, was stopped in his tracks. He slowly took a few steps forward, then said, "Mae... is that a cave?" In front of them was the mouth to a darkened cave, partially covered by foliage. "I'll check this out and if it's safe we can hunker down here till morning. It would be a lot easier to travel in the daylight."

"Sounds like a good idea, but I'm coming with you!" she announced, leaving no room for argument.

Vaughn's heart beat faster as they stepped into the opening, holding the torch as far out in front of him as he could with one hand and his other pressed firmly against the rough edges of the roof. Mae followed with her finger locked onto his belt. The air was more dank and heavy than the outside and after a few steps they could hear water dripping.

"I don't know how much further we should go. We may not be able to find our way back out again."

"I can hear some sort of whistling–like wind–up ahead, and I swear I can feel a slight breeze. Can you use the flame to make a mark on the wall – like Hansel and Gretel breadcrumbs – for us to follow back out?"

Vaughn agreed and they continued further, making their way slowly and stepping deliberately to avoid falling, when they were suddenly hit with a warm, dry gust of air that almost blew out the torch. It startled Mae who stumbled forward, pushing both of them to the cave floor and sending the burning torch flying. When Vaughn looked up, the torch was at the foot of what appeared to be a roughly-hewn staircase rising into the darkness in front of them. He picked up the torch and on hands and knees, with Mae close behind, climbed the few steps to a landing of sorts, where he discovered a chiseled opening about two feet in diameter.

Vaughn pushed the torch through the hole and put his face up to the opening. "There's a room in there, Mae!" he said excitedly, squeezing his whole body through the gap and then reaching back to help her through.

The air was fresh and pleasant, and they could hear dripping water. The floor where they stood was flat and smooth and they realized they could stand up straight. Mae stretched her arm over her head as far as she could reach and could not feel a ceiling, but the darkness was so impenetrable they couldn't see anything around them, and their torch that was burning lower by the minute. Mae moved closer to Vaughn's side and linked her arm with his. "Let's go slow, Vaughn. Who knows what might be out there in the dark."

Then, as they were deciding which direction to move first, a shaft of moonlight suddenly shone onto the cavern floor, startling them both. "Obviously there's an opening above us, so we must not be very far underground," Vaughn said, quietly thanking the Lord for the additional light that brightened the room enough for them to see more of their surroundings. They started to move out when Vaughn stopped in his tracks. "Someone was here before us." Against the far wall was a canvas tarpaulin covering something.

"What do you think it is?" Mae asked as they headed in that direction.

"I don't know, but we better find out fast. Our light is just about gone." Mae held the torch high while Vaughn slowly eased the canvas to one side. Two large wooden footlockers with metal stripping along the edges and corners sat in front of them.

"Do we dare look inside, Vaughn? They must belong to someone."

"Under normal circumstances I would say no, but desperate times call for desperate measures, and I feel the Lord has led us to them for our provision. Forgive me, Lord, if I'm wrong, but I'm going to open these boxes." He took hold of the leather handles on the first one and pulled it away from the wall, then undid the clasp and threw back the lid.

The wooden crate was lined inside with aluminum—no doubt to reduce the effects of humidity and water on its contents. The first thing Vaughn noticed was a tan box with black lettering, 'U.S. Field Ration K', but his attention was quickly drawn to two U.S. Navy yellow-topped, waterproof battle lanterns tucked in the other side of the box.

"Look what's here! If these work we won't need the torch," he said excitedly, lifting them from the box. When he flipped the switch on the first one, nothing happened, but when Mae tried the other, it blinked a few times then sent out a steady beam of light. She placed it gently on the ground and they both said, "Thank you, Lord," several times.

Mae started to take the torch from Vaughn, but he held onto it. "I'll rest easier if I go back out and cover the cave entrance with more brush. We know they're looking for us, and if they happen to make it up that cliff, I don't want them to spot the cave." Mae suggested he take the lantern and leave the torch with her, and she settled in to wait, but it wasn't long till she saw the light and heard Vaughn squeezing through the opening to their sanctuary again. "All taken care of, so now I can relax a bit more," he said, giving her a quick peck on the cheek, just as the torch sputtered and went out. "Looks like I got back just in time."

"You sure did," she said, turning to face the crate beside her. "It wasn't easy, but I decided to wait for you to finish looking through this box, so let's get to it." Vaughn chuckled as he reached into the crate for a second time. In one corner were two olive-green tin boxes with a red cross emblazoned on a white circle. Along the outer edges of the circle was printed, 'U.S. Army Medical Department', and at the top and bottom of each box were the words, 'First Aid – Jungle.' A quick look inside revealed insect repellent, atabrine tablets to treat malaria, salt tablets, a snake bite kit and sulfa to treat dysentery. Other compartments contained a tube of morphine, adhesive gauze bandages, iodine swab and a tightly-folded sleeve of aspirin. Vaughn put this aside for future consideration and returned to inspecting the K-rations.

He was very familiar with K-rations. Even though he had seen certain enlisted men up-chuck at the mere mention of eating these tasteless pre-made battle meals, he knew they were packaged to last and would stay edible for years as long as they were unopened. It wasn't his idea of a tasty meal, but since they hadn't eaten anything since yesterday morning, he decided to give them a try. He supposed Mae was also hungry so he laid out his findings in front of the lantern, beginning with peeling open the can of pork mystery meat with the sardine key. Meanwhile, Mae had selected the pressed graham cracker and malted milk tablets. They could split the fruit bar and would forego the Lucky Strike cigarettes in favor of some Wrigley's chewing gum. When a second pork loaf was found, Mae launched into it as well, to Vaughn's surprise.

They were both quiet as they worked their way through the most satisfying meal they'd had in a while. Mae finished off the last of a Hershey's chocolate bar while Vaughn searched for the source of the dripping they'd heard, hoping to find some fresh water for them to drink. When he finally spotted it filtering through small fissures in the rocks, he used one of the empty tins to catch it. He was counting on their recent bout with island belly to now pay dividends by making them immune to any impurities that might be in this water so they could drink and not be affected. God can work even the most awful things to the good, he thought, and hopefully that will be the case this time.

Of all the treasures they'd found in the footlocker, they discovered the most valuable last. From the bottom of the box Mae pulled a brown paper packet with a dozen individual layers of toilet paper! They were pleased to see they hadn't left all of civilization behind.

Mae and Vaughn were anxious to open the envelope from the Acacia Box and see what secret had been hidden there, but after having something to eat, and being in a relatively safe environment, exhaustion was setting in. The events of the past day, and their weakened physical state from the recent illness, had left them neither the will or the energy to do anything else. They agreed to try and get some sleep and get a fresh start in the morning. It took only a moment after the lantern was extinguished for both of them to be sound asleep.

Chapter 43

Cat Island, Bahamas

Frankie Johnson was livid. Not only had the McIntoshes escaped, but the Acacia box had been burned as well. That bonfire was supposed to be the Salvationists cremation furnace, it seemed a fitting way for them to join their friend, Harry Oakes, but now he didn't have anything–not them or the box! His instincts told him it was Lubeck and his men who were responsible for this fiasco. This was the second time that Kraut had gotten the best of him and he was done playing games.

The only way the Argentinean could have made it to Cat Island undetected was by private boat, and Salming's yacht that had been moored at Lyford Cay was the most likely vessel. He also guessed it was Trevor Sullivan who had tipped them off that the McIntoshes were on their way to Cat Island. He had never really trusted Sullivan, but especially now. Frankie had no way of knowing what else Lubeck knew, but he was taking no more chances. In the next few hours, his men – at least the ones who weren't out looking for those do-gooders who had escaped–would be on the lookout for that yacht.

He figured the best way to find the boat's location was from the air, but a dangerous storm was forecast near the Turks and Cacaos Islands and was supposedly rumbling its way northward toward the Bahamas, which meant there would be no flying today, so he would have to come up with another plan.

The whereabouts of the McIntoshes was also a huge concern. His local contacts had assured him if they tried to use the only passable road in the south from Arthur's Town to Port Hope they'd be spotted right away – not necessarily because of their light skin, but because of those silly uniforms – so they'd most likely travel overland, but that would be a fifty-mile trek that would challenge their survival skills.

If they stayed close to the shore, they would face danger from any variety of threatening fish, and sometimes even sharks, that inhabited the tidal pools, even at low tide, not to mention being exposed to the relentless hot sun on the beach. Frankie didn't think they would risk that, so he decided their inclination would be to move further inland, which presented its own set of challenges.

The forest was thick and the high rocks unforgiving. Moving south along the spine of the island they would encounter rock walls, underwater caverns and hidden sink holes that, over the years, had consumed human and beast alike. Someone else had told him about colonies of funnel-eared rat-bats that congregated in small groups in caves during the daytime and came out to feast on insects at night. To the native Bahamian they were mostly just a nuisance, but they also knew when bad weather hit, or during breeding season, there could be thousands in a swarm and nobody wanted to stumble into that.

As Frankie thought through this he realized the McIntoshes had escaped with nothing but the clothes on their backs—no food, no water, no weapons – so they didn't really stand much of a chance. He slapped his neck as he felt a pin-prick... ah, yes, he almost forgot about the mosquitoes and the sand and black flies.

Yeah, they probably weren't going to make it, but despite the deck being stacked against Vaughn and Mae, Frankie was not taking anything or anyone for granted anymore. There was something special about this couple that was beyond him. The last time he saw them, they were as compliant and meek as sheep, and when bullets started flying they ran across the beach like a pair of startled hermit crabs. They are Salvation Army, for crying out loud, he thought, shaking his head in disbelief. Getting rid of them should have been like taking lambs to the slaughter.

And, what if they knew Harry Oakes' secret? Frankie had everything to gain by going after those two. If nothing else, his curiosity about the full story behind this pair of Bible-thumpers was enough to keep him going. His search party was working from Grape and Flamingo Points in the north toward Alligator Point and Pigeon Cay. He felt sure it was just a matter of time before they would re-capture of them. The island was not that big. What he would do with them once they were caught was the true question. One thing was for sure, he had to beat Lubeck to the punch, and with his plan to use a plane to locate him now grounded, the Argentinean would once again have the element of surprise.

Frankie smiled to himself because he had a secret weapon–Bones Deveaux–who knew every inch of this island. It was time to turn the tables and show Herr Lubeck how a Bahamian surprise was really served up.

———❦———

Hans Lubeck had no respect for the Bahamian way of life. His Aryan background had given him a sense of cultural superiority that fed his Amschel agenda. Here he was, still undetected in the heart of the country after the death of its number one citizen. He had also absconded with the *Southern Cross* and no authorities had even bothered to check on him. In his eyes, these people did not deserve the beauty of the islands, and any prosperity here had happened in spite of the natives.

Lubeck thought that all in all Harry Oakes had been a worthy adversary. Sir Harry had had a chance to kill him, but showed his humanity by allowing Lubeck to live. That, in Lubeck's opinion, was his biggest mistake, but calling his bluff about hiding the gold on Cat Island was masterful gamesmanship. Then, bringing the McIntoshes into the fray was a good move and might have worked if Lubeck hadn't done his research.

He had discovered they were the ones who had bested Picard in Canada in the first place, so once they were on his radar, their effectiveness here was neutralized, but using religious pawns to try and outmaneuver him at his own game was a fascinating play by Sir Harry. There were a few other things, though, that Lubeck was getting tired of dealing with.

First, Frankie Johnson had not taken his advice to leave the islands and stay out of the way–even after he spared the mobster's life. Those irritating hoodlums had to go once and for all. Lubeck had been ready to separate the McIntoshes from the Mafia last night, but somebody, he didn't know who, had beaten him to the punch. It looked like Johnson had a mutiny on his hands and didn't even know it.

It was either that or the McIntoshes were truly the most resourceful people he had ever seen, and since they had been smart enough to pull the wool over Picard's eyes, Lubeck didn't want to underestimate them. In fact, he was looking forward to meeting them. He had no idea what they were doing here, or just how cunning and resourceful they might be, but he was determined that what happened to Picard was not going to happen to him. And after he met them, he was going to take great pleasure in dealing the Salvationists a very slow death. And once he had the gold and they were out of the way he could enjoy his ascendancy to Amschel leadership.

Then, when all those obstacles were behind him, the *Southern Cross* would be perfect to transport the gold. It might take a couple of trips, but he didn't mind since he was totally enjoying being on the water again. He missed his Kriegsmarine days and the adventure of chasing down and destroying allied convoy shipping. He chuckled to think how there really was little difference between a good nautical hunt and chasing down Johnson and the McIntoshes. He would pick off the escorts one by one, and when they were fully vulnerable, he would rush in for the plunder and kill.

He also congratulated himself on the brilliance of providing the false weather report regarding an impending storm that prompted Port Arthur authorities to ground all planes. He had figured that would be Johnson's first plan for tracking him, but the added advantage was that it forced Frankie into rushing to find the McIntoshes. Everyone knew that a hurried reaction usually led to improper preparation and that's what Lubeck was counting on.

The *Southern Cross* was safe in its harbor south of Pigeon Cay, the point from which his men would head north in search of the Salvationists. Predictably, Frankie would pursue them starting from the north. It was inevitable this pincher strategy should flush the quarry out once and for all. He would personally keep his distance and stay out of sight until the gold was found, and then would deliver a little Amschel bombshell.

Chapter 44

Cat Island, Bahamas

As the morning sun seeped through the fissures in the cave roof, Vaughn began to stir. Although there was enough light to get a general picture of their surroundings, the far side where the remaining crate waited was still dark. He was surprised to have rested as well as he had considering the hard rock upon which they had slept. That, along with the sound of trickling water and the constant flapping of birds' wings, should have kept them awake, but the emotional and physical exhaustion they both experienced had caused them to sleep soundly.

Vaughn was reminded of Matthew 6:26: "Look at the birds of the air, for they neither sow nor reap nor gather into the barns; yet your Heavenly Father feeds them. Are you not more valuable than they?" He meditated on the Lord's continued protection until his rumbling stomach distracted him and he looked down at Mae who was still asleep on his coat with her head on his lap. His legs and back were cramped from sitting on the cold rock all night, but he didn't have the nerve to wake his wife just yet.

As she lay there, Vaughn pulled a strand of her black hair back behind her ear. Even in this paltry light, he could see she was indeed wonderfully made. God had given him a great partner, and for some reason, this morning she seemed even more beautiful than usual – almost glowing – and he stretched his tight muscles to give her a gentle kiss on the cheek. The reality of the challenges that were ahead of them was on his mind, but he wanted to extend this special moment as long as he could. He had no idea when, or if, they would ever share this type of personal solitude again.

The cramping in his legs finally got the best of him, though, and he gently slid from underneath his wife's resting body. Grabbing the lantern, he focused the beam on the far crate and saw something he had missed before. On the side of the tarpaulin was black lettering, "U.S. Weather…". He knew that by bolstering the ports of the Caribbean islands, the British and Americans had curtailed much of the early successes of the U-boats. This had included dredging for safe harbors, placing mines in the ports and using radar for detecting U-boats when they surfaced at night to recharge their electric engines. Vaughn felt certain this box had played a part in the strategy of improving communications between spotters on the ground and patrolling aircraft, a key piece in the battle against the wolf-packs.

Mae awoke to the sound of Vaughn examining the second crate, and slowly worked on getting her bearings. She pulled Vaughn's jacket around her shoulders as she sat up, and spent the next few minutes just enjoying watching her husband. His dirty blond hair hung in clumps over his forehead and his cheeks were smudged. The neck of his once-white shirt was open and she smiled to see his sleeves rolled almost to his elbows. His dark blue trousers were caked with mud as he knelt beside the crate, mumbling as he foraged.

Mae spoke softly, not wanting to break the spell. "Good morning, my dearest, do you want two eggs and bacon to start the day?"

Vaughn turned to her and smiled. "Yes, that would be lovely. Could you bring it to me in bed, I'm feeling a bit off this morning."

Mae chuckled. This was the first morning since coming to the Bahamas they had been truly alone, although the accommodations left something to be desired. If nothing else, they could create a memory they might be able to appreciate and share with others one day. She emptied sand from her shoes before putting them on and then stood, dusting off Vaughn's jacket and giving it a shake. Out of the corner of her eye she thought she saw the ceiling move, but quickly dismissed it. The low light was obviously playing tricks on her eyes.

She always started her mornings off with a devotion, so she searched her heart and what came to mind was the time David spent in the caves hiding from Saul. Despite what lay ahead of them today, she had a joy in her heart feeling she was as valuable to God as the then-fugitive David had been. She could only remember bits and pieces of Psalm 57: "I thought I was dead and done for… but, I am hiding out under your wings… I call to the God who holds me together... I am ready God, so ready from head to toe. I am thanking you God...I am singing your praises. ...their teeth are lances and arrows and sharp daggers... but your love is your faithfulness..." With a renewed vigor, Mae was ready to take on the day.

"Vaughn, I can't wait any longer! Let's see what's in this envelope." Mae cried, waving the envelope from the Acacia box in front of him.

"Can you wait till I find us something to eat?" he asked, although he already knew the answer.

"No." was her reply, and he heard the heavy paper tearing. "We have to find out what plan Sir Harry had in mind if we're going to get rid of the Amschel for good!" They stood together in the light of the lantern as Mae pulled out a folded canvas. The handwriting was difficult to decipher so she held it closer to the light. "Vaughn, look at this."

Vaughn recognized the chalky cloth as a hand-painted map of the Bahamian Islands, with a version of Cat Island in one corner–the map that had been on the wall of Sir Harry's library. Mae picked it up, turning it in different directions, then she flipped it over and spread it out on the crate. This was also Cat Island, but an enlarged version of the Port Arthur area. "This is Port Arthur and if I follow along Port Royal beach, where we were last night, I think we must be somewhere in the Orange Creek area," Mae said, pointing out the landmarks.

Vaughn stepped closer and moved the lantern so he could see the rest of the map. "What is that writing beside that blue splotch that looks like a lake?"

"It's labeled 'OBEAH'S MAW,' Mae said, adjusting the hemp cloth to read the text:

"Queen Obeah has found her home
None survive here where they roam.
She churns and chews two times a day
And swallows all who tred her way.
But once a day, she rests and shows
Her open maw only to expose
A path straight to her heart.
Enter in to find her soul
Dark, and yet glimmers of gold

Leave her bowels before she screams
If not, Obeah takes all a-seen."

"I don't like this," Mae said. "It reminds me of Albury's group that attacked Christ's Church. They were mostly from Cat Island. I'm afraid this is their Voodoo complete with an evil Queen, Obeah."

Vaughn continued to study the canvas. "So, judging from this map, it appears we are to head south to this particular large cavern… complete with its own menacing queen. If this is where Harry hid the gold, I can see why he wasn't worried about the superstitious locals finding it."

"Sir Harry and Alex planned this together." Then she had a sudden change of thought. "Have you ever thought about what we're supposed to do if we find the gold?"

"I'm trusting God on that one, but we would have to get out of here and get word to Montagu Norman like we promised. I don't believe the Lord has brought us this far just to fail. Tuck that map away, we need to get going. I found another chocolate bar and a fruit bar–that will have to do us for breakfast – and there was a flare gun and a machete. You take the gun and I'll use the knife."

Showing her true McIntosh colors, Mae lightly proclaimed, "If we can't shoot her or stab her, maybe we can poison Queen Obeah with these K-rations." As Mae reached out to close the lid of the crate, it slipped out of her hand and slammed shut with a tremendous metal bang that echoed through the cave. Suddenly they felt a rush of wind from above their heads. Vaughn quickly flashed his light in that direction and they saw a sea of squirming dark creatures dropping from the ceiling and circling around them. To their horror, they realized they had been sharing this space with thousands of bats that had been prepared to settle in for the remainder of the day.

The bats darted with a driving fury, then swarmed toward the beam of light. Mae screamed as the first cluster of flying mammals bounced off her shoulder and back with the impact and noise of a tennis ball hitting a brick wall. Vaughn grabbed the grimy canvas that had covered the crates and pulled it over their prone bodies while all around them the clicks of a feeding frenzy sounded like rubber pucks hitting a wooden hockey stick. At least they were not coming into direct contact thanks to the canvas.

After a few minutes the flying onslaught subsided but the cave was full of echoes of different bat frequencies, modalities and intonations. Peeking out from a corner of the tarpaulin, Vaughn could see there were only a few stragglers still fluttering about, so he tempted fate by again pointing his beam of light toward clumps of crusty-toothed creatures that had returned to their upside-down roost high above them. The majority of the bats, however, had exited out the cavern roof high into the morning sky in such a great swarm that from a distance it looked like winding grayish smoke from a struggling, wet campfire.

"Well, that explains why the mosquitoes didn't get us last night!" Vaughn said calmly. Unfortunately, he didn't know a short distance away that bat smoke was the only sign Bones Deveaux needed to point Frankie Johnson in their direction.

Chapter 45

Jaws of Death

❧

Cat Island, Bahamas

Arising early in the morning was not something Frankie, or his crew, were used to doing, but the situation at hand required all their attention at a time they were usually just going to sleep. Loan sharking, extortion, prostitution and gambling conditioned them to long, late nights when they eventually got a little shut eye at the crack of dawn, and none of them were happy about it.

Whether entertaining high rollers or disposing of malcontents who threatened the gaming business–it didn't matter if it was in Detroit, New Orleans, New York City, Chicago, Miami, or Cat Island–the Code of the Mafia was always in play. This code, or 'Omerta,' was well known for its emphasis on loyalty, solidarity and silence, but the lesser known statute, 'thou shall not interfere in the business of others' also applied to those outside of the family. When Vaughn and Mae McIntosh had gotten involved with Sir Harry Oakes, they had transgressed this sacred business rite, and then throwing the Acacia Box into the fire pushed Frankie's anger over the top and made the thought of retribution all the more enjoyable.

Hans Lubeck was also high on his list. Not only had Lubeck's men murdered his soldiers, but their continuing aggravation and intervention was a perpetual insult to the *moto*. In his eyes, Lubeck should have a deeply shameful and demeaning exit because he was not a man of honor. Frankie should have been asleep in a comfortable bed with room service. Instead, he was here warding off mosquitoes, sand flies and constant sweat. This added to his ire for the Krauts. Their removal would be a sweet accomplishment.

Just then a startling exclamation from Bones broke his wandering thoughts. "Der... to hill side...be your prey!"

Frankie tilted his tanned, wide-brimmed bush hat off his forehead and focused his brass binoculars on where Bones was pointing. "All I see is a bunch of birds. Anything could have scared them."

"Not so... dey dart like falling kite... not swallow in flight. Da noise be chipper... no song from dis. Dey be bats. Only man move bat like dis...der be your man."

Frankie's men had only been on the trail for two hours but were already succumbing to the early morning humidity and had taken advantage of the brief stop to sit under the shady canopy of a grey-barked tree. They were irritable from lack of sleep and none of them were used to this physical strain in the hot and humid climate – and they let everyone around them know it.

Bones stared at the much younger men in disbelief and offered a remedy. "The nigley-whitey give you da shade... but you need da strength. Take da wax from da bark and smear it on yo legs and back. You be feelin' betta soon."

Although they thought he was crazy, they decided it couldn't hurt to take his advice and after the initial tingling on the skin, the underlying muscles did begin to loosen. To celebrate, they shared a few swigs from a bottle of rum, a local favorite, and in no time were back on their feet and ready to tread on.

Frankie was livid. "I told you not to drink, Clutch! You know what happens when you guys start that! Why did you even bring the bottle along? It'll only slow you down and out here you have to have your wits about you!"

Clutch was equally angry. "Mr. Johnson, what we are doing here isn't exactly what we signed on for. For Hoggie and me, this is a long way from being a croupier and pit boss. Our job was supposed to be to protect The Palace, not to chase down a couple of missionaries and be shot at by some renegade Nazis. If you were gonna have me play Robinson Crusoe, then you should have said so in my contract." He looked to the others for support, but they just looked at the ground, so he barreled on. "But since you're makin' us be out here, then at least let us have some comfort with us. We could always go back to Port Royal beach and work on our tan." Again, the support he sought from the others wasn't there. Then he crossed the line. "You're the lawyer... lay down the law if you think you can!"

Clutch took another drink and confidently looked around with a smug smile on his face. All he got from the others, though, was nervous smiles and mumbling. These men knew what a challenge to authority meant, and they stared at their leader, waiting for his response.

Frankie coolly took off his backpack and wiped his brow with his white monogrammed handkerchief. To the thugs, Frankie was overstepping his authority since he was nothing more than a lawyer for the family, but they were about to learn a valuable lesson. "We are in this together," Frankie said quietly. "I know there's some type of treasure waiting for us when we find these people and we can't afford to have this kind of conversation separate us. There can be no weak link in our plan."

Clutch took a step toward Frankie. "From where I stand, I'm staring right at the weak link. Maybe you should've stayed in Miami with the hookers and druggies."

Frankie was quiet for a just a moment then said, "Where are you from, Clutch?"

"You know where I'm from – Detroit! McComb County... 19 mile road... just like Hoggie over there. We cut our teeth in Toledo at the Club Devon–for Sammy Orrondorf. Good ride till Hoggie and me whacked a judge's son, so Sammy sent us to Miami to cool off. Been there ever since. But you know all that!"

"So, what you are saying is you screwed up in Detroit and we saved your butt?"

Clutch nodded. "I guess you could say that." He patted his pockets, looking for a cigarette, and when he looked up, Frankie threw him a pack of Limited Edition Lucky Strikes. Then, as Clutch fumbled with the package, Frankie threw him his lighter.

"What you don't realize, Clutch, is that you're not the big man you think you are. You were sent to this off-beat little island to prove yourself, all over again. Yeah, I know about your mess in Detroit. I also know it happened because you defied orders to leave that judge's college boy alone, but it seems you two liked the same girl and you wanted him out of the picture." Before Clutch could protest, Frankie continued. "And don't be blamin' Hoggie for it. Our boss, Mr. Lanskey, took you in as a favor to Mr. Orrondorf, but you don't appreciate it. You just keep makin' the same mistakes over and over again."

Clutch disrespectfully exhaled his tobacco smoke in Frankie's direction. "What can a lawyer who ain't never done any serious service for the family tell me about the business that I don't already know?"

Frankie was losing patience with this game. "First, Clutch, let me explain that you don't get to be the family lawyer, without performing service for the family–proving your loyalty to the *Capo de tutti capi*. Who do you think keeps the peace among the families? Why do you think there are no murders in Hallandale and Broward County? Do you know how John Scalise lost his eye? Who do you think taught Kid Twist to use the ice pick? Who do you think planted the gun for the Meyer Shapiro payback?" Frankie paused. "So, I think I have cut my teeth just like you."

Clutch gawked at Frankie as he dropped his cigarette and stood with his arms firmly at his side as a sign of contrition and respect. He finally realized he was in the presence of a legend and knew he had made a deadly mistake questioning Frankie's leadership.

But Frankie wasn't finished. "Second, Osvalda Antonio Stefano "Clutch" Calabria, you have no manners, no reverence, no class and no deference for your superiors. I want you to say my name to show your respect. I want to hear you say, Alberto Ferdigio Rinaldo "Frankie" Abruzzi. Say it!"

"Alberto..." Clutch futilely looked at his colleagues for support.

"Ferdigio..." Clutch's body began to shake.

"Rinaldo..." Clutch felt like he lost control of his limbs.

"Frankie..." Clutch just stared into the wicked eyes of the lawyer.

"Abru..." Clutch dropped to his knees, gurgling, while clutching at his bleeding throat, feeling his life spurting from his neck.

Then *Caporegime* Abruzzi whispered into Clutch's ear. "Good, Clutch, you've finally learned respect and the last words on your lips were reverently spoken. Now go to hell where you belong."

Frankie turned to the others who gathered their packs and started up the broken trail toward the higher cliffs without saying a word. Frankie wiped his knife on Clutch's shirt and returned it to his sheath, then picked up the bottle of rum and tossed it to the shocked Bones Deveaux. "I think you might need this if we are to continue on. What I just did was simply correcting an employee error... and I think you'll see it'll be to everyone's benefit."

Chapter 46

Cat Island, Bahamas

With supreme confidence, Lubeck and company came ashore from the *Southern Cross* with an array of jungle supplies and equipment. They seemed to be prepared for anything they might face. The parameters of the mission were simple: the McIntoshes were to be taken alive at all costs, but the Cosa Nostra were quite expendable, except for Frankie Johnson. Lubeck wanted him captured–he had special plans for the hard-headed leader.

After a final review of the map they headed out. Being south of Pigeon Cay and moving inland, they would only have to hike about three miles to their first stop–Thurston Hill–and should encounter very few, if any, locals. Once on higher ground, the clearing would offer them a vantage point to see any signs of activity in the ten miles north to Arthur's Town. By Lubeck's best estimates, the McIntoshes had started no more than fifteen miles north of them and with no food, water or supplies, traveling was going to be demanding for the couple. Although, Captain McIntosh had military training which might give them a slight edge. Lubeck knew he couldn't underestimate them and was certain they would put up some sort of fight, but he was prepared. If nothing else, he respected the couple's tenacity, but in time the spider web would be set and he would just wait for his quarry to be driven into the trap.

Johnson was a different story. He may have been street smart but that knowledge didn't exactly transfer to this type of setting. Lubeck was fairly certain the thugs had no idea what they were going to encounter and would not have done adequate planning. With the intense, sticky weather, there would be chaffing and blisters, soreness and cramping – and what about a safe water supply? Trekking took calories and Lubeck was sure Johnson's men were fueled by pride and arrogance and not suitable foodstuffs. And, if the city boys failed to reconnoiter the island properly before starting out, they could be wandering around forever, unable to find their way back to civilization. Although he knew they would be armed, Lubeck had very low regard for Johnson and his men. He could have hunted Frankie down and killed him already, but why waste the energy when they would come to him soon enough on their own. He would let the flies chase the 'holy honey' and do most of the work for him.

When they reached Thurston Hill, Lubeck gave the order for a five-minute rest while he surveyed the island below. He had read that this summit had been the original proposed site for the Hermitage Church, but it was moved to Mount Alvernia, the highest point on Cat Island. Lubeck was repulsed by anything religious, and even more so by the name of Jesus Christ, so although the church was never constructed on Thurston Hill, he had a sense of uneasiness and apprehension here. He was much more comfortable thinking about the island's history of spirits, ghosts and voodoo practices.

His reconnaissance complete, he decided to follow the commando rule of taking a rest whenever the opportunity was presented, so, keeping his distance from his men, he sat on the ground and leaned against a wind-swept cotton tree and closed his eyes. He was dozing off when he heard a bell coming from the tree line at the edge of the clearing and was surprised to see a straggly native leading a small herd of sheep and goats. He wore a split-thatch hat, tawny cotton pants torn off at the knees, a sleeveless dirty cotton shirt, and no shoes. He was ringing the bell in time with a song he was singing in praise to his Lord.

"Stop that infernal clatter, old man," Lubeck shouted.

"There, there, young man. You can't expect me to be quiet when the Lord gets hold of my soul!" He began to wail even louder, in love with his Creator:

Sleep on, beloved, sleep and take thy rest,
Lay down thy head upon thy Saviour's breast.
We love thee well but Jesus loves thee best,
Goodnight, goodnight, goodnight.

"It's not going to be a good night for you if you don't shut up." Lubeck's words didn't faze the herder so he stood and moved toward him.

Until our shadows from this earth are cast,
Until He gathers in His sheaves at last,
Until the twilight gloom is over past:
Goodnight, goodnight, goodnight.

"I am warning you for the last time!" Lubeck sneered, reaching for his Mauser and stepping even closer. But still the man sang.

Until made beautiful by love divine
Thou in the likeness of thy Lord shall shine,
And He will bring that golden crown of thine,
Goodnight, goodnight, goodnight.

Lubeck placed his pistol squarely onto the man's forehead.

Until we meet again before the throne
Clothed in the spotless robes He gives His own,
Until we know as we have known:
Goodnight, goodnight, goodnight.

Lubeck pulled the trigger.

Nothing happened. The old man just stood looking at him with a toothless grin.

"You don't like, *Sleep on, Beloved*?" he asked kindly. "It's an old Cat Island fisherman's song about lowering a friend's casket into his grave."

Although Lubeck carried a gun and was a large and imposing figure, the herdsman did not seem intimidated at all. He just cocked his head to one side and asked, "Why do you seek to kill in this place today?"

Lubeck fiddled with the firing mechanism of the Mauser, completely at a loss to understand why the gun hadn't fired. At the man's question, he looked up. "I wanted you to stop singing! You need to learn to follow orders from someone who is your superior."

"Oh, no sir. I only have one Superior and He is not you."

This conversation was really beginning to irritate Lubeck. "You are an annoying little man and are quickly becoming a nuisance."

"So you do not have death on your mind today?"

Lubeck had no more time to waste on this senseless exchange, so he holstered his gun and drew his gravity knife. The insolence of this little fellow had to be corrected. With the herder's back to him, he slowly approached with the intent of making another notch in the weapon's handle.

"The blade will not function, Hans Lubeck," the herder said without turning. "So, please stop with all your threats and menacing actions. Let's talk about truth."

"*Ubergeschnappt*! How do you know my name, crazy old man? Leave this place before…"

"Before you do what… kill me? I think we both know that is not an option. I know all about you, Hans, not just your name. I know about you stealing your sister's birthday money; I know that you cheated on your mid-level exams; I even know the name of your first girlfriend…Magdalyn, I believe!"

Lubeck was becoming unraveled. "And do you also know I have four men only a shout away?"

"Bring a whole army if you want. I can defeat any number of your men."

"Who are you, old man?" Lubeck had that same uncomfortable feeling he had experienced when thinking about the building of the church.

"The question should be, who are you, Hans Lubeck, that you should be chasing my children?"

"Your children? We are not here to harm any children!"

"Think, Hans…why do you feel the need to persecute me so?"

"I do not know what you're talking about! I simply have a job to do here… a destiny to fulfill. Be on your way, *wahnsinnige*." Lubeck pointed to his ear and circled his finger in disrespect.

"But I am here with a warning–you have one last chance to leave this place and be renewed. If not, you tempt a fate you cannot reverse."

Finally! Lubeck heard his men rushing down the hill behind him. Pointing at the old man, he gave the order to shoot. This time the guns did not fail. As the goats and sheep ran for their lives, dozens of bullets tore at the old man's flesh. His undulating body was driven backward against a Casuarina pine tree that held his now lifeless body erect with his outstretched arms tangled in the low-hanging branches. And still they fired–emptying their Mausers in a cloud of powder residue. At last they approached the innocent man who, though hit too many times to count, still remained upright against the tree trunk.

"Let's get out of here," one of the men said. "Move north as far away from here as we can. That noise could have been heard all the way to the top end of the island."

Lubeck felt a nudge on his arm, and then a more insistent prodding. "Wake up, sir! It's time to go. You've been asleep for a while." He shook his head and tried to get his bearings, thinking back over the past few minutes. He was relieved to realize it must have been a dream. "We are not going to wait any longer," he said, finally regaining his senses. "I think we should move north. There is still some high country there with more camouflage. Have the men ready to go in two minutes."

As the men hurried off, Lubeck looked toward the base of the hill where the largest Casuarina tree stood out between two smaller ones. Out of the blue, a single lamb emerged from the foliage. He was stunned for a moment, but quickly shook it off. At least there was no man hanging from the tree.

Chapter 47

Suspended Joy

❧

Cat Island, Bahamas

Mae examined the map to get her bearings. They had been heading south for some time and ran across a myriad of sink holes, tunnels, submerged canyons and water caverns – not to mention the sharp outgrowths of limestone and granite rock hidden by the dense flora–so it was more important than ever for them to keep their wits about them.

"We should be coming up on Bird's Point soon, then we turn west to Obeah's Maw." Mae was the official navigator leaving Vaughn free to create a path through the overgrowth. They were learning very quickly to avoid swarms of mosquitoes around stagnant water pits and to cut down or circumnavigate rash-inducing asparagus fern, thorny cat's claw and cow thorn bushes.

"Vaughn, did you notice the birds seem to be moving ahead of us? I saw a falcon and a kestrel fly past us at a pretty fast clip. Even the swallows seem to be flying higher than usual. You know me and my birds, and even some of the ground animals seem to be skittish. It's as if something behind us is spooking them."

"Well, I can't see anything with all this brush, and neither of us has heard anything unusual so far. I trust your animal intuition, though, so the sooner we get to the Maw, the sooner we can figure out who or what is around us. For now, we just need to keep praying and moving ahead."

The foliage had become very dense, but at the same time, very beautiful. When they came onto a slightly clear rise they could see palm trees and shallow creek flats to the east. "The tide will be going out soon," Mae said. "It would probably be fairly easy to catch some bonefish or red snapper left behind in the tide pools." She knew it was a long shot but they hadn't eaten all day and she was hoping for some food.

"I don't think it's a good idea, Mae," Vaughn said reluctantly. "There would probably be jelly fish and jack fish in those pools, too, and we can't take the chance of being stung, not to mention the exposure of being on the beach. I know you're hungry – I am, too – but if your intuition is right, they could be closing in on us so we have to keep moving."

Mae knew he was right, so turned back to the task at hand. "Look here, Vaughn. Doesn't that look like a path through those bushes? Probably made by animals–but it's headed west." He pushed back some branches and there indeed was a seemingly passable path.

They started moving ahead. "Seems like we're heading into the Garden of Eden," Mae said. "It smells so good and fruity here."

"An Allemanda plant smells like that but it's poisonous, so don't get any of the sap on you. Great to see and smell, but don't touch."

"Hmmm, more of the Garden of Eden analogy?"

"Kind of. Stick to the orange bougainvillea and pink hibiscus – they're touchable."

"Since when did you become such a botanist?"

"Jeremiah pointed them out to me. They grow a few in their garden for pollination. Jealous that I know something you don't about plants?" Vaughn chuckled.

"Not jealous – just surprised!" Their muffled laughter drew them closer for the moment in the midst of their desperate situation, but Mae needed a bit more reassurance. She impetuously grabbed Vaughn's collar and pulled him close for a kiss. When they separated, she said, "Hope that makes up for nearly breaking your nose and chipping your tooth a few winter's ago!"

In answer, Vaughn cut a corner off the tarp they were carrying, scooped up a handful of the pink sand at their feet and tied it up. "I know this might sound ridiculous right now, but some day when this is all behind us, we might want to remember how we survived. Keep this to remind you how much I love and respect you for what you're doing."

Mae gave him another kiss and slid the small packet into her pocket. "Vaughn, I have to tell you something. I don't want you to look at me as a Delilah or Jezebel, but… I must shorten this skirt! It keeps getting caught on branches and thorns, and I think the worst of our journey is still ahead. Please forgive me but I need your machete."

Vaughn laughed as he handed it to her. "Really Mae? Look around! Do you really believe I would think badly of you when we're in this situation? I'm surprised you didn't do it long ago. Hack away!"

When she'd finished, she held out the piece of fabric to him. "Here, wrap this around your head like the fishermen at Potter's Cay – it will help with the sun." She chuckled, "With the machete you'll look like a pirate – my very own Blackbeard–except you would have to be Bushy-Blondebeard."

"Then you can be my first-mate, Anne Bonny, and we're on this island in search of buried treasure." Then in his best pirate voice he added, "You don't want to get caught, so fight like a man so you don't die like a dog…ARRRR!"

In a flash, their levity came to an abrupt halt when Vaughn noticed the reflection from a not-so-distant object. Their pursuers were so close they could hear their voices. "Sounds like Johnson and his men," Vaughn whispered. "We need to make time to the Maw. Are you sure you're alright to run?"

Mae answered by double-timing past him down the path, and he was close behind.

Chapter 48

Salient Forces

❦

Cat Island, Bahamas

Bones Deveaux was stunned by the volatility of Frankie Johnson, and was determined to stay in the good graces of the *consigliere*. Then happenstance smiled on him and he took advantage of it. "No, take de path to the right. I know dis fork...da other takes you to the coast at Bird's Point. Dey haf to be turning inland...we cut dem off."

Johnson's men were in need of food and fresh water and were not prepared for such a trek, and were still reeling after witnessing the brutality of their leader against his own man. When Frankie took the suggested path, Bones tried to appease him even more. "I take you where you find food. I know dis place. I come here when we go to da maw. I know you will find da people der, but you mus' drink and eat first. You can take da bible folk, but you mus' watch for da men wit da gun."

Frankie was pleased that bringing Bones along was starting to pay dividends. He had lamented his failure to prepare his men for the demands of the bush, but bringing Bones along had nearly made up for it by allowing them to track the McIntoshes more easily. It had taken longer than he originally expected, but it was obvious including the native had been a good decision.

"The maw has fresh water, right? And you think they are headed for it?"

"Streams for drink fall into da maw, and if dey go to Bird's Point dey mus go to da maw. You might even beat dem dere, but you mus rest first. I show you what to eat."

Frankie did not want to stop completely, but gave the order to slow their pace. They would eat while they walked so they didn't lose as much time. Bones advised against the guava fruit as it was hard to digest in its natural state, but mangoes were different. Their dense, succulent orange meat gave an instant boost to the men's energy levels. He warned them, however, to eat slowly as the 'nectars be only want'n dem to drink more water.' They ignored his advice and gorged themselves instead, so as the men trod on, dehydration set in very rapidly. Although the terrain seemed to be taking a downward slant making walking easier, the sound of invigorating, cascading water kept getting louder and louder. Frankie looked at Bones for an explanation.

"Obeah's Maw is not for da light-heart. Dis be da home of the mudder of us all–da dark queen who comes from da eart's bowel an' she bring da smell of hell wit her. She be da devil–hear her wail? The good stream feed her our life blood, but she drink and swallow and belch the rotten hell. Do not go if you want to live…we should go around."

Frankie was adamant. "You said this is where the McIntoshes will come, so we stay and wait for them!"

There was no mistaking the fear in Bones' eyes. "Do not go near her water, I warn you. She reach up and swallow you. If da McIntosh go der, dey no come out."

"Well, then, let's wait and see what they will do. Maybe this is the spot our search will end."

The splash of several free-flowing waterfalls resonated all around the group and was irresistible to the parched throats of the men so they started moving toward the sound. Bones warned them to walk slowly but they ignored his plea as they moved faster. Throwing down their backpacks and pulling off their hats and boots, Animal and Diamond Jim began to run toward the sound, tripping over tree roots, boulders and each other in their urgency to reach the water.

Frankie put his hand on Hoggie's chest to hold him back. "Obeah's siren call tells dem to come to her for da cool drink," Bones said sadly. "She promise da life…she beckon wit da taste of it…but she only offer da poison to take der soul."

Animal and Diamond Jim ran with abandon as if being pulled by an invisible force, and suddenly a bright light flashed just as the earth was pulled from underneath them and they disappeared with shrieks of alarm and terror. Frankie, Hoggie and Bones stood in shock until the terrified cries died away and the only sound, once again, was the splashing water falls.

"Obeah be eaten dem up now. Her belly churn and she take da blood from dees folk. I tell you, Johnson, no good come of us bein' here."

Frankie had to see for himself where his men had vanished to, so he started through the trees and brush, with great trepidation, along the path that Animal and Diamond Jim had followed, picking up shirts, shoes and other clothing along the way, with the other two following behind. Without warning the tree line broke and they were balancing on the edge of a jagged precipice. Instinctively, they fell to their knees, fighting to keep from following where their comrades had disappeared before them.

What lay in front of them was a sink hole some fifty yards in diameter. There had to have been a drop of several hundred feet into swirling, churning aquamarine waters. Several falls from feeder streams spilled into the vast abyss with splatters and splashes echoing off the carbonite cliffs. At the edge where they were, they could hear and feel the air being sucked over the crags into the spinning vortex while their senses were assaulted by the smell of repeated sulphur burps as roiled waves cracked against the solid rock face.

Peering down into the cavern, Hoggie noticed the prone bodies of his colleagues being dredged along with the spinning waters and then the air around them began to whistle as the waters began to flush into a deep black nothingness. With a final inhalation of what sounded like a human death rattle, the waters disappeared into a never-ending deep void.

And then it was quiet.

The streams continued to tumble into the hole, but the falling waters looked like cascading stars as they flashed their final opulence, and then disappeared into the blackened vacancy without a whimper.

"Obeah be full," Bones said in a hushed voice. "She at rest for a while in da arms of da debble...now she have two more souls to torment."

Frankie was ready to concede they should move on until he saw the outline of two figures emerging on the opposite side of the maw. "Step back, easy and quiet," he said urgently to Hoggie and Bones. "Look across the Maw." The three of them moved back into the underbrush. "What is it the McIntoshes would say–The Lord giveth and the Lord taketh away? Well I think the time has come for us to do a little taking."

Chapter 49

Cat Island, Bahamas

They had traveled fairly quickly through a wonderland of unspoiled and undisturbed colors and fragrances, but were unable to appreciate their surroundings knowing that Frankie Johnson was close on their tail. Any possible enjoyment was replaced with a driving desire to reach their destination. Now that they were staring into the Maw, the fight response was kicking in. Vaughn thought back to when his Uncle Bert was training him to fight, and his words of advice, "Hit first, fast and be unforgiving, but only as a last resort. A gun is nothing more than an extension of your hand–you use either one first to protect and only last to kill." Going back to his grandfather, the Colonel, all family members were taught fisticuffs. Though he had never known her, Vaughn had been told even his gentile and graceful grandmother, Leah, could deliver a roundhouse blow if necessary. So for a brief moment, Vaughn took comfort that the fighting spirit of Leah, and then Cate, had been kept alive in Mae.

Mae needed no encouragement to stand up for herself or defend her family. Being a farm girl she was very familiar with the circle of life–that death was a part of living – but being a Salvationist, she preferred to turn the other cheek as Luke 6:29 said, when possible. Truth be told, though, she was probably most akin to the Old Testament traits of God's character.

It was quite evident the Creator understood war and killing, but it was always done in the context of the great cosmic struggle between His Good versus Satan's Evil. She had studied Deuteronomy 20 with Vaughn before he went overseas, and accepted God's rule of war for His people including the tenets of justice and kindness in killing. Mae had seen throughout their struggle with the Amschel that evil really did exist, but despite it all she still felt a lingering guilt about knowingly hurting another human being.

Vaughn, on the other hand, knew quite well that the meekness demanded of a Salvation Army officer could be misleading, and he struggled, knowing he had it within his nature to be a cold-hearted killer when forced.

The bottom line was they were armed with minimal firepower, but maximum feistiness.

Holding back a ways from the ledge, they took stock of the retreating waters of the sink hole. There were random crags and ledges along the walls of the cavern, but no noticeable pattern of a path below.

"Maybe we need to circle the hole and see it from another angle," Mae said. "If there is a path to an underwater cavern, we sure can't see it from here, and I don't see anything marked on this map."

"Agreed, but don't go too fast. Some of these ledges seem really soft and could crumble."

Mae took his advice and stepped slowly and intentionally along the edge of the hole. When they got to the other side they still hadn't discovered any sort of passageway to the depths below, but then Mae had an idea. "I'm going to fire the flare gun into the hole. Maybe that will give us more light to see something."

"I'm not sure that's a good idea. The noise will be heard for miles. We're trying to escape, not attract attention!"

"I know that, Vaughn, but what choice do we have? We can't defend ourselves against Johnson from here. There must be some type of path down through there and maybe out of this place."

Vaughn could see there was no use arguing. When Mae put her mind to something, he had learned to step aside. She was going to do this whether he agreed or not, so the least he could do was help her. He took the flare gun from her and slipped the large aluminum cartridge into the barrel, then after a quick review of what to expect from a 10-gauge pistol, Mae was ready to go. She moved to the ledge, and holding the pistol in both hands, fired the gun toward the deepest portion of the far wall.

There was a deafening bang that echoed off the walls of the Maw, then the cartridge careened and exploded with an ear-splitting blast off the rocks producing a bright red glow in the opening.

"Vaughn.... straight across! Are those steps leading down to a cave?"

Sure enough, the extra light had exposed a passageway previously hidden by a curtain-like stalagmite formation. The descending stairway along the basin wall led to what appeared to be a tomb-like opening.

"We have to get moving! I'm sure Frankie knows where we are now!"

Mae tossed the flare gun to Vaughn, and ignoring the dangerous footing, began to zig zag her way toward the passageway with Vaughn close behind. He called out to her, trying to slow her down, but either she couldn't hear him or was simply ignoring him. He could only follow in her wake, slashing indiscriminately at overhanging tree branches and bushes that impeded their progress. Then suddenly, he lost sight of her. He paused to listen, but couldn't hear any movement up ahead. His gut was clenched in fear as he quickly approached the stairway landing.

Unfortunately, his instincts were spot on.

Chapter 50

Cat Island, Bahamas

Lubeck's intuition told him to stay put, but the rational part of his brain urged him to forge ahead – bird movement, animal unrest and now, his sixth sense was picking up ground reverberations–a thunderous noise like a bellow similar to that made by the six-inch guns aboard the *Graf Spee*. With no hesitation, Lubeck gave the order to move on.

"*Los! Los! Los!*" The commandos had also heard the rumble and were quick to move toward its origin. Each man was rested, well-armed and motivated and there should be no surprises if they followed his orders. This pursuit was like chasing a naval convoy in a fog bank – keep moving, steady pace and adhere to the rules to always go after the prize. So when the enemy was sighted, they would detain or destroy the protecting cruisers, stop the target ship, steal the contraband, evacuate the crew, then sink the vessel – all with slight modifications in this case.

Frankie Johnson's crew were to be exterminated with extreme prejudice, followed by a slow execution of Johnson himself. After the McIntoshes provided the location of the gold they would suffer a painful death, then the Nazis would abscond with the gold. With the element of surprise and greater firepower in their favor, Lubeck was confident of the outcome except for one thing. The missing piece was their inability to scout the area of the impending battle beforehand. Lubeck knew that failure to know the terrain and vegetation could be lethal, so he feared this most of all.

History was replete with stories of superior forces being defeated by a lesser foe simply because the latter was able to use the landscape to their advantage. With this in mind, he felt uncertain about leaving the high ground to engage the enemy, but all things considered, he felt compelled to roll the dice anyway. Timing and maneuverability would be everything. This encounter may not have the pomp and circumstance of those other famous battles, but its importance could not be diminished. If he lost, the House of Amschel would collapse, but if he won, he could reshape the entire world for the next generation. Lubeck would not let his name be categorized as a military write-off along with Xerxes, Darius, Cornwallis, and Napoleon.

The two men on the flanks would not be able to keep up with the rest of the group, but their job would not be measured in terms of distance but in how much time would elapse before a rendezvous. The dense foliage would restrict their observation and therefore their judgment and their ability to communicate properly. Where Thurston Hill would have offered ideal firing conditions, the jungle would impede their line of vision and allow the enemy to conceal themselves regardless of inferior numbers and armaments. The more Lubeck thought about it, the more he was concerned that his nightmare might have some credibility.

There was one more thing that gnawed at his soul. An unknown and unseen force that he could feel, something that seemed to be protecting the McIntoshes. The presence was strong, but not unbeatable. He remembered from his dream that in the end his men did kill the old man. With that thought, Lubeck committed himself totally to war. It would be all or nothing. The benefits of moving on were greater than those of hanging back.

When the gold was found, its removal would require special attention. The authorities on Cat Island would be of little concern so he was not worried about any interference on that front before he made the necessary arrangements with his ship. He thought about delegating the gold's transport to another, but that thought was quickly dismissed as he remembered how Major Picard had been duped. He was smarter than Picard, however, so he would be sure to verify the gold's presence for himself. Since the McIntoshes had pulled a sleight of hand before, they could do it again and Lubeck had not come this far to be played for a fool.

As he and his men continued their search, the first challenge was the dense foliage. The vegetation was so thick it took a great deal of the men's energy just to cut through, creating noise that would destroy any element of surprise. To minimize the effects, they traveled single file along a very narrow path cut out by the first in line. This route was taking them around salt ponds and dry salt caverns, and as the afternoon sun grew hotter,

Lubeck worried about their position. He decided they were too close to the coast – their prey would not have been foolish enough to waste energy in these mangrove trees and the ever-present danger of the shallow salt flats. He had to move inland, but before they could change course, natural forces took over.

It began with quivering of the leaves of the scrub brush, and then, as if reacting to a strong wind, foliage on the large trees was being tossed helter skelter as the base of their trunks shook. Hardened sand on top of exposed rocks cascaded to the ground, and as the wave continued to thunder beneath their feet, the rocks themselves burst from the soil. Birds scattered, coconuts fell from tree tops and frightened forest animals hissed and squealed all around them.

As the unrelenting subterranean tidal wave persisted, Lubeck and the men staggered, grasping for anything firm to hold on to. It sounded to them like a train rolling into a station – a rumble and hiss followed by a ruptured boom, then momentary quiet only to be throttled again. Finally, the intensity began to dissipate with what sounded like the final flushing of water beneath their feet. The foundation of everything around them had been shaken to the core, but for the most part, the men were intact – slightly rattled but quickly regaining their composure.

Lubeck gave the order to head inland. They must be close to something big, but this was truly the most unpredictable landscape to ever engage an enemy. He thought about a passage from the Greek philosopher, Heraclitus, that he had learned years ago: "Out of every one hundred men, ten shouldn't even be there, eighty are just targets, nine are the real fighters, and we are lucky to have them, for they make the battle. Ah, but the one, one is a warrior, and he will bring the others back." Lubeck was determined to be that warrior.

Chapter 51

Cat Island, Bahamas

Vaughn shortened his stride as he rounded the last Poinciana tree. Its large flowers and long seed pods had blocked a direct view of the cavern steps, but when he entered the small clearing he saw something no husband should ever experience. Frankie Johnson was holding his struggling wife like a human shield, his arm cranked around her neck and his pistol to her temple. Mae's hair splashed across her face as she tried to pull away, but the much bigger Frankie forced her to her toes with an upward choke hold that made her gasp for air. Mae was forced to stop struggling just to breathe. Vaughn forced himself to hold back, relying on his commando training to curb his baser instincts, and raised his arms in the surrender position to buy time. The monster within him was temporarily being managed, but beneath his calm exterior he was boiling with rage.

Beside Frankie stood Bones. Vaughn recognized him from their arrival at the airport – could that possibly have just been yesterday?! He had thought Bones was just a local showing kindness, but changed his opinion as the leather-faced native began to speak in a threatening tenor,

> "*Round da Jumbie tree, he run*
> *Looking ta catch sometin', someone*
> *But he no luck sees his eyes*
> *Instead he get da big surprise.*"

Then Bones closed his eyes and continued to chant with his hands outstretched over the pit.

"Obeah Maw we all is heah
You open wide and give da feah
We give you souls for you to eat
Horses, pigs, now human meat."

Bones' eyes became blood red as he approached Vaughn, pulling a 9-inch stiffie knife used for filleting fish. The curved wooden handle fit comfortably in his hand as he slowly walked around Vaughn waving the rusty blade.

"Obeah needs to taste da blood
She need a sip to bring back flood
I cut you now and 'troes you in
Den Obeah come to bless agin.

Vaughn felt another presence behind him, but kept his eyes on the local shaman.

"I be da 'HOUNGAN' who give sacrifice
I be her man to take your life
It is a gift you give yourself
Obeah's soul demands none else"

Bones appeared to be in a trance as he moved like a coiled rattler – his thrusting knife provoking fear in his quarry, laughing as he tossed the dagger hand to hand,

"Ah says to you, mon, take yer breath
It be your las' before da death
Do not fear as Obeah needs of you
Your body and soul makin' her new"

Bones had corralled Vaughn against the cavern edge, and with this last pronouncement, he let out a terrifying scream as he ran at Vaughn with the blade held over his head in both hands, destined to give the fatal blow, but Vaughn was ready for him.

He pulled the machete from behind him as Bones rumbled forward, and dropping to one knee, delivered a crossing thrust to the bare abdomen of the evil priest, severing his gut almost to the spine. Then, as Bones, smiling at his personal sacrifice, teetered on the edge before falling into the yawning chasm, Vaughn slowly turned and looked directly at Frankie who stumbled backward a few steps in disbelief. "Doesn't change a thing, Captain," Johnson proclaimed after regaining a semblance of composure. "He was a crazy man. All I need is this lovely lady." Johnson nodded to the figure Vaughn had suspected was behind him as Hoggie stepped from the bushes, brandishing his firearm. "Hoggie, now is the time to redeem yourself. Take care of this business and we'll be square. Then you can go back to your buddies in Detroit with your honor restored." Frankie tightened his grip on Mae who had begun to struggle again. "And you shut up or I'll plug your husband myself."

"Let her go, Frankie and we'll show you where the gold is hidden."

"Gold? I knew it! If it involved Harry Oakes it had to be gold! He must have really hated Lubeck to hide it the way he did. Well, I've just appointed myself Sir Harry's heir so I guess the gold belongs to me now!"

"It can all be yours, but if Lubeck is around, you're going to have one big battle ahead of you–and we all know what happened the last time you two squared off. Your fight isn't with us, it's with him. What do you say? Let's join forces."

"Join forces? You're as crazy as old man DeVeaux. I ain't joinin' forces with anyone! I have to admit, though, Sir Harry hiding the gold from the locals with the cover of Voodoo was pretty ingenious."

"You'll end up with nothing if you don't have the manpower to beat Lubeck. He could have five–or twenty-five–men on their way just to intercept you."

"No... he'll bring the same henchmen he had in the church, only this time I'll be ready for him." He looked at Mae, then back at Vaughn. "I could use you as bait to get him into the open. Bet he'd want to talk to you first."

Vaughn was desperate to get Johnson to let Mae go, so he agreed. "Ok...,I like the idea of bait, but let us do this together."

"Give me one good reason I shouldn't pop you and the Mrs. and send you into the hole after Bones!" Frankie was not going to be caught off guard again.

"Get your man to look in my wallet. There's something in there he should recognize."

"Tell you what–you drop the machete and throw the wallet to Hoggie. Then we'll take it from there. If I don't like what I see, then we bid you ah-dios. And Captain... move really slow," Frankie said, tightening his grip on Mae. "A surprise wouldn't be good for your girl, here."

Vaughn did as Frankie said, then they waited while Hoggie searched through the wallet. He found nothing of significance until he opened the small pouch in the bills section, and suddenly he tossed it to the ground and said to Frankie, "We gotta let them go!"

Frankie couldn't believe this underling was now giving him orders, so he reached out to slap Hoggie on the side of the head, but the younger man stepped aside like a prize fighter and threw out his hand holding a black and red poker chip.

Immediately, Frankie released Mae and shoved her into Vaughn's arms, then took the gambling piece from Hoggie. Sure enough, it was original. "You are *Amico Nostro* – a self-made man... a friend of the family? I don't believe it! Where did you get this?"

Vaughn breathed a quick prayer of thanks before answering. "From Hoggie's boss, Benny Orndorff. I did something once for his son and his father was grateful and said this chip would be good for a favor. Well, I am asking for that favor now."

Frankie was stunned. The *Amico Nostro* chip was universally accepted among the families as a demand to protect the person who presented it. This meant Vaughn was to be protected as if he were Frankie's own son, that he had been weighed and found more than admissible to the *Cosa Nostra* no matter where he went.

"I can't believe I'm doing this, but I will honor the code." Frankie holstered his pistol and gave Vaughn a bear hug followed by the traditional double-cheek kiss. Vaughn stood stoically in discomfort as Hoggie followed suit. "We extend our apologies to your lovely wife as well. We did not know."

Mae was as stunned as Frankie. She couldn't believe that only a moment ago they were mortal enemies – just moments from death–and now they had forged an iron-clad alliance. If it weren't so unbelievably terrifying, she might find humor in their situation.

"So, are we going to work together to take down Lubeck?" Vaughn asked Frankie again.

"Yeah. This sure ain't how I thought this day was goin' to go, but I guess you're right. We need to work together." So, moving back into the bush, the odd group began plotting their defense.

"I think we should stick with the idea that we are the bait," Vaughn said, and Frankie nodded. "So, when we're set, you and Hoggie fire a couple of rounds and let's see what comes out of the wormwood."

Chapter 52

Torn Asunder

❧

Cat Island, Bahamas

Instinctively, they ducked at the sound of the first shot, but after the second one came from the same direction, they realized the bullets were not meant for them. Lubeck gave a move-up motion signaling the men to assault the ravine directly in front of them. Cautiously they criss-crossed their way to the apex of the gully, getting a view of Obeah's Maw for the first time. "This gorge is not on the map," Lubeck told his men. Yet again he was annoyed at not knowing the lay of the land, but he quickly put it aside when his keen eye spotted a motionless body lying near the edge. He waited for a moment to see if anyone else appeared, but all was still. Obviously, this meant somebody had been here very recently, and since Lubeck suspected Frankie Johnson had learned something from their last encounter, the Argentinean was hyper-vigilant.

The rock walls were crusted with limestone travertine, much the same as salt water would scab onto a sedentary ship, which puzzled Lubeck since this suggested the cavern must usually be filled with hotter-than-normal water – a curious observation. Then one of his men pointed to the wall near the body where a staircase of sorts was leading down into the sink hole, and he knew what they would do.

Lubeck visually examined the jagged flight of steps as far down as he could see and discovered a blackened hole in the wall. Although he realized the staircase would be dangerous with loose stones and any number of other hazards, he had an adrenaline rush and was convinced he was nearing the end of his hunt.

Carefully rounding the pit to the clearing, the men stayed hidden as they approached the still body. Suddenly the injured man began to groan and tried to stand but collapsed back to one knee, so Lubeck sent one of his men in to retrieve him. The captive put up no resistance when he was unceremoniously dumped in front of the Nazi. "You are one of Frankie Johnson's men." Lubeck said matter-of-factly.

"Not anymore, I ain't!" he answered indignantly. "Those Salvationists and Frankie went into the hole. Once he got them, I guess he wanted me out of the way–more gold for him! Those goody-two-shoes don't know it yet, but Frankie's gonna bury them in there. I'll have the last laugh!" Hoggie dabbed his sleeve to a bleeding wound on his forehead.

"So we wait here for them to come back out."

"Then you're gonna have a long wait, partner. They got a map and they don't plan on comin' back this way. You must be Lubeck. I'm Hoggie," he said, extending his hand formally. When this was ignored, he added, "They don't want to mess with you right now."

Lubeck nodded, then asked, "Tell me, is the gold really there?"

"Sure is... crates of the stuff. Most boxes marked with a stamp from some place in Canada. The McIntoshes found that pretty hilarious for some reason or other."

Lubeck was ecstatic. The information he had gleaned from Picard was proving to be invaluable.

Then, grasping his head and acting woozy, Hoggie began to mumble and started to fall to the ground. Lubeck shook his arm. "On your feet, *dummkopf*, you are going to lead us there!"

"Sorry, I can't do that. I'm in bad shape–I can barely stand up."

"You either take us there or I kill you myself, here and now."

One of the men roughly pulled Hoggie upright. "All right, all right... don't get pushy! I'll take you just give me a minute." Then slowly the captive began toward the staircase, with the men following and Lubeck bringing up the rear.

"You have to be careful. These steps slant one way then the other–and don't step on the white stuff, it's slippery. Not all these rocks are tight either. Try and get both feet on the step before you move to the next... and stay close to the wall." The further the group moved, the darker it got.

Hoggie continued to mumble deliriously as a result of his 'head wound'. "I knew an old man who wouldn't go down here because he thought this hole is the mouth of the devil, but we didn't fall for all that Voodoo gibberish. Feel that? It's getting' humid. Can't you feel the warm mist? Touch the rocks. They're hot… just like in hell."

Lubeck had had enough. "Shut up and walk. We don't need a travel guide."

Ignoring him, Hoggie rambled on, "…and that smell, sort of rotten eggs…that's the sulphur from the Devil's den. Get used to it, because, *L'inferno e la nostra casa.*" They would all see each other in hell, whether they realized it or not. Then he noticed the cavern entrance up ahead.

Lubeck inched by his men and pushed Hoggie against the wall, keeping his hand firmly on the mobster's chest as he shined his flashlight into a sub cavern. The minuscule beam barely illuminated the spectacular grotto with glass and marble walls forged by nature's fire and water. Releasing Hoggie, he beckoned his men to follow him and soon the room was full of light. They could see several passageways radiating out from the space, but only one caught their interest when, without speaking, Hoggie pointed straight at it.

The men all rushed toward the wooden crates, temporarily forgetting about their tour guide. Lubeck gave the order to place the first wooden box at his feet, but when it was lifted, the wood disintegrated in their hands leaving a pile of clay in its place. He ordered another box to be inspected with the same result… then a third.

Lubeck was furious! He had been fooled much the same as Major Picard, but when he turned to face Hoggie with thoughts of vengeance, there were three bodies instead of one. It took a moment in the poor lighting, but Lubeck suddenly realized Frankie, Mae and Vaughn stood in Hoggie's place.

"Don't even think about going for your gun, Lubeck," Frankie had his pistol pointed directly at the Amschel hopeful. Mae stood beside him with a solid two-handed grip on Hoggie's weapon. Vaughn had a different kind of defense.

"Ahh, Johnson, so we meet again. Why don't you put down your gun since you are the ones who are outnumbered. Have you already forgotten what happened in the church?" As Lubeck talked, his men were slowly moving from his side toward Frankie.

But Mae didn't see it as simply as Lubeck. "Hans Lubeck, what you represent has haunted my family for generations. Your kind has murdered thousands for greed. My husband and I stand here today to put an end to it once and for all."

"Mae McIntosh, I presume. We finally meet face to face. I hate to disappoint you, but even though you had success in the past against that idiot Picard, you don't think you can make it out of here alive, do you?"

Vaughn stepped forward and addressed a power stronger than Lubeck. "We remember His good servants who have gone before: Max, Stuart, Thomas, Leah, George and Cate, and we all call you out in the mighty Name of Jesus Christ. Come out and show yourself, Liar from the Beginning, Father of all Lies, Author of all Sin – BELIAL! I know you are comfortable here in these islands and in this bottomless pit, so show yourself now! Or will you remain a coward hiding behind this mortal who has been doing your work for you? I command you, by the power of Jesus Christ, to show yourself!"

The stone around them began to vibrate, and a steamy, pungent vapor started to seep through every small fissure in the glass and marble walls. The rock floor shuddered and jumped, creating crevices for an oozy slime to form puddles, while noxious gases flooded the room leaving the three dizzy and disoriented. Although the Christians had warned Frankie about what might happen in the cave, it took all the courage he possessed to stand his ground, but he knew there was something happening here that went beyond mortal understanding.

Ignoring the chaos around them, Lubeck's men had stayed on task and moved within striking distance, thinking Mae would be the easiest target and hoping to catch her off guard–but they had underestimated Johnson's lust for vengeance. Frankie's eyes were darting back and forth as he tried to make sense of things when he caught the soldiers' movement out of the corner of his eye. He fired, drawing Mae's attention and prompting her to shoot, both of them emptying their pistols into Lubeck's men, driving their bodies backward into the shadows.

Vaughn had his own target but remained transfixed, unable to pull the trigger on the flare gun. The toxic vapors were affecting all of them making it hard for Vaughn to focus on Lubeck. He rubbed his tear-filled eyes but couldn't get a clear enough view. Mae and Frankie urgently shouted to Vaughn between coughs and vomiting, urging him to fire.

The Argentinean laughed at his hesitation. "What right do you, mortal, have to come into my lair and pronounce the profane name of the *Nazarene*?"

What happened next was something Vaughn could never have dreamed. Lubeck began to grow, ripping through his black commando shirt and pants, to reveal bile-colored lizard skin covered with an immeasurable number of swollen, tear-filled, human eyes. As he grew, his face split into four images–eagle, lion, man and ox–and from his shoulders and back, four bat-like wings with human hands at the edges flapped menacingly.

With a trenchant and soul-wrenching chortle, a flash of lightning shot from the nostrils of the man-face and encircled the three like a golden thread, then plunged its jagged bolt into the chest of an unsuspecting Frankie Johnson. The lawyer writhed as the bolt incised him from nape to abdomen.

"I had a personal vendetta with him that I promised to finish," the voice hissed. "Besides, I owned his soul anyway. How does your God say it? 'I never knew you; depart from Me, you who practice lawlessness!' I liked his lawlessness. He was working for me and now I have him for eternity." Then the face slowly lowered until it was level with Vaughn and Mae. "But you… you are a different story that I am about to change."

Mae yelled, "Get behind me Satan! We are children of the Living God, The Great I Am; the True Vine and the Bread of God!"

Vaughn took her hand and pronounced his praise, "He is the Alpha and Omega, the Bright Morning Star and our Rock of Refuge! Christ defeated you when He rose from the dead – how did that feel?"

"Such insolence! You think you can play games with me? Let me show you the real truth!"

Vaughn blinked and there stood Catherine Martin McIntosh in front of him. He lowered his gun and stood in shock. Her face shone like an angel and his heart longed to hold her, but when she spoke with that lovable, unforgettable accent, her words tore him apart. "You were conceived in sin, Vaughn McIntosh, and your father was a fornicator. I never wanted you and let your Aunt raise you. I left you because you were a spoiled brat–a pompous, self-centered child seed of perdition. You married a bastard and left me to die alone at the hands of a murderer. I never loved you and hated you for spoiling my life. You are a cold-blooded mass murderer responsible for the death of over fifty men."

Then Catherine turned and what Mae saw was the venomous face of Josiah Blackwell– something she thought was long in the past. "And you… you are the product of a rape. Your parents abandoned you because they didn't love you. Your sisters hated you because you embarrassed them with your selfishness. You were responsible for the death of the Skippers and Cate McIntosh. You threw yourself at the first available bachelor like a brazen hussy. Your husband left you because he loved killing more than he loved you. You are a murderer of men and a liar. And that child you carry will never know its father."

Before either could respond, Lubeck's dead men reappeared from the shadows–still in uniform but with the emaciated faces of Joseph Radar, Adderley, Colonel Brisbois and Major Picard–all pointing at the couple with a repetitive pronouncement of "guilty… guilty…guilty…"

The Lubeck man-face then transformed to Bruce Lindsay. "You know everything said by Catherine and Josiah is true! You can't argue with the facts. Your God has no use for you. Admit it! If you have nothing to say in your defense, then come and embrace me!"

Both Vaughn and Mae were speechless, but there were others who could speak for them. Stepping from the mist behind them came numerous forms they recognized, from their past and the present. The smallest member of the group was a little girl wearing a black beret. Her childish voice did not waver as she said, "I see, Lucifer, you are throwing out your usual accusations again." She motioned behind her. "We can all speak in defense of these two, so before you claim victory, let me remind you who you are dealing with. This should stop the declarations of your demons!"

One by one they stepped forward and stared into the eyes of the great liar. "I am Thomas Martin…Leah Martin…Inspector Forsberg… H.T. Schmidt…Wilhelm Gunter… John Forester…"

Many more voices from their past resonated off the glassy walls.

Then the petit one continued, "I am Gertrude and this couple has been washed in the blood of Jesus Christ. You cannot claim them now – or ever–for you would have to deal with the Second Man, Himself. To hell with you, King of Babylon!"

With that pronouncement, Lubeck drew his weapon. Vaughn instinctively lifted the flare gun and fired, but the missile missed the moving target, plunging into the rock ceiling above. The reverberations of the explosion drove them to their backs. Then all was quiet. The mist had receded, but what took its place was anything but reassuring.

Warm water washed over their faces bringing Vaughn and Mae back to consciousness. Staggering to their feet, they could see the cavern was filling up quickly. Vaughn looked around for Frankie or Lubeck, but they were nowhere to be seen. "The maw is returning. She must have had her fill of blood."

Slipping on the wet floor, they stumbled, hand-in-hand toward the cavern entrance. Frothing salt water was pouring through, filling it half way to the top, and when Vaughn attempted to wade through the surging water he was knocked off his feet, tearing his hand from Mae's grasp.

"If you can hear me, grab this!" A voice was shouting from the remaining air pocket at the entrance as a multi-knotted rope appeared. Mae grasped it, but hesitated though the rising water was almost at her chest. She frantically looked around for Vaughn but couldn't see him… she hysterically called for him but he didn't respond… then she cried for him as she was pulled from the cavern.

Chapter 53

Nothing to Give

❧

Nassau, Bahamas

At first, she thought Vaughn was just up early, much as he always was, and would meet her for breakfast after he finished feeding the animals and doing his morning chores. Maybe Liam had spelled him and he was in the kitchen making breakfast for the two of them, then if he wasn't too busy, they could do devotions together to start the day off.

But then it hit her. Lying in bed, staring out the window of the Mackey Street Mission in Nassau, she realized those images were now only memories. Pulling the cotton sheet to her chin, she closed her eyes and tried to wish reality away, but as she expelled a deep sigh of loneliness and remorse, she knew God had brought her to a new life. She didn't know if she could ever go back to Canada without Vaughn. Captain Stubbs had recognized her gifts with the young people and offered to actively apply for her installation as an officer in the Bahamas. It seemed to be a good fit, but she still had some reservations.

She was pregnant with Vaughn's child and she didn't know if this would be a good part of the world to raise a family. When she thought about what had happened in the cavern, she struggled to overcome a sense of failure and guilt. With the death of her husband, she had lost confidence in who she was and what she was supposed to do in life. Mae didn't trust her ability to make decisions anymore. God seemed very distant despite her pleas to Him to show her what she should do next. One thing was a given, though. Her life with Vaughn would never truly be over as long as this child was with her.

Mae tried at times to think of things from an eternal perspective. It made her smile to think of Vaughn talking with his parents and grandparents, but it didn't change the fact that she missed him so very much. This permanent separation was apparently part of God's plan, but she didn't like it at all.

She tried to journal her thoughts to pass the time since her only real task at the moment was nibbling at her food and sleeping indiscriminately. The staff at the mission patiently waited for Mae's shock to run its course, but it would take some time for her to accept two things: that she had failed her husband, and that she had possibly interpreted God's will incorrectly by coming to the Bahamas in the first place. Either way, she was mired in a pit of bitterness.

Another person she had failed was Montagu Norman. Despite all her efforts, she had not retrieved the gold. Maybe she had stopped the Amschels from getting it–and for that, there was some satisfaction–but without the gold there could be no British return to the European continent. She feared she had let down millions who suffered from Nazi tyranny. All her life she had put other people and social causes ahead of herself, but in the biggest test of her life she lost her most important person and let down a great need. She truly felt she was a loser and lower than dirt.

As Mae reached out to sip some tepid tea left on her nightstand, a subdued knock came from her door. Instead of answering, she quickly rolled over with her face toward the wall, feigning sleep.

The door slowly opened. "Scuse'm, but deh be a person to see you wif big, shiny car out front. It almos' be noon-hour and de day is haf gone. Wha' do I tell 'em?"

Mae had no idea of day or time – what difference did it make anyway – but slowly she realized she couldn't go on like this indefinitely. "I suppose you can tell them I'll be there presently."

With a sigh, she rolled out of bed to face the day that was thrust upon her. She put on a long-sleeved white blouse, but could not bring herself to wear any form of the Sally Ann uniform, so pulled on a comforting pair of dark blue dungarees that had been donated from a local clothing store, then rolled and sectioned her hair into a red snood securing all with a few bobby pins. When she looked in the mirror, she thought she looked like she was heading out to clean the barns rather than greeting a visitor – but she didn't care and opened her bedroom door.

Captain Stubbs was there to greet her. "Mae, you have a special visitor waiting in the breakfast hall who is drawing a lot of attention. This is quite an honor." For just a moment she thought he must be talking about Vaughn, but then reality hit once again. She headed to the breakfast hall with a heavy heart – until she walked through the door

"Mother!" Like the little girl she always was in Harriet's eyes, Mae ran to embrace her most welcome caller. Mae couldn't hold back her tears, but Harriet remained unshaken. Stubbs and a few on-lookers smiled at the heartfelt reunion.

"Looks like you lost a few pounds. You're swimming in that barn outfit." Harriet reprimanded until she got a little better look from head to toe. "Actually, on second thought, it looks sort of stylish,"

Mae took Harriet by the hand and for the next few moments was her old self. She made introductions to the mission leader Captain Stubbs and the cooks, Bernadette and Aurora. She could also not forget the colorful Hector Rolle who came to long enough to ask about something to eat. Harriet was treated like royalty, including prolonged Bahamian hugs from several blind children.

When the confusion had settled down Mae took Harriet aside and offered some very important advice.

"Drink only tea or boiled water – no tap water. Do not eat anything scorched on a rock and never, ever be a passenger in a vehicle driven by Hector Rolle!"

Eventually, Aurora and Bernadette went with the Captain back to the kitchen, and Hector fell asleep once again on a wicker chair in front of a circulating fan. They were finally on their own.

"I have another surprise for you, Mae. George is with me. We came as soon as we heard the news."

"I don't really want to talk about it, Mother. I'm just so confused and don't understand God. I saw things I can't share yet, that you will find hard to believe. It all just hurts so much. I don't know what I'm supposed to do or where I am supposed to go."

"Well, we'll take it one day at a time. We're going to have lunch with Alex Ferguson. He's letting us use Harry's touring car. George is like a kid with a new toy in that automobile, although he still has to learn to drive on the left side of the road."

"How long will you be here? This could take a while. I don't want to leave without Vaughn."

Ignoring Mae's comment, Harriet continued with her itinerary. "Eunice Oakes has spared no expense. We would be staying at Westbourne but it's a crime scene and they won't let anyone in there just yet. Press from all over the world are here… seems they've arrested Harry's son-in-law, de Marigny, and charged him with the murder."

Mae seemed unfazed by the news. "Harry was a most peculiar man, Mother. He should have left the island with his family, but he was determined to see things through. We followed his instructions but there was no gold. I don't understand why he led us on such a wild goose chase."

Harriet had seen this same life questioning from her former husband, Josiah Blackwell. Try as he might, Josiah could not make sense of why things happened the way they did in this world. Harriet believed this is what drove him to the bottle and there was no way she would let Mae continue in that direction.

"Some things in life are never meant to be understood, Mae. You just make the best of what's been dealt to you and hope you can move on."

"Hope, Mother? What hope is there? Vaughn dodges bullets and comes home from war only to die a ludicrous death on a deserted island. Where am I supposed to find hope in that?"

Harriet was losing the battle so pulled the ace from her sleeve. "I didn't travel this far to listen to whining. Yes, you lost Vaughn and it hurts, but we don't honor him by moping about and complaining. He was a doer and would want you to get back into the game. Remember, I lost a husband, too – and George lost his wife–so let's go have some lunch and talk. I have some news to share about friends of yours back home." Harriet stopped and gave Mae a sad smile. "So what do you say? Let's take the first step in trying to live again."

She knew her mother was right and would try her best to honor Vaughn's memory by getting back into life. Then, for the first time in days, she smiled thinking about the other reason she had to live again–some news of her own she had to share with her mother and George when the time was right. So Mae grabbed her purse and walked beside Harriet to the awaiting silver chariot where George Beall was entertaining the local boys with pieces of Indian and Sky Bird chewing gum. Problem was, they all wanted the empty packages with the pictures of spitfires and mustangs, and a full-feathered Indian chief and when two boys finally ran off with the boxes, the rest followed leaving George quite relieved.

When he saw Mae, he opened his arms. "There you are, Mae." Giving her a hug, he whispered in her ear, "I think you'll find your efforts have not been in vain." Then he stepped back and opened the car door. "Now get inside this grand old lady. Harriet is itching to drive, but we all know how reckless she was with the Buick – and that was driving on the right side of the road!"

Harriet noticed that Mae had broken from George's embrace with a reassured smile. In thanks, Harriet leaned in and gave George a kiss for his part in Mae's more upbeat attitude. Once they were in the car and on the way, she had one more bit of news to drop on Mae. "Just so you know, Mae, Montagu Norman will also be joining us."

Mae looked accusingly at her mother. How was she supposed to face this man and explain her failure to him? She sat back in the seat, closed her eyes, and tried to pray for an answer that didn't come.

Chapter 54

❦

Nassau, Bahamas

Members of the Bahamian Police Force were directing west-bound traffic off Bay Street toward the docks. Despite their calm exteriors, they were obviously churning inside, as George found out when he was stopped one block from Parliament Square. "Sir, you must turn here and follow our signals. You cannot proceed any further along this street."

"But I can see the Colonial Hotel just up ahead. We are staying there. I could just make a mad dash for it and be out of your way."

"No sir, I'm sorry. The trial for Sir Harry Oakes' killer is under way and we cannot let anybody past this point."

"I know that, Constable. I am an old friend of Sir Harry. In fact, we are on our way to luncheon with his business associate, and we are late. If I could just sneak by, I could make my appointment at a respectable time."

"I don't care if you are the King himself, sir, and I have no time to argue. You are backing up traffic. If you don't move along, I will confiscate this vehicle and arrest all within. Now shove off!" For the British traditions of etiquette, civility, pomp and circumstance to be reduced to such a level, tensions had to be running very high. George's reaction did not help the situation.

He pulled hard on the wheel and recklessly spun down East Street toward the Prince George Wharf, planning to take the back way around Rawson Square and Parliament House. Unfortunately, there was a mass jam of automobiles, motor bikes and taxis blocking this route as well. George laid on the horn but it was roundly ignored as traffic had come to a complete standstill. It was especially frustrating since they were so close, but just couldn't get to the hotel.

Mae looked out the window, observing every person who walked by, hoping against hope that Vaughn would appear. His death had to be a mistake. She took a deep breath to prevent herself from crying, which caught Harriet's attention. She reached out and held Mae's hand, knowing her recovery would be a day-to-day process. After her initial chiding earlier in the day to get Mae moving, the best thing she could do now was to just quietly listen and be there for whatever her daughter needed.

Mae was most appreciative of Harriet's thoughtfulness, but her attention was being drawn down the alley toward the courthouse where a group of reporters and on-lookers were gathering around a newly arrived person of interest. Then, to her shock, she noticed something in the immediate crowd behind Freddie de Marigny that terrified her. She nearly bolted out of her seat.

"Mae! What's the matter? You look like you've seen a ghost."

"Worse yet, Momma. I think I saw the devil." Pointing to the spot, she said, "There! See the dark-haired gentleman in the navy blue suit? Look to his left."

Both Harriet and George looked intently into the crowd and indeed, there was a very distinct person who just did not belong in the middle of the mob. "What's that poor woman doing there? She's going to be trampled. Look at the way that pack of reporters and offi-cers are manhandling her." Sure enough, a squat, elderly woman holding a wooden pole with dozens of straw hats was being swept up by the tidal wave of humanity coming her way. Suddenly the pole came down and the woman was nowhere to be seen. Harriet was appalled. "I hope she's alright! How did she get by the police?"

"No! Not the woman! There was a man there. I know him. He's supposed to be dead but he's alive. He was there, I'm sure of it!" Mae sprang from the car and ran toward Bay Street, pushing her way through the displeased multitude now being refused entrance to the overflowing Supreme Court building. By the time she got there the doors were closed tight and her quarry was gone.

Mae was having a rough go pushing back against the aggressive locals, and eventually needed to take shelter beside the marble statue of Queen Victoria, using it as a bulwark against being trampled. The air around her was awash with the sounds of police whis-tles, unsavory language and obscenities, and derision for both deMarigny and the local authorities. Nobody around was paying any attention to her, so in the midst of this noisy circus-like atmosphere, Mae looked to the heavens and began her own tirade.

All she could think about was Job's wife's comment, "…curse God and die." It seemed rather appropriate to her situation, so she began spewing language that would most likely be offensive to the Omnipotent One, but she needed Him to know how she felt. Why was Lubeck still here? She was in no shape to continue fighting the leviathan, and God was nowhere to be found. He had taken her partner from her – did He expect her to handle this battle on her own? "How much more do you want from me, God? Where is the glory in torturing someone who only wants to serve you? Where are you?"

Then a soft voice said, *"Mae, I am right beside you. I have never left."*

"Why did you send us here to fail when you knew Sir Harry would never leave his home? And Cat Island… why would you allow him to send us there knowing there was no gold?"

"The story is not yet complete."

"And most of all, why did you take Vaughn and give me this fatherless child to raise?"

"The child will not be fatherless… and I am still here."

"I'm tired of doing Your will because all it has done is bring me heartache. Is this some type of cosmic joke You play with us just because you can?"

"Yes, I can because I AM! Job, Abraham, Joseph, Moses, David and many others also suffered for Me, but I assure you, they and many more are with Me now, all wearing the crown of life…"

The answers were not good enough for Mae, and at this moment she really didn't care what He had to say. "Please just give me a sign that you're still there. You've been silent for so long – why did You remove your protection and allow Satan to do his dirty work?"

There was no answer, which only served to harden her heart further. "I don't care anymore, God. You've destroyed me and I don't know why. So go ahead and do what You want! I've read all Your promises and they aren't true! 'Trust in me and I will rescue you'… bunk! 'You are my help and my deliverer'… untrue! 'He delivers them from the wicked and saves them'… rubbish! 'Your love is unfailing'… lie!"

Mae felt an emptiness deep in her soul. She didn't know who she was anymore. Everything was too hard. There was no joy in her life and the feelings of peace that Christ said He would provide were nowhere to be found.

As she ran out of energy and finished her ranting, she noticed the crowd in the square had thinned out allowing her to step down from the statue without fear. She looked around the civic square to get her bearings and gasped. There, leaning on the other side of the statue, was Lubeck, laughing at her with great pleasure.

Mae could only mutter, *"Eli, Eli, lama sabacththani–*My God, my God, why have you forsaken me?" as she turned and ran.

Chapter 55

Never Forsaken

Nassau, Bahamas

Mae decided she couldn't possibly attend the luncheon in the state she was in, and instead, despite her doubts about a caring God, felt inclined to walk the few blocks to Christ's Church. She needed to shut out the world for a while and just be quiet to try and settle her soul. George and Harriet would have to handle the luncheon on their own.

Not very many people visited the church during midweek work hours, especially since the recent horrific events, but things had been cleaned and restored once again so the congregation was slowly returning to their normal schedules. As she walked the newly restored marble tiled floors today, her footsteps were all she could hear in the quiet hall. The clamor of the outside world was silenced inside these walls.

Wiping tears from her cheeks, Mae took several deep breaths to try and ease her anxiety. Even through her pain she couldn't help but marvel at the wonderful renovations Alex had accomplished with the help of Reverend Green and Sir Harry. She ran her hand along the back of a pew that had been oiled and hand-rubbed to a glossy finish, beckoning her to sit and pour her heart out–but she wasn't ready for that yet. She wandered to the back of the room and admired the hand-carved wooden baptismal font that had been used for generations, then strolled the side aisles, studying the series of stained glass windows depicting the Crucifixion of Christ in each phase – from His betrayal in the garden to His ascension to the throne.

When she turned, she noticed an old stone cross leaning near the altar. According to its inscription, it was from the eighth century and had been removed from the ruins of

England's Canterbury Cathedral, somehow finding its way here to symbolize the affection between the two parishes. No doubt Sir Harry had played a part in its transplantation, but Sir Harry was no more. And Vaughn was gone. Just like the dozens represented by the tombs in the floor of this place. Then she stretched her arms wide and looked toward the heavens shouting sarcastically, "But Lubeck is still alive!"

Mae couldn't pray and she'd had enough of the silence, so she stormed out the south side of the church. She passed a marble statue of Jesus with extended hands that she turned from with an impertinent shrug, and suddenly found herself in a garden surrounded by graves and memorial stones. "You say You are with me, Lord, but I don't believe You. Show yourself to me! Make your purpose for me known or leave me alone."

In a loathsome mood she stormed around the garden glancing at the inscriptions when she noticed a moss-covered headstone for a Private Lawrence A. Monroe, Fallen Hero of Vimy Ridge in the Great War, with a withered bouquet of yellow elder leaning against it. Tucked into the flowers was an envelope.

Under any other circumstances she would never have touched another's property, but for some reason she felt compelled to open it. So, after looking around to be sure nobody was watching, she picked up the envelope and sat on a granite bench, and began to read:

To my loving Larry,

It has been 25 years today since you were returned to me. I will never love another and will never forget you as long as I am alive. You never met your son, Peter, but he grew up to look just like you. He even followed in your footsteps and became a missionary. He lives in Halifax dealing with soldiers returning from war. I don't know how he lives every day sharing the hurt of others, but he is a comfort to many families. You would be proud of him.

As for me, I talk to God every day. I like Him better than I used to. For years I pushed him away. I hated him. You would not be proud of some of the things I said to Him. But then I thought of you. What good did it do to hate God when He had been the most important thing to you? If I hated God, it was like I hated you and I just couldn't live with that. But it still didn't take away my hurt. I sleep alone and spend all my evenings without the comfort of your voice. I miss the teasing and the fun we used to have. And I miss your touch. You were my best friend but I've had to go through life without you. I hated God for taking you from me and Peter.

But then I realized it wasn't all about me. Miracles have happened in your honor. On this 25th anniversary, I know you have made a difference in the lives of people because they tell me so. Remember how reserved I was? How I doubted myself and how many others said I was destined for nothing? Without your passing I would have never been able to become the person I am. Some people say I can deliver an invitation to salvation better than most Reverends. I doubt that. It was not easy to come by. It took me years to live again. It took years for me to talk with God again. But it has all been worthwhile. I have to tell you some good news–I will be seeing you soon. Probably by the time these flowers wilt, I will be in your arms. The doctors aren't optimistic and that is fine with me. So, thank you for dying so that I could live. But I am thankful that I am finally going to live again in Christ's blessings. I love you and will see you soon….. Vivian

Mae placed the letter back in the envelope and respectfully placed it back among the flowers then began to clean around the tombstone.

"Miss, can I help you?" a soothing voice spoke above her.

Mae looked up at the frocked clergyman who stood before her, embarrassed at being found on her hands and knees. "I'm sorry. Am I doing something wrong? I was just cleaning up Larry's site."

"No, of course not. Was Private Monroe a family member?" the Pastor inquired kindly.

Mae didn't hesitate. "I just discovered that we belong to the same family."

"Well, please know you're always welcome to visit this Garden of Remembrance."

"Oh, thank you. I feel sure I'll be back. Now if you'll excuse me, I have to replace these flowers with a new bouquet."

"Would you like me to get rid of those withered ones for you?"

"Oh, no! They may look beaten and wilted, but they've produced more life than you'll ever know."

Mae shook hands with the confused Reverend, and he handed her a small card. "Here is the scripture our parishioners are learning this week. I hope it speaks to you. II Samuel 22:19-20: 'They confronted me in my day of calamity, But the Lord was my support. He also brought me forth into a broad place, He rescued me and delighted in me.'"

Mae thanked him with a smile and whispered to herself as she walked away, "And I will again delight in Him."

Chapter 56

Lazarus

❦

Nassau, Bahamas

During the trial of Freddie de Marigny, the *Nassau Guardian* reported that Hans
Lubeck had been dismissed as a possible perpetrator because, according to the
Captain of the *Southern Cross*, he had left the island prior to the night of the crime.
Although the captain verified that Lubeck and his associates, as guests of Axel Salming,
had already set out for Cat Island before the time of death, he could not explain the subsequent disappearance of the Argentinean businessman, but since he had been ruled out
as a suspect, the court had no reason to pursue Lubeck's disappearance.

But Mae McIntosh knew the truth. Lubeck was alive and was out for vengeance, and
she needed someone she trusted to help flush him out. Vaughn was gone, Sir Harry was
gone, Harriet and George were spending time at Westbourne with his family, and Captain
Stubbs was overwhelmed with mission work, so that left Alex Ferguson who had talked
to the Mafia behind their backs and sent her and Vaughn to Cat Island on a bogus mission.
Alex's actions had cost Vaughn his life and she didn't know if she could even talk to him
again, let alone trust him to work with her to catch Lubeck.

With no other options left to her, though, she decided to confront Alex at Christ's
Church during his noon hour ritual. To her surprise, he seemed pleased to see her, greeting
her with a kiss that made her think of Judas. "I know I have some explaining to do, Mae,
but first let me say how sorry I am about Vaughn."

All Mae wanted to do was slap his face, but instead just said, "Thank you. You're too kind." Alex could read the underlying sarcasm, but chose to ignore it.

"You're fortunate to have caught me here. I haven't been taking my lunches at the church lately–for safety reasons. Let's go across the street to the pub where we can talk more freely."

Mae was not inclined to go into a drinking establishment, but then again, she'd had numerous life experiences lately she would never have expected, so decided one more couldn't really hurt – especially under the circumstances.

Mae found the aroma of warm beer and cigarette smoke disgusting as she entered the room, but then caught a whiff of less-offensive pipe tobacco and focused on that. After they found a table and ordered tea, their conversation soon moved from innocuous small talk to the current trial, but neither wanted to open the subject that really needed to be discussed.

"Seems like Trevor Sullivan is in the clear as far as the murder is concerned. I've known him for a long time and don't believe he's capable of such a bludgeoning. He wouldn't want to get his hands that dirty," Alex added with a wry smile.

"What about Sydney–feathers all over the room and the burnt 'sacrifice'?"

"No, I don't think so. He wouldn't have done that on his own. According to their beliefs, a life is only taken with a high priest, or *Houngan*, present. Unfortunately, I saw rituals like this back in the days before I left Cat Island."

"So, how about your former friend, Frankie Johnson?" Mae asked, trying to keep her voice even.

"Why do you say that, Mae? Frankie Johnson was never my friend." So this was what she wanted to talk about.

"Then why did you want him to kill us?" Mae asked, finally putting all pretense aside.

Alex stared at her for a moment before answering. "I never wanted him to kill you. The plan was for him to get the information and then let you go so Lubeck would fight it out with the Mafia – not you. That cavern was the perfect place–it used to be a site for Voodoo worship and sacrifice but since Father Jerome started building churches and giving the people hope in other ways, the locals were afraid of it and avoided the maw; and it was Bones DeVeaux's family who built those stairs years ago, so Johnson working with him played right into the plan. I spent months moving those dirt-filled crates into that cave – the gold was never on the island – but when you threw that box into the fire it changed everything.

"So, now you're blaming it on me?"

"No, of course not. I'm just saying you were too smart for the rest of us. Harry would be very proud of you."

Mae ignored the compliment. "But you sent us in unprotected and we just lucked out?"

"No! Hoggie was actually one of Harry's men and was there to protect you. The gunfire around the bonfire that appeared to be directed at you, came from him. When he found out that Frankie was planning to kill you, he had to improvise. You were supposed to drop the box and run, not throw it into the fire! Hoggie saved your life then–and Hoggie had Vaughn's back when he was fighting Bones. He would never have let Bones kill Vaughn, but as it turned out, Vaughn was more than capable of handling himself so he didn't have to step in."

Mae was stunned. "Hoggie was one of Harry's men?"

Alex nodded. "He originally put him undercover in Toledo when Orndorff was controlling the union dock workers from Sarnia to Detroit and Toledo. Hoggie was there to make sure Picard's shipment made it through uninterrupted to Lake Erie. It was Hoggie who arranged for Sir Harry's gold – or should I say, former Amschel gold – to get through customs without a hitch, piggy-backing on Picard's system. Sir Harry just kept his shipments going through the International Tunnel at Sarnia just as Picard had done. U.S. customs were none the wiser when more construction materials arrived, long after Picard's crates were gone. Let's get some lunch," Alex blurted unexpectedly. "Finally being able to tell you about this is bringing back my appetite."

She nodded in agreement and Alex waved to the waitress as Mae sat in stunned silence while he ordered for both of them. When the server walked away, he continued. "Interestingly enough, it was the U.S. government that helped ship the crates to the Bahamas as part of the lend-lease operation. They were still under the original Picard invoices, but our crates were stamped as weather and air field construction implements, not bridge materials like Picard's. It's amazing how easily the American government will move things in a time of war. Nobody paid any attention as the gold moved from Miami to Nassau, a few boxes at a time!"

"But how did Frankie Johnson get involved in this?"

"Frankie's 'family' has had eyes on the Bahamas–and Sir Harry's wealth–for a long time. He sniffed out something was going on when he didn't get a Customs cut from Sullivan when the 'weather and air field construction parts' passed through Miami to the Bahamas. Sir Harry knew Sullivan was making a sweetheart deal to build airfields in the Bahamas, so he just used Sullivan's operation to smuggle the gold in. If Sullivan was going to use Harry's good name to set up a deal, Sir Harry figured he might as well take advantage of the situation. By the time Sullivan discovered what Sir Harry had done, the gold had been completely removed. Sullivan got his airfield and Sir Harry got what he wanted from Sullivan. They chalked it up to the way business is conducted and moved on. Frankie wouldn't let it go, though, figuring there was a big score somewhere."

"So where does Lubeck fit in?"

Just then their food arrived, and between bites, Alex continued. "Sir Harry was being squeezed between the Mafia and the Amschel, represented by Lubeck. He knew there would have to be a show-down and he was trying to keep himself out of the cross-hairs. So we came up with the idea of luring Lubeck and Johnson to Cat Island to let them fight it out there. Whichever one lost would always claim the other had gotten the gold, and we believed with the huge egos that were in play, whoever claimed victory would want to save face and would never admit there was no gold.

Johnson would use the victory to bump Lansky out, and with Sir Harry out of the way financially, and the Duke and Sullivan in his pocket, he would recoup more than enough money from his gambling venture in the Bahamas. If Lubeck claimed the win, he could steal leadership over the Amschel empire by fiat. At present the Nazis are pumping millions of dollars in gold into his Argentinean banks which he could manipulate as his booty from the Bahamas. If all went as planned, the focus would be off Sir Harry, once and for all."

"But why did you send us? You and Hoggie could have done this yourselves. Why did you put us in danger?"

"Well… please remember you two showed up here uninvited and unannounced, so we changed the plan to include you. At first I was against involving you, but I gave in to Harry's idea when he explained how you all had handled yourselves in Canada. In theory, it was a good plan because it freed me up to carry out an assignment from Harry here while you lured Lubeck and Johnson to Cat. Unfortunately, the outcome wasn't ideal but at least you are finally released from the curse of the Amschel gold. Only thing left is to share some information with Montagu Norman, but you don't need to concern yourself with that."

Mae just looked at him. "And you think that settles it all? Alex, this big scheme you and Harry dreamed up cost me Vaughn's life – and I'm not free yet! Lubeck is still alive! I saw him the other day in the square!" The look on his face told her he had believed Lubeck was dead. "He's stalking me, Alex! He's alive and still thinks I know where the gold is. This isn't over. You have to help me."

Alex lowered his head and sat in silence for a few moments, then pulled a pencil from his pocket and wrote on a napkin before looking up. "Mae, I know you're afraid and I'm sorry. I have no answer for you right now, but I promise I will help you. I need to think first." He passed the napkin to her then and said, "Maybe this will be of some comfort, but until we figure this out, be very careful and keep your eyes open. I'll be in touch." Before she could react, he stood and quickly left the pub.

She picked up the napkin and read his one-word message. What in the world could this mean – Lazarus? She left the pub more confused than ever.

Chapter 57

Abimelech

Nassau, Bahamas

Back in Canada, before all this had happened, he and his associates had been welcomed into her home. It had been such a comfortable evening it seemed Mae and Montagu Norman were long-time friends and had come to an understanding about the need for her to travel to the Bahamas. It had turned out to be a most memorable adventure, but for all the wrong reasons, and now, in the midst of recovering from the most devastating time of her life, Mae was having dinner with Montagu Norman here in Nassau where she had to explain about her failure to fulfill her commitment to him.

Long ago, Mae had become immune to the trappings of power and influence but was still respectful of decorum, so for the first time in quite a while, she cared if her clothes measured up to the occasion. She had only brought her uniform and a few casual outfits on this trip, so she was at a loss to find something suitable to wear to the British Colonial Hotel for dinner with the Governor of the Bank of England. The staff at Mackey Street came to her rescue, though, through Aurora who borrowed an elegant evening dress and jewelry for her from a cousin, and Bernadette who did her hair in a stylish up-do. The gown was a little tight, and by her standards was rather risqué for a widow, but judging by the compliments she received from those around her, she was presentable. She was, however, still very uncomfortable.

Upon hearing of the death of Sir Harry Oakes, Governor Norman had been honor-bound to send formal condolences to Harry's wife and family, but when he learned of the death of Vaughn McIntosh, he was heart-bound to travel the 4,000 miles to visit the young widow in person. Montagu knew that mere sympathy, an apology and a hug could never make up for the damage that had been done to her life, but he wanted to show his gratitude for her sacrifice. His tribute would begin with an exquisite candle-lit dinner at the "Grand Dame of Nassau Hotels,' the British Colonial.

Outwardly, it was Mae's hospitality and dedication to placing herself in harm's way that had won the admiration of the Governor, but secretly, his interest and fascination was with the young woman herself. Being duty bound by the proprieties of his office and his marriage–though dry and simply convenient in these later years–he kept his romantic feelings toward Mae to himself.

Disappointed by her failure to appear for his first proposed meeting, Norman was taking no chances this time and through the graces of the Duke of Windsor, sent a car to the Mackey Street Mission to escort Mae to the British Colonial. Inside the Bentley he had placed a wrist corsage of sweet smelling frangipani flowers, and another small box with the message, "For Your Canadian Palate." Mae smiled and opened the box to find one package of O-Pee-Chee Gum, a Willard's Sweet Marie Nut Roll and her favorite, a Nestle Coffee Crisp bar. She couldn't remember the last time anything had looked so good to her.

Upon arriving at the hotel, Mae was escorted through the door by a pistol-carrying Sergeant who passed her off with an open-handed salute to a stiff-necked concierge who had a camera in his hand. He immediately snapped a picture of her, explaining that her host for the evening had requested the snapshot, and since he was such an influential guest, could not be denied. As if she weren't already uncomfortable enough, this exchange was almost more than she could handle and she toyed with the idea of turning and having the driver take her straight back to Mackey Street.

Before she could act on her impulse, however, the doorkeeper took her arm and led her further into the lobby where Montagu Norman was waiting. Mae stopped abruptly, knowing she had missed her chance to escape, and tried to put a genuine smile on her face, but didn't feel she had quite accomplished it. Montagu thought it was the most beautiful smile he had ever seen.

Removing his hat, he dismissed the concierge with a pound note and grasped Mae's hand. These were hands that had milked cows, slopped pigs, cleaned toilets and sorted dirty laundry, yet Montagu barely noticed its roughness when he kissed it, and then pulled her to his side. "You look lovely, Mrs. McIntosh," was all he said as he led her to a pre-arranged private dining room.

Mae was feeling so out of place that all she wanted to do was run, but made herself keep going, and once they reached the reserved room and were away from prying eyes, she felt much better. Before her was a lace-covered table set with lead crystal, bone china and polished silverware, and once the waiter had placed the serviette on her lap and left the room, Mae finally found her voice. "Thank you so much for this invitation, Mr. Norman. I'm very sorry I missed our previous meeting. I was on my way but was overcome by a circumstance."

"I appreciate your position, Mae. Perhaps I should have been a bit more sympathetic and allowed you more time before approaching you, but as soon as I heard of the unfortunate situation with Vaughn, I knew I had to come to Nassau to see you. It's totally understandable that you would be overcome."

"Oh, no, you misunderstand me, Mr. Norman, I was not overcome by Vaughn's death. It was because I had failed to catch Hans Lubeck when I had the chance." Although the incident had nearly destroyed her at first, after her experience in the Remembrance Garden she had been able to move on. Besides, she had to think of baby now, and he, or she, would need a strong mother, not a grieving widow. Her response to Montagu must have seemed cold and callous.

"My dear girl, you are allowed a time of mourning, and don't fret about Hans Lubeck now that he is dead. Alex Ferguson related the whole story to me in our last meeting."

"Lubeck's not dead," Mae said matter-of-factly. "I saw him in the square that day." At Norman's look of doubt, she continued. "You know his body was never found, so it's entirely possible. For that matter, neither was Vaughn's – so if Lubeck's alive, maybe there's a chance Vaughn is, too."

"But the water… and the cavern. From what I understand you barely made it out alive yourself. If it weren't for this Hoggie person you would have suffered the same fate."

Mae was not happy with the direction of the conversation. "It doesn't matter what anyone told you. I was there… I saw things in that cavern you wouldn't believe." Then her voice got very quiet. "I even killed a couple of men, myself."

"And so you did – good for you – job well done. You are to be commended." His patronizing attitude was beginning to annoy her.

"You can believe me or not, but I saw Lubeck the other day in Nassau. He is alive and is here, and he promised he would kill me."

Montagu's condescending attitude didn't change. "Mae, you're not making sense. According to Ferguson's man there were no survivors, other than you. Yet you maintain that Lubeck resurrected himself in Nassau?"

"Mr. Norman, you don't have to believe me, but I know what I saw."

"But you are going against facts and common sense. I want to help you…"

Mae was tired of his arrogance and cut Montagu off. "I came to this country at your request to convince Sir Harry to leave, but now two very good men are gone, and I am sorry to report there is no gold on Cat Island and I have no idea where it is."

"You're saying there was nothing in the cave? Are you sure you checked it out thoroughly?"

"Yes. There were crates there, but nothing but dirt inside."

"But surely someone else checked them out," he persisted. "Did Sir Harry's man not see the gold?"

"He never made it that far. He was the bait to lure Lubeck to the cavern and had to stay outside."

"So, you're the only one who came back to tell the tale?" Norman said, skepticism in his voice for the first time.

Mae was indignant. For a man of taste and culture, he was now sorely lacking in manners. "Are you saying I am a liar?"

"No, certainly not! I am only saying you were under extreme duress and you could have missed something. Could there have been other places the gold was stored?"

"We had time to inspect all the passageways even though we were in a terrifying situation. There was nothing there – I assure you. I'm surprised Alex didn't tell you that himself. After all, he was the one who planted the empty boxes there."

"My deal was with you Mae, not one of Sir Harry's chauffeurs. I understand he is from Cat Island. Did you ever consider he had the gold hidden somewhere else out there?"

"No, I did not. I believe Alex Ferguson is an honest man who loved Sir Harry and fulfilled the wishes of a creative and eccentric man to rid us of the gold once and for all. And Hoggie was a guardian angel to us. If it weren't for him, I would be in my own watery

327

grave right now. Alex told me he had something to take care of that he could only do if we lured Lubeck and Johnson to the out-islands. My suggestion is to talk with him again."

"The King and Prime Minister will be most displeased with this outcome."

"I'm sorry, Mr. Norman. We did our best, but don't put the responsibility for carrying out the war on me. You are going to have to find someone else to blame."

The charming and courtly Maitre d'Hotel approached the table with fluted glasses in hand. Living up to the Colonial's fine reputation, he was prepared this evening to delight his guests with a fine *Chateau d'Yquem* that had been the preferred wine of George Washington, Thomas Jefferson and Napoleon Bonaparte. The Governor rebuffed him with the back swipe of his hand. "I'm terribly sorry, but I believe Madame will be leaving us now, Phillipe. You may send this exceptional wine to my suite."

As the waiter walked away, Mae said, "So, you actually were using me... and my husband. With all your friendly gestures, you didn't care about us at all, only the gold. You are really the loser here, Mr. Norman, for I believe we could have been friends, but you don't believe me about the gold or the return of Hans Lubeck."

"Mae, you shouldn't take this so personally. I am duty bound to find that gold, and I truly am sorry about Vaughn and all you are going through."

"Enough to help me find Hans Lubeck?"

"I'm sorry, Mae, but he is gone forever. I cannot help you find a ghost."

"Then I suggest a compromise. If you humor me and help me trap Lubeck, I'll work on finding out what Alex Ferguson has done with the gold."

Montagu tried to hide his relief. There was still some hope. All he had to do was pander to her ghostly story for a while and she would continue to look for the gold. "That seems reasonable Mae. Shall we meet again tomorrow?"

"Yes. Mrs. Oakes is holding a formal gathering at Westbourne for George and Harriet – it's been in the society pages for days. You can be my escort. I don't think you'll want to miss this event. It should be quite a memorable evening."

Chapter 58

The Unfolding

❦

Nassau, Bahamas

Since Eunice Oakes' soiree was a formal, society affair, Montagu had made arrangements with the Colonial Hotel for a rushed dress fitting for Mae, and they had pulled out all the stops to outfit the companion of a man of his stature. Mae was totally out of her element, but agreed to go along with it, and at the end of the day was glad she had. The black lace evening gown fit her blossoming figure perfectly, unlike the dress she had borrowed the evening before, and with the bolero jacket she had insisted on for modesty, she felt the look suited her status as a widow. Turning several times in front of the mirror, she had to admit she looked rather good. Then she pulled the picture from her purse that Montagu had handed her this morning – the one taken in the lobby last evening before their dinner–and was disappointed the photographer hadn't captured her in this dress instead of the one she had borrowed. But that was just vanity, and she quickly put the thoughts out of her mind. After all, she had plenty of more important things to think about – like what was going to happen tonight.

Lady Eunice was a demure and charming woman. Her Aussie accent had been quite anglicized during their years in Canada, but was still evident enough to give her an air of sophistication that, despite being quite a bit younger than her husband, allowed her to handle their social calendar with ease. Harry, on the other hand, had detested society and all its trappings, so would oftentimes find himself in situations that required Eunice's adept touch to smooth over. Her even temperament, whether in the presence of the former

King of Great Britain or in the company of an uncomplicated Salvation Army cadet, was well-known and most admired. She knew it was awfully soon after Harry's death to have a party, but the family, and Alex, had agreed it was the right thing to do – and she felt she would have Harry's blessing.

This gathering was officially being held in honor of George, Harriet and Mae, but the family also wanted to show Bahamian society that even though Sir Harry was gone, the remainder of the Oakes family was alive and well. When Mae and Montagu arrived, there were plenty of whispers among the guests about the connection between the two, though none were spoken directly. Most had no idea how a Salvation Army cadet had come to be in the company of the Governor, but Eunice felt a little mystery was always good for a party. After they had mingled for a while, Montagu got into a discussion with Trevor Sullivan about Italian Dictator Benito Mussolini's mountaintop rescue so Mae excused herself and headed for the patio for some fresh air.

Alex had been waiting for a chance to talk with her, so when she walked outside, he followed. "I see you finally met up with Montagu Norman," he said, stepping up to the railing beside her.

Mae turned briefly and looked at him, then focused once again on the ocean. "You know you'll need to talk to him soon." The two of them had met earlier in the day and thought they had a plan to deal with Lubeck once and for all, and it was almost time to put it into play.

Alex ignored her comment, and instead removed his jacket, undid the collar of his shirt and began to roll up his French cuffs. "That's enough formality for me. There was a time when the fanciest thing I wore around here was a pair of oily grey coveralls." He threw his jacket over a chair and took a deep breath. "See that light in the back of the garage? That's where I slept back then. I'll never be able to repay this family for what Sir Harry has given me, but there are times I miss those simpler days."

This was a side of Alex that Mae had not seen before, allowing her to relax and be a bit more open with him. "I feel so out of place here–especially without Harry."

"You shouldn't. Lady Oakes is very gracious and you are, after all, Mr. Beall's daughter now, so you're family. You have as much right to be here as anyone and I'm sure she would rather spend time with you and your mother than any of those self-righteous political blood-suckers. She must keep up appearances, though, for Nancy's sake."

"It's all about appearances, all right. A swank formal evening with American con-gressmen, corporate presidents and engineers–I even met a Colonel and a Major in there. I wouldn't have been surprised to see Prime Minister Churchill himself walk in. Mrs. Oakes seems to have put everything she has into this."

"Well, we must all do our part," Alex said, then looked at his wrist watch. "It's time, Mae. You should probably get down to the beach house. Do you still have your gun?"

She nodded. "How can you be sure he'll come?"

"It's been in the paper for days and this would be the perfect time and place for him to attack. I bet he's already on the property, watching you, waiting for you to be alone. Are you sure you want to do this?" When she nodded, he added, "Just remember, I'll have eyes on you. There's only one door to the beach house and I've got it covered."

"And you didn't tell anyone else about our plan? We agreed to keep this low-key and to ourselves."

"Yes, I followed the plan," Alex said quickly, though he was having second thoughts about their agreement.

Mae made her way to the beach house and settled into a cushioned chair that faced the door. Then, smoothing her dress comfortably over her legs and double checking that her gun was handy, she prepared to wait.

Looking around at the opulence even in this beach house, she thought about the life-style of these people who had become her friends. She could enjoy this for a while but didn't think she could be happy here forever. She would always long for dungarees and a summer evening lounging on the farmhouse porch reading a novel or just visiting with friends. She thought of what Peter had written about the beauty of a woman: "It is not fancy hair, gold jewelry, or fine clothes that should make you beautiful. No, your beauty should come from within you–the beauty of a gentle and quiet spirit that will never be destroyed and is very precious to God." The only thing in that description Mae really had a problem with was a 'gentle and quiet' spirit, especially considering what she was about to do this evening. Accomplishing her goal tonight would require her to be neither gentle or quiet.

She could see the sunset out the window–a glorious deep yellow sky with palm trees silhouetted behind several black-crested terns skimming the placid waters. The intense heat of the day was beginning to dissipate to be replaced by a cool ocean breeze. She slipped further into the chair as the last golden rays drifted across the water and disappeared below the horizon and twilight settled in.

Suddenly, the door was kicked open by what appeared to be two drunken lovers hoping for a secluded spot for a secret tryst. Mae jumped up and stopped them just inside the door, making it clear simply by her presence that they needed to find a different place for their assignation. With earnest apologies and more laughter, they headed back down the beach. She watched until she was sure they were gone, then pushed the door closed and turned back to her chair. The man she had been expecting stood before her.

"Good evening, Mae. I am delighted to be with you again." Dressed in a full black tuxedo, the very essence of evil stood with his hands clasped behind his back. On the surface he did not present as something scary, dark or ugly. Hans Lubeck was tall and blonde, with blue eyes and an impressive physique. His very presence was intoxicating. She felt an inner stirring as he spoke with warmth and love – as if from God himself. "I see you still possess the beauty that all men desire. I do hope my use of the young couple as a distraction did not upset you, but I had to be sure we would be alone. I want you to enjoy this evening to its fullest!"

She didn't want to fall prey to the evil one's allure, so she closed her eyes and said a silent prayer until her mind felt clearer. What she needed was her gun so she could put an end to this monster, but unfortunately her purse, with the gun, was still on the chair directly behind him.

If she was going to finish this task, she needed him to think he was winning her over. She looked him in the eye, and as she started moving very slowly to the side, told him what he wanted to hear. "You are the very being who enraptures my soul. Seeing you in this light again, my Prince, my heart is here to do as you please."

Lubeck cocked his head and carefully regarded Mae. He was a bit surprised at her quick compliance, but he trusted in his powers of persuasion and believed he had gained control. "It has been so long. I believe the last time I was so wonderfully appreciated was with the Tsarina Alexandra of Russia. She and I became very close, in fact, I persuaded her to convince her husband that he could stop the Revolution. Sadly, it cost both of them their lives, but I was most appreciative of her cooperation right up to the end. The gold was worth all my efforts and she is with me eternally because of her loyalty.

"And then there was Josephine. While Bonaparte was in Egypt she became mine, and when he was confined on Elba she gave me the keys to his treasury. I missed her until I met you. Now you will join my Queen and my Empress."

Lubeck unclasped his hands and moved toward Mae, pulling a white cloth packet from his pocket. When he looked down to unwrap the contents, Mae made her move, lunging for her purse on the chair behind him. Unfortunately, with a quick side-step he was able to block her and she stumbled to her knees.

"Oh, Mae. I wish you hadn't done that. We were beginning to get along so well. Unfortunately, now that I see you aren't as cooperative as I'd expected, I'll have to change my plan."

Lubeck took hold of her arm and pulled her to her feet, while his other hand that held the open white cloth moved in front of her face. She noticed a small mound of white powder in the center, but before she knew what was happening, Lubeck blew the dust in her face. She coughed once then blacked out, sliding onto the floor.

"You will only be asleep for a moment, and when you awake you will be totally in my control. We are about to become one, now and forever." Lubeck stood in front of Mae and took a deep breath, then tilted his head back, closed his eyes and allowed himself a satisfied smile.

The room became dark as the inside of a swirling tornado – as still as death. A bitter odor made it difficult for Mae to catch her breath as *Sammael* placed his sinewy arm at the small of her back, drawing her closer. An incantation that at first seemed to be coming from a distance, grew louder and faster as more and more voices joined in:

Abigor, Andras praise Your name,
Botis, Furfur do the same
Ronove, Pyra hail you King
Shax and Stolas, Yang and Ying

Inside out and wrong is right
Come our Lord, Dark of Night
Be our master, Beast of Light
Quench your lust, win the fight

Grab this beauty, and rip her soul
Thamus, Uvall, steal it whole
Tear the good that's yours to take
Do it now! Make no Mistake

The time is ripe, the time is nigh
She craves you deep, she whines on high
Coil her tight, let it be done
Verin demands that two be one

Wipe the light that hurts our eyes
Destroy the Nazarene of lies
Son of Adam, Second son
Cut away so there is none

See she wants you now more and more
Control her flesh, we all implore
Take her spirit from this final act
Do it, Dragon, seal the pact!

His eyes were glazed over and his head tilted back in ecstasy. She was his for the taking. A Christian life rebuked was worth more than gold. He felt the yearning to draw her soul into his body and shivered with the delight of her life force beginning to invade his dark form, but suddenly his eyes flew open and he knew. Something was holding her back.

Chapter 59

Nassau, Bahamas

Alex was fully armed and had full view of the beach house door from his perch in the garage. Ever since Sir Harry's murder he had stepped up his fire power–with Lady Eunice and the children returning he could take no chances. The Duke had provided a detail to stand guard at the entrance to Westbourne this evening, and several of the attending dignitaries had brought their own security. In addition, the general Bahamian Defense Force were also on patrol throughout the grounds. Alex knew how slippery and resourceful Lubeck could be, however, and was taking no chances.

The Argentinean had a personal score to settle with Alex since he had poisoned him and left him on the beach to bake in sun. It was one thing to best this staunch military man professionally, but a totally different story when he was humiliated personally. Sir Harry had dealt with Lubeck as a businessman, but it was Alex who had carried out the final blow. Lubeck's response would be lethal, as a well-trained Nazi officer but also an Aryan racist who could not live with being embarrassed by a lowly black colonial who would need to be taught his place.

As Alex stood watch from the garage, he thought through events of the past few days. He believed Hans Lubeck, with the help of his men, had to be Sir Harry's murderer. They had the commando training to slip into Westbourne undetected, and could have easily arrived by boat in the foul weather. He suspected the guards weren't expecting anyone to be on the water in the storm, so had not been as vigilant at the dock as they should have been. The men most likely stood guard outside–some at the boat, some outside the doors–while Lubeck crept into the house to take care of Sir Harry.

Nobody who had lived in the islands for any length of time bought the ploy of the Voodoo sacrifice. The feathers had been from Sir Harry's expensive down pillow, but a Voodoo ritual demanded the use of chicken feathers; and there would have been chicken feet somewhere, too. He had to admit it was smart of the killer to open the windows so the rain could cover their tracks and muddle the evidence. In Alex's mind, Lubeck was the only suspect who could have carried off the precision execution.

But what finally convinced Alex of the Nazi's guilt was the sadistic finale of the crime. Lubeck's type of revenge would have been to inflict the same type of pain on Sir Harry as he had suffered, only more so, and in his twisted mind that was the torching of Sir Harry's flesh while he was still alive. All Alex wanted was a chance to see him pay for what he'd done.

Every few minutes, Alex scoured the grounds with his binoculars. His attention was momentarily drawn to the mansion where a few of the guests were preparing to leave, and he thought about Mae being used as bait once again. She was doing this of her own accord and on her terms this time, and after tonight, if all went as planned, she would be done with the gold forever, leaving it in Alex's competent hands. This was a trade-off they could both live with. He looked back toward the beach house, realizing it was getting dark and he would soon only have the light of the moon to see by, but he was determined to keep Mae safe, no matter what.

He perked up when he saw a young couple approaching the beach house, and was ready to run when they forced open the door, but Mae was there and stopped them from even making it inside. Within a moment they had backed off and were moving further down the beach, and Mae closed the door behind them. Alex took a deep breath waiting for the adrenalin rush to subside. He checked the safety on his gun and watched the errant couple disappear into the sunset – literally. He couldn't believe it, but one second they were there, and the next they were just gone. Then he saw flashes of light coming from the beach house.

Chapter 60

Nassau, Bahamas

Lubeck had underestimated Mae's resolve. Although he had felt her beginning to surrender, her redeemed spirit was now intensely fighting. So, the Father of all Lies tried to reach her psyche one more time. "You should come to me now. You are as abandoned here as you were when you came into this world, Daughter of Perdition. What type of God says he loves you and then lets you suffer? Let me care for you and love you as he could never do. Come to me and be free from all the pain and sorrow."

Mae had opened her eyes, but had to fight to remain conscious. She could feel the essence of who she was being drained from her, but a remnant within would not let go. It was like someone higher had control of her heart – someone she trusted–and she gave up the struggle and commended herself to that power.

Lubeck writhed in disgust, pounding his fist into the air. "This is your fault, Nazarene! It must stop here and now. I may not be able to steal her soul, but her mortal body is mine for the taking."

"Have you not learned by now, Lucifer, that when I claim someone for my own, you will never have them!"

"Show yourself, Nazarene! Let us put it to the test one more time. I can still destroy her fleshly body through my servant here who is tested, tried and true. Who will you bring against me?"

It began with golden shafts of light and mist seeping into the room through any available crevice, and soon became a pillar of cloud growing larger and larger until it enshrouded Mae and pushed Lubeck back against the wall. A voice from within the cloud boomed. "*I give you my helper.*"

Then, as quickly as it had appeared, the cloud was gone and the room returned to normal. Lubeck stepped away from the wall as if awakening from a dream and assessed the form that stood before him. He recognized his opponent.

"Your God is stupid to think you can best me. You tried it once but failed to have the courage to carry it through. I can sense the struggle within you and even now you have doubts about killing me. That will be your undoing."

He showed no signs of fear. "Let's get this over with, Lubeck."

Mae's eyes flew open when she recognized the voice. She tried to move, but her head was spinning and her body wouldn't cooperate. All she accomplished was a prolonged groan. Her rescuer heard and said, "It's OK, Mae. I'll end this now. Let the church mouse guide you. All you need to do is pray. Pray as you have never prayed before." Then he turned back to his opponent. "How do you want to do this, Lubeck?"

"It appears the only weapons at hand are our guns," Lubeck began, "but that would end things entirely too quickly. I want to prolong your pain. I want to see your blood flow when I cut you. I say hand-to-hand, face-to-face is still the best. That way I can watch the life force ooze from your body at my own pace." He stepped back and smiled as he pulled something from his pocket. "Look what I found!" he cried gleefully, taking his time unfolding a glove and slipping it onto his hand, then he shoved it in front of the helper's face. Imbedded in its knuckles were shards of glass and metal.

"Do what you must, Evil One, but know this: one way or another, you will be defeated tonight."

Mae's body had slowly been waking up, and luckily, Lubeck hadn't noticed. She had been doing her best to find her purse, but her vision was still blurred and she could see nothing but vague, shadowy shapes. Though she was powerless physically, surviving Lubeck's spiritual onslaught had empowered her divine strength, and her prayers for the helper were heartfelt and deep, and included pleas to reveal the whereabouts of her weapon.

Then without warning, Lubeck tendered a back slap with his gloved hand across his opponent's chest, drawing blood from the razor-like slice. "One little whack and you bleed like a stuck pig," he laughed. "Even Mrs. McIntosh put up a better fight than you." The taller and bigger Lubeck cut his shorter opponent off with his long strides.

"You look tired already, Helper, and you move slowly. I am not surprised since you claim the same heritage as the Nazarene. He was a most effeminate creature spending his time with widows and tax collectors. All his talk about love was most unmanly!" Lubeck gave a derisive sneer as he threw a round-house into the side of the helper's head, decimating his ear. He winced as blood ran down his neck, but did his best to keep his head up. "Look at you, Helper, what a fine example you are!"

The helper just smiled. "Proud fools talk too much, Lubeck. You should know that those who guard their lips preserve their lives and those who speak rashly come to ruin."

He tried to shuffle and jab, but Lubeck was too quick and countered with a slash along his extended forearm. "Do not think that I have come to bring peace to this earth." Lubeck mocked. "I have not come to bring peace, but a sword. How did that feel?"

"I am here for His glory. It will take more than a mere cut to do me in." Despite his injuries, the helper stood tall, resting in his Maker's overriding power.

Riled by the reference to the Creator, Lubeck lunged, shoving the already injured man to the floor. As the helper rolled onto his knees, Lubeck grasped his right arm at the wrist and pulled it up and out straight behind him, dropping all his weight onto the helper's back. "There is nothing more gratifying than the sound of an arm being ripped from its socket. You want to be like your Christ? Let me help you. He felt this pain on the Cross." Lubeck yanked and twisted. "One more push and your arm goes numb, then your fingers tingle before they feel nothing ever again." But before Lubeck acted, the helper thrust himself forward, driving his own face and shoulders to the ground, freeing himself for the moment.

"Good move, but I fear your arm will be useless. Now I'll take care of your legs." The helper's immobile arm dangled loosely, so he turned to protect that side, but in so doing, exposed his leg as a target. "You can no longer punch and soon you will not walk. Why don't you give up and admit the Nazarene is no match for me?" Lubeck jumped and came down with both feet on the outside of helper's knee with a force so great the joint's popping echoed through the room.

The pain was excruciating but still he attempted, but failed, to stand. Lubeck laughed. "Do you hear that crackling sound when you move? I've severed what holds your leg together. They say your Christ has felt every pain you could ever experience in this life, but He is a liar! He never experienced a leg broken the way I just destroyed yours! That was personal, just for you."

Mae knew the helper couldn't hold on much longer, and in desperation called out, "My God, my God! In the name of Jesus Christ, let your power come forward to protect this man."

But Lubeck wasn't finished. With unbridled contempt, he drove his bloodied fist deep into the small of the helper's back, grinding the glass and metal into his flesh and ribs. The victim collapsed once more to the floor. Lubeck circled to the front, and kneeling in front of him, grasped him by the throat, pressing his fingers to the outside of his neck while his thumb pressed down on the hollow of the windpipe.

Lubeck's spittle splattered across the helper's face as he laughed and even though his body was torn and bloody… even though the flesh had been ripped from his form… the helper continued to smile at his enemy. In frustration Lubeck released his grip.

Even though his opponent had physically destroyed him, he knew without a doubt he had fought the good fight and was forgiven and loved by his True Father on High. His pain-glazed eyes shone like the noon-day sun as the helper looked at his conqueror with an unconditional love that would never fluctuate.

Lubeck stood over the motionless body in awe, then screamed in terror when he heard the next words, "Father, into Your hands I commend my spirit."

Through the screams, several gunshots rang out.

Chapter 61

Nassau, Bahamas

When guests at the main house heard the shots, Lady Oakes was immediately rushed to a safe room by Bahamian Defense personnel, while Godfrey Higgs, the attorney for Freddie deMarigny, asked for calm as the colonels and majors helped to sequester the American politicians on the second floor. Security forces for Governor Norman advised him to leave the premises under the watchful eye of British Regulars, but he refused to go until he knew that Mae was safe. He hadn't been able to locate her, or Alex, for the past few minutes and couldn't shake the feeling that something terrible had happened to them.

Once Defense Force members determined the incident had taken place away from the mansion, and was now under control, guests were released from their safe areas, but the soiree had come to an abrupt end. A few decided to leave, but many were curious and began to wander toward the commotion. Harriet and George had been looking for Mae and Alex, and like Montagu Norman, had an ominous feeling as they pushed their way through the crowd to the open door of the beach house. George got close enough to make out two still bodies on the floor before a policeman forced him back from the crime scene.

"George, was she there? Did you see Mae?" Harriet begged.

"I couldn't get close enough to see anything," George lied, not wanting to worry her unnecessarily until he had more information.

Harriet bullied her way through the crowd, screaming for her daughter, as George wrestled with the constables attempting to restrain his wife.

"Let them both go!" came a demand in a British accent. "They are the parents of this woman here!" Montagu Norman had his arm around Mae, and quickly handed her off to her parents. "As the highest ranking official of Her Majesty's government, and acting on the behest of the Duke of Windsor, I want this place cleared out... now! I need to speak to the Chief Inspector."

It took a while till the rank and file finally realized this man actually had the authority to make these demands, but once the chain of command was clear, they quickly ushered the onlookers back to the main house. The Chief was a bit miffed that Governor Norman had taken charge, but when George joined them, at Montagu's request, he realized he had no recourse. "Mr. George Beall is Sir Harry's family attorney," Norman informed him, "and has advised me to clear this up at once." Montagu spoke with the authority of his office. "My understanding is that Mrs. McIntosh was taking a break in the cabana when she happened upon Hans Lubeck, a person of interest in the Harry Oakes murder. There was a struggle and Alex Ferguson, Mr. Oakes chauffeur, came to her rescue. He and Lubeck tussled, whereupon shots were fired. The best we can tell is that during the brawl, Hans Lubeck was shot by Alex Ferguson, but unfortunately, Lubeck was able to do the same to Mr. Ferguson before he died."

"Thank you Governor Norman," the Chief answered, still a bit skeptical. "We will cordon the area off and formally confirm the findings at first light. Please take Mrs. McIntosh home. We will be in touch."

Mae was in shock and still suffering the effects of the drug Lubeck had given her, but her hearing was perfectly fine. "No, that's not what happened! I shot him after he killed my husband!"

Governor Norman was quick to clarify her perspective. "Yes, Mae, we know he killed your husband, but that was a while ago."

"No! Vaughn was there. He stopped Lubeck from hurting me. I shot Lubeck and Alex told me his secret."

"It's true, Mae, that Alex was shot. But it wasn't you who did it."

"But I have to tell you my secret!" she pleaded, grasping Montagu's arm.

The Chief was quick to recognize her behavior as signs of shock and disregarded her rantings. George and Harriet sandwiched Mae between them in the back of the Bentley along with Norman who gave the driver the signal to drive on. Mae's last words, though, resonated through the car. "Vaughn is not dead! He completed his job and will return for all of us. We must be ready for him." With that she collapsed against Harriet's shoulder.

The rhythm of the tires on the asphalt was soothing, and Mae soon fell into a deep sleep, but not before they heard her final whisper, "But of that day and hour no one knows, no, not even the angels of the heavens, but my Father only."

Chapter 62

Render to Caesar

Nassau, Bahamas

The rest of the world was basically being ignored by the Bahamian people in favor of all the exciting things happening right on their doorstep. The trial of Freddie de Marigny for Sir Harry Oakes murder had become a farce. The prosecution had so badly mangled the evidence that the smart money was on his acquittal. After giving his testimony, Trevor Sullivan had set off for parts unknown claiming to be looking for future investors in the Bahamas. Axel Salming had decided to extend his time in Mexico, and to top things off, the Duke of Windsor had muzzled the press and indicated he would not re-open the case if de Marigny was acquitted.

Mae McIntosh was concerned with neither the war or the trial. She had been exposed to a reality most people would classify as ridiculous and insane, and some even felt she needed to be institutionalized. Authorities had been convinced to drop the incident at Westbourne involving the mentally-deranged cadet, and advised the *Guardian* to do the same to avoid denigrating the fine work being done by the Salvation Army in Nassau. Yet, Captain Stubbs visited with Mae every day as she walked him through her spiritual journey and encounters, and he knew she was not insane. They both understood what it said in Ephesians: *"For our struggle is not against flesh and blood, but against the rulers, against the authorities, against the powers of this dark world and against the spiritual forces of evil in the heavenly realms."*

Unfortunately, there were still many without Christ as their center who would never understand, so she took to heart the words of the Psalmist: *"I will guard my mouth as with a muzzle, While the wicked are in my presence."* They both knew that in the end the Lord's Word would cause every knee to bow and every tongue to confess, but until that day they kept the events Mae had been through to themselves.

Mae was growing stronger and recovering nicely from her ordeal, but she still had one obligation left to fulfill involving Governor Norman Montagu. It was good to put on her Salvation Army uniform again, even though she had to let her skirt out a bit and deal with a tighter blouse. It was worth it though, since this wondrous form being knitted inside her allowed her to feel Vaughn's presence. Despite what the world and logic told her, she knew in her heart that Vaughn was still alive and would come back to her someday.

The last time Mae had come to Christ's Church, Alex Ferguson had stopped her from entering. His decision had seemed odd at the time, but now that she knew his secret, it all made sense. It made Mae sad that neither Sir Harry or Alex would be present to put the capstone of their efforts on the plan, but in an odd sort of way, she was reassured by the fact that both her friends were gathering with loved ones on high to see this closure. It also meant a great deal to her that Sir Harry had seen the importance of God in his life and had used this peculiar, yet brilliant, plan to utilize God's resources to free her family from the Amschel curse.

Montagu Norman had arrived first and was admiring the baptismal font in the back of the sanctuary, and he was delighted to see her again. He had experienced Mae in dungarees to evening gowns, but never in her official garb looking so prim and formal. With her hair pinned up under her cap, sporting a long blue tunic with red collar, she exuded an elegance and deportment even secular people would admire.

Mae could hardly wait to reveal Alex's secret to him. "Did you know, Mr. Norman, that this church has been rebuilt at least five times since the 17th century?"

"No, but I do know this place is truly a shrine to both Bahamian and British history. Have you spent any time in the Remembrance Garden?"

Mae smiled. "Oh yes. I learned quite a bit from a friend there, although we never actually met."

Norman looked at her curiously as if she was talking gibberish again, but he quickly pushed the thought aside when she added, "Now, before you think I've gone a bit balmy again, I assure you there's a perfectly good explanation for that statement–and don't worry, it doesn't involve spooky surprises and ghostly apparitions." If only Mr. Norman were able to grasp the truth, Mae thought. "But I think it's time to get down to business. Please indulge me, but my revelations begin with the night at the Westbourne beach house."

Montague sat down in a pew near the font and placed his hat on the perfectly polished veneer. "Even if your story did involve apparitions and ghosts, I think we are protected in this place."

"Bravo, Mr. Norman. I do believe you're hiding a deeper spirituality."

"I am a Jew, Mrs. McIntosh. My heritage is full of stories of miracles. How can I not acknowledge the spiritual?"

"Then this may make more sense to you than I expected," Mae began. "I remember Lubeck attacking me and then he drugged me. Then, when I started to come to, I vaguely remember someone fighting with him, then I heard two gunshots. All I remember after that was emptying my derringer and a body falling near me."

"Where does Vaughn fit in?"

Mae shook her head. "You know what I believe and I don't care what you think about it, but I know for sure Alex was there and he told me something that didn't make any sense at the time, but I've figured out what he meant. And that's why I brought you here today."

"You're not going to try and tell me that Mr. Ferguson will return from the dead, are you?"

"No, but he's alive for sure, just in a way you wouldn't understand, no matter how much you make fun of me." Montagu was enjoying baiting Mae, but wiped the smirk from his face and motioned for Mae to continue.

"What would you say if I could make the Amschel gold magically appear right here? Would you call it mumbo-jumbo?"

"Mae, I grew up believing Moses parted the Red Sea, Joshua tore down the walls of Jericho, Gideon had his own conquests and David killed his tens of thousands. If you could make the gold appear here and now, I would have to be a believer of those fairy tales forever."

"And what would be in it for you on an earthly level if you could provide Mr. Churchill and the King with the gold?"

"You know we've discussed this already. The only thing that matters to me is defeating Hitler and bringing down the House of Amschel. That is my only real passion in life anymore, but if I could help Bertie and the Bulldog it would be a major plus. I want this war to be over."

"I see your true heart and I assure you the miracle you are about to receive is truly remarkable." Mae put her hands on Montagu's face and gave him a quick kiss on the forehead, which surprised and unnerved the old man, then she took him by the hand and led him to the baptismal font. "Do you see the carving of the mouse?" When he nodded, she added, "Push hard on it."

Norman placed his freckled and shaky hand on the wooden figure and pushed. To his amazement a spring door popped out revealing an object wrapped in a clean white linen cloth. He looked back at Mae who encouraged him to retrieve the treasure.

"Oh, my God!" was all he could say as he peeled back the cloth, exposing a singular gold bar.

"Yes, Mr. Norman, my God is the right response."

"This is one bar, but where is the rest?"

"While I was recovering I spent a lot of time talking through my experiences with Jeremiah Stubbs. When I got to the part about what Alex said to me before his fight with Lubeck, I suddenly realized what he was trying to tell me. So, later that evening, I came here and played around with that mouse till the door popped open. I wondered, too, why just one bar was hidden there, till I looked deep in the back and discovered a crumpled piece of paper that explained it all. After I read it, I burned it so nobody but you and I will ever know the secret."

Montagu's face had gone white, so Mae closed the trap door and led him back to the pew. He sat beside her with the gold bar resting on his lap as she told him the rest of the story. "When Sir Harry bought the British Colonial, he hid the gold there as it arrived from Miami, but then they had this idea. It took him a very long time, but Alex took one bar each day and came to this church to have his lunch. Day after day he deposited the gold, bar by bar, in various repair sites around the building. He couldn't come with me to Cat Island because the last crate needed to be emptied and the renovations completed. Here's your gold, Mr. Norman," Mae said, waving her arms in all directions. "It's sealed in the font, the walls, the foundation and the tombs."

The Governor sat in stunned silence, then said, "But how am I supposed to get it out without tearing this church apart?"

"That would be another miracle and is not up to me to figure out. I've completed my part of our deal so now I leave it to you. I believe you'll figure something out to appease those back home."

Montagu sat transfixed, pondering Mae's words as he blindly rewrapped the bullion. She stood humbly, with her hands clasped in front of her and Montagu could feel her deep personal loss that had resulted from this Amschel fiasco. After all the years, and all the family members she had lost, it was finally over.

He stood, and as he made his way toward the door with the wrapped gold bar under his arm, he stopped beside Mae. His final words to her surprised even him. "You've left the gold to me now, but you're the one with the fortune."

Chapter 63
Faith's Fortune

Wellburn, Ontario

P halyn Purdue picked up the crying baby and gently rocked and soothed him. "You
have a way with children, Phalyn. I guess in a couple of months you can put this practice to work." Mae hugged her best friend from the side because of her protruding tummy.

"If I have a child as good as yours, it will be incredible. Young William, here, seems to
love his sleep more than anything else.... sleeping through the night already?"

Mae was indeed grateful that her son had fit so well into both her day and night schedules. His birth had been without complication and for the past three months he had done
remarkably well. What was particularly gratifying, though, was seeing him respond to her
touch and voice. It was, for sure, the beginning of a strong mother-son bond.

"I think he's so good because you named him after his favorite uncle... me!" Will knew
this would get a reaction from the women and Mae was quick to oblige.

"You can't take all the credit! William, in Irish, is Liam, so he gets his name from both
of us!" Liam was quick to add.

"You both remember, of course, that his name also comes from Vaughn's Uncle Will,
don't you?" Mae laughed. "William, as the Bible says–Bold Protector – is another reason,
and his middle name is just as important."

Despite Phalyn's lighthearted warning look, Uncle Will continued the teasing.
"Lawrence... Larry? He's named after a drunken convict? Vaughn told me that story from
his Chicago days. You surely could have done better than that!"

Mae was not to be shaken. With chin held high she very calmly rebuffed the claim. "Lawrence means 'Victorious One' in old English circles, and that is just what he is...a Victory!"

Amid all the laughter, Liam turned up the Philco. "Listen everyone, it's finally happened!"

"...Peter Stursberg reporting for the CBC...The long-awaited push to tear down Fortress Europe has commenced...Overhead the hum of thousands of our planes could be heard last night droning their way to liberate France. But unheard were the hundreds of gliders being towed by C-47s, Dakotas and Short Stirlings to key sites behind enemy beaches. As I speak to you today, some 150,000 brave soldiers are launching a direct amphibious assault over a 60-mile beach in Normandy, France. The world's greatest armada has been assembled to free Europe from Fascism, and our boys are there in the thick of it! The press has been asked to curtail our comments to protect our fighting forces, so as information is released, we will pre-empt your regular programming to keep you updated. In the meantime, keep those lips tightly sealed and pray for our boys!"

Will turned down the volume once again as the late Tuesday afternoon city and regional news began.

"Liam, you and Vaughn would have been in this operation."

As with many men who had survived combat, Liam had no response. Mae sat straight with her tea cup suspended in front of her. "I hope what Major Forester and you all did at Dieppe will pay off."

Liam knew where his gratitude lay. "We learned a lot on that mission. Our boys should be better off because of the information the Major and Vaughn gathered. We'll still lose lives, but they'll push inland. You heard Eisenhower – we're like a coiled spring ready to launch into Europe. We'll drive them back. Vaughn saved my life then and will save many lives today. I'm sorry, but what he did was necessary." If only Vaughn could hear the vindication. Yes, he had continued to struggle with the incident at Notre Dame, but in the long run the sacrifice had a greater purpose for the success of this massive military invasion.

It seemed that Governor Norman had struck an agreement with the Americans over the gold that was built into the very foundation of Christ's Church. Captain Stubbs had written her to say the new American Embassy would be located right across the street where the Shutters Pub used to be and Mae figured that was their way of keeping an eye on their investment. She took great delight in knowing that if someone wanted to go after the gold, they would have to go through God's house to get it. And there were only a few people in the world who would understand the irony of the epitaph that Alex Ferguson had suggested to be inscribed over the threshold of the newly-dedicated Church: *"More valuable than gold, we are built on the fortune of faith."*

Since coming home, she had chosen not to share many details of her time in the Bahamas. Because she still believed Vaughn was alive, Harriet and George had taken on the responsibility of informing those in the know that Vaughn had drowned while protecting his wife from a common thief on Cat Island. Mae just avoided the subject and had no desire to rehash the past. Besides, she had needed to prepare for the birth of her child and catch up on farm life and what was happening at the St. Marys Citadel. She had always envisioned working together with her husband in a life of service based on the words of Evangeline Booth: *"Service is our watchword, and there is no reward equal to that of doing the most good to the most people in the most need."* But now she didn't know if she could do it alone, especially with a baby in tow. Only time would tell.

As advised by the radio broadcaster, Mae reached for her Bible and went to her room for some study and prayer. She was all about prolonged, intensive Bible study and was not prone to erratically flipping through the Scriptures to a random chapter and verse, but tonight, that's just what she did and happened upon the ordeal of the Apostle Paul when he was shipwrecked off the island of Malta.

In all the times she'd read the story, she had never thought much about the two-week storm during which their boat was adrift, or the three months he was stranded on the island before his two-year imprisonment in Rome. Vaughn hadn't been gone that long yet. This started Mae thinking about the Maw and how she had only seen him washed away, but not drowned. The bodies of Lubeck's men had washed up in smaller sink holes and salt ponds, but their ringleader had escaped only to be done in later. Wasn't it possible that Vaughn was still alive? She knew it was a long shot, but she chose to embrace the belief. After all, the Lord had allowed Jeremiah, Jonah, Joseph and Job to survive impossible trials!

Then Alex's note on the napkin at the Shutters Pub–'Lazarus'–popped into her mind. The inference could not be more obvious and for the first time since she had come home, her hope was revived. She went back downstairs and asked Phalyn to keep an eye on William so she could take a walk on her favorite backwoods trail to think about what the Lord was putting on her mind.

This was like her prayer closet where, for so many years now, she communed out loud with God–sometimes in gratitude, sometimes in fear, sometimes in anger. When she walked in silence, notions came and went in her mind, but usually by the end she had a clearer picture of what God was telling her. It had been a while since her last trip around the loop, and she was excited to see what might be revealed.

At the last concession break on her way back to the farm, she recognized an old man sitting on a hewn tree stump. It was Mr. Knowles, wearing blue coveralls and a short-sleeved red checkered gingham shirt. When he saw Mae, he removed his grey fedora to acknowledge her presence. "Hey, it's the Blackwell girl. You sure are looking pretty these days. How is Josiah? Haven't heard much about him lately. I think he may be behaving for a change."

Mae was quick to divert the conversation, "Did you know I got married, Mr. Knowles? I have a baby now, too. He is a sweet young boy named William."

"I saw your wedding picture in the Journal-Argus. My boys told me he's an American. What were you thinking, girl? You can't marry an American. What will happen to that boy of yours? The breeding is not exactly right…"

Every Canadian made fun of Americans so it wasn't worth the hassle to explain Vaughn's real heritage. Besides, Mr. Knowles' awareness came and went so he would most likely forget this conversation anyway, but today she thought he actually seemed quite lucid and glib, till he made his next comment. "You need to keep better tabs on your man – I saw him down at the dam the other day and he wasn't exactly looking or behaving right. See? This is what happens when you get involved with an American."

"You think you saw him in St. Marys, at the dam? That's not possible, Mr. Knowles."

"Don't be telling me what I saw and didn't see, Missy. His beard is straggly and he needs a haircut – it's touching his ears, it is. I would think a Salvation Army officer would take better care of himself. And why aren't you taking better care of his clothes? The man's pants didn't have a pleat or a cuff. And when I said, 'hello', he just ignored me.

Had some shady lookin' guy with him, too. I told the police because I was worried about him, but when we got back there he was gone."

Mae's breath was coming in shallow gasps. "What time did you see him?"

"Around noon, I think. Saw him in that same place more than once when I'm down-town for lunch – just staring at the Prince Eddie across Trout Creek. Once when I got close I heard him mumble 'the gold should be movin' out right about now.' Just sat there with his friend flippin' some kind of coin. It didn't make any sense to me. What's going on with him?"

Mae was in shock. She thanked him and blindly began running back to the farm. Mr. Knowles just shook his head when she took off and threw up a prayer as he adjusted his neck scarf. "Father, this is one very strange family. I'm not so sure Mae isn't becoming a little bonkers herself. So, do me a favor? I know it would take a real miracle, but could you please watch over that family? They've got some deep issues and you're the only one who can help them. Maybe once you get them straightened out you can use them for something really important!"

Chapter 64

Assurance

❧

St. Marys, Ontario

She didn't want to tell the others about her discussion with Mr. Knowles and get their hopes up, and besides, you never knew if you could trust what he said these days anyway. She needed to check it out for herself and pray he was right.

She arranged for Phalyn to take care of William the next morning, and headed for St. Marys. Although, based on what Mr. Knowles had said, Vaughn generally appeared around the dam, she decided to look around town on her way there. If he really was back, she might find him at one of the other places that held meaning for them.

Heading in on Water Street, she slowed down as she passed between the two quarries. Even in war time the town had invested funds to modernize the one open to swimming, and some kids were already there this morning, diving off the cliffs and hanging out on the rafts in the middle of the pool. Across the street was the quarry where Picard had tried to kill George and her mother in the Buick. That car was still in there, where it would stay unless somebody decided to tell the tale and haul it to the surface, but she didn't expect that to happen in her lifetime.

Further on she noticed that construction of the ice rink for a new Junior B hockey team had been put on hold, but the new car raffle Will had organized should bring in the additional funding they needed to finish it. She smiled to think that maybe someday her own son might play on that team.

Here was Cadzow Park. This had always been one of Vaughn's favorite places but he wasn't there today. She kept driving then parked behind the Boy Scout Hall at the St. James Anglican Church and quietly entered the Narthex. She thought about the singing competition she had been in years ago, and how nervous she was that day. And to think, at the time she had thought that would be the scariest thing she would ever face in her life!

Since Vaughn was not in the church, she walked across the street to one of her childhood homes – the old Blackwell house on the corner of Peel and Jones. She and Vaughn had made wonderful memories in that garage, some very innocent and some that brought a blush to her olive skin. No luck finding him there now, though. Still trying to keep her hope alive, she went back to the parking lot for her car.

At the corner of King and Queen was the new Furtney block building – the brick Phoenix arising from the ashes! This was where she had first met Vaughn and where her working relationships with Cate and Mrs. Skipper had grown into warm friendships. It was also the place Vaughn's mother had died. He wasn't there, but until she had exhausted every possibility, there was still hope Mr. Knowles wasn't imagining things. She looked west on Queen Street past the station where Mr. Vorstermans would soon be attending passengers arriving on the noon train; past Peaker's restaurant with its unbelievable burgers and shakes; and then pulled over to the curb.

Across the street was the Citadel with its new concrete steps and social halls named after Vaughn's mother and the Skippers. Vaughn would be so proud of its success. The ladies of the IODE were talking about hanging his picture beside the one of Mr. Skipper in remembrance of his unconditional gifts of service, but Mae had asked them not to dedicate a spot yet. They had kindly honored her request even though they didn't necessarily believe, as she did, that he would return. There was the Thrift Shop, still closed. She realized she hadn't been back here since leaving for Nassau, but seeing that closed sign now was a reminder that one way or another, it was time for her to get back to work.

Past the Windsor Hotel... Town Hall... the Library... there was the spot, behind the memorial of the Great War, that her singing had first attracted Vaughn's mother's attention... Mancinni's barber pole was twirling its tri-colors... Corporal Thompson, with his immaculate handle-bar mustache was directing traffic... further up Church Street, Purdue's old bowling alley was still for sale... but still no sign of Vaughn.

The large billboards in front of Mr. Eedy's Journal Argus announced the Canadian Forces were fighting for the French town of Caen. The Essex-Scottish, Vaughn's old fighting unit, would be in the middle of that battle.

On she went through town, past the five major banks the town was known for. She refused to acknowledge the Bank of Montreal, however, with its foul memories of Bruce Lindsay and the Amschels, just as she refused to register for a box at the new Post Office that opened in the old Lindsay building.

Even the Salvation Army mail delivery had a Wellburn Post Office address. She would leave it to the new Captain of the Citadel to make that change.

Then finally, she turned north toward the dam just as the Andrews Clock chimed the noon hour, and in sixty minutes the Cement Plant would blow the whistle to bring all their employees back to work, signaling, in her mind, her last hope of finding her husband.

She parked in front of the Prince Edward Hotel and stood for a moment to catch her breath. So much had happened in this part of town, but it still looked so normal. The mill race was underground now, and there was no longer access to the inner workings of the dam from the hotel's basement. The Journal-Argus touted structural engineer, Phalyn Tremblay-Purdue, with heading up the project that permanently sealed off the foundational sore spot. She looked around and thought, if the people in this town only knew how close they had come to ruin. Fortunately, that was all behind them now, but her moment of truth was at hand. She took a deep breath and walked through the building and out the back door.

There was the confluence of Trout Creek and the Thames River. The water table had dropped so low this year the willow trees were barely able to lick the water and there was nothing to cascade over the spillway. Children ran along stretches of dry stone at the base of the dam catching salamanders in the smaller ponds all the way to Victoria Bridge.

The Flats were still the Flats. Acres of rich, thick, well-manicured and well-watered grass where fall lacrosse was replaced by hard ball and soccer in the summer, and hockey in the winter. But Mae saw something completely different – RCRs everywhere with their tents and cordoned off fields. This war couldn't be over soon enough for her so the military would never again have a presence in this town–at least not one headed by the likes of Brisbois and Picard!

A new path had been created around the outside and the grass had been cut back exposing the secret retreat that had once been claimed by the Purdue family. Now everyone had access and kids ran and jumped over the large granite boulders. Mae was instinctively drawn to the spot and walked the short path to the river's edge where they had first been stopped by Picard and his men. The water lilies were still thick as white trumpeter swans and an assortment of pintails and mallard ducks scooted among them.

But there was no sign of Vaughn or his friend.

Dejected, Mae continued to walk the river's edge and then climbed the stone causeway of the Water Street tunnel onto the Sarnia Trestle. She was concentrating on the tracks under her feet and trying to keep from crying, but it was a losing battle. Why had the Lord brought her to this point just to shatter her hope of seeing her husband again? She had looked everywhere, and finally had to admit Mr. Knowles was just a senile old man who didn't know what he was talking about.

But when she lifted her eyes to heaven to cry out to the Lord, something in the distance caught her eye. There were two people sitting on the railway ties overlooking the river. She froze in place, barely breathing, as one of the men began to walk toward her.

As he got closer, she recognized him and couldn't believe it. He didn't say a word, but took both her hands in his and, leaning forward, placed a respectful kiss on her cheek. "I've been waiting for you to come – he wouldn't let me contact you. I rescued you once, and now you need to rescue him." Then he slipped a black and red gambler's chip into her hand. "I've completed my obligation. Mr. Orndorff now considers this matter of honor completed."

With that he walked away. When Mae said, "Thank you, Hoggie" he never turned, just waved his hand in acknowledgment.

It had been the better part of a year, and so much had happened to turn their lives upside down, but as Mae approached Vaughn, her hope returned. "Hello, Stranger," she stammered through her tears. "Nice beard."

Vaughn kept his eyes on the view in front of him. "I had a long time to grow it, far away from here."

She carefully sat on the tie beside him. "And now are you back home?"

"I'm home if you'll have me," he said slowly, "but I'm not the same person you fell in love with... or who fell in love with you and this town."

Mae thought carefully about her next words. "I just took a trip through that town down there – looking for you–and it's mostly the same place as it's always been. But you're right about one thing. I'm not the same girl. I am, in fact, the proud mother of your healthy son."

Vaughn finally turned to face her, shock and wonder in his eyes. He looked very tired and much older, but all Mae saw were those deep blue eyes that she loved. She quietly sat on the cross-tie beside him, allowing him to take things at his own pace. When he reached out to touch her hair, she gambled and took his other hand in hers, and he didn't pull back. "But even though we've changed, I will always be your girl, Vaughn, and William will always be your son."

"I'm afraid you won't recognize me, Mae. I've aged a hundred years while I've been away. You'll see I can barely walk–I have trouble feeling my feet and I stumble a lot. My fingers are cold even in this summer sun, and I have trouble remembering things. What kind of father can I be for... William, was it?"

Mae caressed his hand. "I have never stopped loving you, Vaughn, and never will! And you will be just the father William needs, and wants to love. One of his namesakes is your uncle, by the way."

With tears in his eyes, Vaughn tried to hug her, but they suddenly realized how silly it was to be sitting in this ridiculously dangerous spot. Then, to Mae's delight, a spark of the old Vaughn came through. "We haven't come this far to fall into that river. Let's get off this trestle." She helped him to his feet and he began his slow walk, dragging his right foot behind. Mae's heart melted and all she wanted to do was love and care for her imperfect warrior.

When they were out of danger of falling, they walked side by side and Vaughn started talking. "Lubeck pulled me under the water and we were both carried out through a passageway into the ocean. I've been told I washed ashore and was found by an old goat herder who took me to Father Jerome in the Highlands. By the time I came to, Hoggie was there. He had come back to search for me. My thigh was fractured so I couldn't move and I was in and out of consciousness for a long time. And I had the strangest dreams! In one I was fighting Lubeck....and then you shot him!"

"I can assure you, Vaughn, when you've had some time to recover, I want to hear your whole story and I have a lot to tell you, too. For now, though, let's go home and meet your son."

Epilogue

❧

St. Marys, Ontario

Phalyn was just drifting off to sleep when the nurse walked into the room with a bundle in her arms. "Sorry to wake you, Mrs. Purdue, but it's time to feed Ellie."

"Don't apologize," Phalyn said, smiling at the girl. "I love holding and feeding her. I've been preparing for this for nine months, after all, so I'm ready to take over."

As the nurse laid the baby in Phalyn's arms, Will stood to look at his two favorite girls. "I just have to tell you again how much it means to me that we named her after my mother. I know Elspeth is a mouthful but shortening it to Ellie is just right for this tiny one."

"Well, since I never had a family to speak of, I love that we can remember yours. Now, I hate to say it but you should probably leave. Visiting hours are almost over and these nurses frown on having anyone but the mother in the room when the babies are eating. I can't wait till we can go home."

Will leaned down and gave each of them a kiss. "It's Ok. Vaughn wants me to stop by the farm and help him tonight. Something about the well. I'll be back in the morning." With that, Will walked out leaving her to relax and enjoy her time alone with her new daughter.

Ellie was only half-way through her feeding when Phalyn looked up to see a strange woman standing in her doorway, just watching her.

"Can I help you?" Phalyn asked, wondering why the nurses had let a visitor in at this particular time.

"You have already helped me, Phalyn. Your family has provided some of my best workers through the years."

Phalyn was confused and had an ominous feeling about this woman. "Do I know you? You don't look familiar? And, how do you know my name?"

"I've known you for years, though you weren't always aware of me. And now that a new Amschel generation has been initiated, I'm here to claim my future."

"I think you should leave now. Please, or I'll call the nurses to escort you out."

The woman chuckled. "Why should I turn and run when I have you – and now your daughter? You are an Amschel, not a Purdue, and certainly no Martin or McIntosh. I created you. We have the same blood and can never be separated."

Suddenly, Phalyn knew who this was and what she had to do. "No! Jehovah has me now and I am washed in His Son's blood."

"But I am stronger than the Nazarene," the woman scoffed, walking further into the room. "I am the greatest of all God's creations. There is nothing like me in the entire universe. Even the Father says I am the seal of beauty and wisdom. He anointed me. By his own words, I am the holy mountain of God–blameless from the day I was created. You and I are blood kin."

Phalyn was not shaken. "Except for one big difference – no righteousness was found in you, Satan!"

"I am greater than Michael and Gabriel. I am the true loving son. Let me embrace you," the woman said, moving closer to the bed.

"Never! You have had your way with others in my family, you have attacked this family with doubt, death and destruction for years, but it stops now! You may have posessed my earthly father, but he is dead and now I have a new Father–I put my trust in Christ Jesus."

The woman staggered back as if she had been struck. "I will never give up, Amschel! I will go after your seed and all your generations to come. They will become mine."

Phalyn was feeling stronger by the minute. She was ready for this spiritual battle, and knew she would win. "You, Satan, want us to give our life's blood for you, but the One I claim gave His life blood for me. You will not have my life - or my children! So, in the name of the true and living Christ, go from here and leave us alone."

"This is not over Amschel," the woman hissed.

"Go and roam the world for other lost souls, but as for me and my family, we chose Christ, now and forever."

"Your loss, Amschel. You're passing up power and riches. I could have given you the world, but there are many others who will take what I have to offer. You may think you've defeated me, but I'll be back. I don't give up easily. And when your God lets you down, I will be there to embrace you with open arms."

Phalyn looked at Ellie, then back to the woman. "I know you won't give up, but you are defeated. I am a new creature in Christ, I'm wrapped in His love forever and you can't have me. After all I've been through do you think anything would cause me to stumble back to you? I don't need your riches – my faith is my fortune and I will never give it up."

Selah and Amen

Leah and Cate Martin
in Germany

Leah Martin in England

Thomas, Leah, Cate, Will,
Bert Martin in Sweden

Cate and Will Martin in Sweden

Martin Family on holiday
In Black Forest, Germany

Bert Martin in England

Will Martin in England

Harriet and Josiah
Blackwell, Wellburn Farm

Vaughn McIntosh and Leah Martin,
Chicago, USA

IODE Ladies, St. Marys, Canada

Essex-Scottish Barracks, Windsor, Canada

Vaughn and Mae
McIntosh, Wedding Day,
St.Marys, Canada

Vaughn, Mae and Son, William, McIntosh, Wellburn Farm

CPSIA information can be obtained
at www.ICGtesting.com
Printed in the USA
LVOW04s1141090417
530156LV00004B/90/P